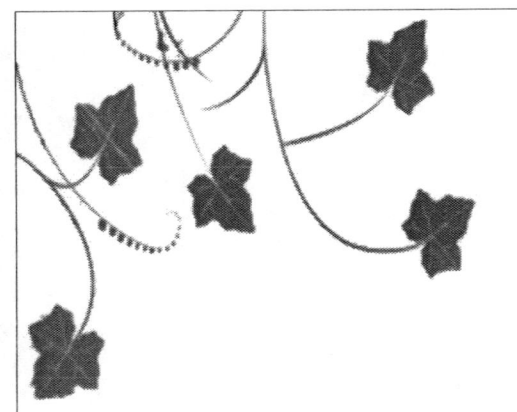

The Bitten Word

The Bitten Word

Edited by Ian Whates

NEWCON PRESS

NewCon Press
England

First edition, published in the UK March 2010
by NewCon Press

NCP 022 (hardback)
NCP 023 (softback)

10 9 8 7 6 5 4 3 2 1

ISBN: 978-1-907069-06-2 (hardback)
978-1-907069-07-9 (softback)

Front Cover Art and Dark Ivy Motif by John Kaiine
Back Cover Art by Les Edwards
Cover layout and design by Andy Bigwood

Invaluable editorial assistance from Ian Watson
Text layout by Storm Constantine

Printed in Great Britain by the MPG Books Group, Bodmin and King's Lynn

For Natasha

Contents

The Bitten Word

An Introduction

Ian Whates

To say that the vampire is an iconic figure is so obvious that it verges on tautology, but I think it's something that bears repeating. Over the years vampires have on occasion been figures of fun, satirised and lampooned in countless comics, films and books. Yet somehow the image of the dark, brooding lord of the undead manages to rise above all this unscathed, and vampires still evoke a sense of mystery and deepest dread, not to mention seductive allure.

Perhaps this latter quality goes some way to explaining their unique appeal. After all, zombies are pretty terrifying, but sexy…? Hardly. As for Frankenstein's Monster – the creature that spawned a thousand imitations – well, no. But *vampires* are capable of charming, they court and bewitch, and finally they kiss – invariably with dire consequence, but still… There is something inherently attractive, erotic at almost a primordial level, about this ultimate bad boy or wanton woman, an appeal which horror's other iconic figures simply lack.

9

I've long toyed with the idea of producing an anthology of all original vampire stories, without ever seriously committing either time or resources to the project – there were always so many other things to do. Then came the announcement that World Horror Con was coming to the UK in 2010, and I realised that if there was ever a right time to produce such a volume, this was it.

I knew instantly the cover image I wanted for the book – a wonderfully haunting piece of mist and shadow produced by artist John Kaiine, which I'd loved from the moment I first saw it. The fact that John's wife happens to be one of the finest writers of dark fantasy ever to put finger to keyboard made this the obvious place to start, so I contacted the couple and was delighted with their enthusiastic response. Within a matter of days I had the hardcopy of a fabulous new vampire story in my hands. No need to wonder whether the submission proved to be good enough, after all, this is Tanith Lee we're talking about.

Next I approached a select few authors I knew to be capable of producing something fresh and original within the well-trod genre and invited them to submit, and from there things gathered a momentum of their own. Discussing the book's launch with Steve Jones (in a pub, strangely enough) he wondered why I hadn't approached Les Edwards, who was also present, to do the artwork. I already had the cover image I wanted, but I'm also a huge fan of Les's work, and was delighted when he agreed to provide the back cover art (also included as a print within the book's special edition). Chatting with Jon Courtenay Grimwood (in another pub, as it happens), about future NewCon Press projects, I mentioned this one, and he told me that the new trilogy of novels he'd just been commissioned to write was to be a historical vampire sequence…

Certain authors were automatic choices; I'd never dream of producing a vampire anthology without inviting Storm Constantine and Freda Warrington to submit, and Chaz Brenchley's rich, lyrical prose also put him high on the list. Word spread, and writers began to approach *me*, which is always a bonus, particularly when the anthology hasn't been generally announced and you know full well the quality of those asking.

Traditionally, NewCon Press anthologies have been very much British affairs, but I wanted to make this one more international. Steve Jones had already recommended Canadian writer Nancy Kilpatrick, who was due to be at World Horror Con, and I saw that Gail Z Martin was to be Guest of Honour at 2009's Fantasy Con in Nottingham. I approached both ladies, who seemed extremely pleased to be invited. Then I heard that Kelley Armstrong was to be at WHC. There was no way a writer of her international standing would be interested in contributing to a book published by a UK small press, surely. But, it's amazing what can be achieved simply by asking. So I did, and, to my delight, Kelley said, 'Yes.'

No project such as this ever runs entirely smoothly. A computer crash nearly spelled disaster and led to my mislaying one of the first stories I'd read and marked for acceptance – Gary McMahon's. The piece was only rediscovered after the special edition's signing sheets had been produced, with no time to redo them, which is why Gary's signature floats mysteriously on the back of a sheet rather than appearing on the front where it belongs. Not everybody who was hoping to submit for the book was able to, and not everybody who *did* submit produced a story of the quality and type I was looking for.

However, what emerged from the submission, selection and editing process was a set of stories that I'm genuinely excited about. Here is a collection that demonstrates not only how good a vampire tale can be but also how diverse its form.

From the smooth cutting edge of Kelley Armstrong's urban adventure to Donna Scott's clever weaving of vampirism around Bram Stoker's theatrical career, from the searing bleakness of Gary McMahon's haunted suburbia to the richness of Chaz Brenchley's colonial gentleman returning to England, from the saltiness of John Kaiine's (yes, cover art *and* a story) sailor in dangerous exotic climes to Gail Z Martin's occult adventure in Antwerp, from Storm Constantine's tale of fey children to Simon Clarke's doomed archaeological expedition, from Tanith Lee's tale of an unappreciated writer to Kari Sperring's story of vampirism in a society of sentient insects, from Freda Warrington's tale of misfortune across generations to Jon Courtenay Grimwood's version of what came *after* Wuthering Heights, from Nancy Kilpatrick's story of transformation and linguistics to Sam Stone's suggestion that Jack the Ripper wasn't the only killer haunting the streets of old London, from Andrew Hook's politics in an alternative reality to Sarah Singleton's tale of an artist's obsessive love... there is variety here aplenty. In the special edition, this is then topped-off by a slice of intelligent but mad-cap humour as only Ian Watson knows how.

Yes, there be vampires here, but vampires with a difference

I'd like to thank everyone involved in the production of *The Bitten Word*. This is a volume I believe we can all be proud of. I only hope that the reader takes as much pleasure in discovering the book's various treasures as I have in compiling them.

Ian Whates
January 2010

Vampithecus

Simon Clark

The railroad of our pre-human ancestry spawned many a branch-line that terminated in evolutionary dead ends: the ill-starred Neanderthal; the Cro-Magnon, fated for racial re-absorption into the Homo sapiens *family. And of utter, morbid fascination, the deadly* Vampithecus *— dare we suppose, a creature of the night, and a consumer of hominid blood?*

From Violent Souls *by Carveth Zuckerman, 1928*

4th September, 1931

My wife is beautiful. Her blonde hair is gold ablaze. I fired four shots from my revolver. Shot one missed. Three bullets struck her. One in the shoulder. Two in the forehead.

"Help me, Gerald," she murmured quite softly. "Don't leave here. I want to go home." The fifth bullet entered Rowena's mouth as she pronounced the long *o* in 'home'.

The pistol shots didn't stop her. And there, in the light of the Arabian moon, she continued to climb the mooring line to the airship.

"Gerald, please help me into the cabin. I don't want them to hurt me again." Rowena's voice emerged from her slashed lips as

13

gentle and as rational as I'd first heard it at university three years before, when we began our research. Five feet below me, her slender form swung on the rope that ran down to the anchor, which prevented the airship floating free above the desert. She steadily climbed the line, hand over hand, her pale face upraised. I leant out of the gondola, my pistol aimed at her right eye. "Ever since they took me," she sighed, "all I could think of was you holding me tight. I'd touch the side of my face and imagine my fingertips were your lips. When I was held in the cave I never thought I'd feel your kiss again."

The voice – that of my wife, my beautiful wife, with a flame of yellow hair – was unchanged. Yet it emerged from the mouth of a monster. Five bullets from a revolver failed to stop her. A sixth would do nothing, either. Her arm extended from below; she'd almost reached the doorway that led into the airship's forward cabin. Her eyes were smouldering things. A blaze of hunger and hate.

Then in contradiction of what I saw beneath me, her soft voice. "Gerald. I love you."

With furious speed I wrenched the release-lever. The mooring lines parted from the vessel. My wife… or rather the monster she had become… dropped, as white as a pearl, sixty feet to the sand below.

The airship lifted. As it rose toward the moon my mind seemed to rise faster than that envelope filled with hydrogen. Dizzy, I tottered backwards before slumping to the floor.

Eighteen months ago there had been great excitement at the university. Professor Carveth Zuckerman returned from an expedition to Arabia, bearing astonishing finds; not to mention sporting a gargantuan white beard of Biblical dimensions and patriarchal gravitas. That same week Rowena and I fell in love. She elevated me from timid, bookish boy to a man with a roaring hunger for what this great world has to offer. I learnt that one of the greatest gifts of life is the ability to feel surprise. In the laboratory, there were constant surprises as we painstakingly assembled fragments of bone to rebuild the skull of Zuckerman's astonishing discovery, *Vampithecus*. This man-like creature possessed a head that rose in a smooth dome; its eye sockets were abnormally large, perfectly round, and widely spaced. We were amazed to discover that whereas we humans have a bone palate that forms the roof of the mouth, *Vampithecus* boasted a rigid floor to its mouth. I should add that the entire bottom jaw consisted of solid bone. Professor Zuckerman, had found incomplete skulls of *Vampithecus* before in the 1920s. He calculated that this creature, which dwelt in the mountain ranges of Arabia, had become extinct some one hundred thousand years ago. Furthermore, the bone plate that enclosed the bottom jaw had such a restricted opening for the gullet that it would barely admit a pencil. Therefore, he concluded, *Vampithecus* couldn't have possibly swallowed solid foods of any description; consequently it must have existed on a liquid diet. Zuckerman, gloriously adorned with that huge white beard, would declaim in the lecture theatre thus: "In the time of yore, what unique fluid contained all the nutrition a beast requires to live, mate and conquer its domain? Why, the answer is obvious, my dear students. Blood! *Vampithecus* – like the mosquito, the leech and the vampire bat – gorged itself on the lifeblood of its victims."

And didn't I say that a great joy of life is the gift of surprises? Rowena and I married. The wedding party arrived at the chapel on punts; they glided along a river threaded with green plants. In our hearts, Cambridge and Venice became one on that Summer's morning. Later in the day, Professor Zuckerman pressed a letter into my hand as Rowena and I boarded our honeymoon train. A rich Greek aviator, so the letter announced, had been so excited by the Professor's discovery that he offered his marvellous new airship, *Greco,* to transport an archaeological team to search the Arabian highlands for yet more *Vampithecus* bones. Professor Zuckerman closed the letter with an irresistible PS. *Promise me, my dear fellow, that you and the* brand new *Mrs. Foy will join this expedition*

15

of a lifetime.

And surprises aren't confined to palaeontology, weddings and fabulous journeys through the heavens aboard Greek airships. An interval of sixty days remained between the honeymoon's end and the beginning of the expedition. Rowena had her own uncharted territories to explore, too. On many, many occasions I would smile and say "Of course" when she murmured: "Dare I ask, my love, would you care to employ a new method tonight?"

I need not trouble you with mundane descriptions of the voyage to the Red Sea port where we boarded the *Greco*. For it's here that our extraordinary adventure truly began. This silver bullet of an airship pierced the blue sky with ease. Twenty four hours later we entered the arid borderlands between the Asir Mountains and Ar Rub' Al Khali or 'empty corner.' The desert lies in the south of the Arabian Peninsula (known by the Romans as Arabia Deserta); it is untravelled, treeless, grassless, waterless, and shunned by even the most resilient Bedouin traveller. An ocean of sand, some say it comprises a quarter of a million square miles. Temperatures soar to 130 degrees Fahrenheit at noon. Its dunes stand a thousand feet tall. And yet here there are surprises, too. The lost City of Pillars. Black meteorites speckle orange sand. And in hollows, between thousands of dunes, the desert air pretends it is freshwater. As Rowena and I gazed out of the gondola, we could see a perfect mirror image of the *Greco* reflected from below, as if from a lake. The sleek, silver airship glided at an altitude of three thousand feet. We could discern the cruciform tail fins in the reflecting glass of searing air. The four engines purred smoothly. In the front gondola, suspended beneath the gas-filled envelope, the pilot and the engineers tended to the machine's every want. In the rear gondola, lightweight cane chairs, sofas and academia. Glasses of cold lemonade adorned a card table. Professor Zuckerman's team studied the plaster cast of *Vampithecus*. The holes in the eye sockets troubled them. The hole in each orbit, which admitted the optic nerve to the brain, appeared very large –

so large it made Mother Nature appear downright eccentric.

Oh, for historical accuracy I should add that, in all, there were eighteen of us. Ten crew; eight scientists. The *Greco* is three hundred feet in length; top speed forty knots, and boasts, not least amongst so many technical innovations, an ice chest that enabled us to enjoy deliciously refreshing gin and tonics.

Rowena and I waved from the gondola. Far below, our mirror images waved back. I could even make out Rowena's excited grin. She threw a coin into that wilderness forsaken by humanity.

"For luck!" She watched her offering of sterling silver tumble, twinkling through our reflections. Ar Rub' Al Khali, that king of all 'empty quarters' absorbed the coin into its gritty body – just as it had swallowed many an expedition, camel train, and even entire cities in the past.

"You throw one, Gerald." Her girlish delight shone brighter than the sun… or so it seemed to me.

I shook my head. "Do we need to buy luck? Can't we make our own?"

"Go on, throw a half crown."

"I can't."

"Spoilsport."

"It's not that. I put all our money under my bunk."

Professor Zuckerman stroked his silver beard. He never attempted to conceal his admiration of Rowena. "Take this, my dear."

"A gold sovereign?"

Eyes twinkling, he said, "I'm not above bribing the gods. If a sovereign should, by strange magic, purchase me a complete skeleton of *Vampithecus*, then I'll boast for years to come that this was the bargain of the century. What say you, chaps?"

The rest of the team sang out their hear-hears. As they did so, a whistle came from the Marconi speaker fixed to the cabin wall. The captain used this device to communicate with us in the rear gondola (this saved a scramble up the ladder into the body of the airship, then walking one hundred and twenty feet to the ladder that descended through the latticework of metal into our little domain).

Excitement intensified the Captain's Greek accent. "Professor Zuckerman, sir. Will you look out to port and confirm that we have found our destination?"

The professor rushed to the window, excited as a child on his birthday. "There it is, by God! The Mount of Three Towers. Look! Clear as day they are."

Our team joined us at the gondola's observation windows. The Asir mountain range stood like a fortress wall. Forbidding ramparts of grey rock, seven thousand feet high. Where desert clashed against the range one mountain, alone, had been adorned by the work of man.

"See the towers?" The professor eagerly pointed. "In this place you can never tell whether a building is fifty years old or five thousand years old. But I'd swear those structures are Roman. Probably observation towers to check on the Bedouins moving along the old camel trails."

"You mean people could survive down there?" exclaimed Doctor Meadows. "The place is a furnace. There isn't even a blade of grass."

"Bedouin caravans could negotiate a path between the mountains and the desert. Wadis ran at intervals that provided water for the next leg of the journey, but eventually even those dried up." Professor Zuckerman tugged a curl of beard as he recalled past adventures. "I've managed to reach this place three times with Bedouin guides. We had to carry every drop of water we needed. And it's a six day journey on foot to the nearest oasis. Those water supplies were contained in goatskin bags, I should stress – ye Gods it made the water taste foul. And all the rations permitted were two days at the site where I found the skull fragments." He beamed. "With this miracle of the air age, the *Greco*, we can reach our destination in twenty-four hours. And we have food and water and tools in abundance."

"And mountain climbing equipment, I notice," said Doctor

Meadows.

"Absolutely. It isn't wise for a scientist to make public where he finds his valuable artefacts – nothing so unseemly as fellow academics being struck by the equivalent of gold-rush fever. But now we're here I can reveal we won't be digging into the earth. We will be ascending." He smiled. "I found my *Vampithecus* at the bottom of a rock face. Fifty feet above that point is an opening to what appears to be a large cave. Of course, on previous expeditions, I lacked the time and the equipment to climb a vertical cliff. This occasion will be different. Mister Kennedy and Doctor Goldstein are accomplished mountaineers."

Rowena said, "So you believe that the bones fell from the cave?"

"Indeed I do, my dear. Moreover, dare I add what I expect to find in the cave?" He smiled. "The necropolis of *Vampithecus*. Or so I pray."

The gondola tilted; the airship had turned toward the mountain range.

"Hold on tight," I warned. "We're about to land."

The afternoon sun cast long shadows. Mountains turned from pale grey to darker shades. With the *Greco* anchored to the arid earth, we prepared to disembark for the half-mile walk to the Mount of Three Towers. The captain couldn't risk taking his ship any closer due to the turbulent air generated by the Asir Range.

"Asir means 'difficult', so whoever named it chose the apt word," Professor Zuckerman declared. Then he noticed what was absent from my hip. "Don't neglect to take your pistol, my dear boy. We're not ambling through Jesus Green now."

"But the nearest village is five hundred miles away. Surely, there's nobody here to give us any trouble?"

"Don't rule out bandits, and there are certainly leopards. I saw one pounce on a lame camel the last time I was here. Take your gun with you, there's a good chap. If not for my sake, then for your wife's."

Rowena flashed a smile. "We'll start walking, Gerald, so don't dilly-dally."

The eight members of the team were joined by five crew members, who'd help carry the formidable array of picks, shovels, climbing gear, cameras, and, of course, that most precious desert essential: water. The Professor descended the ladder to the desert, his white pith helmet gleaming as bright as polished bone in the afternoon sunlight. Rowena followed. Then the crew members and her fellow adventurers shimmied down to the soft, orange sand.

Quickly, I retrieved the pistol from my locker, then exited the craft. The heat stole the moisture from my mouth the second I began my descent of the ladder. As soon as I alighted, I rushed to join our expedition and find what surprises this fabulous wilderness had to offer.

Kennedy and Goldstein were indeed accomplished climbers. They soon scaled the cliff face to the cave's opening. After that, the sound of hammering as they drove steel pegs into rock. To these pegs they tied a rope ladder. With a shout of "Watch out below," Goldstein rolled the ladder over the edge. It spooled out as it fell.

Kennedy called down. "Don't climb up yet. Two of you jump onto the bottom rung. Test it will hold fast."

Goldstein added, "And come up here one at a time. And carefully does it – fifty feet is a long drop!"

The setting sun now turned the rock a russet brown.

Professor Zuckerman had attached cord to the lantern handles, so he could carry four from his shoulders. "I'm sorry to have to ask you to work at night, but to do this in the heat of the day would be impossible." He smiled. "We oh-so pallid Caucasians tend to keel over when the temperature climbs anywhere above one hundred degrees."

We took it in turns to scale the rope ladder. And, believe me, that fifty feet of rock was still almost too hot to touch after being roasted by the Arabian sun. I confess that I watched Rowena ascend with nothing less than a pang of anxiety. The airship seemed frighteningly tiny as it sat out there in the desert. The mountain range loomed above us. Those three towers jutted out from the slopes – to me they resembled the thighbones of giants; an odd comparison to be sure, yet this place unsettled me. The Ar Rub' Al Khali desert scorned man. These forty thousand square miles of mountains were just as menacing. We human beings are such fragile things to be pitted against those two implacable enemies of life.

Nevertheless, with my load of equipment, I scaled the ladder. Perspiration evaporated so quickly it chilled my skin. My tongue had become as dry as paper. Even my eyes tingled as the desert air robbed them of moisture.

Nervousness? Anticipation? Awe? I don't know if any of these affected my companions. However, nobody spoke; that is, beyond the essentials of ensuring everyone had safely climbed onto the ledge at the cave mouth. Could the quality of Earthly gravity be different here? Because my arms and legs felt unusually heavy. The weight of our heads drew them down; we walked with our chins almost touching our chests. Even to breathe became arduous. My heart didn't so much as beat in my chest. The muscle squelched as it pushed sluggish blood through arteries.

Rowena saw my troubled expression. She squeezed my hand. I agreed with an, "It will" when she gently whispered, "Everything will be all right."

The cave. A gloomy vault of huge dimensions. Torches revealed a dark roof high above our heads. This chamber had all the vastness of a locomotive shed. Yet its floor wasn't level. Instead, it contained perhaps two hundred columns of rock that stood ten feet in height and were roughly four feet in diameter. Their distribution suggested the spikes protruding from that fabled 'bed of nails' beloved of Fakirs in India.

Professor Zuckerman rushed amidst the columns with breathless excitement. "They can't be natural." He shone the flashlight about him as we lit our lamps. "See! Handholds! These aren't pillars, they're platforms!"

"Bones, Professor!" Rowena had been caught up in the excitement, too. Eagerly, she picked up pale, stick-like objects from the floor "Are they hominid?"

"No… no, they're baboon – those creatures would have been plentiful before the wadiis dried up." Recklessly, he climbed one of the columns.

Other members of the team, including the crewmen, were infected by the fever of discovery. For they all climbed their own stone protrudences that imitated tree-trunks. Rowena chose one, too. Everyone had forgotten the uncanny gravity of the place. They shrugged off anxiety. Caution was well and truly flung aside.

If I hadn't been so concerned for my wife's safety, as she clambered up the vertical rock, I'd have probably found my own column to climb. That curiosity burned within me, too. What lay up there on the elevated platform? What marvel?

Yet I made a point of staying beneath my wife and held the lantern high so she might safely ascend.

The professor was the first to reach the top of the rocky stump. "Great Scott!"

"What is it?" I cried. "What have you found?"

Rowena hauled herself onto the platform ten feet above my head. "Gerald. Hurry! Climb up and see what's here."

The Professor ran his hands through his hair, almost overwhelmed by his discovery. "We've found it!" His eyes blazed with such intensity. "This is the tomb of *Vampithecus*!"

Rowena called out to the men, as they each stood up on their respective columns, some fifteen feet apart, "I expected bones… fragments of bones… not this."

"What's up there?" Inexplicably, fear brushed aside excitement. "Rowena, you've got to tell me."

"No bones, Gerald." Her eyes blazed, too. "Mummies!"

"Rowena, come down."

"Gerald, fetch the camera," she said by way of answer to my

plea. "We must get as many photographs as possible."

"Please, Rowena…" and then I added these words – I can't say why, other than instinct compelled me: "Come down at once. It's not safe."

Of course, fatally, she did not come back down to me. Memory of what happened next has become dream-like. Perhaps the emotional intensity of it all prevented my senses engaging fully with what occurred in the cave.

Goldstein asked me to take the camera to him; he was designated the expedition's photographer. In a dull way, I might even say 'detached' – for some premonition of danger threatened to overwhelm me – I picked up the satchel that contained the camera and film. As I climbed the column of rock to Goldstein the echoing voices washed over me.

Professor Zuckerman shouted his theories, "Without a shadow of doubt! This is *Vampithecus*. See? Each column of stone provides a platform for one elevated burial. Unlike Egyptian mummification these bodies are intact. The hot air in the cave dried out the flesh to preserve the creatures perfectly." Like some strange circus act the men and one woman stood atop their individual pillar, with their own individual mummy – which I had not yet seen for myself.

Mr. Kennedy declared, "They have bone floors in their mouths."

Dr Goldstein: "See the state of preservation? Even the hair is intact. Look how it radiates from the skull, causing them to resemble dandelion clocks."

"What about the eyes?" asked another scientist. "What could account for the enlarged canal for the optical nerve?"

"I'll check," called Rowena. "The light here is best."

No! That's the word I wanted to scream. I didn't want my wife to touch those creatures. Dread engulfed me. All I wanted was to grab her hand and rush from this wretched tomb.

Yet, my scientific training propelled me, quelling the panic, stifling complaint, and robbing me of common sense!

"Take this." I'd reached the lip of the platform so I could hand the camera satchel to Doctor Goldstein. "Stand back. I'll haul myself up."

"No room, I'm afraid. I don't want you standing on our sleeper."

"Sleeper? What makes you say that?"

He gave me a kindly smile. "Sleeper? Oh? Just a turn of phrase."

I had an eye-level view of the mummy. And the neighbouring mummies lying atop the dozens of stumpy towers. Each four foot wide platform supported a mummified *Vampithecus*, curled foetus-like, as if in a womb. Knees held tight to chests, the cadavers could have been fashioned from brown paper. Those gaunt relics were complete down to their creamy fingernails and curious hair which, although very thin, radiated evenly from their heads by ten inches or so. Surprisingly for an ape-man, the lower jaws were small, quite delicate really. The eyelids were lightly closed. Their eyes must have sunk into their heads, for where our closed eyes bulge smoothly out, theirs were slightly concave. Above each eye, a bristling dark brow.

And my lovely wife peeled back an eyelid of the creature on her platform. She raised her lantern; let out a shout. That shout echoed on and on throughout the cave. Its sound disorientated me. I had to clutch at Doctor Goldstein's ankle lest I topple backwards as I stood with my head just above the platform's edge.

"They don't have eyes," she cried.

Everyone on his platform checked their own desiccated corpse.

"Ye Gods, she's right. They don't have eyes," called Mr. Kennedy. "Ouch. Careful, their eyebrows are sharp as thorns. Great Scott, they've even drawn blood." He sucked a bloody fingertip.

"We should come back here in the morning," I told them (though in truth I wanted to be away from this nightmare vault –

forever!). "We can't work here at night."

Professor Zuckerman waved away my comment. "Nonsense. It's cooler. And we have lamps."

"This is most peculiar," Rowena said. "There is a fleshy membrane where the eye should be. And it's pierced with a small orifice."

"A night creatures," declared the professor. "*Vampithecus* didn't need eyes."

"The lack of muscle development in the lower jaw shows they didn't chew food."

"That proves my hypothesis," the professor declared grandly. "They consumed fluids – nothing but fluids. And nutritious fluids equals blood."

"It must be getting cooler," Mr. Kennedy announced. "The flesh of this mummy is contracting. It's making the fingers move."

"As is mine," Dr. Goldstein added. "Egyptian mummies often writhe when exposed to sunlight for the first time in centuries."

"These must have lain here for a hundred thousand years." The professor crouched in order to gaze into the dead face. "Imagine the world these creatures dwelt in. Mammoth and sabre-toothed tigers roamed. Neanderthal outnumbered *Homo sapiens*. People could walk from Asia to America."

Dr. Goldstein sighed. "This movement is almost life-like. The lips of my specimen are tightening. It's as if my friend is smiling."

"Get out!" I shouted, not able to quell that primal scream of warning inside my head. "Rowena! Climb down from there! You're in danger!"

"Really, Gerald..."

That's all she said. Because the mummies erupted into a frenzy of movement. On every platform where a human stood, the mummy attacked. My vantage point was only inches from Dr. Goldstein. The *Vampithecus* seized that gentle scholar's head in both its hands – and even now I remember those creamy oval fingernails that belonged to the creature – so perfect, so delicate.

Then the thing acted according to its nature, first tugging the doctor's face forward as if to kiss it. Yet rather than bestow a kiss, the creature rubbed its forehead against his cheeks... no, not forehead: eyebrows. Those thorny eyebrows scourged the doctor's flesh. Blood immediately ran from the wounds, slicking his entire face in crimson.

The creature fed. Not lapping or sucking. No. Its eyelids slid back to expose a moistly pink membrane. Still holding Doctor Goldstein's head the *Vampithicus* rubbed its eyes against his face. As eye brushed skin a white track-mark appeared where the blood had been drawn away.

This wasn't a necessary observation. To my ears I heard hysteria in the words, but say it I must: *"They're absorbing blood through the eye sockets. They drink with their eyes!"* But there were no eyes, of course. Merely a now bloody membrane with its petite orifice where a pupil would normally reside. At that moment it must have been madness that burst inside my head. Screams drenched my ears. Emotion flooded my mind. But my own eyes locked on the form of my lovely wife.

Rowena struggled with the creature on the plinth. Insanely, I experienced such jealousy at what appeared to be another kissing her. But this wasn't kissing, was it? No lips were involved. No, it was all in the eyes.

All around me, the vampires came to life. They grabbed their victim. Tore open their flesh with eyebrow hair that must have evolved into thorn-like spikes, designed to slice their victim's skin and so release the blood-flow. Then they ingested their prey's blood directly into their monstrous brain. Or so I surmised.

As the crew and scientists died they shrivelled. Equally, the vampire men started to swell. Blood filled their desiccated bellies. Limbs became engorged. Tumescent. Wrinkled skin smoothed out as blood inflated their bodies. They fattened, just as the mosquito fattens when slaking its thirst.

The vampire finished with the doctor then turned on me. In my precarious state, clinging to the top of the column, I didn't so much escape with that clichéd 'mighty bound'. Instead, I fell in an ungainly flutter of limbs to the cave floor. My head smacked against a boulder. From the back of the cave shuffled dozens of figures. I saw turbaned Bedouin, Roman legionnaires in corroded helmets; there were the chain-mailed warriors of ancient Himyar and Sabar; and mingling with them, European explorers and African traders. Then came hairy, hobgoblin ape-things that must have been yet more of our pre-human ancestors. At that moment I knew this fact: *Vampithecus* did not breed. It recruited.

This was confirmed when I saw Kennedy, Goldstein and Zuckerman slowly rise to their feet next to their demonic companions. Moreover, one of the crewmen had escaped *Vampithecus*, yet Zuckerman leapt down to grab him in an instant and fixed his teeth on the man's throat. Quickly, the professor gnawed through the skin to greedily drink his victim's blood.

Rowena stood up, too. "Gerald. I need you." Such a plaintive voice. "Don't leave me." Oh... the raw hunger in those eyes.

I fled the cave. A bright moon lit my way as I raced down the rope ladder, then ran full-pelt to where the *Greco* was moored. By moonlight, it resembled a silver bullet. The airship seemed so tranquil as it hung there – in utter contrast to the storm of emotion that raged inside my head.

I've already described my wife's return to the balloon. The gunshots. Then my dead faint to the cabin floor as the airship, now released from its moorings, soared upwards.

The captain and the remaining crew of four left their cabin to find me as mentally adrift as the *Greco* was physically. Later, I tried to make them understand what had happened. But they hadn't seen *Vampithecus* with their own eyes, had they? They hadn't gazed upon those shambling progeny of *Vampithecus*, either. Or that my wife, and Zuckerman, and the rest were now like them, too. Undead. Hungry for blood. Monstrous.

One truth rang clear, however: *we were safe.*

But did I want safety? Rowena had brought the dormant man

inside of me to life. Before, I'd been that bookish boy who was as good as sleep-walking through the world. So safety wasn't my personal priority. However, it took hours to persuade the crew. They speculated about bandits. About them kidnapping our colleagues. Did that bruise on my forehead hint at concussion and attendant hallucinations? But at last they accepted my plea of "Take me back."

Dawn broke. The captain delivered me to the Mount of Three Towers. The sunlight turned Ar Rub' Al Khali a delicious orange. So much so that it seemed to shine with an inner light all of its own. I equipped myself with a full water bottle. A pencil. A notebook (my pistol remained onboard). Then I waved as the *Greco* returned to the outside world. The gleaming vessel hove westwards – gradually growing smaller and smaller until it became a silver star in the blue sky.

I'm confident *Vampithecus* won't be able to follow the *Greco* to civilization

The creatures are effectively marooned here in these forbidding mountains. Even they can't cross these peaks. Nor can they negotiate the dunes of the 'the empty quarter.' As evidenced by their confinement to this relatively small section of mountain range.

I have what I need. The pint of water will last me until sunset. I will sit here in the shade beneath the cave's entrance in the rock face. There is sufficient time to enable me write in my notebook, and tell you what happened the night we found *Vampithecus*... *Vampire Man*, if you prefer.

Not long now. The sun will dip below the horizon and it will be night; I will end this account in the time-honoured way with: 'The End.'

When Rowena emerges from the cave I shall greet her. Her capacity to surprise me is eternal. Memories of those weeks following our marriage, the nights of wonder, those embraces in the hidden meadow, the excitement – they still resonate so powerfully in my mind. Therefore, without a shadow of doubt,

my heartfelt response will be "Of course" when she murmurs: "Dare I ask, my love? Would you care to try something new tonight?"

THE END

Young Bloods

Kelley Armstrong

The man on the subway car was dead. He looked like he was just passed out drunk, but Roger wasn't fooled.

The dead man slumped against the window, eyes closed. His mouth hung open, his cheek damp with drool. A teenage girl started to slide in beside the dead man, then stopped, nostrils flaring as the stink of BO and booze hit her. She quickly moved on.

The man hadn't been dead long. The blood dripping down his neck still glistened. Three drops of it had fallen on his dingy white shirt, forming an ellipsis. To be continued, the mark said. Fate's idea of a joke, Roger supposed.

When Roger saw the twin puncture wounds on the dead man's neck, he'd thought of finding another seat. But by then, the vampires had spotted him and he'd had to sit down. Pretend he didn't realize the old man was dead. Pretend he didn't know they were there.

Roger never doubted that they were vampires. He knew what those neck wounds meant. Any fool should. The fact that the local media failed to draw the same conclusion when two other blood-drained corpses had been found proved the suspicions he'd already had about their collective IQ level.

He supposed the real question should be: how did vampires manage to drain a man's blood on the subway? A tragic reflection on modern society. The bigger tragedy was that Roger wasn't surprised.

He looked around at his fellow commuters. The teenage girl had taken a seat across the car, ear buds planted, music blasting, gaze fixed on the nothingness zooming past her window. Opposite Roger, a businesswoman's fingers flew over a smart-phone keyboard. A man in a coal-gray suit was trying to catch her attention, a mission as futile as flirting with the metal pole between them. Two more men sat farther down, hidden behind their newspapers. They shared a subway car, but they might as well have been in hermetically sealed pods for all the attention they paid to their surroundings.

The only ones who were paying attention were the vampires. Two of them. Boys. Neither looked like he'd passed his twentieth birthday. Both were dressed in leather jackets, motorcycle boots, worn jeans and tattoos. Their fingernails were clean, though, and even their beard stubble was carefully cultivated. Wannabe thugs, the kind you could find on any city street corner, attracting girls who thought they'd be a safe walk on the wild side. All bark, no bite. These boys, though, had plenty of bite.

He'd known they were the vampires the moment he'd realized what happened to the old man. It wasn't the flush of colour on their pale cheeks. It wasn't even the faint smear of blood in the corner of the older youth's mouth. It was the eyes of the younger one. Hard, vacant eyes.

The train slowed for the next stop. A transfer station. The businesswoman snapped her phone shut and walked past, giving Roger an appraising once-over glance that earned him a glower from the would-be suitor dogging her heels. The other two men got off, too. Roger should do the same. That would be the smart thing, he supposed, under the circumstances, but that would mean leaving the teenage girl alone with the vampires. So he'd stay.

As the train pulled away from the station, the younger vampire said, "What are you looking at, old man?"

Roger checked over his shoulder, thinking someone else must have gotten on.

"I mean you, old man."

He turned and met the boy's empty eyes. *Old man?* He could have laughed at that. The businesswoman certainly didn't seem to think he was old. But, he supposed, to this boy, he was.

"I asked what you're looking at."

Roger thought of saying "not much," but it didn't seem wise. Nor did denying that he'd been looking. So he murmured an apology and fixed his gaze on the dead man, then quickly shifted it to the window.

The seat beside Roger squeaked. He glanced over to see the older vampire sitting there, arms crossed, staring at him.

Roger nodded. The vampire scowled, and thumped his leg down on the seat opposite them, blocking Roger's exit and smirking a challenge. Roger nodded again and returned to gazing out the window.

"That old guy's really tired, huh?" the vampire beside him said.

Roger considered pretending not to hear him, but settled for a vague, "Hmm?"

The vampire waved at the old man slumped in his seat. "Dead to the world."

Roger managed a small laugh. "Looks that way."

"Maybe he's not sleeping."

Roger peered at the old man. "I think you're right. From the smell of him, he's passed out drunk."

The vampire caught his eye. "Should I check?"

Roger shrugged. "If you like."

The vampire didn't like that. He said nothing, though, just squirmed in his seat, glancing over now and then, waiting for Roger to realize he was sitting across from a dead man.

Roger took out his planner and flipped through it, checking his appointments for the week.

"You'd better not be planning to get off anytime soon," the vampire said.

"I'm not."

A pause, then the vampire called to his friend across the aisle, "Tasty, isn't she?"

Roger looked over to see the younger vampire sitting beside the teenage girl. She was still staring out the window, music cranked up, oblivious.

"Very tasty." The younger vampire leaned over until his nose almost brushed her neck. He inhaled. "She even smells good."

Roger returned to his calendar. Out of the corner of his eye, he watched the younger vampire poised over the girl, his gaze shunted Roger's way, waiting for a reaction. When none came, he growled and the older vampire snatched the calendar from Roger's fingers.

"You won't be needing this." He tore the book in half and dropped it on the subway car's floor. "Something tells me there won't be any more appointments in your future, old man."

The younger vampire laughed. The train slowed, pulling into another station.

"Actually, I believe this is my stop," Roger said, standing.

The vampire didn't remove his feet from the seat across the way. "No, I believe it isn't. You're going all the way to the end of the line, old man." He flashed a smile, fangs extending.

Roger froze. He glanced out the window and waited until the train stopped, doors opening. Then he scrambled over the vampire's legs. The younger vampire lunged, but Roger dodged and made it out the doors, the vampires on his heels.

As the door closed behind them, the younger vampire let out a string of curses, realizing he'd lost the girl. Roger barrelled through the sleepy, late-evening commuters. A guard shouted. Roger looked back, but the man's gaze was fixed on the vampires behind him – the thugs chasing the middle-aged businessman through the station.

Roger smiled, broke into a jog and raced out the exit as the guard called for backup.

Roger made it to the road, only to find he'd exited into a section of downtown that had closed hours ago. Office buildings lined the road, only the occasional lighted window suggesting signs of life.

He looked up and down the empty street.

"No cabs out here, old man," a voice called.

He turned to see the two vampires sauntering toward him, teeth glittering under the sickly glow of the streetlights.

"No cabs, no buses, no cops..." the younger one said. "Guess you should have stayed on the subway. And let me finish the girl. Maybe I'd have let you go. Now I'm hungry. And the more you make me run, the hungrier I'm going to get."

Roger took off.

After ten minutes of running, Roger began to reflect that he really needed to add a workout routine to his daily schedule. Seemed those boys were right. He was getting old.

He veered down another back road. His shoes thumped against the pavement, as loud as a locomotive chugging along the tracks, the sound echoing through the emptiness.

That was the only sound he heard, though. Had he lost them? He turned into an alley, gaze fixed over his shoulder, watching and listening for—

A thump in front of him. He spun to see the older vampire standing there, the fire escape overhead still vibrating from the force of his leap.

"Gotcha," the vampire said, flashing his fangs.

"Actually, no. To get me, you needed to jump down after I passed you and found myself trapped in a dead-end alley."

The vampire frowned, momentarily thrown. He recovered with a grin. "Maybe I don't want to trap you. Maybe I like running."

"True, but I don't. Getting old, as you so graciously pointed out. Which is why I appreciate what you've done – trapping *yourself* between me and that dead end."

Roger smiled. A wide, teeth-baring smile.

The vampire blinked. "What the—?"

He didn't get a chance to finish the sentence.

Roger crouched on the fire escape. He could hear the younger vampire stalking along the empty street, calling to his buddy, his tone taking on a crackly edge of worry.

Roger stomped on the fire escape floor. The metal twanged, and the boy raced into the alley, then stopped and looked around.

"Tim?" he said.

Roger dropped from the fire escape. He didn't thump when he hit the pavement. You didn't reach his age by being noisy and careless.

"Tim?" the boy called, louder.

"Over there," Roger said.

The boy whirled, stumbling. Seeing Roger, he tried to find a suitably menacing glower, but couldn't quite manage it.

"Over there." Roger pointed at the trash bags littering the end of the alley. A boot stuck out from behind one. "And over there." He pointed to a lock of blond hair peeking from behind another. "I think there's part of a hand over there, too, but that was an accident. Getting old. The reflexes are the first thing to go."

The boy looked from body part to body part, then turned to stare at Roger.

"You know what else happens when you get old?" Roger continued. "You get comfortable. Set in your ways. You find a city like this." He waved around them. "You settle in. You make it your own. And you really, really hate it when some young bloods waltz in and crap all over the place." He ran his tongue over his teeth, letting his fangs extend. "It's very inconvenient."

The boy backed up. "I-I didn't know. . ."

"But you should. It's basic respect. You don't have it and, I'm

36

sorry to say, it doesn't look like anything you're capable of learning. Now I need to clean up the mess you made."

The boy bolted. He managed to dodge Roger and raced onto the road. But he didn't get far.

Roger was finishing up when his cell phone rang. He checked the call display. Leslie.

"Please tell me you're on your way," she said when he answered.

"On my way...?"

"To Fresno's? For drinks? At eleven?"

He swore.

"Forgot, didn't you?" she said with a chuckle. "You're getting old, Roger."

"So I've been told." He sighed and finished tucking the young vampire's body behind the trash bags. "So I've been told."

A Winter's Tale

Sarah Singleton

A mountain of ice from the northern ocean – all blue-glittering towers and turrets, high valleys and plunging chasms – followed a steam ship to the city. It floated in the harbour for a night, a restless Arctic monster harnessed with spikes and ropes and chains. In the morning a team of twenty horses dragged it to the city park for the winter festival. The horses sweated and struggled, hooves slipping on the churned snow. Drivers tugged at bridles, clung to leather collars, urged and coaxed and cursed, cracking long whips. Inch by inch, the iceberg climbed the slipway, lurched onto wooden rollers and along the harbour road. People stood and stared.

After midnight, officials, sightseers and horses long gone, the ice stood monumentally still. It was blue-striped, like a sweet-shop lozenge. The shape of the ice had captured the motion of the sea – the surge of deep currents, the ramps and troughs of waves. The polished surface glittered.

The city's church bells, in succession, chimed the single hour. Frost sealed the surface of the ice and in its salt heart, like a knot of moonlight, something moved. A curling, like a white tadpole sewn up tight in its ghostly jelly. A twist and wriggle. The ice flexed, softened, creating a smooth aperture.

A girl stepped out.

Her skin was translucent – a freakish sapphire blue. Her hair, black as the deep ocean, flowed over her as smooth and glossy as sealskin. She brushed a lingering powder of ice from her narrow, newly-formed body. Then she placed her tiny feet one in front of the other, leaving footprints in the snow. First steps.

At the park gates a chestnut seller slept in his booth, his back to the brazier, head muffled against the winter weather. The girl was drawn to him – to the heat of the dying embers and the salt-heat of his blood. His eyes opened as her hand stole through the canvas opening. He made an odd sound, query or protest perhaps. Moonlight passed through the girl's ice face. The old man crossed himself, trying to speak, but the face moved towards him. Her kiss burned his forehead. When she walked into the street her transparent blue had become a soft white.

The city lay all around. Snowy roofs rose and fell like billows on the sea. Here and there, a church spire stabbed and, in the west, the cathedral dome curved like a whale's belly.

The tidal river, black and serpentine, held the scent of the sea in its breath, along with rot and sewage and the chemical tang of effluent from city factories. A hotchpotch of tethered vessels jostled along the banks, some beached and tilting: coal-dusted barges, battered rowing boats, residences from which beads of yellow light gleamed. She followed the river upstream. Docks and warehouses gave way to teetering residences, tenements that leaned over soiled lanes. The occasional sound of voices strayed from shuttered windows. Yellowed posters, like the wings of dead moths, peeled from wooden walls.

A door opened beneath a painted mermaid on a shabby sign. A young man stumbled out. Angry words followed him but the man shrugged them off and pulled together his long, tattered coat against the cold. When he passed beneath the streetlamp, she saw the copper hair curling over his collar. He looked back once as the pub door slammed shut, sniffed loudly, and set off with an uneven stride along an alleyway, the river at his back.

The girl followed. He left a trail of warmth and scent behind him like a ribbon fading on the winter air. His heat drew her, perfumed with gin, tobacco and the complex olfactory signature of his body: blood, perspiration, red wine and the partially digested meat he'd eaten two hours before, now passing through the organic machinery of his guts. Beneath a second lonely streetlamp the young man halted and looked back, perhaps sensing his follower. The girl retreated into the shadows. She was close enough to see the scattering of freckles on his face and paint stains on his tapering fingers. The man shook his head, wiped his nose on the back of his hand and crossed to a door. It wasn't locked because he opened it without a key and stepped inside.

David Newton pushed the door to and climbed three flights of bare wooden stairs to his attic room. He fumbled with matches to light the oil lamp waiting inside the door. A daubed canvas stood in front of him. He was so drunk the colours swam in an ugly, angry cloud. A cold wind rattled the window and he swore out loud when the door banged against his back. He'd been uneasy all day: the frustration of painting, the row in the pub and then the paranoid suspicion that Albert had followed him into the street. It persisted still, this sense of a pursuer.

Too late to set a fire. He sat heavily on his bed behind the screen in the corner of the room. The water in the jug had frozen. Ornate coils of ice furnished the window panes. He should remove his coat at least, but drink and fatigue had the better of him so he pushed off his boots, curled up under the blankets and plunged into a drink- sodden sleep.

David woke suddenly. White light filled the room, morning sun filtering through the frosted windows. It was late, wasn't it? Midwinter, the sun didn't rise till eight. His mouth was sour and dry; his body ached. He heaved himself out of bed.

He'd forgotten to lock the door and it gaped, revealing the tiny landing and the stairs descending into shadow. A thin, needling draft whistled through the room. He pushed the door to and turned to look at the painting again.

Curled like an ammonite, white as a pearl, a woman lay on the floor beneath the canvas with its swirls of cobalt and turquoise and aquamarine. At first he thought she was dead – stiff and chilly, like a piece of marble. She had her back to him, the spine visible like a string of beads. Pale skin skimmed narrow hips and small, boyish buttocks. A flood of glossy black hair streamed over the bare boards.

David blinked. He was holding his breath. He stepped towards the woman – a girl, she was young, surely? – and reached out his hand. Remarkably, a delicate veil of snow lay on the skin. But as soon as his fingers brushed the apex of her bony shoulder the girl twisted towards him, opened her eyes and stared into his face.

Such eyes! Crystalline prisms of jade and moss and bottle green – the colour altered as the light moved on her face. David drew back his hand and they stared at each other. Her arm lay across her chest and, though her gaze did not invite, it held no embarrassment either. His heart thrummed against his ribs. Something about this face filled him with a visceral unease – her eyes – the sense that the presence behind them was a blank nothing, or else vast beyond imagining. Limitless in either case. Inhuman, certainly.

"What are you?" he said. What, not who. "Why are you here?" He heard the edge of anxiety in his voice, a show of bravado. Inhuman? What was he thinking? Some slattern from the streets who'd broken into his room.

The girl sat up. The sleek wash of hair hung over her shoulders. David shook his head and strode over to the screen where he scooped up his second shirt and best jacket for the girl to put on. He lit the fire and ushered her into the single chair by its side. Perversely, she started to shiver, soaking up the fire's heat, this swan with her black hair and jewelled eyes.

"I'll make us some tea. Then you'll have to go." He was brusque, putting aside his earlier misapprehension. He didn't want to get saddled. She seemed more ordinary, covered in his clothes. How to be rid of her? He couldn't let her leave dressed as she was. He'd have to find her something more suitable even to get her out of his room. That would take money, and bother.

"What's your name? Where are your people?"

The girl didn't speak. She stared at him like an imbecile. Was that the reason for the vacancy he'd noticed before? Perhaps she'd escaped from somewhere. He should just throw her out.

But… but what? Something inside him resisted. The image of her coiled beneath the painting burned in his imagination like a white-hot coal. He could use her, couldn't he? Place her in the picture, the figure his painting so sorely missed.

"What's your name?" he repeated. Still no answer. Perhaps she was mute.

"Well, I'll call you Blanche. I'll get us something to eat. Would you like that?"

David hurried out to the bakers and bought hot rolls. The idea had caught hold of him. He would use her as a model. She was a gift, wasn't she? Once in the street anxiety overcame him. What if she slipped away while he was gone? He should have locked the door behind him.

But she hadn't gone. She was as he had left her, sitting on the chair by the fire.

"Here, have something to eat. You must be hungry." He buttered the roll and passed it to her on a plate. The girl picked up the bread but she didn't bite it. Instead she cradled it in her hands. David ate hungrily and drank a cup of tea though he hardly tasted it, his mind fired up with idea of what he would paint. As soon as he'd finished he jumped to his feet.

"I'd like to paint you," he said. "I'd like you to be my model. Do you understand?" He moved from foot to foot, energy brimming over. "You can stay here as long as I need you. And I shall pay you of course. Some shillings, you'd like that wouldn't you?"

Blanche was immune to his enthusiasm but she seemed to

understand. She placed the bread roll on the hearth and rose to her feet.

"Take off the jacket," David commanded. "Here – put it here. And stand so. Can you turn? Yes, like that." He took out his paper and charcoal and began to draw.

He worked all day in a pleasurable fever. Blanche was patient and compliant, seemingly impervious to the cold. When darkness fell he relit the lamp and a host of candles so the work could continue.

Later, exhausted, he locked her into the room and went out into the city. He stopped at the Mermaid to see his friends Albert and Claude, fellow artists. He fell on a meal of beef pie and boiled potatoes. They drank beer in the pleasurable fug of the pub and David, tongue loosened by drink and the euphoria of his day's work, confided that he'd found a new model. The picture he'd been struggling with for half a year was going to be a triumph.

When he returned, half drunk, Blanche was asleep in the chair by the fire, lying under his best jacket. The bread roll he'd given her that morning still waited, uneaten, on the hearth but evidently she had boiled a kettle and made herself a hot drink. Should he give up his bed? Ah, why disturb her? She was asleep already. He undressed quickly and slid under the blankets.

He dreamed of the sea, of drifting in black, arctic waters under mountainous waves and above immeasurable, abysmal depths. The weight of the ocean pressed against him and the endless cold sucked heat from his body. He seemed to be dissolving, losing himself, as flesh and bones melted and blood seeped into the circulating currents of the sea. David woke a little, slowly, slowly surfacing from sleep. He became aware, distantly, that he was no longer alone in the bed. Blanche had climbed in and lay curled against him with her arms around his neck, seeming to hang from him, dragging him down. The room was black, except for the hanging square of the frost-encrusted window. David shivered, hands and feet like blocks of stone, but Blanche was fever-hot, her skin burning. He put his fingertips on her face, feeling the closed eyes, the curves of nose and brows, the soft mouth. She stirred sleepily and moved against him, shallow breasts brushing against his chest, narrow legs slipping between his own icy thighs. Her face reached up and she pressed her mouth against his, a curiously cool, salty tongue pushing between his lips. Her hands tightened around his neck and his pulse thundered, desire like a furnace blazing to life in the pit of his belly, sending out ropes of renewed heat through his shivering limbs. She didn't make a sound but she clung to him, half choked him, stopping his breath. He tried to release himself, to unwrap her arms from his neck but she was tenacious, stronger than he would have credited. He rolled over onto his back, gripped her bony behind and slid inside her while she thrashed and struggled on top of him like a huge, white bird, making odd guttural noises that didn't stop till he'd spent himself inside her. Then, in a moment, her body relaxed and she folded over, pressing her face into his chest.

When David next woke, the room was light and he was cold again. Blanche lay next to him, spread-eagled over the bed. Her skin had lost its unnatural pallor and her lips, partly open, were a dark, fleshy red. He leaned over, smelled the stale salt and iron perfume of her breath. An intricate lacing of veins was visible through the translucent skin on her neck and shoulders. His appetite stirred a little, but not enough. He clambered out of bed and tugged on his clothes, shaking and desperate to be warm. He set a fire and heated water for tea, glancing at the numerous sketches from the previous day. He sucked his lip, tasting blood. The lust to paint blazed and he forgot tea and cold, snatching up his brushes and stirring sluggish paints to embroider the figure of his new model in the vortex of blue on the canvas.

It was midwinter's eve – the night of the Winter Festival. The shops and banks closed early.

A night of perfect black and white. The day's new snow lay over the city, the sky a black lake swimming with stars. A narrow moon swung above the cathedral dome.

Blanche walked beside David. She wore a long, velvet coat with a spiral of ivy pinned to the lapel, a black fur hat on her head. David had procured these items from a second hand clothes shop in one of the many unpromising alleys near the river several days before but their shabbiness faded when Blanche put them on, and under the cover of glamorous night.

In the Regent's Park, not far from the harbour, the darkness of the longest night was broken by a hundred burning torches.

Thousands of feet had churned the melting snow into a muddy slush, here and there covered by pathways of hemp carpet where the ladies walked to save their hems. So many people. It seemed the entire city had arrived for the festival – the rich, dressed in furs, sitting around braziers in armchairs within canvas pavilions, the traders with barrows of chestnuts, sausages, mulled wine, spiced potatoes, the working men and women released from the factories.

Blanche's eyes widened as she and David made their way among the crowd to the arena. They moved through a stew of sound – laughing and talking, the shouts of children, stray notes from the barrel organ and the deeper tones of the city band playing Christmas carols. David took her arm and kept her close beside him but he'd nothing to worry about. She seemed fearless – exultant almost – soaking up the atmosphere of the event, watching everything.

Then – at the heart of the festival – a glittering winter palace.

The city's sculptors had carved the monstrous iceberg into an elaborate fairy castle, phantasmagoric in the blaze of torch light, fit for the Snow Queen herself. How many men, how much work, to carve this fantasy of ice? The mountain had been hollowed out and embellished. Towers and turrets, arched doorways, glistening gargoyles – ice dragons – throwing themselves from embellished parapets, spires leaping from spires, and a huge silver dome help up by fluted columns.

Festival goers wandered like children through arched

corridors, in blue-icy cloisters and shining hallways, the most marvellous thing they'd ever seen.

Blanche stared and gripped David's arm.

"So you want to go inside?" he said. Blanche didn't answer but her eyes widened. They stepped through a gateway beneath battlements.

The stars blazed, bright and distorted, through transparent ice-windows. The warm breath of so many wondering visitors filled the rooms like a mist. At the heart of the palace they stepped into a courtyard where ice tumbled silently from a fountain beneath the central dome.

"Do you like it?" David said. Blanche raised her face, reached for him, pressed her lips against his. There they stood, surrounded by revellers, in the heart of the palace of ice.

"David! David!" A commotion broke out on the other side of the hall, young men's voices, a woman's shrill complaint.

"It's Claude and Albert," David said. He hadn't seen them for days. Time had blurred, becoming a sequence of light and dark during which he either he painted and lay in bed with the girl.

Two young men ran over to him, faces bright with drink and excitement.

"David, where have you been? You've been working, haven't you? The picture, it's taken you away from us." Albert glanced at Blanche, and glanced again.

"Well, won't you introduce us?" A sly smile crept across his face.

"Yes, of course. This is Blanche, my new model. Blanche, this is Albert, and Claude."

Lanky Claude frowned. He was less drunk than Albert; he reached out to pat David's arm and said: "My god, what's happened to you? You look dreadful."

"Oh, working like a demon. You know how it is."

Claude shook his head. His eyes searched David's face. "It's more than that," he said. "Have you seen yourself? You look haggard. Have you been eating?"

David brushed it off. "Another few days, the picture will be finished. Then I can rest."

"Come with us, come and have a drink," Albert urged, clutching David's sleeve and jumping up and down. "I'll buy you one! I'll buy us all drinks."

"He sold a picture, the money's burning holes in his pockets," Claude said, over his friend's head. "I can't stop him. He's been drinking for three days straight." He rested a friendly arm on David's shoulder. "But you, what have you been doing with yourself? And the girl, where did you find her? She's quite something."

David shrugged.

"She came to my studio, looking for work," he said. "Just what I needed. Come and see it, Claude. The picture is nearly finished. It's the best I've ever done."

A brace of fireworks exploded in the sky, releasing plumes of blue and silver. David gripped Blanche's gloved hand as he followed Albert through the crowd to the Albatross, a sunken pub off a narrow walkway near the park. Inside, a fire burned in a huge hearth. They sat together at a table crammed in the corner of the room. Swags of holly and ivy hung from the rafters. Albert called for drinks. Blanche took off her hat, and her hair, never bound nor pinned, poured over her shoulders in two long, black stripes. Albert stared, mesmerised.

"You look like a fairy," he said. "Doesn't she, Claude? La Belle Dame Sans Merci. I should like to paint you too. May I borrow her, David, when you've finished?"

David, overwhelmed by the heat of the fire, had slumped into his seat as though Claude's concern about his health had made the symptoms manifest. He barely shook his head at Albert's suggestion.

"Well, girl, Blanche – La Belle Dame. What do you think? She doesn't say much, does she?" Albert wriggled in his seat. A girl deposited cups of hot spiced wine on the table.

"She doesn't speak at all," David said. Albert was beginning to annoy him. He wished he wouldn't stare at Blanche.

"Doesn't speak? Why, the perfect model. No moaning, eh? In fact, the perfect woman." Albert's eyes continued to feed on Blanche and David felt a rising desire to smash his fist into his friend's face. Why had he taken her to the festival?

"I need to go out," he said, rising abruptly from the chair. He pushed his way through the bar and out of the door into the tart winter air. It was better here, in the cold: at least he could breathe. David took a cigarette from the case in his pocket and lit up; for the past few days he had all but forgotten about smoking. A further banner of fireworks hung in the sky. Distantly he heard the noise of the crowds in the park, stray notes of music from the brass band. He shouldn't be too long. God only knew what Albert was saying to Blanche. They'd shared models before, of course. They were a loose bunch, the girls who hung around the artists' studios, always on the make, looking for the best chance. Blanche was not like them. He had no intention of letting her go, not even when the picture was complete. He would paint her again. Besides, he had grown accustomed to having her in his bed at night.

He dropped the butt of his cigarette into the churned snow and took a deep breath. He was never cold now. On the contrary, the bitter night air sustained him and the prospect of the pub's close, overheated interior was not a pleasant one. Perhaps he should simply retrieve Blanche and they could walk home together. Three men barrelled out of the door as he was about to make his way back inside. His eye caught the reflection in the fly-blown, gilt-framed mirror hanging over the fireplace – and he stopped short. He saw a man standing among the oblivious carousing crowd, so gaunt his clothes hung from him like a scarecrow, face hollow and dead-white, mauve and grey shadows under red-rimmed eyes and around his mouth, like three-day-old bruises. David stared. Did he look so bad? No wonder Claude was worried. He took a long, slow breath, and then he put his hands on his chest, and his belly, and his thighs, feeling the

49

tenderness of his flesh. Were there other bruises? How could he have paid such scant attention to himself that he hadn't noticed the wreckage of his body? It was the picture of course, the work consuming him. Well, it was nearly finished. What did it matter if he pushed himself to the edge?

He sat down again, beside Blanche, and took a mouthful of hot wine.

"Your hands are shaking," Claude observed. "You're sick, David. You should go to the hospital."

David lowered the cup to the table. He shook his head. "I'm fine. Tired, that's all. You know how it is, you forget to eat. I'm nearly done now."

The ice palace took weeks to melt in the long, hard winter. It decayed in slow increments, sliding bit by bit into ruin, melting in the sunny days, freezing again during each cold snap. As time went by, respect and wonder dissolved too. Soot and graffiti spoiled the walls. Youths loitered in the still marvellous halls, lit bonfires and kicked at the walls. Silver-blue ice became grey and soiled. Melt water lay in a lake in the park.

The days lengthened. The first frail cherry blossoms appeared on the trees. Snowdrops broke the icy soil, then waves of gold and mauve crocuses. These impressions of spring David saw vaguely. He strayed from the apartment only briefly, consumed by his work, painting, scraping the canvas, painting again. The white figure emerged from the coil of water, arms uplifted, the cloud of black hair swirling from her head into the sea, while above, just a line above the mass of water, loured a stormy grey-blue sky.

Blanche stood before him as he painted. She hadn't tired of her role, never fussed or sulked as any other model would. She had altered over the weeks, the boyish slenderness becoming sleek and womanly though she ate little. She didn't ask to go out, but sometimes, as the spring drew on, she would stand at the dusty window staring out at the city, watching the pigeons and sparrows on the rooftops, listening to the voices on the pavements below. She was waiting for something. What was it? Perhaps he delayed the completion of the painting because he was afraid that once the picture was done, she would be gone. Somehow, alchemically, he was binding her in cords of paint and colour, making her his own, creating a trap. What would he do when she left him? When the picture was finished? The prospect was unbearable. His life had contracted to the twin obsessions, the girl and the mass of paint spreading over the canvas. Nothing else mattered.

The moon rose, slight and pink over a skyline of roofs and spires. The evening sky glowed with the day's last light. David put down his brush. Blanche lay on the bed, her eyes focussed on some indeterminable distance, making an odd, tuneful humming noise.

"I'm done," he said. "No more work today. You're getting bored I think. D'you want to go out?"

She shook her head. David sat on the bed beside her, stretched out a paint and oil-stained hand to touch her face.

"Good, I'm glad. I don't want to go out either." He stared into her eyes, the witch's brew of greens he'd seen that first night now flat and solid. A wave of desolation passed through him, an aching premonition of loss. Shaking it away, he slid his hand down into the front of her dress, reaching for her breast, wanting the heat of her. For the first time Blanche didn't respond. He pressed a kiss on her face and pushed her back on the pillow. He laid his head on her chest, beneath her throat but the pulse he felt was slow and level. He kissed her again.

"You don't want me now?"

She turned her face away from him, green eyes still open. Wordless, entirely still, she was casting him off. Her body had closed itself against him, like a locked door. David stood up and pulled on his coat, sick to death. He hurried out of the studio, strode into the city and didn't return till the small hours. Drunk and stumbling, he crashed through the room and collapsed on the bed, wine-sodden, head reeling. He woke in the hour before sunrise. A narrow white shape moved through the swimming light. David squeezed his eyes shut and opened them again. Was it Blanche? He was dreaming. The figure before the window turned and raised its arms, a milky, opalescent shape with long, inhuman limbs. He blinked again, wanting to clear the mist from his mind.

The sun rose above the rooftops and its first rays pierced her, the translucent woman. He couldn't see well, blinded by the sun's dazzle and the curious fog in the room but like a piece of moonstone she stood before him. Within her belly, at the root of her, hung a blood-red purse. Inside it, a foetus curved like a fossil ammonite.

Blanche – except that she was no longer Blanche, shedding the limitations of a name – placed a protective hand over her womb. She turned her face to David on the bed but her features had smoothed away. Then, fluid as molten glass, she moved to the open door and disappeared into the shadows of the stairway.

Claude walked through Regent's Park, past the lake of salt water and the last, sad stumps of the ice palace. Spring sunshine has released the suppressed perfume of the city, garbage and horse manure, the river's stink, the breath of cherry blossom. He headed through the maze of narrow streets to his friend's studio. He hadn't seen David for weeks, and he'd looked so ill during winter. The girl he'd picked up hadn't been taking care of him. Clearly David had been working too hard, not eating or keeping himself warm. No doubt the girl had been taking all his money, sucking him dry. Well, Claude had some money now. He'd take David out for dinner and buy him a few drinks, check out the painting David had been raving about.

The sun was warm on his face and he hummed as he walked along the pavement. He turned into the tenement and climbed the stairs to the top floor.

"David?" he called. When he knocked, the door swung open.

"David?" he said again. The place was quiet. A draught from the room carried a peculiar odour. Stricken with unease, Claude stepped inside.

A huge painted canvas dominated the room. A mass of swirling blue and green in which a pale female figure twisted, arms outstretched, face tipped back exposing the line of a long, pearly throat. A spray of foam leapt from the sea's surface into a narrow strip of stormy sky. Energy burned in the picture, in the sea and sky, and in the strained, exultant torso of the woman whose motion seemed to generate the stirring of the elements, like nothing Claude had seen before. No wonder David had been consumed by it.

Claude stepped closer. David had scrawled his name in uneven letters in the bottom right corner of the picture. On the other side, he'd written: Undine.

But where was David? Claude poked around the room. It didn't look as though anyone had lived in the room for days. The fire was cold and dead. A stone-hard loaf rested on the tabletop. He peered behind the screen.

A figure lay on the bed. Famished, face blackened, already caving in on itself. Claude's breath choked in his throat. He let out a shocked, inadvertent moan. That was David, wasn't it? The clothes were David's but impossible to recognise his face. Claude rallied, calming himself then stepping closer. What had happened? The body resembled the mummy he'd seen at the museum, except for the horrible frostbitten blackness on the face and hands. Had he died of cold and starvation?

And the girl – the girl was long gone.

Those Damned Kids

Gary McMahon

Fading autumn sunlight. The distant sound of motorway traffic. Dying birdsong. Suburban streets dimming slowly to grey; yellow lights sparking on in the cosy front rooms of row upon row of ordinary semi-detached houses. Newish cars parked on gravel drives. Bikes locked up in garden sheds. Everyone is home from work, relaxing in front of the television after a family meal. Good children are toiling over their homework at the dining room table, their parents chatting in low murmurs in another room about the events of the day. Old folks nod in the growing gloom. Newsreaders' voices are set to a low volume, talking about high oil prices, more job losses, the influx of Polish immigrants, teenage stabbings, the housing slump…

And outside, the kids begin to gather.

"How are you this evening, babe?" Lucy watched her daughter from the doorway, almost afraid to enter the small dark bedroom.

The curtains were closed – as always – and she struggled to make out Jessie's small form amid the tumble of bed sheets.

"Okay." Her voice was tiny, like an imitation; a failed recording. According to Jessie, she was always "okay". Whatever agony wracked her frail body, whatever new and painful drug the doctors gave her to try; everything was always "okay." She was the Okay Girl; never a word of complaint would pass her permanently chapped lips.

Lucy slipped into the room and approached the bed, stepping over books and toys which always reappeared in the same spot, never mind how often she put them away. She knelt down by the side of the bed, hands smoothing the bedclothes over Jessie's small bony frame.

"Really, Mum, I'm fine." Jessie's smile was pale in the gloom. Her teeth were little white squares.

"I know you are, but it's a mum's job to worry." She kissed a damp cheek and stood, crossing to the window. Opening the curtains an inch, she looked out at the street. The lamps had come on, casting their vulgar white glow, and held in their light a lone kid loitered at the corner, kicking a stone about. She glanced back over her shoulder and noted that Jessie was staring wide-eyed into the darkness, and when she looked back to the street a second youth had joined the first.

They were like the crows on the climbing frame in that old Hitchcock film. Each time you looked away, a few more appeared, until there were dozens of them, scuffing their shoes on the kerb and peering out at the night from under the brim of their standard-issue baseball caps. But they never *did* anything, except maybe make a noise, block the road and footpath, or kick a football. Nothing *overt*. They were a sign, a symbol of the times. Those damned kids simply stood around as if they owned the street.

"I'm thirsty," said Jessie, shifting on the mattress.

Lucy turned to face the room, hope rising within her. "You want a drink?"

The girl stared at her, eyes large and almost on the verge of tears. "No."

"How can you be thirsty and not want a drink, baby? Can you tell me that?" Lucy stood over the bed. She found that was shaking with an emotion she could not even name – a strange combination of hope and despair.

"I…I don't know. Juice makes me sick. Too much water hurts my throat. You know that."

"Hush now. I'm tired." She'd spoken a little harshly, but her patience was running out. She knew it wasn't Jessie's fault that she was ill, but who *could* Lucy blame? The doctors kept telling her that they were close to identifying what was wrong with her baby's blood – but they also tried to convince her to leave Jessie in the hospital, and Lucy would hear nothing of it, refusing to let her daughter out of her sight. Doctors weren't always right; sometimes they had as little clue as anyone else.

She was halfway down the stairs when the phone began to ring. Hurrying into the living room, she answered the call.

"Hi, love. Any news?" Her friend Brenda always launched into a conversation without any preamble.

"Hi. Not really. I spoke to the hospital again this morning, and all they could tell me was the usual vague stuff – impurities in the blood, foreign matter, recommendations for another round of chemo… but at least the rash has gone."

"Shit. I'm sorry. I'd hoped…"

"Yeah. Me, too. These days, I spend my whole life hoping."

Their talk drifted to less vital things: the minutiae of everyday life. It didn't last long, and Lucy found herself hanging up the phone without remembering any of what they'd discussed. Just as the receiver hit the cradle, there was a sound outside. Laughter. Voices. She went to the window and lifted one of the slats of the venetian blind, searching for the source of the ruckus. Three youths of indeterminate gender stood at the end of her drive, heads close together, skinny faces almost touching. She could hear them whispering but could not make out a word of what

was being said. They stood there for some time, then two of them began to mock-wrestle and the group moved slowly away.

The area of footpath where the youths had been standing looked damaged, as if the paving stones had cracked. It had not been like that earlier, when Lucy arrived home from work. She closed the blind. Her mouth was dry and her palms were moist.

She walked into the kitchen and took a bottle of wine from the fridge; she'd only opened it last night yet there was little more than an inch remaining in the bottom. So she was up to a bottle a night now: how fucking predictable. Her own mother had been a borderline alcoholic, and now she was repeating the cycle.

Unmoved by her observation, she opened another and returned to the living room, where she watched bad TV shows until she was drifting to sleep in the chair. Before turning in for the night, she glanced out of the landing window. The kids were no longer there, but the street looked shabbier, more run down than ever before. Not trusting her wine-fuzzed eyesight, she went to bed and dreamed that Jessie's father had never left when she was eight months old, and that they lived in a nice house in a decent part of the city, where the streets were quiet and empty.

"Sorry I'm late." Carla, the respite nurse, was breathless. A hefty girl, she was unable to hurry anywhere, and this often made her unpunctual.

"Don't worry about it," said Lucy. "I'm sure my boss will understand. Again."

She headed for the bus stop wishing that she'd given Jessie another goodbye kiss. She felt guilty about being so uptight the night before, and the hangover was making her sentimental. When she reached the stop the shelter was a mess. The Plexiglas frontage had been shattered overnight; bright little shards decorated the verge like scattered diamonds.

"Bloody kids," said an old woman as she glanced up from her newspaper. Lucy smiled; there was little she felt able to add to the woman's observation.

The bus was full of school kids. They'd taken over the entire upper deck. The noise was raucous, a cacophony of screams and laughter and stamping feet. The bus driver did nothing to intervene; he simply stared through the dirt-tinted windscreen, blocking it all out.

The streets on Lucy's route to work looked cleaner and brighter than her own. It seemed to her that over the past few weeks a change had occurred: there was more graffiti where she lived, the cars rusted quicker, the houses where falling apart. Before those kids started showing up after dark the place had been fine, but these days everything looked badly neglected.

Her boss was far from happy that she was late. He threatened her with an official warning before leaving the office for a meeting. Lucy had always enjoyed her work before Jessie had fallen ill, but now the job was simply another hassle to add to the list. She sifted through endless piles of paperwork, typing up letters and reports, answering telephone calls and emails, and all too soon it was time to go home. She was glad that she only worked three days a week, yet she also wished that she could stay out of the house longer than she did. Guilt trailed her like a backwash.

Carla had already left by the time Lucy arrived home. The bus was caught in traffic; apparently there had been an accident somewhere up ahead, but she witnessed no evidence of wreckage once the cars started moving again.

The dingy street had never seemed so unappealing; gardens were unkempt and littered with discarded food wrappers, the kerbs were shattered, weeds growing out through the gaps. Lucy passed some strange graffiti on a garage wall. Big white splashes of emulsion paint formed a figure or symbol that wasn't familiar to her – could it possibly be a foreign letter or numeral? She hurried on, sensing the dark pressing at her back. She almost sighed with relief when she reached her gate and the carless drive.

"How was today?" She once again found herself kneeling by Jessie's bed, holding her hand.

"Okay."

Lucy smiled, despite the exhaustion. "No worse?"

"No worse. No better. Just the same." Jessie's eyes widened. The room was gloomy, the curtains closed, the lights off. Jessie hated the light; it made her eyes hurt, she said, and her skin itch. The doctors claimed it was a psychosomatic reaction, but Lucy could not help thinking it might have something to do with the drugs her daughter was taking.

No one seemed to understand how or why she'd caught the mystery blood disease. They all agreed that this was a form of cancer, but ideas as to what might have caused it differed. Despite her usually rational mind, Lucy often found herself wondering if Jessie had contracted the disease from someone at school. Polish and Romanian immigrants had brought new strains of the flu virus into the area, so why not this? She knew this sounded xenophobic, yet something at the back of her brain, where the dark things lurked, insisted that it was as good a theory as anyone else had yet offered.

Prior to the onset of her illness, Jessie had spent a lot of time playing with a Romanian girl – what was her name, *Alina*? Perhaps if that girl were tested something might be found. But Lucy's suggestions, as always, fell on deaf ears and prompted only cagey replies. The one time she'd tried to track down the girl on her own, she had found no trace.

"I ate a little today." Jessie's voice pulled her from her thoughts.

"What did you eat?"

"Just some dry bread."

Hope surged within her. "Did it stay down?"

Jessie closed her eyes and turned her head away. "No. I puked."

Lucy's worst fear was that she'd have to put Jessie on the drip again. The sight of that transparent plastic tube slotted into her daughter's arm made her panic; it was like a glimpse of something she knew would happen further down the line, a snapshot of

Jessie's death.

"At least you tried, baby. That counts for something."

Jessie's thin wasted smile was a travesty, but at least it *was* a smile and not a grimace of pain.

After dinner Lucy had a long soak in a hot bath, drinking more wine and reading a supposedly inspirational book about some woman who'd overcome her disability to carve out a successful career in advertising. It was rubbish, but served as an adequate diversion, albeit a temporary one. Still she could hear laughter through the thin glass of the bathroom window; raised voices drifting on the evening air.

She dried off and put on her pyjamas, then stood at the bedroom window watching the street, glass in hand, book lying forgotten on the bed. More than a dozen youths were out there, standing in the middle of the road. Two of them sat on bicycles, leaning their arms across the handlebars. They were animated, excited about something… their heads moved up and down and their hands gesticulated wildly.

Glancing away from the group, Lucy noticed a couple of dark figures standing on the lawn across the way, staring into the window of her neighbour's house. Lucy wasn't sure who lived there, directly opposite her own home, but thought it might be the middle-aged man who walked his dog every morning. Come to think of it, she'd not seen him for a couple of days, maybe even longer. More like a week.

She watched the figures as they stepped down off the high-level lawn and onto the pathway which ran around the house. They were bold, brazen; they didn't even look around to see if they were being observed. Gradually, as she watched, their dark bodies began to stretch, to elongate until they looked at least seven feet tall…and thin; so very, very thin. Their long hands hung down to their knees and their fingers were like talons. The grass beneath their feet withered and the walls of the building seemed to buckle as they moved towards the side door.

Slinking into the shadow of the house, they disappeared from view. Lucy heard a loud bang, as if something heavy had made contact with the door or the side of the building, and then nothing more. The house looked older, more decrepit, than only moments before, as if something vital had been taken from its very fabric.

She was torn between phoning the police and feeling silly and paranoid. What if she did call them out and it was all for nothing; she was simply drunk and stressed? Would the youths then target her for interfering with their fun? But if she did nothing and the old man was in fact being terrorised, could she ever forgive herself?

Coming down on the side of caution, she watched the house for almost an hour, straining to see or hear anything out of the ordinary. Nothing happened. The street was empty: even the other kids had moved on. Finally, she went downstairs and opened another bottle, wanting to drown her fears but knowing that they'd still be there when she surfaced.

Morning announced itself with grey skies and the promise of rain.

Lucy stared out at the street, wondering if there'd been some kind of incident overnight. Previously undamaged windows were boarded over with planks; telephone wires sagged from their fixings; a couple of ruined cars sat on piles of bricks; a riot of weeds had sprouted from the broken boundary wall of the house across the road, the one she'd watched so intently the night before. Was she losing her mind? Had Jessie's illness snapped something inside her head and brought on these visions of decrepitude?

A solitary figure shuffled along the street, head down, skin pale, clothing torn and dirty. He stumbled occasionally, as if drunk or tired. Lucy assumed it was some homeless man, a passing vagrant, until the fellow walked into the garden across the street and let himself into the now-shabby house, almost collapsing through the doorway as he pulled his evidently failing body inside. His little dog wasn't with him, but Lucy's immediate fears for the old man could now be put to rest.

She sat down on the edge of her bed, put her head in her hands, and wept, although she could not say why or for whom.

"What's happening?" she asked the empty room, still feeling half drunk from last night's wine. "Is this a nightmare?"

She slid off the bed and went to Jessie's room. The girl was still sleeping, wrapped up in her shroud of bedding. "Jessie?"

There was no answer.

"You okay?"

Jessie shifted, her body rolling, but her face remained covered by the blankets. She snorted something – more of a sound than any specific word – and, satisfied that the girl was resting, Lucy shut the bedroom door and went downstairs for coffee. She checked the cupboards and found that there was enough food and supplies of Jessie's medication that she wouldn't need to leave the house for several days. Checking that the doors and windows were locked and bolted, she settled in for the long haul. Things were getting weird out there; she preferred to stay indoors and see how everything developed.

Days later, or so it seemed, someone knocked on the front door. Lucy got up from the sofa and went into the hallway. A long, blurred shadow stood behind the glass of the front door, one arm raised. Whoever it was knocked again.

"Lucy? Please let me in, love. I'm worried about you!"

The voice was familiar, but it took several moments for Lucy to identify it as belonging to Brenda, her best friend in the world. She took a step forward, clutching at the stair banister, and then paused, unsure of both herself and the situation.

"Please, Lucy. Open up. I can see you through the glass."

She approached the door and removed the security chain. Then, taking a deep breath, she opened the door.

"Fucking hell, what's happened to you? You look like shit." Brenda powered into the house, grabbing Lucy by the shoulders and ushering her along the hall. "Come on. I'll make some tea and we can talk."

Lucy allowed herself to be led back inside and sat in an armchair while Brenda busied herself in the kitchen. She stared at the wall above the cold fireplace, wondering what had gone so badly wrong with her life.

"Here. Take this." Brenda thrust towards her a mug of hot tea, and Lucy took it without comment. "What's been going on here?" She sat down opposite Lucy and waited.

"It's difficult to explain," said Lucy, between sips of tea. "I'm not sure where to start."

"Just try me. Please." Brenda smiled, but her eyes remained serious.

"About six weeks ago a bunch of kids started hanging around. Strange kids, ones I'd never seen before. Shortly after that the street started looking run down." Lucy tugged her hands through her knotted hair, blinked her eyes…anything not to look at her friend's face.

"Little bastards. Vandalism, eh?" Brenda touched Lucy's bare arm; her hand was warm and soft.

"No," continued Lucy. "It's more than that. More than the usual graffiti and empty crisp packets. The entire street seems to have gone grey, lifeless, and the people have turned inward. It's like these…these kids…" She could go no further; she knew how crazy she sounded, yet somehow it all made a kind of grim sense.

"Lucy…"

At last she felt able to look directly into Brenda's eyes, to hold the other woman's gaze. "No. I mean it. What if they do this all the time, killing places slowly, street by street? We would never notice, would we? Whenever you see a group of rowdy kids on a street corner, you look away, scared that they'll single you out, turn their attention on you. And they're everywhere these days, like some sort of blight on society."

"Lucy, don't. You sound like you're losing it." Brenda let out a low whine, as if something was stuck in her throat.

"Maybe I am. Maybe I have. Maybe we *all* have, and it's much too late to get it all back. Think about it, Brenda: think hard. The last time you were here, did the street look this dirty? Were there so many boarded up doors and windows? This used to be a nice area, such a nice street. Lucy's hand had strayed to her friend's knee, to grip the flesh through the faded denim of her jeans.

A moment of silence followed, in which Lucy could hear the clock ticking steadily on the mantelpiece, the shocking clink of cup on saucer, the terrifying sound of her own laboured breaths.

"How's Jessie?" said Brenda, as if to ignore, or even cancel out, their previous exchange. "Can I go up and check on her?" She stood and went for the door, not waiting for permission. "Be back in a minute."

As Brenda climbed the stairs, the wood creaking beneath her weight, Lucy went to the window and gazed outside. Twilight was settling over the street but no lights came on. A lumpen mass lay sprawled upon a lawn on the other side of the road, perhaps a bundle of rags or a pile of sheets fallen from a washing line. She refused to believe that it stirred, trying to raise itself from the overgrown grass. She watched a police patrol car cruise along the silent street, its occupants seeing nothing out of place. The car turned the corner and was gone. Lucy had never felt so abandoned.

"She's sleeping," said Brenda, coming up behind her and placing a hand on her shoulder. "She seems peaceful enough. But when did the doctor last see her? Maybe you should see someone, too…"

Lucy tensed, pulled away. "It's nearly dusk – you should leave. They'll be here soon, to finish what they started." She moved to the centre of the room and pointed at the door.

"Just think about what I said – about seeing someone." Brenda began to say something more but words failed her, so she simply turned and left, closing the front door behind her. Lucy followed and checked the locks. Then she slowly moved around the ground floor, checking all the doors and windows, making sure the house was shut up tight. As she left the kitchen, the suggestion of movement drew her back. She stared at the square window set high up in the back door; at the dark figure which stood there, pressing its face against the glass. The head was long and much too narrow and began to widen considerably as it pressed against the pane.

Lucy reached out to turn on the light but the power was already dead. She left the kitchen, closing the door on that terrible sight.

It was dark now. Shadows stretched across the walls as she inched along the hallway, panicked and with no clear plan in mind. She knew they were here, and that they were after her – possibly the last remaining resident of the street – and her thoughts turned to Jessie, asleep upstairs and unaware of the danger. The house creaked, the old construction settling, and amid the usual groans and whispers she caught new sounds, unfamiliar clicks and clatters.

Then, taking shape in the darkness ahead, a lone figured stepped forward to block her path. Behind it, the front door was nothing but a curtain of rotten timber, the swaying tatters of a failed barrier.

"No," she whispered, but denial was a luxury she could no longer afford. "Who are you?"

The thin, angular shape crept towards her along the length of the hallway, moving with a grace and beauty which at first took her by surprise. They had finally shed their costumes. The street had perished, so they no longer cared about concealment. Whatever they were, wherever they had sprung from, they were not teenagers. But they were hungry.

The thing cackled, and then emitted a sound like air escaping from a punctured tyre. It dragged obscenely long fingers along the wall as it moved towards her, and behind them the wallpaper darkened, blistering and curling away from the plaster. The carpet beneath the creature's feet turned to dust and the very air was polluted by its breath.

When finally the thing spoke, its voice was an urban hymn of breaking glass and crumbling foundations; the dull boom of tall buildings falling to earth; the roaring of the blood in her veins; all the sounds of her sorrow.

"We need your home. We need your lights. We need your pride in the nests you make for yourselves. We need the bricks and mortar, the relationships you build. We need the ground beneath your feet. We need the places where you gather and the things you do there to pass the time. We need it all. *We need to feed.*"

Lucy felt hypnotised by the dark lullaby of the creature's words, and as it drew closer she found herself being slowly seduced by the promise of emptiness...

The connection was broken abruptly – thankfully – by the sound of glass shattering in an upstairs room and the dull thud of something limp hitting the floor directly above her head.

She pulled herself free of the grip of the thing in the hall and fled for the stairs, taking them two at a time as she rushed to save her daughter. Nothing blocked her way; no other entities pursued her. Even the thing downstairs waited, as if all of this were merely inevitable, an indulgence on her behalf. She hesitated for only a moment outside Jessie's door, then pushed it open and lunged inside, ready to battle whatever she found there skulking in the darkness.

The bed was empty, the covers mussed and scattered. Jessie was kneeling on the floor at the side of the bed furthest from her position. She could see the girl's narrow shoulders, the top of her head as she twisted it back and forth. Slowly, cautiously, she walked around the end of the bed, hands gripped into fists, legs tensed for flight either towards or away from something monstrous.

When Jessie came fully into view, Lucy could barely conceive of what was happening. Her daughter was straddling a narrow figure on the floor, one knee on either side of its spindly body. Her back was bent, head bowed, as if she were kissing whatever struggled beneath her. But no, this was no kiss, no act of

passion… not when it was accompanied by such strange sounds. *Tearing. Slashing.*

This was something different, something primal.

At long last, Jessie was taking sustenance.

There were no fangs here, no supernatural powers or clichéd graveside metaphors. Just a sick little girl caught in the act of tearing open a thin dark throat with her bare hands, and drinking of the black-red fluid which even now gushed forth. Lucy watched in numbed fascination, emotionally detached from the scene.

Jessie paused in her feeding, turned, and spoke: "Mummy." Her eyes were wide, lips dark as sin against the ivory skin of her cheeks. "Mummy, everything's going to be okay. I think I've found a cure."

Then the Okay Girl returned to her meal.

What happened next was as swift as it was brutal. The terrifyingly reinvigorated Jessie went through them like a blade through water, using her hands and her small, square teeth to rend and open; to let out what was inside so that she might gorge herself. All that remained were the shells, the husks: the empty carcasses of ugly young things not quite ready to tackle the ancient terror that Jessie had become.

After the frenzy, Jessie lay on the floor, satiated. She had not looked so healthy in months.

"My baby," said Lucy as she cradled her child, stroking her matted hair. Lucy's gaze flicked between the top of that small sodden head and the dead street beyond the dirty, cracked windows.

"We can't stay here," she whispered. "Not now. Not anymore."

Jessie nodded, the movement small and inconsequential in all that still silence. Even in this strange state the girl was aware enough to realise that they must move on. Brenda would contact someone – social services, or even the police – and before long unwanted visitors would come calling, asking questions which Lucy knew must never be answered. *Could* never be answered... certainly not by any sane explanation.

So they must leave this place and build a new life: a life of darkness. There was work to be done – something which Jessie had begun in hunger but would now continue out of necessity and the remnants of a sense of community, however vague and fragmentary.

Lucy packed in minutes. All she owned, and everything that owned her, was here, in her arms, hanging onto her for dear life.

They walked into the street, into the welcoming night, side by side, hand in hand. With luck on their side, Lucy thought, they might even reach a safe haven long before daybreak.

"They will make cemeteries their cathedrals and the cities will be your tombs."
– movie tagline for *Demons*, directed by Lamberto Bava

Red or White

Andrew Hook

Is she red, is she white?
Is she promised to the night?

Traditional circa 1890

I find myself searching through the dark and daylight hours. Hoping I can find her in both and not only in one. The sun was so good to her, accentuating her looks, her perfect cheekbones, making her raven-dark hair shine with an almost luminescent fluidity. She cannot have lost that, I tell myself, when I am too tired and too scared to remain wandering the dark streets alone. I need her back with me. Back with her old man.

Amanda was the first. I could hardly conceal my disappointment when she was born. I won't deny that I was looking for a son, someone to run the wine shop alongside me, and eventually to take over once I was dead. It took me two years to accept her as my offspring, all the while hoping that my wife, Katherine, would bear another child, one who might be more suited to carrying on the family name. Sometimes I wonder whether it was such a hope that displeased God, or whether my bitter confused rationale leant itself to abuse from another source. Whatever it might have been, it couldn't stifle the anguish I felt when Katherine died in childbirth, and my new son only a few hours after that. The midwife cried openly – she knew us both well – but I kept it tight inside me; fool that I was to think I could hide my grief.

Outside, I can see the red rivers of another sunset streak the horizon. A beautiful sight now that the Machine has cleared our skies, even though this signals the night that I now abhor. A clockwork horse rattles along the cobblestones pulling its black cab, the occupants glimpsed briefly in an embrace as it passes by my window. I open the wooden drawer beside the counter and look at the key to the shop. Dare I close early, start my search for her right now? As if in answer the sun sinks lower over the horizon and casts a shadow inside the shop that temporarily vanishes the key. I sigh, reach into another drawer for a taper, and enter the backroom warmed by the fire. By the time I return with the lantern, the bell over the door has rung, and something is in the shop.

At first I can see nothing, then a shape moves in the shadows, and under the velvet of a black cloak the red silk lining flashes back the light from my lantern, reflecting a gaunt face and thin body. I catch my breath.

"Good evening, sir." My voice is strained, nervy. "May I help you? We're just about to close."

"I'm looking for a red." His voice, contrary to mine, is sharp, distinct. "A British wine, if you please. Perhaps from the vineyards of Castel Coch. If you have some."

I know where the wine is, but am less sure of his intentions. Is he who I think he is? This is the first time one has been in my shop, and the thought repulses me, but if it might assist in leading me to Amanda then surely the risk is worth taking.

I cough to clear my throat, regain some composure. "Those wines can be rather expensive."

I feel him bristling with anger, then reduce it; calm down; as I knew he would.

"Do you not think I can pay?"

"You can have two bottles for nothing," I say, "in exchange for some information."

He laughs. The sound is eerie, not in the slightest bit amusing. When I return his laugh, my own is hollow.

"And what kind of information would a shopkeeper like yourself be looking for?"

I pause. Then take the risk and turn around, reach up for the two bottles, leaving myself completely unprotected should he wish to strike. I hope my bravery will impress him, or, at the very least, intrigue him.

I place the bottles on the counter, keep both of my hands tight around their necks. "I'm looking for a girl."

When he smiles this time I can see the tip of his elongated incisors, gleaming white. "Shopkeeper, I am not in the profession of running a brothel. And the girls that I keep acquaintance with would not be to your taste."

"Not just any girl," I say. "A specific girl."

He shakes his head. "I will choose to pay in the usual currency rather than give you such information." He reaches out a smooth white hand, which, under the lantern light might have been bone itself. "Now give me the wine..."

"Wait..."

But I am too late. In an instant coins are clattering on the table top, and the bottles have left my hands, my palms sting with the speed at which they have been taken, the shop door open with its bell ringing madly as though a Peeler's whistle. Gone. Already he has gone.

It was my sister who had brought Amanda into womanhood. Suffering a facial disfigurement caused by a swinging Tube train door, she was destined never to marry and for a while she lived with me; tending to Amanda during the day, and berating me with her tongue during the evening hours. She never had a good word to say about me, which I attributed to a sibling jealousy of my own looks and business stature; but I couldn't ask her to leave as Amanda would have left with her.

Despite the ill will I felt towards my daughter at her birth and for several years after, I couldn't deny that she was my flesh and blood. And more importantly, the only flesh and blood I would ever have.

When my sister died of the plague it was I who burnt her body. I won't lie and say that it gave me no pleasure to do so. By that time Amanda was almost a grown woman, fourteen and fully budded. And despite her sex she had taken a great interest in the wines. I pinned my hopes on her, and for that maybe I was just another fool.

Whenever I was sick, Amanda saw to the shop. She became a favourite with my customers, brightening up the place with her laughter and her knowledge. Under her guidance we added other products, cheeses that might complement the wine, and glasses into which they might be poured. She had a wider vision, there was no doubt about that, and soon enough she had her share of suitors.

Of course, being her father this sat uneasily with me, as doubtless such things have with every daughter's father that came before me and likely all those that will go after. Not simply in terms of honour, but for what would happen to the shop should she ever leave.

London was a sprawling metropolis, larger – we were told – than Rome had ever been. It bustled with myriad people, was filled with new technological advances, and was naturally at the hub of my world. Yet, within this seething morass of culture, this shop - my business – retained its identity as the finest purveyor of wines. Orders flooded in from all corners of the capital. With only Amanda to help me - God forbid I would allow another man's *child* to interfere in my business – what would I do if she were to go? So I put my thumb down on many of her suitors, without realising as I did so that it just drove them underground.

I take my cloak from the hanger and slip it over my shoulders. I lock the front door and place the key in my pocket, then turn out the lantern and enter the backroom. Amanda should be sitting by

74

the fire, going through the accounts, and her absence creates a vacuum in my heart. Will I ever again watch her features as they are illuminated by firelight, without an accompanying fear that they would turn to dust in daylight? But I can't sit here waiting to be told the answer to that question, and as usual there is nothing for it but to go and look for her.

I leave by the back entrance, pull my cloak tightly around me. Push my hat down over my forehead so that almost all that can be seen are my eyes and slanted nose. London has regained some of its night-time passion over the past few years. When they first arrived, there was panic, confusion, sheer terror. Now there sits an uneasy truce, even attempts to enter Parliament! Their red insignia is a stand, they say, against whomsoever it was that first cursed them. But no one is sufficiently convinced by these political arguments to accept them. No one, that is, except the young.

I take a right through the alley and enter the street that runs across the front of the shop, glance up at the painted sign that announces: *John Bamford, Purveyor of Fine Wines*; and remember first my disappointment that it would never read *John Bamford & Son*, and secondly my lack of courage to make it *John Bamford & Daughter*. It wasn't as if I didn't acknowledge her. I treated her as an equal. She had nothing to rebel against, yet this had come to pass.

I bite down on my lip, push myself forwards, try to convince myself that all is not yet lost.

I stop at my usual haunt, *The Slaughtered Lamb* on Landis Avenue. George fetches me a tankard of ale and we have our usual argument about alcohol that always ends in agreement. He is the only one I have told about Amanda's absence; if the others are aware of it then they have had the courtesy to stay quiet.

"Any news?" he asks, when our banter about wines and ales has run its course.

I shake my head, then tell him about the last customer of the day.

"They're getting bold," he says. "Don't underestimate their political weight. The Ministers aren't daft, they'll use them to their advantage; there was even talk the other day that they'd make good Peelers."

My body shakes at the thought. "You're not serious?"

"Why not, John? They have the height. They command the terror if not the respect. And should they agree – as has been mooted – to feed only on the criminals, then what's to stop them taking on the role of law enforcement?"

"Common decency?" I mutter, almost under my breath but not quite. "How can we trust them?"

"Ah, now there lies the secret of their success," George nods, pouring me another ale. "We can't."

The night plods on. I venture further than my local, to places I wouldn't ordinarily go. Here, amongst strangers, I feel that I might be able to show my photograph of Amanda without fear of arousing suspicion as to who she was; thus avoiding some kind of retribution. Families have been driven to the outskirts of the capital once it is known that their relatives have turned. Instead, I make suggestions that she was no more than a runaway, no doubt prostituting herself on the streets after a silly family argument. To elicit sympathy, I say my wife is out of her mind with worry.

Most people I approach shake their heads. More than a few hold onto the photo for longer than is necessary, but I withhold the urge to pummel their lascivious faces with my fists. Several times I skirt the entrance to the Underground tunnels, knowing that my answers might be found within, but too scared to enter there with the equal knowledge that I might well never return. Just as I hope and pray Amanda is simply walking a thin line between light and dark, I also tread that same line between red and white.

I remember clearly when her interest was piqued. Too young to appreciate the fear that first came from the plague and then the vampires, her reaction to the official announcement of their existence was the same that one might attribute to a new invention. Something which one might visit at the Crystal Palace and gasp with wonder at its intricacies, whilst at the same time knowing next to nothing about how it worked. I could see her intrigue bubbling there, but never sought to deflect it. I thought talking about matters openly might more likely negate the myth.

If there were warning signs then I disregarded them, but even I couldn't fail to see the attraction these monstrous beings held for the general public. The newspapers were full of such things; Amanda's hands were blackened by the print. But are conditions truly so bad for some of the lower classes that they would voluntarily join the undead to improve their lot? Are there really secret societies amongst the higher classes where vampires and Lords mix cocktails, and talk politics; later indulging in such orgies that would put the Hellfire Club to shame? Speculation is rife, facts are few; no one seems to differentiate between the two.

One night, Amanda put her accounts to one side, stood up, and went towards the window where the darkness fell softly against the pane, only our fire keeping it from the room.

"I want to go out," she said.

I ask you, what kind of father could possibly acquiesce to such a request?

Now I find myself amongst the prostitutes of Whitechapel, who stand in twos and threes, afraid to move out of their little groups for whatever reason might scare them. I show the photograph guardedly. Few of them have even seen a photograph before, and it's all I have of Amanda to keep her in my memory. I don't get much response, and only a handful of inappropriate offers that I'm too tired and much to focussed to take seriously.

Around the corner from here, as I well know, the Fabian Society is no doubt debating the morality of the vampire. Wells, Bernard Shaw, the sexologist Havelock Ellis. Don't they realise that some kind of acceptance of vampire lore is tantamount to accepting them into our homes? Once I heard as a fact that a vampire might only cross a threshold if it had been invited, but now it's become a myth as its authenticity has been eroded. Does knowledge beget knowledge, or does it, in fact, create knowledge? All I know is that a vampire entered my shop today and left with two bottles of wine.

I glance up at the lit windows. Emmeline Pankhurst might well be in there. And how much might she also be culpable in Amanda's curiosity and disobedience? *The Woman's Franchise League* was unnecessarily empowering women. Christ knows that my relationship with my own daughter is forward-thinking and not backward. The perpetuity of my own business depends upon it. But what Pankhurst is doing is simply opening a can of worms. Freethinking has lent my daughter a political mind. And from that has created interest in the disenfranchised.

I spit on the street outside their door and move on quickly.

The night seems blacker now than it has ever been, although I know this to be my imagination. Is it the possibility of my daughter's death that has drawn a veil across my world, or is it the fear that she might be alive but not alive? Again, actual hard facts about the vampires' habits are hard to find within the city. No one trusts the newspapers to know the truth, yet everyone has a different answer. Is the *Blood Cell* part of that myth, or does it really exist? As I continue to walk I push such things out of my mind, try to remember my daughter whilst I still have a mind to think with.

It is true that I had only begun to notice her since my sister's death. During the daylight hours I had toiled in the shop, heard only occasional squeals of play behind the door that led to my back room; and even more occasionally my sister admonishing her for some misdeed. Invariably she loved the child, who had almost been my gift to her, and at the time I didn't resent their play or their companionship. But now... if things had been different? Would I have spent more time with Amanda as a child? Would it have made a difference as to how much time I would spend with her as an adult?

The questions foam as thick in my brain as did the head on George's ales. As I turn yet another corner I am so consumed by my thoughts that I don't see the gentleman until I am already on top of him.

Quick as the one who had left my shop earlier that day, I am lifted off the ground and held up against the wall by my throat. My feet kicking at air beneath me, my nostrils clamouring to be away from the stench. Raised from the ground as I was, we were at the same height. His breath rancid, his teeth an abomination. Yet I withhold the urge to spit in his face as I had done the doorway, and instead I meet his gaze as his anger cools and he lets me down.

"My apologies," I splutter, as my breath returns to me.

He begins to walk away.

"Wait."

He turns. A look of dreadful curiosity on his face. I doubt whether anyone has ever told him to wait before. I have to speak quickly, to outrun his impatience.

"I'm looking for my daughter. She may have joined the *Blood Cell* either willingly or as a victim. I suspect the former, but either way I need to speak to her. I need to know."

He looks the way a dog might look, quizzical but not particularly bothered.

"This should concern me?"

"Please," I say; then I notice he is wearing a wedding ring on his finger. "If you ever had a child yourself, then you will know."

He had followed my gaze. God knows what kind of memories these creatures hold, but I knew he had to have been something once, before he had become what he became. A certain trigger pulls taut within him, although I wouldn't speculate that it was compassion.

"This daughter of yours. What does she look like?"

I remove the photograph from my breast pocket with trembling hands. He takes it from me as someone might pick a playing card. Uncertain as to whether he was being tricked.

Then he flicks it back at me, the corner nicking my face, drawing blood.

I put up a hand to defend myself, but he is already upon me; knocking me to the floor. His tongue grazing the length of my cheek.

"Don't be concerned," he whispers, as I fight my rising gorge,

"no one ever died from a lick."

I close my eyes tight. Pray.

When I open them he is standing above me. "I know her," he says. "When I last saw her she was still human. She was assisting us in our political campaign. Look for Goulston Street."

"Goulston Street? But that's..."

Too late. Already he is gone.

The night isn't over yet. I get to my feet and stagger over to the wall, feel my face. The blood in my wound has coagulated, but I don't know whether this is a good sign. I bend down and retch, bring up the ale and the remnants of my lunch. I feel no different, and after a few moments I realise I haven't been turned. For whatever reason, for the moment I have been spared.

Goulston Street isn't far from where I am. It is infamous, of course. The Ripper had reportedly left a message chalked on the wall there, but whether that holds any significance to my personal quest I don't stop to think. Instead, I search the dark ground for the photograph of Amanda and soon find it, thankfully intact. I tuck it back into my pocket, then go on my way.

I remember a quote I had read, attributed to the poet John Dryden: *Death in itself is nothing; but we fear to be we know not what, we know not where.* And as I walk I wonder what I might fear the most, losing Amanda or losing myself.

I come upon Goulston Street easily enough. It is not deserted, as I expected, but filled with an angry mob, some of them bearing lighted torches. Many of them with makeshift weapons. A few of them with guns. It seems I wasn't the only one looking for something this night. The city has been polarised, no doubt by ale and outrage, the usual proponents of unthinking behaviour. On another night I might happily have joined them, but looking up at one of the windows of the wooden tenement building, I think I catch a glimpse of raven-black hair and a familiar face.

"Amanda!"

My shout is lost in the crowd, which even now pushes

forwards, dragging me with it as I stumble and try to regain my balance. I look at the faces of the men alongside me; wretched every one of them. Nothing to lose, but perhaps a bit of fame to gain. It is impossible to fight against the mob, so I turn with them and begin to force my way into the building, into the front; hoping I might reach Amanda before the rest of them are able.

I can see in their eyes that they would make no distinction between vampire and political assistant. What tarred one, would surely tar the other.

And as I carry myself forward I pray to the God that I have always believed in. Not the one that had killed my wife and son, nor the one that is worshipped in the churches. But the little one that lives inside of me, the one that I can talk to through the bad times even though I might neglect him during the good. The one who has given me the strength to search for Amanda, when a lesser man with a lesser God might have given up.

We climb the stairs. At the top is a corridor with several doors to the left and right. If my bearings are correct then Amanda must be in the room nearest to my right, facing the street, maybe deliberating whether to jump. The door is wooden and locked. An axe is thrust into my hands, and I use it aware of the irony that I might be letting her murderers into the room as I am trying to save her. I don't dare call her name aloud, but repeat it constantly in my head.

And then we are through, spilling into the room. Which is empty.

A few sticks of furniture, some papers, little else. And then the noise starts. A horrific, grinding noise that sends cries of terror amongst the men. I run to the window and look outside. The building is being vacated, fast. Yet outside of it the vampires are feasting, maybe as they have never done so before. In front of the entire mob, whose attempted blows are met with speed and laughter. Who are being cut down and turned into ribbons.

I look up, away from the scene. Look out over a London that stretches as far as the eye can see. How long would it take them to take this city? They don't need the political campaign. It is breathtaking. The city is here, right in their grasp, in all its magnificence. They only need the numbers. They need recruits.

Someone shoots me in the back.

As I fall I turn to see the man who had fired. I see from his face that he realises his mistake. And then he is off. I close my eyes.

Pain spreads out across my lower back like a bloodstain. Maybe this is how she knows I am there.

When I open my eyes again I see Amanda bending over me. She is spotless, smooth, either herself or a good imitation. I can't quite work out what the look means in her eyes, but at the moment of my death I know I don't want to die.

Her lips part, and I beg the God inside me that I might see that she has fangs.

So that she might save me.

Or damn me.

Or both.

Where the Vampires Live

Storm Constantine

For Connor

Zenna knew where the vampires gathered after sundown. She could climb out of the attic window, jump onto a limb of the ironwood tree outside and be free of the house, unheard and unseen, in minutes. She would run like a white hind between the dappled shadows of night, perhaps shape-shifting as she ran; hind to girl to hind. Her feet would seem barely to touch the ground. Her hair would be full of moths, drawn to it as if to a white flame.

Ariel would watch secretly from her own window, further down the house, full of envy, wistfulness and other aches she could not identify.

Ariel was Zenna's cousin, and she had come to live in the Green House in the spring, right at the edge of the forest, far from town. Ariel's father had died many years before and recently her mother had suffered some kind of disgrace that had affected her ability to be a mother – apparently. Ariel did not know what had happened; all she knew was that her mother had seemed to become someone else, a stranger in familiar skin. This troubled her so much she couldn't bear to think about it, so it came as rather a relief when her uncle and aunt had offered to take her in for a while.

It quickly became clear to Ariel, who was well-mannered and prudent, that she was the kind of daughter that Maeve and Darn would have liked to have had. They tried very hard not to show it, but Ariel was aware of the irrepressible leaps in their spirit when she asked for things politely, or did chores without being asked. Zenna was a wild creature; wilful, often bad-tempered, but seductively fascinating. When she turned on her light, none could fail to be blinded by it, hypnotised into adoration. Getting her own way was a trait inbuilt into her being. She had magic in her that made it happen. No one could dislike her, because it is impossible to dislike a beautiful wild thing, a rare spirit of nature, just because it is naturally wild. But sometimes, watching her cousin, Ariel could not help but remember something her maternal grandmother had once said. 'Some people are cursed in life, darlin'. Watch out for them. When a soul touches you on the inside, so that the whole world goes black but for them, take care. For they can take you to a doom.'

There had been more to this conversation, one of many lectures Granny gave on the potential horrors of life, but Ariel had forgotten the rest now. All she could think about, remembering those words, was what it would be like to be black on the inside, as if a hooked finger had poked through your skin and bone and had touched your heart, leaving a dark spot that grew and grew.

"Do you believe in vampires?" Zenna asked Ariel that one summer afternoon, as the girls sat by the pond in the garden. The day was hot. The air smelled green.

Ariel laughed politely. She always did that when she didn't have an answer.

"Well, do you?"

"I don't know... Do you?"

Now it was Zenna's turn to laugh, and this was a very different sound from Ariel's. "Do you know," she said, "people always say 'you can't be too careful'. But the fact is: you can." She jumped to her feet. "Come on," she said.

Come where? Down to the greenwood, where the shadows are brown and gold. Down to where the earth breathes so loudly you can hear it with human ears. Step through a barrier from here to there. It's where otherness comes alive.

Zenna took Ariel to a place deep in the forest. They passed a tumbledown wooden shack covered in ivy. Zenna said the body of the woman who had lived there was still lying on the floor behind the door. No one knew that she had died. She had become mostly ivy. Ariel shuddered and ran on. When she held Zenna's hand it was as if her feet too barely touched the ground. If they ran fast enough the world became a blur and it was possible to see another world beyond this one – always there, but you can't see it normally.

Zenna's destination was a dragonbark grove. The trees there were ancient; they were tall yet they stooped beneath the weight of their own age. Five of these trees were still alive; three dead, lying on the ground and riddled with insect nests. Zenna sat down on the spongy wood of one of the dead trees. There was a dampness to this grove, even though the sun was hot and high summer reigned in the greenwood. It was the breath of the earth, oozing out through mulch and mold. The canopies of the living trees were immense, the wings of dragons. Despite the absence of breeze the leaves fluttered high overhead as if impulses from the roots shivered through them; impulses to fly.

Zenna swung her legs, leaning back on stiff arms.

"Are they *here*?" Ariel whispered. She wondered whether this was a game, and whether she was playing it right.

"At this time of day? Are you kidding?" Zenna sighed. "I wonder if they sleep beneath the dead leaves, but of course you'd never find them, even if they did. They would just become part of the soil, or would look like soil anyway. They are not what you think."

Ariel wasn't sure what she thought vampires to be. In her mind, all she saw was a flash of red eyes, some fangs glinting, a hiss of silk. "What are they?" she dared to ask.

"Very much creatures of earth," Zenna replied. "They are not about death, nor come from death. They are the greatest example of life. They live on life itself."

"Blood..."

"Well yes, everyone knows that." Zenna stood up.

"Have you actually *seen* them?" Ariel asked.

Zenna glanced at her cousin over her shoulder. "It is actually very difficult to see them. They are camouflaged. At night they must be clustered on the roofs of houses, standing beneath the trees in gardens, watching and waiting for a place of entry."

"That's horrible."

"Why?" Zenna pulled a scornful face. "They don't kill people, you know. That's just made up, because people are scared of what they don't understand. But if you are bitten, you are never the same again."

"You become like them?"

Zenna paused. "No. You are never the same again because you *don't* become like them."

"But have you *seen* them?" Ariel persisted.

Behind Zenna's silence, Ariel could hear the cracklings and rustlings of the forest. It was never silent. It seemed to be quiet but was full of noise. Things moved unseen.

At last Zenna said, "You can only see them for yourself. This isn't something that can be told."

Perhaps it was just a game, the wild fancy of a girl at the cusp of womanhood, seeking romance and danger in the breathing forest. If Zenna had come across a strange creature in this place, it might not be a vampire, but something else, far less mysterious and far more dangerous.

"I would like to see for myself," Ariel said.

"Then wish for it," Zenna said. She held out her arms and turned slowly in a circle, head thrown back. "Wish for it with all your might. But you will never know when it might come true." She was clearly in love: with the place, with an idea, with life itself.

Ariel did what she thought people were supposed to do when making a wish. She closed her eyes, very tight, and thought hard. *I want to see the vampires*. Even as she thought this, half of her was playing a girlish game, but the other half was standing at the brink of fear, holding out a tiny flickering candle into the dark. This half was actually a very old part of herself, who was wise enough to know even the most outlandish wishes can come true.

Two days later, Zenna shook her cousin awake in her bed, in the dead hours of the night. Ariel awoke from a dream of red flowers, something to do with a white dog, a star that could speak. She blinked at the pale vision of Zenna, whose eyes were wide and dark. "What? What?" she hissed, suddenly afraid. Was the house on fire?

"I need you to come with me," Zenna said.

"Why? Where?"

Zenna pursed her lips, screwed up her eyes and shook her head briefly. "It's your wish," was all she'd say. "Please hurry."

Ariel got out of bed and put on her clothes. Were there vampires on the roof now? If she listened carefully enough, would she hear them scratching at the slates? Part of her was lecturing the rest of her many parts with a quiet and patient voice. *Don't go with her. Whatever she's found, whatever she wants to show you, it won't be what she thinks it is. A good girl now would say 'no'. Why are you putting on your shoes?*

"Don't put on your shoes," Zenna said. Perhaps she could read minds and could hear the measured voice of Ariel's inner good girl. But her reasons were different. "We must go barefoot. It's quicker that way."

At night, the forest dares to speak aloud. As Ariel ran with her cousin, she could hear the immense creaks and groans of the trees, as if they were flexing their stiff ancient spines, pulling painfully their twisted roots from the possessive soil. The breath of the forest was now loud in Ariel's ears. All manner of creatures might lurk in the darkness; humans were interlopers in this particular time and space. But when Ariel held Zenna's hand and ran so fast, she felt she became something other than human and that this would protect her. She would not let go of Zenna's hand, whatever happened.

The dragonbark grove felt as if something had just finished there; it had the air of a room where twenty people had just walked out of the door. All that is left is the smoke of their conversations, wisps that will eventually fade away. The bright moonlight made it possible to see almost as clearly as if the sun were in the sky.

"The vampires were here," Ariel whispered. It was clear to her now that Zenna had wanted to share this experience and had come for her quickly. A pang of affection went through Ariel's heart. It felt like a long, white-hot pin.

"It's not just that," Zenna said. She let go of Ariel's hand and immediately Ariel felt fear, not affection. The pin was cold in her heart, making her breathless. Zenna was already walking away through the dappled moonlight; she was like a white hind again, lifting her feet delicately. Ariel blinked. She ran after her cousin.

Zenna had come to a halt before the greatest of the dragonbark trees; it must be their queen. "Here," she said. "Look." A pause, and then, with the slightest tremor of doubt: "Can you see?"

Ariel came to stand beside her cousin, and Zenna took her hand again, lacing their fingers lightly. With her free hand, Zenna pointed gracefully at the foot of the queen tree.

For a time Ariel could see nothing. She realised she didn't believe, and that in itself was quite shocking to her. But then she *could* see: there was someone curled up among the knuckles of the roots. As she looked closer, she could see that this someone was trembling. They were half covered with leaves, perhaps their shadowy garments were actually made from leaves. Zenna dragged Ariel nearer, her fingers had closed tightly about Ariel's own.

"It's a boy," Ariel said, half relieved, half disappointed.

Zenna glanced at her, said nothing. Again she let go of her cousin's hand and hunkered down. "He's hurt," she said. "They left him behind."

"He's a boy," Ariel said, in a voice that sounded to her like her aunt's. Maybe she was shattering magic, but if the boy really was hurt, fairy tales were no good for him.

You can't be too careful... you can...

Ariel went to the boy and touched him. He uttered a sigh and shuddered. He reminded her of a wounded dog, but it was too dark here to look for injuries. "We should take him back," she said.

"Into our house?" Zenna sounded afraid, and for once Ariel felt older and more confident and capable than her cousin.

"We can't just leave him here. He needs to be looked at... a doctor..."

"We shouldn't do that. They'll come back for him. It would be stealing..."

"Zenna!" Ariel sighed heavily. "Stop it. I don't know what he's doing here, but this lad is very much flesh and blood like us. Help me get him to his feet."

Ariel put her arms about the boy and tried to lift him. It surprised her how light he was, almost insubstantial. "He's half starved," she said.

With clear reluctance, Zenna came to help. He didn't resist them. He uttered soft whines, like a puppy. All the other sounds of the forest had faded away. For the briefest moment, Ariel thought how they might just have dragged this boy into the mundane world. Perhaps he didn't belong in it. But this was just a fleeting thought.

Maeve and Darn, and the doctor who came to inspect the boy, decided he must be a traveller lad, somehow separated from his people. He did have an injury, yes. He'd been shot in the thigh.

"No doubt caught stealing from some farm," the doctor said as she put away her things.

Everyone was gathered in the small spare room at the top of the house; an attic full of light that remained golden-brown even when the sun shone right through the window. The boy lay on a narrow bed. He was dark of skin and hair, slight of form, more like an elf than a boy. No wonder Ariel and Zenna had been able to carry him home as if he were no more than a handful of leaves.

"We'll call the police," Darn said.

But Maeve said, "No." She was Zenna's mother after all, and perhaps the sight of this fey, dark creature affected parts of her that had been asleep for many years. "There's no need for that. Not yet. Let him speak first."

The doctor had cleaned the boy's wound and stitched him up. There was no bullet. It had gone right through him. No one spoke again of official things, such as hospitals and authorities. They lived right on the edge of the forest and things were different here.

The boy slept for two whole days, and Maeve stayed with him, sitting by the narrow bed reading a book, or else curled up on the mattress that Darn had carried to the attic room. Zenna was often there too, frowning at the boy on the bed. No one really spoke about things, not even Zenna, although Ariel guessed her cousin's head was full of unspoken thoughts. It was as if they were all waiting for something. The weather became hotter and all around the Green House was a narcotic humid atmosphere that slowed movement, that stilled voices.

Ariel found sleep difficult during that time. At night, she lay awake breathing quickly, listening to the soft pound of her heart, her ears straining for other sounds. In particular, her senses extended upwards, out through wood and slate, to the roof. *I am too many people,* she thought. She wasn't sure what was real; the sort of world where common sense held sway or the sort where you could run so fast you could flash into another world. She sensed nothing on the roof, and in some ways that worried her more than if she'd felt the opposite.

On the morning of the third day, the boy opened his dark eyes and for some time lay staring at the ceiling. Maeve heard him sigh and put down her book. It was as if an invisible call shuddered through the Green House and everyone who lived there was drawn to the attic so that by the time Maeve murmured softly, "Who are you?" Zenna, Ariel and Darn were in the room also.

The boy looked at Maeve and there was no expression in his eyes that Ariel could interpret. If anything, he just looked resigned.

"Water," Maeve said and Darn brought a cup of it to the boy. They held his head so that he could drink, and he did so.

Zenna flicked a glance at her cousin, and Ariel was able to interpret what it meant. *Maybe we shouldn't be giving him that.* But both girls remained silent. He was drinking. Perhaps he needed it after all.

"Can you remember anything?" Maeve asked the boy.

He shook his head very slightly, still looking at her.

Maeve smiled at her husband. At least the boy could understand them. "You were hurt," she said. "Everything will be all right. Don't worry. We'll help you."

"What's your name?" Darn asked.

The boy shook his head.

"Where are your people?" Darn continued, voice firm. "We'll need to find them."

Now the boy looked cornered, eyes wider, gaze flicking from the window to the door.

"Stop that," Maeve said. "He's only just woken up. Give him time, Darn." She stroked the boy's hair, hushed him as you would a baby. "It's all right. Nothing to fear. I'll bring you some soup." She stood up. "Help me, Zenna."

The family left the room, leaving only Ariel behind. No one had noticed she'd stayed back or that she hadn't been given her a job to do. She wanted to tell the boy she was only a visitor too, but what was the point of speaking? She could sense it displeased him. So she sat down on the chair where Maeve had sat for the past few days and began to hum a tune. She closed her eyes and made the tune green and cool, like the forest depths.

She heard a soft sound, like water running over stones. It was the boy's laugh. "We *can* speak," he said, hardly more than whisper, "but only when it's needed. And we rarely answer questions."

Ariel opened her eyes and stared at him. "This is a question you must answer," she said. "Will your people come for you?"

"I'm not lost," he replied. He would not speak again that day.

Everyone knows that if you bring a changeling child into your home, or some creature of the otherworld, the otherness rubs off. It drifts like pollen through the still, summer rooms, and what were once just shadows take on feet and walk.

It was inevitable that Zenna was most affected by what had happened. Ariel felt she was destined only to be a witness to whatever transpired, nor would she affect the inevitable outcome in any way. She told herself firmly not to lie awake listening for sounds on the roof, because there wouldn't be any. She must not be infected by Zenna's feyness. The boy himself was like the summer light of the forest, sometimes green-gold sunlight, sometimes almost invisible in shadow. They named him Jack, because he would not tell them any other name. Most of the time it was easy to believe he was just a boy, separated from his family, but then his wound healed so quickly. After only a couple more days he was back on his feet. He did the chores that Maeve asked him to do without hesitation. He whistled to the geese that strutted around the pond, and they came to him, wings held out like arms. Maeve watched him from the kitchen window, smiling.

Jack was quiet, inhumanly so, but no trouble. He kept himself busy, and did not interact with the girls particularly, other than to nod his head in greeting should he come across them. Zenna could not keep her eyes off him. She speculated about him continually; it was naturally the topic that consumed her, and Ariel mostly played along because Jack interested her also. She just didn't want to think he was anything but a stray, albeit an intriguing one.

Every afternoon, they would sit by the pond and Zenna would talk about Jack. "He walks in daylight, he eats the food we eat," she said one day, clearly perplexed. "I had thought they would be white as ghosts, like moon people, but he is dark like the trees."

"Maybe that's because he isn't a vampire," Ariel had to say.

Zenna tossed her an annoyed glance. "I don't know why I bother telling you things. You just strip the magic out of everything, so the world will never be like that for you. How can you possibly think he's just a normal boy? Look at him."

Jack was stacking logs he had just chopped in the shadow of a shed attached to the house. Ariel could see nothing abnormal in his behaviour or movements. "He's a gypsy boy," she said.

"But what does he want with us?" Zenna continued, ignoring that response. "He's not spoken of his people or even questioned what he's doing here. He simply *is*, part of our lives now, living here amongst us. I wonder if we're foolish."

"He's fed well, he's got new clothes, and probably has a better life," Ariel said. "If he was thieving when he got shot, he's not going to tell us about that, is he?"

"He could steal from us, but he hasn't," Zenna said. "He could take everything we own and run away and sell it. But he stays, and chops logs, and does what Ma asks him."

"Then it's because that's what he wants. Perhaps he likes it here."

"No, he's just waiting," Zenna said firmly.

"Then why don't you just ask him what for?" Ariel asked, somewhat tartly, because she was feeling impatient with her cousin. She didn't think Zenna would do any such thing because Jack had an air about him that turned questions to stones in your throat. Even if you wanted to speak to him, and imagined it vividly, actually doing so was another matter.

Zenna gave her cousin an arch glance and jumped to her feet. The geese were startled and bustled off, honking. Ariel watched Zenna walk to the shadow of the shed. She was a girl in a fairytale about to reach out to a wolf, about to prick herself on a deadly thorn, about to change the future. Ariel also got to her feet. She didn't want to miss what might be said.

She was still some feet away from the shed when Zenna said to Jack, "What are you waiting for?"

Jack didn't pause in his work; there wasn't the slightest hesitation.

"Well?" Zenna persisted. "It's not that you can't speak, it's that you won't. But you're living here in our house, eating our food, sleeping in our attic, and I demand that you answer me."

Still there was no response. Zenna grabbed hold of Jack's right arm and shook him. Ariel fully expected him to retaliate then, to bare his teeth in a snarl, to show a darker nature. All he did was cease working. He let Zenna shake him and when she had finished he turned to face her. He reached out with the arm she had grabbed and touched her, very lightly, with one finger just above the heart.

Zenna shot backwards a couple of feet as if he had punched her. She staggered a little then fell on her back.

Ariel couldn't help uttering a cry. Jack looked at her for a moment, then carried on stacking the logs. "Tell her she cannot come," he said.

"What?" Ariel had heard the words very clearly. She didn't know why she queried them.

He walked away, round the side of the house.

Zenna had scrambled to her feet. She ran past Ariel in the direction Jack had taken, but presently returned. "He's gone," she said. 'What did he say to you?'

'Are you all right, Zenna?' Ariel felt light-headed. The day no longer seemed quite so real.

'Never mind that. What did he say?' Zenna rubbed her chest in the place where Jack had touched her.

'He said to tell you that you cannot come. I don't know what he meant."

Zenna frowned and pulled down the neck of her dress. "Did he mark me?" she asked.

Ariel leaned forward. "Yes," she said. There was a small mark on Zenna's pale skin, in the shape of a crescent moon. He must have dug his fingernail into her, and yet the touch had appeared to be so light. "It's just a scratch, I think. Not even that. What did it feel like?"

"I can't remember. I simply found myself on the ground." Zenna shook her head. She didn't appear to be upset about the incident, just puzzled. "Tell me now you think he's just a boy," she said.

That night, very late, a wind came up from the east. The moon was nearly full, but the clouds rushed past her, didn't pause to carry her like they sometimes did, edged in silver. The Green House creaked in the arms of the wind.

Sitting sleepless by her bedroom window, looking out, Ariel realised that everything had a voice; houses, forests, wind, even, impossibly enough, silence. The wind was singing and Ariel knew what it meant. A song of searching, for the wind never stops, always going forward, asking: Who? Where? When? There were feathers in the wind, glowing white. It had its own wings. And in that moment, Ariel realised her true nature. Stubbornly refusing to believe in something did not make it go away. The world had a secret life and some people could see it. Perhaps her mother had.

Then she saw them. Four of them. Down in the garden,

among the rhododendrons, shapes in the dark. There were no glowing eyes, no vivid flash of white teeth, just shapes. They looked like beasts, crouched and waiting. They had come for Jack. He would leave now.

In an instant, Ariel was on her feet. She ran out of her room and down the stairs and her feet made no sound. They didn't even touch the stairs. Sure enough, Jack was in the kitchen and no one else was there. She had to ask a question. She couldn't help herself. "Who are they?"

"My father and his brothers," Jack said. He opened the door to the garden, where the wind was hurrying past. "Will you come?"

"Yes," Ariel said. She took the hand he offered her.

"It will be just this once," Jack said. "Do you understand that?"

"Yes."

Walking across the wind was difficult because it wanted them to go the way it was going. It seemed to take a long time to reach the other side of the garden. Jack's hand was hot and dry. He was speaking in a language Ariel did not know, a constant sibilant murmur; "ah kaya, hala, hala, mah kah nay."

Jack's kin came out from the foliage, huge and sinuous. They were cats and yet not. They had golden hoops in their tufted ears, and manes that were plaited with feathers and beads. They stretched and groaned and rubbed around Jack. One of them looked at Ariel, and breathed upon her. Its breath was hot and moist. Ariel reached out and laid a hand upon the enormous dark head. It smelled of the earth. The animal raised a paw and then, with a swift and unexpected movement, slashed Ariel with its claws across the chest, above the heart, tearing right through her shirt. Ariel did not stagger back, nor felt any pain, but saw she was bleeding. Her blood looked black. She looked at the beast and let the questions fall from her eyes: Why? Had she not trusted? Had she not believed and so allowed the true sight to come to her?

The cat reared up and then it was a man standing before her, dark and wild, a creature of the hidden places. "You can't be too careful," he said.

Jack put a hand upon her shoulder. "It's all right," he said. "Let me, not him. His tongue is too rough."

So Ariel let him lick up her blood, which he did neatly, as a cat would savour a saucer of cream. These things were really happening to her, there might be no future, but she didn't care. She was dreaming on her feet. Jack's voice brought her out of her reverie.

"You see, you're fine. Now we can run." He took her hand again.

"Where?"

"With the wind."

When she awoke in her bed, Ariel knew she was supposed to believe it had been all a dream. Then she would get out of bed and her feet would have soil between the toes, her legs would be scratched from brambles, there would be a wound above her heart from where a vampire had supped her blood. She lay in bed, breathing quickly. Above her, the ceiling was covered in sparkling motes that did not disappear when she blinked. She heard Maeve call her name. So she slipped from between the white sheets and looked down at her feet. They were clean. Perhaps he had licked them clean after he'd carried her to her bed, exhausted. It hadn't been a dream. There were her clothes, thrown over a chair, and the shirt was torn and bloody. Ariel picked the shirt up and stuffed it into the back of the wardrobe, among dozens of pairs of old shoes that perhaps Maeve had worn, many years before. Ariel looked at her wounds; they were nearly healed. She hoped the scars would not vanish.

The first words Maeve said to her downstairs were: "Have you seen Jack?"

This was ridiculous. How could she? She'd been in bed. Ariel shook her head.

Zenna came in from outside. She looked like someone lost. "He's gone," she said. "I know. They came for him."

Ariel could not look at her cousin. She was thinking of fast paws, galloping along the wind, of hot moist breath, of the time when true sight came to her and made it so that she could never be the same again.

"You must be glad," Zenna said to her. "Everything can be all normal again now."

"Stop it," Maeve said. "He might be taking a walk." But the tone in her voice showed she didn't really believe that.

How can you love someone who is so beyond all that is real it is impossible even to give them a name? If a person stands up in his real skin and shows you his real self, and you see it is not human, but something more beautiful and wondrous, even though it is potentially deadly, is that enough to change a life forever? But it is a fairy-tale, just words in the dark. How can you feel grief when that is taken from you?

The women of the Green House were struck down by grief. Even the geese by the pond lay down and stretched out their necks, spread out their white wings in the grass.

For a week Ariel was not entirely in the real world. The east wind had brought rain, dark and heavy, so that every day felt as if it was weeping. Ariel didn't think about whether Jack and his people might come back for her or not. It was impossible to think about anything. She lived in memory alone, like walking through a gallery of pictures, studying each one, experiencing it, but without having any opinion. Her memories brought her great pleasure; her secrets. No one knew. No one suspected. Ariel was the sensible one. It was Zenna who would have strange things happen to her; be taken under the hill by the faery folk, and be allowed home for only six months of the year.

Ariel drifted through the weeping days, while Maeve and Zenna comforted each other. They drew closer in a way they never had before. They were changed too. But the spell over

Ariel eventually began to melt away. She could feel the real world coming back. She could not turn into a beast and walk the wind. She could not drink blood and become 'other'. That was the tragedy of it. She would never be the same again because she *couldn't* be like them. Zenna had been right about that. But at the same time she was not how she'd used to be. She was marked, lines down her torso the colour of mulberries.

On the night of the next full moon, Ariel climbed onto the roof of the house. Summer was ending, already the air smelled of decaying fruit and smoke. Autumn air would always smell that way, even if there were no fires, no fruit trees. There were no vampires on the roof, or down in the garden. How cruel they were. And how stupid was she to have believed that once would be enough. Of course it wouldn't, but even so she had consented.

It was no surprise to her that Zenna wriggled out of her window and used the limbs of the ironwood tree to reach the roof. She did not speak to Ariel at first, but just stood beside her, hands on hips, gazing at the forest behind the house. Eventually she said, "Are you going to tell me or not?"

There seemed no point in being arch and saying, "What do you mean?" Ariel sighed. "I will show you," she said.

Zenna turned round. Ariel could see she was full of pain and jealousy. She had guessed, no doubt, because Ariel's secrets were written all over her; she smelled of them. Ariel took off her shirt. In the moonlight her skin was parchment and the claw marks looked like burns.

"Claws, not teeth," Zenna said.

Ariel nodded. "When they take your blood, perhaps it is something in their saliva that makes things happen. But it doesn't last. You were right about that. It does change you, though; enough to feel a stranger in this world, but not enough to belong in theirs."

"Tell me what happened," Zenna said. "Please."

Ariel did so. She spoke the words of a story so unlikely, she

99

could hardly believe it herself, yet it had happened.

"I should hate you," Zenna said, "because it feels like you took something that was mine. But I'm glad it changed you. We are similar now."

Ariel tried to smile. "We can outrun time."

"For now." Zenna held out her hand. "Come on. Maybe we are not as stupid as they think."

Hand in hand, two girls run through the moonlit forest. They run so fast they are merely blurs of light. They run so fast they cause cracks in the bark of trees that leak a green-yellow radiance. It is the were-light of seeing.

English Spoken

John Kaiine

Where to turn when there are no corners?
"Pluperfect" by R.S. Thomas

The Passenger becomes the Stranger when he leaves the ship and steps ashore.

There are no others, no travellers or tourists to join him in this tropical darkness and warm rain, just the crew of the immense container ship, cheap labour, milling past, out onto the harbour quayside and beyond.

He has not spoken a word for the four days and nights of the voyage and his mouth is, now, terribly dry.

He has come ill-dressed for the journey, with a small battered suitcase and the rest of his belongings wrapped in brown paper. The past – his shirts and photographs all creased. He has a destination, an address in a foreign hand, the scrawl of numbers, a company name. The promise of overseas employment passed on by a drunken, well- meaning, brief acquaintance. His mode of escape. A new life – Office work, 9 to 5. *A speaker of English required. Agents worldwide.* He looks down at the back of the faded, torn envelope to a map of sorts, a design of lines, arrows, an X marking his journey's end. Thumbing his collar, he sets off under the wet shadows of gantries and giant, rotating cranes.

Lorries rumble by.

Moths spill about him.

As he walks to the far side of the port, the Stranger watches the full moon, rising low. Curious, blue. But now, a corner turned and the moon is eclipsed by the steel metal glow of huge floodlights on a towering chainlink fence. Closer, he peers through. It is a ship-breaking yard. Barefoot workers dissect the white hulk of an aircraft carrier that tilts in dry dock, a vessel of 60,000 tons. As swarming ants would strip flesh to bone, so the men slice through its insides, picking it clean. The red eye of an oxyacetylene cutter sparkling there, and fires burn within. Music radio played loud. Boys and dogs scavenge along the *folded* remains of old merchant ships. Vast rusted chains hang all around. A scorched metal taste in the rain. Shivering, he moves on.

Out through the exit gates, he follows the map. A long line to walk, held either side by seething jungle dark. A pitted black track washed in puddles of old monsoon rains.

His expectations? – a fresh life, routine, keep his head low, stay hidden in this place, perhaps, most importantly, take a wife and start another family. New mistakes to make.

He thinks, *I am afraid*, as he begins down the path, the only route left to him now. Battered Dodge-truck headlights illuminate his way; melon seed rosaries draped from every rear-view mirror. One driver, a woman of many years, slows her vehicle and through the downpour gently casts out a bunch of feathers twined with thin blue wire – an offering at a roadside shrine. Passing the shadow of her hand across her face, she bows her head, drives off. Windscreen wipers dragging on the rainfall.

He witnesses this but does not understand.

As he goes, the Stranger sees a lot of shrines. Crude stone bowls lit by flame where wild land meets rank tarmacadam. For all the rain, their fires still burn. Effigies, some tall as stunted children others no bigger than dolls, balanced in mud or standing upon altars of plump coconut leaves. Clay and stone gods placated with chocolate bars, gum, some scented cigarettes. (He recalls church on childhood Sundays and the pretty painted statue of *The Virgin*.) The icons are many – a carved white bull, perfect, but having the hands, eyes, mouth of a man. And there, a squatting mammoth, its broken tusk garlanded by Jasmine. Further along, an object, faceless, winged, smeared with turquoise blue, wrapped in ribbons and the roots of a tree, a miniature bottle of *Smirnoff* nestled in its chipped, alabaster lap. Next, a plastic Bubastis, all weeds about her trimmed neatly away, looking like a well-tended grave. Her offering is one of money and *hair*? U.S dollar bills so tenderly tied within a child's trimmed locks. Who would do such a thing – and why.

Suddenly, a Coconut Crab scuttles out before him. Transfixed, sickened, he has never seen anything like it. Doesn't know what it is, or what to do. A colourful grey crab the size of a monstrous dog. Trucks slow, stop to let it pass. Clicking its enormous claws, it sidles gracefully off across the road and is gone.

Nauseous now, hurrying on down the path he sees a pack of cheroots rested with great care against another shrine and wants one; should he take it, strip it of its gaudy wrapping, or steal a nip of vodka from that god, over there? Some chocolate maybe? He is hungry, but who knows how long this stuff has been sitting with the leeches and heat of this godforsaken place. His stomach lurches. Rummaging through his pockets for something, he finds nothing, sniffs. Sweat is beaten from him by the rain. Head drooping, not looking anymore – doesn't want to see – he continues. Wet feet in deep puddles. Shoes with no socks.

The Stranger finds scant fascination in where he is. Knows nothing of Sacred or of belief and the strength and power in believing. Never did, was always distracted by the pretty statues and golden goblets during the service, just as then, he wants his sweeties, small comforts to stave off bad thoughts. Pretends he cannot notice from the corner of his eye that looming red mountain propped there in the darkness; a Soviet whaler dumped inland, shrouded by vines, broken by overgrown night. A ship nobody wanted, not even in pieces.

He doesn't like the moths, the clacking of pincers all around, or the plump, warm pulse of rain so akin to the sting of being called crude names, over and *over* again. Little wet slaps, running down his back, filling his ears and senses. Thick diesel fumes there too. Raucous music from every truck radio. He does not grasp why the drivers do not just run down the monstrous crabs. It is beyond him, why cheap sacrifices are made to makeshift gods. The Stranger has no conception of the thing that has brought him to this raining land – *Something* bred on superstition, a psychic nightmare driven from caves of Pre-History, cast out with fire, enslaved for Caesarian Rome, thus cheated by Empire, exiled to this swollen equatorial hell, unseen, left to rot with only words to feed upon; language, thoughts garnered, all tangled in air. The gaffes of ages – slavery, pilgrimage, revolution, brought in tide after tide – misery, doubt, guilt, and at the base of it all, curled beneath hate, and long dead love, there is *fear.*

Something grown fat on prayers and screams and sour song, sifting the ether with frail scratchings through endless war, World Service propaganda and Bollywood hokum.

Keep going, he tells himself. Ignoring the flapping prayer flags hung high in the twisted boughs of silent trees. Black flags, tatters. Ignore the thousands of candles blazing in the depths of jungle.

Keep going…

Spirits surround him, energies *beyond* him in so many ways. Primal, in the croaking of frogs to the lost greens of dark. He is ideal; there is nothing in him, nothing of any worth or substance. A life lived in other people's margins – a debt called in, overwritten and shunned. He is one of hollow many. Each and every one of them reaches this point, eventually. Perhaps once a week or twice a year they will arrive. (It will always be waiting.) Passing, as those on countless ill-shod journeyings before, into this easy unknown. *Somebody else's husband* or *another man's wife*, taking the short cut to the end of the line. Already dead. Treading emotional water, drowning. Going under, slipping away. Washed up. Beached. Nowhere left to turn, best just give up. And *'all that love'* that came to nothing, so much walking away, *running* away, far from home, to some distant town in a land you never hear of now. A continent mislaid on maps. The final destination known, unspoken in the blood.

Nearly there…

Perfect. Another empty life lived burnt at both ends. Those friends and lovers kept so close, and enemies closer still. The whole of his words come to naught – Dreams, wishes, hope. The weary communication of life, translated: Age, remorse, wrong turnings, debt. *Worthy of no mocking sigh. No tearful expression.*

The Stranger kicks at an armoured sun fashioned of tin that has fallen from the long grass on to the path. Was this another offering, or a god in a simpler form?

Coughing, he notices the insects, crickets, are shattered by the weight of the rain, but that the moths somehow skirt the onslaught.

Finally, breathing heavy, standing at the edge of the jungle – he has made it this far – there are shanties before him, the sea behind him. In the distance now, the breaking-yard spitting white and fierce, grinding moonlight into long shadows.

Storks go picking through the night.

Ash-grey-gold mists rise up before him – from reeking tanneries, pumps and engines. Sodden shapes move there in the teeming slums, on foot, moped or bullock cart. The sickly scent of incense is everywhere. Rain is dripping from neon strips, hammering on flimsy walls and roofs of plastic tarps and rusted, corrugated metal, turning red soil floors to mud. The lanes and passageways flooded with sewage. Dogs too thin to piss shelter in backstreet sandstone temple ruins. Misplaced in a distorted mass of radio rhythms, the underlying chorus of chanting and the ringing of small hand-bells.

His first impressions are not filled with hope.

He enters the night market, pushing through low hanging lines of drying laundry, grim sheets and garments of rag strung high, spread wide, across, on bamboo: the bones of haunted ships that had finally found their sails.

The long sprawling wooden stalls of the night market are ramshackle surfaces cobbled together from the dismantled contraptions of ships gangways and flotsam. Vendors and buyers shift patiently from stall to stall, bartering, smoking, handling the merchandise with infinite care, from dried corncobs to colourful swathes of silk and cotton. The Stranger can't help but stare. They look at him too, but some look away. Expressionless. They are *not* patient, but *deliberate*. Slow and ashamed, their voices, even though he cannot understand their speech, are low, whispering. Their faces, born beneath umbrellas. Faces drawn in lines of age. Skins the colour of clay. Hennaed nails, wispy beards. Pallid turbans, baseball caps. One vendor slicing jackfruit with an old putty knife. Another, with a panther cub curled upon her lap. A little bow-legged man rushes before him, briefly nodding his bald head, indicating the way forward. It is only then that the Stranger glances aside, down, seeing his drowned reflection in an oily puddle, then that he *knows* – not *sees* – that his is the one white face there, and that someone has scattered pink rose petals before him on his well-swept path. They lead on and along the same direction as is penned upon his tatty map.

From somewhere, a cockerel monotonously calling out the hour. Whichever one it is.

On, passing stall after stall of guava, lemon grass, cinnamon sticks, cardamom and cloves. Water fowl and porcupine – killed, skinned, hung, waiting to be cured. Sacks of sugar, bottles of second generation *Bells Whisky*. One stall featuring brass ship portholes, polished, gleaming. The next covered with wide, shallow baskets filled with mobile phones. Radio voices blur as he passes, static crackling up, seeming to follow him. More stalls – antique flintlock rifles side by side with greased, locked and loaded *AK-47's*. And moths everywhere winding through the rain drops.

Things cooking, spicy, pungent. Sweet and sweaty. Bowls of black rice. Hooded women there, sparking *Zippo's*, drawing deep on *Camel* cigarettes.

Ravenous, his stomach turns. Head thumping from thirst and the past. From all that had brought him there – the unfaithful lover, graceful, even *humorous*, after the event; the false words down the line, the tremble in the welcoming hug. The grubby hearts broken, the livers washed with regret. Hand over hand, the untruths told and built upon. The lies by omission, *all* those little excuses. Better not to dwell on it.

Strange, he thinks, his pathway is moving. A line of ants march ahead of him, picking up the petals that have been scattered. Now where does he go?

The lines of the map have faded; squinting, he can just about make out that alley there, two turnings, left and right and then.

And then.

Hesitant, he ventures forward, out from the market toward the maze of alleyways too narrow for the bodies of tourists, squeezing himself sideways on, in, and through to walls of tattered planks and thick, stitched jute bags, the mark of a turquoise blue painted hand-print smeared on every surface there, and within the hand, the crude design of an eye staring out. The eye is glowing: fluorescent paint. Lost in this enclosed space of rain, with his back to these backs of shacks, he peers through a broken window of sorts, only to witness a starving dog licking a sleeping baby's face. He staggers, gagging on the sudden stench of rank meat and human ordure, vision fixed on shattered clay roof tiles, trodden down, barely visible through the filth of the ground, and *there*, petals.

Making little animal noises of relief, the Stranger rushes on.

Moths rush after.

Past shipping offices with bright-lit facades and endless steaming, buzzing sweatshops, following the strewn flowers. ...

Breathless, knowing he is close to his agreed destination, up this street hung with lights, little twinkling spots of ice blue electric, and dull burning lanterns draped in white saris, just a few more yards, turn the corner and there it will be, this will all have been worth it, the longest journey of his life, and *tonight*, and its entire, disgusting spectacle. In the morning, he thinks, this will all look much better – cleaner and clearer – and he will probably even laugh, at how things seem *so* distorted at night and brighter and normal in the pure light of day.

A rail of drenched gents' full dress suits (circa 1920) waits unattended outside a closed Halal meat emporium. Headless, handless, footless. Pockets full of rain. Bow ties wilted like badly inked lilies.

He continues.

Orphans and prostitutes of many a gender line the street, hands outstretched, open, or blowing kisses. Winking. Behind them, a bland concrete building, and inside its four walls three generations whoring out of one room. *So* many brides. Eating with their fingers in the dark. And they smile with their teeth.

Unseen faces lurk in doorways, grinning, chattering to him in their eager sing-song voices as he crosses by, '*No harm on you, sir*,' Gesturing forward, pointing. He takes this as a good sign.

Only a little further now, the noises all around him – black kettles whistling on back room stoves, radio hiss, wind chimes and the insipid beat of rain on tin baths and pails – becoming strangely muted.

The rose petals have ended and have been replaced by peach stones.

He follows them around this final corner.

It is suddenly all so very clean and *well mannered*, if landscapes and buildings can be so. This street is empty, bare of trash, pedestrians, rain even. The uniform offices are all fierce lit – clay-blue-white sodium streetlights. The last peach stone rests, split in two at the foot of a rusted black iron staircase. It would appear that the Stranger has, indeed, arrived.

He checks, looking at the map of envelope he has been clutching, but the map has dissolved. Pulpy. Just the X marking the spot, a dark mark in the palm of his hand. One last kiss goodbye.

His package of belongings wrapped in brown paper has disintegrated too, its contents spilled, drowned in puddles; the string which wrapped it has also slipped, twined round by vines, swallowed by snakes. Gone. All that remains of the battered suitcase is the tiny plastic handle which he grips on to for dear life.

He brushes himself down, runs fingers through his thinning hair. He has travelled halfway around the world for this, the very least he can do is to try and give a good impression of himself. If he were wearing a tie, he would be busy straightening it.

Moths swirl by, spiraling up and onward between the iron steps. He follows them. Dull modest echo of his footfalls on the rust.

The ringing of small hand-bells…

Outside the office door now – there is a sign on an old cord – a faded partial rectangle of card that had once belonged among the stiff-backed white packaging from a man's shirt. There are words, letters, italicised upper case, black and bold. The sign *originally* read **ENGLISH SPOKEN HERE**. But **HERE** – isn't there. That word had been folded and torn neatly away.

No need to knock. He turns the handle and steps inside.

There is no one in the room. No welcoming committee in that simple surround of stark plaster walls, neon strip light and worn wooden floor – Alaskan pine. In the centre of the space a large desk dominates, bundles of documents, unread, unstamped, rest upon it. No chair though or any type of seat. What, he wonders, could be present in the drawers of that desk? On the far wall, a closed door. A key in the lock. To his left, a filing cabinet of gunmetal grey. The office is without a clock. No time. No fan either to move the dry, heavy air.

Outside, all the dogs and babies have fallen silent.

109

He bleeds rain upon the floor.

Behind him, moths enter through the unclosed door.

Perhaps the person he needs to see or speak to is hard at business in the backroom. Yes, that must be it; they would certainly have known that he was coming. Probably they are tidying the office *he* will be working from.

He tries the handle.

Locked.

Face flushed, sweating hard, the Stranger turns the big brass key. Clanking heavy, difficult, the bolt shifting. Open now. Best go in.

As one door opens, so another – the main office door with neat torn sign – closes.

The backroom is in darkness, he fumbles for a light switch, fingers brushing a wall-fitting, clicking down hard. In the instant between pitch black and illumination, images fill his head: closing doorways, the beginnings or ends of staircases, the steps of planes, the backs of car windows, loved ones waving. *Smiling.* Train windows. Hospital beds. Waving. Farewell. The blown kiss leave-taking of all those never again seen (unless in grim-lit mortuary or undertaker's chapel of rest). Too many images land-locked in life, unknowing, walking hand in hand with death. *Fare well.* So few do. Some, fresh off the boat, wander down this route; streets of rag and thin neon. *Agents worldwide,* an address scribbled in a hurried hand. – Strange, he had never before *thought* in pictures.

The backroom is shabby and empty, save for a garbage sack slumped in a corner. The room is lighted now by a bare bulb hanging overhead like a little electric suicide. Moths skim around the light, hundreds of them, crawling about the floor, walls, ceiling. The Stranger's vision is blurred by wings and movement. Something stirs and rises in the room. He sees – the garbage bag – what is it? Unfolding, veiled, faceless, a *woman* of sorts (The Hand Maiden; *The Twenty-First Daughter*), all bones, or bones of shadows beneath, in an ashen shroud; it clutches something to its breast. *Something* boiled maggot white, a gross, limbless infant, held there as if suckling through the spills of old dark stains.

Moths pour in, darting, swarming about the bulb, burning up, one by one, on glass and heat. Thousands upon thousands beating out the light. An insane hive, flapping, falling, as the ghastly swollen shape shifts itself to peer languid at the Stranger.

Its terrible corpulent head is sunk into a shapeless stump of body. Its features are flat, as if what once could have been called a face has been trodden on and down. The mouth is a small crooked line but as it smacks its black, sticky lips, its lower jaw drops sloppily into the mass of gut, showing a huge, toothless, dry drooling maw of darkness. There are deep rings and bags around and beneath its eyes. Its eyes are Roman coins. Folds of thin fat are draped about them. It squints. It reeks. Stagnant white, the hue and texture of its flesh are of something that has lived its life in rain. The enormous mouth moves, sickeningly slow, as if it were a gull attempting to laugh.

A knuckle's reach, a shadow's length – *it* motions 'Nearer' without moving.

The Stranger cannot budge. Drawn as moth to flame, he stands, somehow respectful. Watching, knowing *It will always be waiting,* and that it always was.

It feeds, gluts, and is at once afflicted, inertly squirming. Love would kill it. It nests in fear and the superstition of fear. It doesn't want blood. It wants failure. *All* the mistakes ever made. Each wrong word, deed, turn.

Feasting on the psychic shit of every fruitless defeat, breakdown and emotional blunder.

This is its cave now.

Perhaps once a week or twice a year they will arrive – losers world-wide tempted by the promise of a new life – a name, address, passed on by endless servants, 'Brief acquaintances', scribbled maps on the inside of cigarette packets. Those already lured – centuries ago – last July – yesterday. Those who had journeyed over oceans, through jungles and shrines, to be in this room, where the banquets of their pathetic lives could at least be feasted upon. And afterwards – cast out again. Search, send. Other strangers. Nourishment, to what is waiting, *always*. Agents: some purpose, finally.

The scene is woefully sad. All his stinging tears uncried, they are cried now. The rivers that melt the mountain. The weakness in his knees and the retreat of gravity on the Stranger's arms and shoulders, pulling his head forward, as if nodding once and no more. Silently howling, not wanting to move from this very spot. Cannot. It is not fear that holds him, it is truth. Everything he has ever done has brought him to this point, *this* is where he finally belongs. He is so, *so*, very sorry. For everything. His sobbing vision, misty, powdered and crowded at the edges by disintegrating moths. The vile stench of insect flesh burnt on electric light. The brave little bodies collapsed around his cheap brown slip-ons and in the badly-machined turn-ups of his summer slacks. The wings, without. All those nights flown, grown, to end, charred and crisped, sacrificed in the mad spiral to man-made light. Sacrificed to a stranger in a drip-dry shirt.

What was it all worth?

There are pink petals stuck on the soles of his shoes.

The piss all drained from him, the bile, bubbling, no need for hunger. Not anymore. It is like some religious experience.

All those nights, thoughtless, loveless human thing, wasted, lost, finally found in a back room in a foreign land, with moths eating light and a pale flower cradling a bloated, *ancient* child to her barren breast, greedy for all of life's fuck-ups.

Error, then, not terror.

Turn and turn again. Useless.

Gulping, swallowing.

Known. Unspoken.

Moth mouthed, terribly dry. *"Mammy,"* the Stranger wants to say. But finally only the word, *"…I"* flutters out.

there are *no corners*

HERE

Hothouse Flowers

Or The Discreet Boys of Doctor Barnabas

Chaz Brenchley

It has been rightly said that travel as you may seek where you can, risk what you dare, never shall you find anything to match the horrors that wait for you at home.

I have been a solitary man and a restless one, by nature and by practice both. Being blessed in the possession of a good fortune and far, very far from the want of a wife, I found myself able to indulge both those predilections as far as I chose. At the age of twenty-one I engaged a man of business and left my affairs cheerfully in his competent hands, to nourish as he could. Myself, I promptly departed this damp demi-paradise with a thousand pounds in gold and notes and promises – it seemed a fortune to the callow youth I was – and the firm intent of returning only when I lacked the funds to keep away any longer.

That noble experiment took me thirty years to realise.

I did come back at last, as I had always known I must. The John Furnival who stepped off the packet steamer in Southampton was as light of frame as the boy of the same name who had departed the same way three decades earlier, if not so light of heart. He was more sallow of skin, malarial, and inclined to limp in wet weather; he carried a record of his adventures in scars both public and private, both visible and otherwise; he had a fund of stories on which he rarely drew, and nothing of value besides, except experience dearly bought and highly prized.

I rode north, two days on a hired hack. My destination was a spa town in the hills, the name of which need not detain us. Once there, and with my pockets entirely to let, my first enquiry was necessarily for my man of business. He, it transpired, had in my absence become a company. I paid a call, then, upon the firm of Alshott, Stroud and Alshott; presented my card and asked for Mr Alshott; and was ushered into the presence of a stripling, a mere youth whose attempts at gravitas were mocked by the very desk he sat behind.

"Ah," I said. "I think, perhaps, your father...?"

The boy laid my card – cheap Indian pasteboard, florid print, itself sufficient to declare my history, my status and my recent impoverishment to anyone with eyes to see – upon his blotter, rose to his feet and walked around that imposing edifice of a desk, smiling ruefully.

"My father is in Suffolk, sir, enjoying a very comfortable retirement. I am sure he would wish me to remember him to you; had we but notice of your coming, I am sure he would have written. I am Sylvester Alshott."

We shook hands, but I was shaking my head. "You were... not born, I think – heavens, I think your father was not married! – when I left England. And retired now? Good grief! I had not supposed him to be ten years older than myself."

"Oh, barely so much, sir. A number of happy years in the business induced him to relinquish an active role with us far sooner than might otherwise have been the case. Or at least, to relinquish a <u>public</u> role. His name, you have seen, remains on our letterhead; he himself remains deeply interested in our activities. It might fairly be said that his retirement is more comfortable for him than for those of us who toil beneath his vigilance. If you are concerned about your own investments, Mr Furnival, let me assure you that my father has been assiduous in overseeing my endeavours on your behalf, and that your position is... robustly healthy, shall we say?"

By now I was laughing internally, and trying to disguise it for the sake of his *amour-propre*, while still being grateful to his father for that careful and no doubt onerous supervision.

"Thank you," I managed, knowing the little phrase to be hopelessly inadequate to the occasion – either of the two occasions, indeed, his injured pride or my own relief.

He offered me sherry, of course – that utterly English ceremony that I have acted out a thousand times, from Gibraltar to Kuala Lumpur to Hong Kong – and bade me sit with him at a fireplace, where we could talk without that monumental furniture between us. We spoke of trade, of 'Change, of my various properties and his investments on my behalf; at last, rather diffidently, I asked whether I might actually still have a house.

"Of course, sir!" For a moment there, he looked like a startled owl. Had we not been speaking of houses, among other benefits, all this half-hour gone? "Did I forget to mention that Minscombe has been let this last year on most advantageous terms?"

Minscombe was my childhood home, a bare ten miles north of where we sat, and he knew quite well that he had not forgotten to mention it.

I smiled at his blushing awkwardness, and shook my head. "I'm sorry, I have confused you now. I have been attending, I promise, despite this intriguing sherry wine," and despite the more simple pleasures of watching young Sylvester Alshott as he strained to impress upon his most senior and unexpected client how very much he justified his father's confidence. "What I mean is, do I have a house that I can actually live in, without dispossessing any of my tenants or disrupting your other arrangements? Preferably a house close at hand, that I might occupy this week? Tonight, even? To be frank, Mr Alshott, I find myself embarrassed – *temporarily* embarrassed, thanks to your excellent stewardship – to the point where even a room in a posting-house is a strain on my resources."

Again I had startled him, again he had to struggle a little with his composure. This time, I thought, he was trying not to laugh. My mind had perhaps not yet caught up with my new, my *resumed* position. After one has spent many months counting every copper coin and ekeing out every meal – after one has spent the better part of a year, indeed, travelling overland because the cost of even a third-class sea-passage had proved beyond one's means – it is not easy immediately to shrug off habits of parsimony.

"Mr Furnival," the boy said earnestly, with a glance at the clock, "it is too late now, but a visit to your banker in the morning will resolve any such difficulty, and should quite set your mind at rest," in a way that, to his clear chagrin, he had failed to accomplish himself. He was back to thinking me a little simple, I suspected. "In the meantime, I hope you will consider yourself my guest."

"No, no, there is no need for—"

"Please," he said. "I insist. My father bequeathed me his house when he departed for the salt air of the Suffolk coast, and to be blunt with you I rattle in it alone. I should be glad of the company, and you will find it more comfortable than any hotel in town, let alone a posting-house. That is, assuming that you can tolerate the bachelor lifestyle...?"

This was rather neatly done; the question of course made it impossible for me to refuse. Laughing, I drew his attention to the fact that I had myself lived the bachelor lifestyle for more years than he had been alive, and a rather rougher version of it recently. Then I graciously allowed him to buy me dinner, on the grounds that my fortune had been the foundation of his father's and hence his own. Conversation proved easy, and by the time his front door had closed behind us both we were on the way to becoming fast friends; by the time the sun surprised us the next morning, we had ventured rather further.

It was nothing but curiosity – my besetting sin, I confess it – that took me north the following week, on a hunter borrowed from Alshott, whose hospitality I continued to abuse. I meant no more than to overlook my former home from a convenient hill, a childhood haunt of mine. Minscombe was let out now to a philanthropic gentleman, Alshott had told me, who took in orphaned boys; I had half an idea that I might run into some of the lads playing as I used to play myself. Perhaps I wanted to find one alone, who might stand in for me exactly.

The oak was there yet, the particular oak that overhung the cliff above the house. Some days I used to sprawl panther-like on a branch for hours together, to the voluble horror of my anxious guardian, just watching the slow passage of life below. My tree was untenanted this day, though, as was the hill entire. I took my mount as near the edge as was comfortable for him, and looked down. The house seemed as empty as the countryside around. It had never bustled even in my time – my guardian having been of a retiring disposition – but I saw not a soul at work in the grounds, not a servant crossing the yard, not a boy running through the park or capering on the leads or indeed anywhere about.

Perhaps they were all at luncheon. My pocket-watch had stopped and I kept misreading the sun, forgetting how low it lies even at noon in northern latitudes. Or perhaps the philanthropic gentleman was a tartar who laid all his charges down for a nap in the early afternoon. Or he was a generous soul, and had taken them on an expedition for the day or for the week – there seemed no more life in the stable-block than there was in the house, neither hands nor horses shifting the light – and the staff was taking advantage of this opportunity to idle. Or—

I could list half a hundred reasons if I cared to. Nevertheless I thought it curious, unless I was simply disappointed not to find that analogue of myself. Perhaps I had built too much on a dream of continuity, as though there must always be one lonely boy at Minscombe, hopeful and bereft...

One lonely horseman on the road below drew me down unexpectedly. It might only have been that the glimpse of movement in an otherwise still world acted as a trigger to my own need to move, or as a reminder that I could not sit there all day gazing into the pool of memory and speculation. It might have been coincidence that I emerged from Home Wood just as he rounded the last hedge before the boundary wall.

His horse shied at the sight of me, but she was nervous already. That was his doing, I thought, the fat man who sat her, who sweated in her saddle and shied more dramatically than she did.

He huffed with relief when he saw my face, when he saw that I meant no harm, or else perhaps when he saw that he didn't know me. I saw that he was clumsy with his horse, but not unkind. Once they were both settled I saw another thing, that he had a doctor's bag strapped to the saddle at his back.

"Is someone unwell here, sir? One of the boys, perhaps - or their benefactor?"

It was a fair guess. This road was practical no farther than the house, petering out in farmland. The river beyond was neither bridged nor fordable for three miles in either direction. And sickness would explain the quiet, perhaps.

His eyes narrowed none the less. "Do you have some connection with the house, sir?"

His question was equally fair, and I might fairly have said *no, none at all*. Certainly I had no legitimate interest in my tenant's doings, so long as he paid his rent and kept his children orderly. Still, I had come too far this morning to be willingly balked; I took advantage of the way the question was framed. "You might say so, sir, as it belongs to me."

He frowned. "I understood the owner to be expatriate?"

"Indeed. I have just now returned to this country, after a life abroad. My name is Furnival."

"Ah. Barnabas, Rowland Barnabas."

We shook hands, there with our horses restless beneath us. I said, "You are a doctor, I collect? Unless the shape and significance of a man's saddle-luggage has altered significantly since my last days here." When he still hesitated, I added, "I have no connection with the Minscombe tenant, sir, except that he lives in my house; but I confess to a growing curiosity, and perhaps a hint of unease. And, well, he does live in my house..."

"Yes." He came to a decision, visibly; I had been confident that he would. He was a few years younger than me, I thought, and not a confident man himself. He carried a burden he would like to share, once he was sure of my *bona fides*. Perhaps he wanted to confess; he looked to me unquiet in his conscience.

He said, "You are right to be uneasy. Your tenant" – he was quick, I thought, to attach me to the situation – "is not a man to inspire ease of mind. Nor do the orphans thrive in his care. My whole concern is for the boys, you understand," in a sudden outburst.

Mine too, but I did not intend to say so. "Will you explain this to me?"

He was hesitant again, thinking perhaps of his Hippocratic Oath and his duty of confidence. At last he said, "I would prefer to show you, if you will come in with me."

I thought he would be glad of company, as well as of witness. "I think," I said, "my tenant would find it difficult to keep me out."

"So do I, by Jove! Come on, then!" His mood suddenly and inexpressibly lightened, Dr Barnabas actually led the way down the road, that last hundred yards to the gatehouse.

The gatehouse was unoccupied and the gates stood open, as they never had in my late guardian's tenure. The drive, I was sorry to see, was unweeded and the park unkempt; did my tenant's lease not require upkeep of the grounds, or was he a cheeseparer, had he endeavoured to save money by depending on his boys to do the work? If so he must have been disappointed, and so was I.

We rode to the house, where all the windows were shuttered or shrouded, as though there had been a death. Again that would explain the stillness, but I thought my companion would have forewarned me. Something there was, that he wanted me to see for myself; I thought death did not fit the case.

Nothing here seemed to fit the case. We rode around to the stable yard, and no one stood to our horses' heads, no one came to the house door to ask our business here. Dr Barnabas clearly expected this neglect, sliding ungainly down from his mare and himself leading her to an empty stall, loosening her girths, fetching her a bucket of water. I did the same by my own mount, apologising to him the while for the inadequacies of service. He was a fine animal, and deserved better. Meanwhile, the stout doctor was apologising to me: "I am afraid it is always so these days. Mr Royce seems quite unable to retain a servant, inside the house or out."

"Ah. Mr Royce is my tenant's name?" Matters did not bode well for Mr Royce, if he wished to retain his lease. I had not especially wanted to live at Minscombe myself – I had no particular fondness for the place and, while not a great house, it was a monstrous edifice for a man alone, who had neither interest in nor prospect of children – but I would not willingly see it fall to rack and ruin.

Doctor Barnabas confirmed the name but said no more, only beckoning me to follow him in through the house door.

"Oughtn't we to announce ourselves?" I murmured. "A knock, perhaps...?"

"There is no need, no point. No one would come."

It felt strange to walk in uninvited, even here; it felt exceedingly strange to heel another man into what had been my home. After the first minute, though, the strangeness was entirely the other way about. This place was not my home, and everything I saw reminded me of that.

To begin with, the house was cast into unutterable gloom, even at this height of the day. Nary a broken beam of sunlight found its way in to play with the dust – and there was a great deal of dust. Filth, too. Mud beneath our boots, tramped heedlessly into the house.

Well. Barnabas had said that Mr Royce could not keep a servant. I would have countered that boys can dust and scrub as well as maids, if they are put to it - but perhaps he lacked the discipline to do so. Or perhaps there was another reason. The doctor was here for the boys, after all...

More mildly than I meant, I said only, "Do they never draw a curtain in this house?"

"Nor open a shutter, sir, no. The sun is an affliction here."

Lamps and candles stood everywhere, with tapers and lucifers to hand, but there was enough indirect daylight to show us our way; more than enough to show me the grimy condition of my property. I should have been angry if the doctor weren't so imperative, if he hadn't given me to understand that there were worse things here than disregarded dirt. Besides, to criticise my tenant were to criticise my man of business, and I was disinclined to do that. Soap and water and elbow-grease would soon restore Minscombe to her rightful state; no house falls to ruin in a single year.

Dr Barnabas led me up the back stairs, up and up to the servants' rooms in the long attics. He puffed and gasped at the climb; I reflected that Mr Royce was not generous to his orphans in their accommodations. With no one else in the house, he might decently have slept them in the guest wing, even in the family wing. Perhaps he was a practical man, not wanting to give them expectations which must inevitably be disappointed when they moved on into the world beyond the gates. Or – with no servants in the house – perhaps he was practical in another consideration, thinking that the sparse comforts of the attic rooms would be easier of maintenance. Or – if the boys were indeed sick, as Dr Barnabas' presence and anxieties must suggest

– perhaps this was a measure of quarantine, mark of a sensible mind...

The good doctor sweated and hauled his bulk upward, and needed a minute to recover at the head of the stairs; before we ventured the jute mats of the corridor. At least, he wanted me to believe so, lifting his hat and patting a handkerchief across his brow. My suspicion went unvoiced, that in truth he wanted only to delay the moment of discovery a little longer.

Even up here, the dormer windows had been masked with some thin stuff that kept the sun at bay, though it did let in light enough to see by. Dr Barnabas opened the first door, to what had been a housemaids' room in my day. Here were the twin iron beds, the worn rug on bare boards, the washstand and dresser, just as I remembered.

And here were the promised boys at last, one to a bed, pale and clean in the shadows: quite startlingly clean they seemed, in all this gloom and grime. Their nightshirts too were brightly, unexpectedly white.

"I have my girl wash these," Barnabas murmured, fingering a pristine collar as though he read my mind. I hope not so; he wouldn't have liked where my mind went next, as his fingers strayed through the boy's dishevelled hair.

The boy didn't wake or stir beneath these attentions. Nor did his brother in misfortune, though Barnabas was heavy-footed, heavy-handed too, and made no great effort at discretion.

I opened my mouth to ask what ailed them, what could keep lads seemingly unconscious but not apparently sick otherwise, in no apparent need of nursing; but Barnabas forestalled me, moving to the door and beckoning, *onward, more to see...*

Indeed there was, but it was all the same. Room after room, two or three boys asleep or comatose, oblivious. It needed a dozen before at last I could stop Barnabas and put the question; he needed me to see, I think, the scale of what faced him.

"Dr Barnabas! What disease is this?" Something infectious, surely, to strike so many – and yet he seemed quite unconcerned about his own danger, fussing intimately over each of his patients, touching where there seemed no need.

He sighed, straightened, shook his head. "I... do not know. It is like anaemia in some senses, a particularly pernicious anaemia – but anaemia does not produce an aversion to sunlight, photophobia, such as these boys exhibit. Even in this state, if I pulled back the scrim across that window, you would see them flinch. They will rouse at evening, a little: enough to take whatever medicines I prescribe, but my best endeavours do no good. One boy was so weak I transfused him with my blood, my own," and his big hand stroked the arm of the boy he stood above, while his eyes gazed at the blank of the window, while his mind I thought saw another boy altogether, "but he died regardless. He might have died anyway, there are five in the churchyard now," death after all and he had not warned me; "but for all I know, my actions helped him on his way. I cannot tell. I am..." *I am out of my depth*, he meant to say, but a shake of the head was all he had to offer.

"And their guardian, Mr Royce? What does he say?"

"Little enough. Nothing, in recent days; I rarely see him. He pays my bills, and perhaps thinks he has done his duty. And, true, they are only parish boys who would be in the poorhouse else, but I feel their loss most dreadfully, I for one..."

The only one, he thought himself. I thought he was probably right.

And might have thought little more about it, except for wishing this were not happening in my house and wondering how soon we might revoke Royce's lease, Alshott and I – but Barnabas went on, speaking half to himself, touching another boy at the throat. "They have these contusions, too, these sores that form on their necks; I've never seen anything quite like—"

"What? Show me!"

It must have come out in a bark, most unlike my previous sickroom mutter. He startled physically, but turned back the high collar of the nightshirt to let me see.

I looked, I saw.

He said, "Your face...! Do you know what this is?"

"I... have seen its like," I admitted, though I hated to hear the words come from my mouth. "More than once. In India, years since, and in the Carpathians just this December gone. The snows came early, and closed the road; I was obliged to overwinter. The valley folk were kind to me, but they were much afflicted by just such a fell plague as this. Happily, I was able to offer my assistance."

"How, oh, how...?"

I am a hunter: the words were on my lips, but I was merciful. What would he benefit, from knowing? I shook my head and said, "Because I had seen it before, in India. Come, Dr Barnabas. We can do no good standing over these poor boys. You have done magnificently, but this is not a case for you," *you are out of your depth*. "Let me gather what I need to treat this scourge and I promise you, by the time of your next visit, your boys will be on the mend."

It took more work than that to remove the doctor from Minscombe, but not much. He was frankly eager to be gone, only that his professional curiosity was piqued and perhaps his pride also, in a way that flattered him less. I gratified neither, keeping as obscure in my responses as I could achieve.

I put him on his horse and saw him off the grounds and away down the road. Then I turned Alshott's fine hunter to the fields and a wild ride, partly for his satisfaction and partly for my own, to chase the megrims out of my head. This was no disease – no wonder the doctor had been baffled! – but a devil: a foreign devil, by all that I ever knew or dreamed. I had never thought to encounter such a thing in my own county, in my own house yet...!

Here it was, though, and at least I knew what it was. And how to address it. Horror might drive me, but that horror was tempered by experience.

We came hot and hard into Alshott's yard, his horse and I. I tossed the reins to his stable lad and jumped down, to be met by the man himself in his doorway. His face showed disapproval, as he gazed at heaving flanks and a sweat-soaked crupper; he said, "I suppose I should thank you for giving him a good work-out, but truly, Furnival—"

He cut himself off abruptly, as he saw my own face for the first time. "Good God, man, what is it? What's happened? Your house...?"

"Minscombe is very well, or will be when I have her in my care again. Her current tenant, though – he is the devil!"

"Oh! Have I been mistaken in Mr Royce?" His expression changed again, as he thought himself at fault. The young are so mobile, and so revealing; therein lies their charm, I think, far more than in personal beauty. "I might have taken more care over his references; but he settled so quickly on the first sum I asked, I was perhaps too hasty..."

"No, no. Be easy on that score, his references could have told you nothing." I would much have preferred to have done the same thing exactly, told him nothing; but I had said too much already, in my heat. There could be no backing away now. I consoled myself briefly with the thought that I knew my host already to be a sportsman, a huntsman, and one who kept a vigorous and testing stable; he would not resile from a grim task, if I could only bring him to trust me.

I thought I could do that. I believed it, indeed, profoundly; I had amassed evidence enough, these days beneath his roof. Sylvester Alshott was a young man who inspired confidence, and deserved it.

Even so, I begged his indulgence while I washed and changed my clothes. Nothing could happen yet in any case, and whether or not he believed the tale I had to tell him it would be briefly told.

In my absence he'd had his man clean and press my dinner suit, and lay it out ready for me. I had grown unused to such service in recent years; now I felt an unexpected surge of sentiment, as though somehow I had come home. That was inappropriate, of course, in another man's house. Also, it was only too easy to see in relation to the danger that would confront me this night – confront us both, if I was any judge of men – and still I was absurdly moved by such a little, such an ordinary attention.

I couldn't speak of it, of course, when I met him in the library. Besides, we had other graver matters to discuss. I cursed his lawyerly sherry and demanded a brandy and soda; he laughed at me and mixed a strong one, but would not be bullied – he said – into joining with my barbarity, when his father had laid down three dozen of a fine oloroso and this was the last of it.

Unchallenged, then, by each other's tastes, we sank into heavy leather chairs and a brief silence while he waited, while I reached for words.

"I have travelled," I said, "far and far. I have seen strange things, dreadful things, most of them the work of men. This, though: this is something other. Bear with me, while I try to explain - and if you can, suspend your rational mind, which must revolt at what I have to tell you.

"There is a... creature, a spirit; a more godly man than I would call it a demon, no doubt. It inhabits the dead, I think. Certainly it is not human, although it can act so, although it is intelligent enough to pass. Certainly it kills. It feeds on the blood of the living. I have met it in the slums of Calcutta, and again in the mountains last winter; I told you of that before, though not in these terms. Not honestly. I spoke only of a beast that had to die, an endless hunt through snow and storm. You must forgive me, but I did not see the need for more, where more is always worse.

"Now there is a need. This day I have seen its spoor again, at my own Minscombe, and I would ask your help."

"Of course," he said. Instantly, unquestioningly. Ignorant as he was – and knowing exactly how ignorant he was – he yet gave me blind trust, quite untrammelled.

I might have melted, I think, if I hadn't had the fires of hell in mind.

I leaned forward, nursing my glass, and told him punctiliously what lay before us, what we would have to do. If we could achieve it.

He listened gravely, nodded, laid his life in my hands.

I would have prayed not to abuse that, if only I believed in anything good enough to pray to.

So it was, then, that two men rode out late that night, still in evening dress. He had protested, laughingly, until I pointed out that black clothes would help us pass unseen on a moonlit night, and in the shadows of a dark house. After that he was quiet and thoughtful for half an hour together.

Minscombe had been my childhood home, the setting for all the adventures of my youth. Of course I knew where we might leave the horses in a grove of trees, where a natural spring would give them water, where deep grass would offer them both forage and rest. Of course I knew the path that would bring us unseen from there to the boundary wall.

Minscombe wasn't a bridewell; the wall was high, but still a statement more than a barrier. As a lad I used to slither over it without a second thought, to save myself the trek around to the gate. Sometimes, indeed, to avoid questions at the gate. I didn't always want news of my excursions to reach back to my guardian.

Alas, that boy was long ago, and my body had seen hard uses since. Alshott eeled up the old stone with a young man's easy grace, then perched atop and reached down a hand to help me. I might have ignored it, might have snorted pride and hauled myself up alone; I may be twice his age, but a rugged life keeps a man limber. That I chose not to do so, that I gripped his hand and depended on its warm steel grip as I scrambled to the top, I think that says as much as I need to about trust and commitment. On the night, I think it said it all.

Side by side we let ourselves down, into the moonshadow of

the trees. Broad lawns stretched between us and the house, but no need to expose ourselves: again I knew a way, my old poacher's path home, following the treeline until it met the wall of the kitchen garden. As a boy I'd have shinned over that and helped myself to a peach or a pair of apples on my way to the scullery window with the broken sash, paid for them with a rabbit left in tribute on the long deal kitchen table for the cook to find in the morning.

Now, though, we had another end in view. Literally in view: there was light in the old library window, where the shutters had been flung back. Some creatures love the night.

I beckoned Alshott forward. We crept along the wall to my guardian's sacred rose-bed, let run now to ruin in neglect. Runners tangled our ankles, thorns ripped at our trousers: no matter. I was overdue new clothes in any case, and I suspected that Sylvester's suit had come down to him from his father. Certainly from a man broader than he was, and not so tall. My memories of the elder Alshott were grown vague with the years, but would accord with that description. Also with that habit of mind, to pass on an old suit to a new-grown son sooner than send him to a tailor. Parsimony is no doubt a useful trait in a man of business – but I thought I would ask Sylvester to recommend me a good tailor, and then take him along. I could legitimately point out that he had ruined his good clothes in my service, so I was duty-bound to replace them...

I should probably not have been thinking about clothes just then. Nor plotting my way through an inevitable argument with young Mr Alshott. The human mind is a curious artefact, in both what it is drawn toward and what it resiles from.

I did not want to look through that library window. But we were here now, just beneath the stone lip of it, and we had come for this. Exactly for this. I lifted my cautious head above that lip, and looked. And ducked back down, and would have kept Sylvester from looking if I could: only that he needed to see it, to confirm his faith in me and the needs of the night.

So he looked, and I watched his tender young face change in what lamplight spilled out of the window. He shuddered and dropped back to my side, wordless.

Silence was just as well; such creatures have preternatural hearing. I had told him that. Everything that I knew, I had told him and he had seemingly accepted, at least to come this far on an adventure. Nothing that I had said, nothing that I could have said would have prepared him for the actuality of that room that night.

It was worse for him than for me. I had seen such sights before, and grimmer ones than this. Also, he had seen my tenant in other guise, the man he knew as Royce.

No one could mistake the creature for human tonight, for all that it wore a human shape and human dress. It seemed nothing more than beastly, hunched over the white-gowned body of a boy; nothing less than demonic as it lifted its face from his neck, its mouth and chin painted with fresh blood.

I was glad, I had to be glad that Alshott my companion had seen this; I could be nothing but sorry that Sylvester my new young friend had had to see it. I wished that my hand could express those opposite feelings, both at once, as I gripped his upper arm. I did think that perhaps he was sensitive to my wishing, that at least, as his fingers closed over mine.

We had no more time for sentiment. I led him away from the window, softly, softly: back through the rose-bed, back to the walled garden, this time over that wall and swiftly up to the house, confident that the scullery window would still be just as yielding. I could only hope that some at least of the boys now resident had had the chance to discover it before the monster's teeth began to steal their joy, their energy, their life's-blood.

What will let boys out, will let grown men in: even if their shoulders have grown broader than they knew. I went first, my own mute insistence. It took more squirming than was perhaps dignified – especially as Sylvester had my rear half to watch, my helpless kicking legs – but I was through soon enough, and had the resentful pleasure of watching him ease himself after me as if he'd been greased for it.

That was the last of our light for a while, what moonlight fell through one small window that we dared not leave open. Again, though, I had all the years of my boyhood to draw upon. Nothing in this house was a stranger to me in darkness. Or the whole house was strange now, rather, a devil's home and not my own: but the walls and doors and stairs remained untouched, the furniture was much the same in more or less all its arrangements. I could find my way, and Alshott could follow me.

To be sure of him, I took his hand and set it on my shoulder, held his gaze until he nodded compliance.

Like that, then - the blind leading the blind, except that I was blind but knowing - we made our way through the kitchen to the back stairs. The monster in the library would never come this way; it would be beneath his dignity to use a servants' passage.

There was a greater danger that we might meet a boy. The one we had seen in the library might never stir again, but Dr Barnabas had said that his patients grew more lively in the evening. Even so, I was not expecting to find them careering about in the dark.

And did not: wise or lucky, we made our way unchallenged to the Great Hall on the first floor.

The name was a joke. My guardian and I had felt – or I had asserted, and he had agreed – that an establishment so large as Minscombe merited a great hall, and that our own dignity demanded it. Lacking anything suitably baronial or mediaeval in a house that could claim nothing older than ramshackle Jacobean – and that was doubtful – we had settled eventually on the ballroom. Neither of us was much inclined to dancing. So my ancestors' surviving weaponry and military paraphernalia went up above the fireplace, eked out – I have always suspected – by judicious purchases on the part of my guardian, and the Great Hall became an established fact. On wet days my friends and I enacted battles all up and down its length, to the constant complaint of servants who had polished the sprung floor for a generation or more.

Maids and footmen were gone now, but little else had changed. I had counted on that. I picked up a candle on the way, I had a lucifer-case in my pocket; Alshott closed the doors at our backs and I struck a light.

Chairs lined the walls, and at the further end was a stack of. Otherwise the long room was clear, as it always had been.

Alshott took the candle and made his way methodically from one wall to the next, lighting every lamp and sconce and candelabrum.

"If we're going to have light," he said, "we might as well have *enough* light..."

There was sense in that, of course. I didn't argue.

There was danger in it, too. There was danger in everything, in our simple presence here and in every telltale. The least glimmer of spilled light could catch a wary eye; the lightest footfall could carry on a quiet night; the best-laid floorboard could creak unexpectedly, the best-laid plan betray. Even the smell of a smoking candle could reach too far.

The library was directly below us. I watched the high doors almost in expectation. Surely, however little we spoke and however carefully we trod, surely he must hear something...?

I suppose that must have been right, I suppose he did. But for all my vaunted knowledge of the house and of his kind, still he confounded me.

We were watching the doors, waiting for him.

He came through the window.

Our eighteenth-century ballroom was mirrored – forgive me! – on the famous *Galerie des Glaces*, at least in its barest bones. It couldn't hope to rival the ostentation of Versailles; happily it hadn't tried. Nevertheless, there was the run of mirrors along the inner wall, standing opposite a matching run of windows. Outside our windows was a balcony, where guests could cool off with fresh air and long views over the park.

131

He must have heard us overhead and come the quick way: out through the open window and up the wall, scuttling like some spider-thing, inhuman; and so over the parapet and onto the balcony, and then straight in through the window.

Through the *shuttered* window, through glass and wood and all, monstrous strong and monstrous unheeding. Any man would have turned aside from such a mad act; any man who persevered would have taken dreadful hurt in the doing of it.

This creature came through in a tempest of shards and splinters, as careless of its skin as it was of its clothes.

Its eyes glittered in all our lights, as we swivelled around to face it. Did manic fury twist its face, or was that manic glee? I couldn't tell. Perhaps it was nothing at all, perhaps the creature was beyond all such human emotion.

Certainly it thought itself beyond us, unreachable.

It charged, directly for Sylvester. It moved dreadfully fast, but even so I managed to interpose myself and what I carried. Neither of us had time to think, or to change our purpose.

It ran, then, directly onto the point of my spear.

I have enjoyed my share of pig-sticking in India. I was ready for the shock of the body striking steel, the sink of blade into flesh.

I wasn't ready for the cold bitter intelligence that glared back at me from a six-foot distance; nor for the mocking gleam of its smile.

The spear's blade was steel, and it takes wood to slay such a creature, wood piercing its dead heart...

I smiled mirthlessly back, and pushed harder.

The spear's blade was sharp, and my strength was desperate.

The spear's blade might be steel, but its haft was ash.

I had no idea whether this would be effective, but I drove that spear right through the creature's body until the blade stood out between its shoulders, and what pierced its heart was good plain wood.

The creature stood its ground, stood on its feet and stared at me, transfixed.

Perhaps it had no idea either, whether it was dead or not.

It needed Sylvester to decide the matter.

Sylvester, swinging my guardian's old cavalry sabre, taking Royce's head clean off his shoulders at a blow.

Then there was mess, a foul mess. Neither of us was much inclined to clean it up, but needs must. I don't wish to say too much about that: only that there was a sack from the gardener's shed; and a pit dug far from anywhere that mattered, something slung in and buried deeply.

"We," Sylvester said, and stopped; and tried again, speaking not quite at random, not quite. Said, "We should go up, and see to the boys. Don't you, don't you think...?"

"Like this?" I said, with a gesture to show him his clothes, his condition, mirrored in my own. Ripped fabric was the least of it; mud from the digging mattered not at all. What mattered was the grue that had spilled from the creature that we slew. No neat dissolution, no crumbling into age and desiccation. All the blood it lately swallowed had come erupting, mixed with less wholesome effusions, acid bile and I knew not what sprayed out from its pierced body and severed neck. I had been in trouble often and often for spilling on the ballroom floor, taking off the polish. Now I thought nothing would do but to take up the boards and begin again.

Sylvester and I had been sprayed as much as the floor. We both stood in urgent want of a bath. To be blunt, we stank, and our clothes were stained where they were not soaked. We were neither of us in any state to interview sick children, to whom we would be entire strangers. Sylvester acknowledged that, with a rueful expression.

"Besides, they'll be asleep," I said. At least, I trusted so. They must need sleep more than anything: wholesome sleep, not the induced trances of their late master. With his influence lifted, I thought they ought to drift from the one state to the other, first steps on the road to recovery.

"First thing tomorrow," I said, "I'll bring Dr Barnabas here. They know him, they'll respond to him far better than to two filthy strangers in the dark."

"We could light lamps," he said mildly. "We could wash, even."

He didn't mean it, though, he didn't urge it. He was as keen as I was to remove ourselves from that house. Also he was as reluctant as I was to leave the boys unwatched, unguarded, but I thought the alternative was worse.

One thing we could do, we must; together, we laid out the dead boy on the library table and left him wrapped in a linen sheet, cleaner than we were ourselves.

Then back to the grove and the horses. A quick splash in the stream there because neither of us could bear the state of ourselves any longer, though we made the upset of the horses our excuse; and our first move when we reached his house was to fill the copper and boil water for a bath. Sylvester didn't so much as offer to rouse his man. We could perfectly well do the work ourselves, and attend each other.

Our dress suits both went into the furnace, to make their last contribution to our comforts.

Clean at last, there seemed small point in bed. We lit a fire simply for the comfort of it and sat talking over stiff brandies until the easterly sky turned pink. By then Sylvester was on the carpet at my feet, drowsing against my leg like a much younger boy. I smiled, took my hand from his shoulder and sent him upstairs, pointing out that Barnabas knew only me and wouldn't need two of us to conduct him to Minscombe.

So I rode out alone, and roused the good doctor from his warm and solitary bed. I told him something of what had happened, an abbreviated tale with no mention of a supernatural monster, or of a body flung into a pit; rode with him to the unguarded gates of

my house; and bowed reluctantly to his wisdom when he plied
my own logic against me. The boys knew only him, he said, and
wouldn't need two of us to wake them. If they could be woken, if
they weren't too far gone. The dead child in the library would be
his care, he insisted. Truly, he said, he would prefer to go on and
deal with this alone.

I didn't doubt him for a moment. Nor that the boys would
prefer to have him and him alone to deal with, for all that I
doubted his motives. A known face, a kindly soul would always
be better than a stranger.

I left him, then, and rode back to Sylvester.

"What will you do about Minscombe, John?"

In our ongoing attempt to feel clean – "clean on the *inside*,"
Sylvester said, "where I feel most befouled" – I was introducing
him to the greatest pleasure of a spa town, the public steam-bath.
It was late now and we had the place to ourselves, but servants
came and went in the swirling, unpredictable fog; we were
accordingly as discreet in our conversation as we were in our
persons, sweating a yard apart and swathed with towels.

I said, "I'm not sure. There's no hurry, at any rate; but – well,
if Barnabas offered to rent it for the sake of those poor boys, if
he felt it would be best to keep them there, I would have no
objection. I don't feel any great yen to live in it myself, if that's
what you're asking. I don't know where I will go, but no doubt
you can find me a house..."

"I don't need to," he said definitely. "You'll stay with me, of
course." And then, stumbling over his own eagerness, "I mean,
that house is far too big for me alone, and, and..."

"I know what you mean. And thank you. I'd like to stay." I
had almost depended on it.

I was determined at least to give Barnabas some time alone with
the boys, to recover those he could. If he needed me, or when he

wanted me, he knew where I was to be found.

Days passed, a week, two weeks. I heard nothing. When I did encounter the good doctor, it was by chance, and at first I failed to recognise him. I was meeting Sylvester for luncheon, at an hotel close to his place of business. With time on my hands and eager only for his sweet company, I was irredeemably early; but there was a man already at table, eating alone, making swift work of a plate of rare sirloin.

One ought not to criticise the manners of another. That was a remarkably large plate, though, and heaped high, and he was - well, gobbling. I did look twice, I confess. The second time—

"Dr *Barnabas*?"

He looked up, almost as startled as I was; I wondered if he had come in so early in hopes of avoiding anyone he knew.

It took him a moment to remember the courtesies. Belatedly he set his cutlery down, rose to his feet, held out his hand. "Mr Furnival! You must excuse my not having called on you before this, but, well, my charges are demanding of my time, and..."

"And I think you have been unwell, my dear doctor," I said. "Please, do continue with your meal. Don't mind me; I'm meeting Alshott here, but not for an hour yet. I'll sit with you, if I may," taking a chair before he could think to offer it. I beckoned a waiter over and ordered a pink gin, to root myself in place. Barnabas had a bottle of claret, and had made fair inroads already. "Tell me truly, doctor, how do you do?"

Truly, he looked terrible. He had lost extraordinary amounts of weight in such a short time, but men who drop stones are supposed to be the better for it. Barnabas seemed utterly fagged, dragged down; *drained*, I should have said.

"Oh," he said, applying himself to his meat again with that most extraordinary appetite, "I may have slipped a few pounds. Those young devils take it out of me, you know. Still, I have such a hunger on me, I'm safe to make it up again."

"The children thrive, I trust?"

"Ah. Some of them. Some, alas. Others I could not save, they were too far gone. I have seen too much of the vicar. He wanted to come round and bless each of the surviving boys, but I could not have that, no, I could not have it..."

He rambled as he chewed, and I grew more and more worried the more I watched, the more I listened.

Dr Barnabas ordered another plate of beef, and despatched it as keenly. Then he called for the reckoning, rose, made his excuses and left me.

By the time Sylvester arrived, I was on perhaps my third pink gin, perhaps my fourth. He greeted me cheerfully, said, "You look as though you were mulling over something terribly serious, John."

"Yes," I said, in no mood to equivocate. "Yes, I was. I'm sorry, Syl. Will you take a ride with me, this evening...?"

And so we found ourselves riding out again, the same mounts on the same route. They seemed almost to pick their own way to that private grove, and to settle happily to an hour of their own company in the grass there.

I led Sylvester by swift familiar ways to the wall – no nonsense this time about my needing help, or his offering it – and thus the kitchen garden, the library window. It had to be the library. I knew it, and so did he.

Light spilled from the window, as before. We rose and looked together; and ducked back down, and stole away again without a word, without a thought of staying.

We rode halfway home in silence, before he said, "What will you do?"

I said, "I know... some people, who should be here in England now. Army men, from my India days. I will find them out and install them in the gatehouse, with instructions. And let the doctor know what those instructions are."

"And they will be?"

"To let no one in or out of the grounds, except himself. They have *shikari* skills; not the most lightfoot boy could get by them, where they have set themselves to patrol. And each of them is a killer, that's why they were sent home."

He mulled that over, at last said, "You will let them live, then, if you can keep them penned."

"Syl, they're *children*. If he can... keep them fed, I can let them live, so long as they threaten no one else."

Which was the closest we came, the closest we could come to discussing what we'd seen: how the doctor sat in the library chair, willingly, arms and legs spread wide, while half a dozen boys swarmed all over him, biting, lapping, sucking...

Traditions in Future Perfect

Nancy Kilpatrick

"I'm not sure I'm completely comfortable with the idea," Mrs. Ellison said. "It seems a bit… unnatural."

"I can assure you," the vampire offered, a small tilt of his head, the hint of a sympathetic smile on his cold but sensual lips, "that nothing is more natural than death."

"Yes, but, *this* way? I'm not sure…"

After handing her a cup of Earl Grey tea, the vampire sat down opposite the woman and crossed his long legs, a small tug at the Armani suit pant. The style and cut of the suit spoke of sophistication and permanence. And money. He knew Mrs. Ellison thought that he looked like a 1930s movie star, the type of hero she had watched as a girl on the TV with her grandfather every Saturday night. He had that effect on most of the elderly women who came to the offices.

The vampire not only knew his effect on Mrs. Ellison, but he played on it. His gestures were deliberate. Besides choosing his clothing carefully, he had sculpted his 'look', and imitated emotional responses that conformed to what so many of the company's clientele held tightly in their memories when they left here. The combined effect told them that these fragments of experience were as important to the vampire as drops of precious red vitae, and it was crucial they believe that.

He could read Mrs. Ellison's mind if he chose to do so, but there was little need. Most of the breathers who sought out the offered services were of a similar generation, sharing a collective consciousness. They wanted to believe him. Needed to. Convincing just took time and he had plenty of that.

"It's just that I don't want him to suffer." She was about to open her purse in search of a tissue but he offered her a boxful, placing it at the edge of the small table between them, closer to her. She removed one and dabbed at the corner of her left eye.

"Of course you don't," he said. "You care deeply for him."

"Yes. Yes I do." She pulled a second tissue from the box and blew her nose. He knew from having gone through this before that these actions preceded clarity, or what passed for it, and that led to capitulation. His role was to pause long enough for the desired effect.

"Please. Tell me again how it's done."

"Of course," he said, smiling, the picture of empathy. "Ask as many questions as you need to ask. That's why I'm here. To help."

She had the wide wet liquid almond-shaped eyes of a trusting doe unaware that it was making eye contact with a predator. But he had no intention of preying on her. At least not today. "It's very simple," the vampire said. "Your husband is suffering."

Her face creased, so he hurried on.

"You have the power to alleviate that suffering. I know you've heard this before, so it's not a shock," he said, giving her direction on how she should feel. "If you think of the ancient Greek mythologies, and the Greeks had it right, Mrs. Ellison, make no mistake. They were, after all, the founders of democracy, they nurtured physical beauty and complex thinking – did you know that in Greek grammar there are many tenses, only some of which touch on Cronos or chronological time?"

Mrs. Ellison looked a tad befuddled as if she was unsure what any of this had to do with Mr. Ellison.

In the English language, we have, to name but a few tenses, past, present and future, with variations on each. The Greeks have those, progressive and conclusive, including perhaps the most intriguing tense, certainly the one related to our services here at *Charon*. Future perfect tells us that based on actions of the present, a state of completeness can and will exist but only in the future, not, of course, in the past. For the Greeks, future tense is... how do I put it... *emotive*."

Mrs. Ellison's face expressed total bafflement. The vampire knew he must conclude.

He laughed gently. "We admire those ancient Greeks their foresight and fuller perspective, one that relied deeply on tradition. This is why we named our service *Charon*. In honour of the Greek being who gingerly guided souls to the other side. To the afterlife, if you will. In our small way, we attempt to imitate that most noble and necessary of services, respecting tradition."

Mrs. Ellison, who had been sitting tensely forward in her seat, suddenly fell against the back of the Queen Anne chair and sighed, as if exhausted from trying to understand what he was saying. The vampire knew that she had followed little of the subject matter and had lost touch with the context long ago. But the presentation never failed to elicit a sense of continuity and permanence laced with benevolence, what breathers long for, have always longed for, would forever desire. It was the word 'tradition' that cinched it.

"The doctors say..." And he let her ramble about diagnosis (spreading disease), prognosis (bleak) until she came full circle back to the reason why she was here in the first place. The ads that bombarded the newspapers, magazines, televisions, the internet. The ads that said: *CHARON – WHEN TRADITION*

MATTERS.

"I suppose you… people…" She looked embarrassed. He gave her a reassuring nod accompanied by a smile. "You… know things. About the end."

"Yes, we're adept at determining the exact time of death with a 99.9% success rate. That is, of course, death which is not interfered with."

"Oh no, it won't be. Harry signed a DNR form before he… before his brain shut down. He didn't want to be resuscitated."

"Wise," the vampire nodded. Then, "May I offer you more tea? A sandwich perhaps?"

"Oh, thank you but no. I must be getting back to the hospital." She checked her watch, then glanced up at his eyes. He knew that the contact lenses helped provide a semblance of familiar life in what otherwise would have been to any breather a mask of inhumanity.

"Why don't we go ahead and sign the forms," he said, opening the leather-bound folder and removing the consent form in triplicate.

Mrs. Ellison looked panicked for a moment, but accepted the Mont Blanc pen and signed the quality linen paper on the dotted line, three times. The vampire signed too, using his breather name Neophities Thanopoulos, although that name would not be found on any birth records of any country. Back when he was born as a breather, records had not been kept.

Once he had neatly folded a copy and placed it into an envelope for Mrs. Ellison, he stood, holding out the envelope. "Please be reassured. We will take care of everything. And the ashes will be yours, a *memento mori*, if you will."

Mrs. Ellison stood too, confused again, nervous now, dropping her purse, which he stooped to pick up. As he handed the bag to her, the flesh of their fingers made contact for only a split second. The chill was enough to strike fear into her heart.

The vampire did not relish spending more time with this breather and used his visual powers of persuasion to lock onto her will through eye contact and suggest with softly spoken words, "It's time for you to return to your husband's side."

Mrs. Ellison, like a child repeating a lesson, said, "It's time to return to my husband's side."

He ushered her towards the door, saw her through it, then turned and walked back beyond the sitting room to the office where he filed the two copies of the consent form. Then he headed down the hallway to the private rooms, removing the contact lenses as he went. He didn't feel eye irritation – his body wasn't tuned to that type of pain – but he didn't like wearing the lenses on principle. Still, as with so many modern innovations, they were necessary, or at least the collective had deemed so. It annoyed him that they had given up their own traditions in order to convince breathers that they respected theirs. Still, he had accepted the argument that compromise was necessary if they were all to share the same planet.

He found Carolyn and Michel at the back of the building, the former rooting through the freezer for some O Positive – her preferred type. When she saw him, she lifted a vial, but he declined. She placed the glass tube into the microwave for 5 seconds, enough to eliminate the chill. Carolyn, like so many of their kind, preferred glass storage to plastic. The elders were from the past, plastic-free eras, and they did not appreciate the aftertaste of polymers.

"We have another," Neophities announced. "Someone needs to collect."

"I've got a breather on the edge. I can't do it," Michel said.

"I'm scheduled to give yet another 'talk' to the neophytes at midnight," Carolyn said, licking traces of red from her sensuous lips. Her eyes glittered preternaturally.

"Well, what about—"

"Sheldon and Chris are out in the country for a few days and Marilyn has that annual visit to Copenhagen."

"I'd forgotten. And Damon?"

The two looked at him and said nothing. Everything was said

in those looks.

"I suppose that leaves me."

"Sorry," Michel said, without a trace of regret. None of them liked collecting.

Neophities sighed, turned, and walked back through the building. He picked up a copy of the consent form and a kit en route to the door, re-covered his corneas with the contact lenses, and then slowly made his way to the hospital.

The streets were quiet tonight, as dark as city lighting permitted. He preferred muted sound and dim light. Perhaps it was his age. Must be, he thought. He recognized that new converts did not necessarily share his love of solitude and peace.

He reached the hospital within ten minutes. It had been clever to set up shop near the largest care facility in the city, the one with the most close-to-death patients, and a special ward for the elderly, who could always be counted on to die.

Visiting hours were over and Mrs. Ellison would have gone, although the institution usually permitted relatives of the terminal to remain as long as they wished. Still, he knew that the woman was exhausted and didn't like sleeping in the hospital – she had told him that during the chit-chat part of the sales meeting. Likely being in hospital not only reminded her of her spouse's impending demise, but her own as well.

He climbed the stone steps of the Victorian structure, remembering when this building had been new. That was about the time he'd first come to this city, long before 'vampires', as breathers referred to his kind, had stepped out of the proverbial closet and integrated into society. It was a two-edged sword, that bursting onto the public's consciousness in a new and relatively benign way, but he often felt like Damocles and would not have been surprised to have the falling blade implant itself deep into his heart. The others told him he was paranoid. But Neophities had existed far longer than most of his kind and distrusted breathers much more. More than two decades had passed since the 'revealing' as his own kind liked to call it. And during those years, few major problems had occurred, at least that he'd heard about. There were, of course, the normal skirmishes during any transitional time. Initial distrust on both sides with consequent fatalities.

But now, in the Enlightened Age, as breathers liked to refer to the integration, things had levelled out between the two species. His kind ran death houses, combining euthanasia – recently legalized – with funeral services and breathers had adapted to the idea that death, while frightening, could be a smooth segue if an Expiration Provider were present. His kind had taken on that quite natural role. The benefits were many. But there were a few drawbacks too, such as collecting.

The elevator brought him to the ninth floor. Fortunately, the nursing station was empty. Neophities walked down the hallway of the terminal ward barely glancing at the numbers on the doors; he had been here so often. The stench in the building – of creeping decomposition, acetone, necrosis, soured milk, fetid breath, digestive fermentation, faeces too long in the bowel, the vile and odious expulsions from bodies desperate to release the poisons eating them alive – all of it mixed with the medicinal smells of dissolving pills and capsules, saline solutions, alcohol rubs, chlorine soaps, and harsh disinfectants. And yet, despite the rancid effluence, the strong fragrance of blood wafted its way to his nostrils and stroked his olfactory nerve, charges his senses to high alert. As he had thought so many times over the last two millennia: there is *nothing* like blood!

Mr. Ellison was asleep in the semi-private room, the bed across from his containing a comatose patient. Neophities moved soundlessly to his client's bed. He listened for a brief moment and his acute hearing told him that no hospital personnel were in the vicinity, not that he didn't have a right to be here. But there had been occasional unpleasantness in the past.

Quickly he opened the case he had brought and extracted a butterfly needle which he inserted into a vein. He had no need to feel for a pulse, deflated as these blue lines were. Centuries of experience allowed him to find one with his eyes closed.

Once the vein had been pierced, he removed a collection tube from the case and inserted it into the other end of the needle, watching red liquid flow in. When the tube was full, he replaced it with another. He repeated the process until he had a dozen vials, all the while feeling a ferocious ache at the roots of his eye teeth. Every instinct in him demanded he sink his fangs into this vein, or another, or better still an artery, and allow the blood to fill his mouth and slide down his throat. A hunger so intense he saw his hand shake. *Wait*, he told himself, *wait. Wait wait wait!!!*

Repeating the mantra worked but the control was hard won. It was no wonder only the elders were permitted to collect. If *he* experienced this much pressure, a newbie would have no grip whatsoever.

Mr. Ellison slept through all this, the only sign of disturbance a slightly faster heartbeat. When Neophities finished and closed the case, he assessed his latest client. Mr. Ellison could struggle on for another week but no more and likely quite a bit less.

That would work out. Michel said he had one on the edge. It was infrequent that two of their clients passed the same night, but it had happened before and might happen again. And, as always, timing could be manipulated.

Neophities returned to *Charon*. He cold-stored eleven of the vials, carefully labelling them with Mr. Ellison's name and the date. Then, slowly, he drank the remaining vial, savouring the richness of the blood, despite the necropholic elements adhering to it.

As always, the nutrients flooded his cells. He could feel himself filling out, plumping internally. His mind became clear, senses sharp but relaxed. It was always this way, always had been, and so it would be in future. Yes, there was nothing quite like blood!

Within four days, Mr. Ellison reached the point of no return the same evening as Michel's breather Mr. Morrison hit the twenty-four hour time frame. Both vampires had ingested their client's blood through the vials they'd collected and knew the precise moment of impending demise.

Neophities and Michel decided that they would proceed at the same time, since there would only be two or three hours between TOD and also they could not wait because dawn came too soon and there was no sense missing opportunities. Fortunately, Messrs Ellison and Morrison had been assigned to the same wing.

Paperwork in hand, Neophities and Michel approached the nursing station near the elevator, their respective clients just down the hallway. The nurses were never happy to see them, but legalities were legalities. The spouse of Mr. Ellison had been summoned and the son of Mr. Morrison, both of whom were seated by the bedside of their failing loved one.

Ridding the room of Mrs. Ellison would be the most difficult task, of course. Michel would have the same problem with Mr. Morrison's son; although, being several centuries younger, Michel had adapted more easily to palliative care techniques and the lingo of caregivers.

"Mrs. Ellison, I'm so sorry," Neophities began.

The woman looked up, startled. "Oh. You've come," she said, tension straining her voice. She had barely had time to dress, that was clear, her coat askew, blouse buttoned wrong at the neck, legs bare on this cool night. "You're... you're early," she said, false hope imbedded in her tone.

Neophities placed a hand on her shoulder. "I'm not, Mrs. Ellison. We both know that. Your husband is about to complete his journey. I'm here to help. We don't want him to suffer."

Tears gushed from Mrs. Ellison's eyes. Her head shook from side to side but likely she wasn't aware of the movement. It was at this point that Neophities' instincts told him to throttle her. Despite all his centuries walking the earth, he could barely tolerate the denial human beings exercised in the face of the inevitable. He should just look her in the eye, mesmerize her, get it over with. But that type of control always created an odd appearance that other breathers noticed, and he did not want any run-ins with the nurses or doctors – sunrise was but three short hours away. And he had a right to be here. She had signed the papers. Her husband was close to death. Still, discretion being the better part of valour, he must play by the rules.

"Mrs. Ellison, I think what needs to happen is for you to say your goodbyes now. Let your husband proceed into the hereafter in the most painless and peaceful manner possible. I know that's what you want for him. Now is the time for that."

As if on cue, Mr. Ellison's face contorted and his good arm tensed. Mrs. Ellison's hand went to her mouth and she barely stifled a gasp.

"You see," Neophities said, "he's in pain. You've got to let him go now."

Unconsciously she began nodding. Noisy tears gushed from her eyes, down her cheeks, spilling onto the bedding then onto her husband's face as she kissed him and whispered words of endearment into his ear. This went on for what seemed an eternity to Neophities. He repressed a sigh but at one point gently took her arm to pull her away.

"No! Not yet!" she cried.

He released her, fighting the urge to throw her across the room.

Through the small glass window in the door, Neophities watched the son of Mr. Morrison zombie-walk past the room towards the elevator. Apparently Michel had had an easier time of removing the next-of-kin.

Mr. Ellison twitched again, then his entire body convulsed. The heart monitor spiked. Mrs. Ellison cried out. This time, Neophities took both her arms and pulled her back from the bed. "You must leave now," he said firmly, turning her face so that she was looking into his eyes. "Your husband is in pain and there is no medical relief available. He can suffer for hours more or you can undertake the kind and loving act of leaving him to me so that I can guide him over now, before he suffers further. And trust me, Mrs. Ellison, the suffering will only increase."

Without a word from her, he steered the woman to the door, led her through it, and moved her down the hallway to the elevator. The nurse at the station scowled at him and he wanted to rip out her throat. But patience prevailed.

"He'll be all right?"

"Of course," Neophities said softly. "He will pass quietly and peacefully and without suffering. You've given him the most loving of gifts. And I know he thanks you."

He let go of the elevator door and it closed on the distraught face of Mrs. Ellison.

As he passed the nurse again, he bared his fangs, just for the hell of it, but she did not look up. Good instincts, he thought. A survivor.

Just as Neophities reached the room, Michel was closing the door to Mr. Morrison's room. They nodded to one another and Michel said as he passed, "I'll start the paperwork downstairs."

Neophities re-entered Mr. Ellison's room. The pallid skeleton in the bed was beyond hope now and would die shortly after sunrise. Neophities was certain of that because he now knew the blood intimately, having drunk it for four nights. It called to him from the man's veins and arteries, sending weak pulsing signals.

Enough procrastinating, he thought, removing the needle from his coat pocket. He injected the contents into the Y connection of the IV which uselessly dripped antibiotics and anti-inflammatories into the vein of the doomed man. The opiate derivative which Carolyn had developed joined these prescription drugs along the feeder tube and entered the body. Within ten second Mr. Ellison's heart began to slow.

Neophities bent so that his incisors could sink deep into the carotid. The body convulsed as the heart tried to pump faster in the face of blood loss. But the opiate had subdued the pounding heart so the pulse could only return to what was a normal pace, recorded on the heart monitor here and at the nursing station.

The blood, sick though it was, still tasted of ambrosia and he

149

felt it replenishing the cells of his body as if they were depleted from starvation, the opiates hardly a bother. He became living sensation, stroked, nearly overwhelmed by the scent and taste as his ears heard only the sound of the pulsing heart that slowed its beating by the moment. While he drank, much of his brain temporarily shut down, leaving him vulnerable. But a small part of him was busy calculating the volume he took, and assessing what that was doing to his client.

When he had taken enough, his consciousness returned. Everything looked brighter, clearer. Sound reached him from the corridor, from the floors above and below. He not only could smell a myriad of pleasant scents drifting through the hospital air, but also resin of the pine trees on the lawn. Yet he had no time to really savour these sensations. He must finish so that Mr. Ellison could be removed from the hospital and brought to *Charon* as rapidly as possible.

He retreated to the scream of the heart monitor's flatline. Mr. Ellison, not much more than a husk, was still alive, but not by the criteria of the medical establishment.

The two bodies were dispatched to *Charon* that night and, fortunately, arrived an hour before dawn, not that this was always the case with the arrangements. The hospital staff tended to take out their resentments on *Charon* too frequently and delay shipment. But more often practicality won out – they needed the beds.

Little time remained before sunrise and Carolyn hurriedly took charge of the preparations. While she did, Neophities and Michel sat together drinking the remaining vials of their clients' blood.

"I never tire of this," Michel said. "Never will."

Neophities nodded. He felt the same. "But taking directly is the only real way to enjoy vitae." He paused. "I wonder about this strange co-existence with humanity."

"Most of us favour it," Michel reminded him blithely, and Neophities knew he must tread carefully.

"We're protected," Michel went on, repeating the party line. "And it's an easy way of gaining food. We also have what's rejected by the blood banks, tossed out by labs..."

Neophities' mind drifted. Perhaps he was too old to really adapt. Certainly that had been so with Damon, who indicated many times that he could not continue within such narrow parameters. And now he no longer existed--the fate of so many of the elders.

Neophities wondered if he would end up like Damon and the other 'old schoolers'. The ones who had roamed when their kind was feared. Hunters who were hunted and yet were nearly invincible. Predators that instilled terror in their prey, which made the blood rich as it raced through the living body and then into eager mouths. The hunt, the chase, the capture, the succulent breathers... What could those newly created experience that would be anything like what he knew to be the true nature of his kind? Would he, one day, feel as Damon had? Would he grow weary of this false mode of survival? Survival without passion, traditions watered down or lost forever? He did not know. At times, all of it bothered him immensely. Drinking from vials and blood bags! Stealing from the veins of the weakest, not the arteries of the strongest! What in their nature encouraged that? But at least he was one of the lucky ones. As an elder, he was permitted to experience a facsimile of the kill when he took the blood of the dying during their final hours.

The weight of sleep pressed upon him and he was glad when Carolyn finally entered the room and said, "Come."

The basement led to a hidden sub-basement, a concrete room thirty feet square. Neophities and Michel took their positions on either side of Carolyn. Across from them stood half a dozen new recruits, those created within the last six months. They looked young to him. In the past, youth had been desirable, but not everything. He had been in his fortieth year when brought over. Most of the elders had been over thirty. Now, it seemed, the preferred age floated between fifteen and twenty-four.

Carolyn spoke, mainly because neither he nor Michel enjoyed giving speeches and she didn't mind playing den mother.

"We are old," she began. "Our species has existed since the dawn of recorded time. We were first referred to in the *Epic of Gilgamesh* 4,500 years ago, when breathers called us Death Bringer."

The new ones looked on, respectfully wide-eyed, but Neophities couldn't help but wonder how much they cared for the origins of the species. Or if they had even heard of the *Epic of Gilgamesh*, let alone read it.

"Our traditions are long ones that speak to the core of what we are. We *are* the Death Bringers. We know it. Breathers know it. And you, the virgins among us, tonight you will know it too.

"In the past, we lived apart from breathers. We were scorned, hunted, destroyed en masse whenever they found our nests. But now we have forged a bond and the result of that cooperation is our self-preservation, with new traditions evolving.

"This night you are christened as one of the undead, welcomed into the fold. And these are your gifts."

Carolyn gestured dramatically to the two bodies lying naked on the floor. Both Mr. Ellison and Mr. Morrison looked to be sleeping. Or dead. But they were not dead. The opiate slowed the heart to create a state mimicking death, and Neophities and Michel had taken just enough blood from their clients to solidify this death-like state, one that recorded on medical equipment as life terminated. But a kernel of life remained. Blood still flowed through the veins of these men.

Neophities glanced at the new ones and saw a familiar look in every pair of eyes. It was not by chance that this ritual took place just prior to dawn. They would need to sleep very soon and that pressure insured they would not frenzy, a normal reaction to indulgence.

Carolyn said more, about breather traditions, the traditions of their kind, but Neophities could see that none of the six was listening. Only one word got through to them. Finally, Carolyn commanded: "Drink!"

Like a colony of vampire bats, they swooped down onto their prey without hesitation, piercing flesh quickly to get at the blood. The small room filled with growls, howls, cries, groans and moans of ecstasy. Flesh tearing. Bones snapping. Lapping tongues and smacking lips forcing out the weak vitae that remained in these two frail breathers.

The smell reached Neophities, but he Michel and Carolyn had all drunk enough to blunt the hunger. The fledglings, though, they had never before fed on human blood. They had been intentionally starved with only animal blood to sustain them. Until tonight.

But what did it mean? Neophities knew that the ritual, devised to retain tradition in a time where tradition could no longer be explored freely, was not nearly what those from the past had envisioned as the future of the species. There was no comparison. Two decrepit men, prostrate, incapacitated, inching towards death, thin and diseased blood filled with chemicals, unable to resist... Where were the cries and screams? Muscles straining to escape or beat back the predator? Where was the hard thrust of blood through the vena cava, desperate to reach the heart and lungs for purification, then the burst of the vitae out through the aorta, all of it at three times the normal pace? The tangy scent of adrenalin went missing, the sweet-tart aroma of fear. All of that and more were not present in this controlled lab experiment, this imitation of destruction.

When they finished and Mr. Ellison and Mr. Morrison no longer existed but for bone muscle organs brain, finally the new ones licked their faces and hands, and even licked the blood off one another – something Neophities had only seen done in private intimacy prior to this generation. Sated, the newbies went off to bed like children who had gotten their first taste of candy. It was an experience that would stay with them eternally. Now they understood the traditional act of their kind. And now, unknown to them, they must learn a substitute for the act — restraint.

While they all slept, the former-breather bodies would be incinerated together and the following evening the mixture of ashes scooped into two tasteful urns which would be presented to the next-of-kin. Obligations concluded, no breather the wiser. The entire process — from contract to urn — was logical and organized and never failed.

But oh so clinical! Neophities thought grimly. Passionless. He understood Damon. And the ones before him who had ended their own existence. But Neophities was not ready for that outcome. Not yet. He still believed in tradition. They had, after all, only developed this one recently. Perhaps it could be refined, expanded. Perfected in the future.

But, even as he tried to convince himself of this, his mind automatically shifted from future to future perfect, where the actions of now have already resulted in conclusion. Like an oracle of old, Neophities intuited that future unfolding. A personal and collective future, grave, *im*perfect, and, as decreed by the present, preordained.

The Fall of the House of Blackwater

Freda Warrington

She enters the room, luminous by the light of the candle she carries. In the darkness beyond her curtained bed, I wait unseen. No one ever sees me until I want them to; I'm less than a whisper, a dream. The bedroom is cavernous. Its heart glows orange from the fire banked in the grate, but this weak radiance cannot reach the massed black shadows around it.

She is luscious, barely eighteen. Her hair falls like honey over the white shoulders of her nightdress. She's quite short, slightly plump; completely desirable. Her eyes are darkest violet, her mouth so deep a red it looks almost purple, like a ripe plum. Her name is Elizabeth.

She's the only surviving child of her parents and they've arranged a marriage for her, so I've learned, to some cousin who will come here to live and thus secure the future of the family estate and fortune... A respectable Christian marriage, designed to provide mutual wealth, a place in society, a new dynasty... all that stuff. I don't care for the dry details.

She's a virgin, trembling on the chasm lip of marriage. That's all we need to know.

She sets down the candle beside her bed and climbs in. Clutching the sheets around her chin, she stares with those enormous pansy-petal eyes at her future. A pulse ticks in her temple. Can she sense me watching?

A maid bustles in, causing me to draw back with a faint hiss of annoyance. This young, freckly intruder chatters as she pokes the fire, then wipes her hands on her apron and fusses with the bed-covers even as my prey sits prettily against the pillows, waiting for her to leave. The maid brushes dangerously close to me as I draw back behind the heavy bed-curtains. She has no idea I'm there, inches from her. She says things like, "Ah, it's soon you'll be married! You look like a child still. Before you know it, your own children will be running around the place, and you a grand lady!"

The girl smiles enigmatically.

At last the maid is gone, taking her bustling energy with her. The fire fades to a red sulk. Elizabeth bends towards the candle, her lips pouting to blow it out – then she hesitates. Looking over her shoulder, she asks, "Who's there?" She speaks lightly, as if she feels foolish at her own sudden fear.

If ever someone introduces himself to you by saying, "Don't be afraid," my advice is to run, run like the wind! Why would a stranger anticipate fear, unless it was they who posed a danger? Yet that is what I say. I even speak her name.

"Elizabeth. Don't be afraid."

She startles, clutching the bed covers to her chin. Her eyes are pools of astonished innocence. I catch her warm scent; soap and rosewater, with a hint of smooth female musk beneath. She's terrified – not in a make-a-screaming-rush-for-the-door sense, but in the deeper way that turns the victim deathly still. Yet there's fascination in her gaze. Before she acts, she needs to know what I am. And that's the space I have to work in.

"How did you get in?" she whispers. "Who are you?"

"A ghost," I reply. I move just enough to let her see me. Her lips open. I glimpse myself in the looking-glass on her dressing table – it's a myth that we cast no reflection – and I see what she must see; a high, curved cheekbone, shapely nose and jaw, long black lashes. Pallid features a sculptor might have chiselled with idealistic fingers, shaded by hair that is dark, formless and too long. My eyes are deceptive; they're the green-brown of hazel nuts and they look gentle, pensive. They tell you nothing about my character.

"Just a shade, fair child," I tell her gently. "I need your help. Would you help me?"

There's so much history in this house, Blackwater Hall. I should know, for I built it.

Eight years the construction took me, and in 1704 the Hall was finished, standing magnificent beside the River Blackwater amid the rich landscape of County Waterford. My wife Mary was weeks from giving birth. Years, it had taken us to conceive a child! Now all my dreams were close to fruition. Soon we would be leaving the decrepit tower of my Norman and Anglo-Irish ancestors and moving into the new mansion, a place grand enough to befit our heirs. Such struggles I'd had to keep my estate from the hands of the conquering English! I even changed faith from Catholic to Protestant to save it from confiscation – and yet it slipped from my hands anyway. All gone in one terrible night.

Perhaps this was divine punishment. To me, it meant little to betray my religion, since I never was devout. All I cared about was keeping my lands – not out of greed, but passion. I loved my birthright so deeply, I valued it even above my immortal soul.

Some say Irish Catholicism is only one step away from paganism, that the faerie folk were never destroyed, only assimilated into the new faith and given the names of saints so the people could still worship without heresy. I believe in those darker, older gods; devouring black mother Callee and her ilk. They never went away, only vanished into sea and stone, tree and sky. And that dreadful night, three of them came to wreak vengeance. Three ancient gods with burnished skins and writhing hair and terrible golden eyes.

They took me, and reforged me into what I am.

The trinity who chose me personified that very peculiar delusion some vampires have – that they have become mythological personalities, demi-gods. And who's to say they are wrong? We slip into another reality when we change, a soup of dreams and nightmares that some call the Crystal Ring. It swarms with archetypes born from the human subconscious (and from the subconscious of other beings, too, I don't doubt). Who is to say that the thought-form of a god or an archangel can't take over a newly-made vampire, fusing with a soul that has been broken apart like a raw egg?

I digress.

When I recall my human self, I peer through a veil. I recall Mary as beautiful, a tall fine woman. We loved each other, I thought... I'd been patient with the long time it took her to conceive, as I had with the long construction of the house. Wasn't that enough to prove my devotion? Apparently not, by her standards. Mere days before the house was ready for us, it came to pass that I discovered her in the old tower house in the company of some stuttering, milkweed clerk from Dublin. She was packing, ready to run away with him.

Each time I return to Blackwater Hall and stand once again in the courtyard, the grey walls rising like thunderclouds above me, I relive that night. The yellow ropes of Mary's hair hanging over her breasts, the swell of her belly beneath her clothes as she made her confession. *"The child is not yours, Sebastian. In ten years, you could*

158

not give me a child. You care nothing for me – all you love is the house! My lover has come for me and we're leaving."

She shrank away then as if I would strike her, but I didn't. Instead, I ran into the courtyard of the new house and screamed my rage at the heavens. The black sky split open, the deluge of rain sent me skidding to the door of a cellar. Somehow I'd gashed my arm in my anguish and blood was dripping from me.

In a few fatal minutes I'd lost everything. I had no wife, no child, so what now was the use of a grand hall? There was wood stacked inside and I meant to set light to it, to burn my dream to its foundations.

The darkness inside the cellar was absolute, but I knew its shape; a long chamber with racks set ready for storage. Only a store-room... yet it felt in that moment like an ancient torture chamber, silent but for the drip of water and the sobbing of the damned. I remember sinking down against the wall in my despair, my last moments of being human...

Then someone shut the door.

They'd been shadowing me for months, years. In retrospect, I felt they'd been watching me all my life. They had marked me as 'special' in some way, prime raw material for vampire-hood. Who knows why they chose this moment? Perhaps it was my anguish that drew them. Or merely the scent of my rain-watered blood.

They were vampires and yet they were angels. I mean that they *believed* they were angels, messengers from a punishing God, something more than mere demons. Simon, a magnificent golden man with extraordinary deep yellow eyes like a cat's. Fyodor, an attenuated male with silvery flesh and snow-white hair. Rasmila (Callee?) a woman with dark brown skin, her hair a fall of blue-black silk.

In that annihilating moment, all my human concerns fell away in a blast of lightning from heaven.

"Sebastian," they said, their voices as mellifluous, amused, and coldly sonorous as bells. "Don't be afraid. We have come only for your blood and your soul."

Only.

I remember how different the world looked, afterwards. Nets of light webbed a clear deep sky; I'd never before seen with such clarity, never dreamed that such crystalline beauty was hidden from mortal eyes. I could see for miles; northwards to the Galtee and Knockmealdown mountains, to the towers of Cahir Castle, the Golden Vale of Tipperary and Cashel of the Kings; closer at hand, my own beloved estate. The stump of the old stone tower was a shadow behind the new house, which appeared a great, pristine mansion like a gold casket swathed in deep blue twilight. Three storeys it has, with tall imposing windows, a pillared portico that soars the height of the frontage. All was wrapped in night-colours I'd never seen before. The air was sweet and icy, like wine.

How unutterably beautiful it was, the home that I built for myself. For us.

And then I walked away.

I left, only because of what I became. What need had I for anything of the mortal world? I needed no wife or child, no home, no land or wealth, none of that. All I needed was blood, and the wonder of my new senses.

I had no intention ever of coming back. And yet...

Here I am again, unseen in the shadows, a ghost haunting the ruins of my own life.

There are two ways I might proceed with Elizabeth. The road of instant violation and swift death; or the slower path of enthrallment, followed by a wasting decline into madness. Each has its own pleasures, so I am undecided. I live in the moment, watching how the warm light gilds the swell and dip of her breasts, the way her tongue flicks out to make her lips glisten.

"A spirit?" she whispers. And then, "I know you. I've seen you before."

This shocks me. No one is meant to see me! Her parents never have, nor their servants nor any of their numerous visitors and relatives. They're aware of me; I am the guilty secret that no one mentions. They shiver and start at shadows, but they don't *see* me. "When have you seen me, fair one?" I ask very gently.

"When I was a child. You never spoke to me before."

When last I was here, Elizabeth had indeed been a small child. Her older brother lay dying of a mysterious wasting disease, so crazed by strange ecstatic nightmares that they called the priest to exorcise him... Ah, memories. She doesn't know that I was responsible. Obviously she glimpsed me, yet never connected my appearance to his death.

"What did you think, when you saw me?"

"I don't know. You were just a face in the shadows. A sad and restless soul with such beautiful eyes."

"You weren't afraid, then?" I smile in relief. "You know I'm a friend."

"Yes," she murmurs. So, she has some dim memory of me, which has imprinted itself favourably upon her. And thanks to that – after her initial alarm – she's receptive. She sees me, not as a threat, but as someone familiar, fascinating. A lonely, mysterious phantom!

The idea of killing her, swiftly or slowly, loses its appeal. Instead – to win her trust! Her love. There's a novelty.

"You are the ghost of Blackwater Hall," she says, speaking as decisively as a child.

"Yes." I laugh softly at that. "I suppose I am."

Her eyes grow more intense. "You're him, aren't you? You're Sebastian Pierse, who murdered his wife and her lover, and then disappeared."

"And been in torment over it ever since," I concur. "She betrayed me most sorely, but I wronged her the more. Now I seek atonement."

"My parents and grandparents have always feared you," she whispers. "They are always looking over their shoulders in the dark. They brought in priests to cleanse the place – but it didn't work, did it?"

I try not to laugh at this, since she's so sincere. I speak with quiet, desperate need. "Elizabeth, it is the dearest wish of my heart to trouble the household no longer. But I'll never be at peace unless you help me."

"Help you, how?" She is trembling. We're half in love already. The warm weight of her body so close is driving me mad. "Should I pray for you?"

"Yes. Let me come to you at night like this, and we'll pray together. A link with the living…"

"I can't have a man in my room!" she says in a panic. "I'm to be married."

"But I'm not a man, I'm a soul in torment. Connection with a living being, that's all I need."

"All?"

"And a sip of your life-blood."

She blinks. It doesn't sound much, put like that. She touches my hand, doesn't flinch when I sit beside her. "You're very solid, for a ghost," she says.

We talk like this for a long time, a game of thrust and parry that grows ever more intense. There are soft touches between us; my fingertips on her hand, hers on my sleeve. Confidences are shared. She holds nothing back.

I gather she is dreading this marriage to a man older than herself. It is no love match, clearly. As our dialogue strays into more intimate areas, she confesses that she fears the wedding night. "George will expect me like this – all pure, untried and nervous. But I…I don't see why I should be lying here ignorant and frightened!"

"You deserve pleasure," I tell her. "He will not give you pleasure; you are just a possession to him."

"How do you know?"

"I can tell, from your words, exactly the sort of man he is. Domineering, certain of his rights. He will have despoiled a hundred women in his time and yet expect his wife to be a perfect innocent. He will use you brutishly." My outrage is genuine. "I can't bear to think of him hurting you."

She chafes her lip with her teeth. I want to bite that rose-pink pillow. I see in her eyes a violet fire of rebellion. At last she asks, "Will you show me, then? So that when the time comes, I'll know what to expect and I won't be afraid. Will you, Sebastian?"

"Nothing would please me more." I speak with complete sincerity.

"But he must never know!"

"He won't," I reassure her. "It will be our secret. After all, with a ghost, it doesn't count."

At last I lean in and feel the sweet, fresh warmth of her neck against my mouth. She sighs. I am lost.

When I became a vampire I walked away from Blackwater Hall. I left others to find my wife and her lover in the old stone tower, where I had left them marinating in pools of their own blood. I took ship to America, like the long wave of Irish emigrants after me, thinking never to return. I put an ocean between myself and the old country; I wanted no more of its shadowy magic, its religions and superstitions, its wars and the endless struggle I'd had, just to hold onto what was mine.

In those early years of my new existence, I was savage and bitter. Yet as time passed, as bitterness faded and I brought the bloodthirst under control, I began to think of the house again.

Some sixty years after I left, I came back. Just curiosity, you understand. I discovered that the scandal of Sebastian Pierse – who'd murdered his wife, her lover and her unborn infant before vanishing – was local legend; a folk-tale told by old men in their cups. My estate had been claimed by the British and awarded to a family of English Protestant settlers. They were decent enough folk, I concede, who looked after the estate well and were fair to the tenants. I'd no argument with the way they ran my affairs.

And yet, they had no right to be there. I owed it to the house and to myself to haunt them a little; to frighten the old men, to feed on the young and strong. To turn a capable wife into a crazed neurotic, to kill a first-born son here, a beloved daughter there. Just to darken their lives once in a while, as the generations came and went.

So every few years I return to Ireland for old times' sake, and listen with pleasure when people say, "That Blackwater Hall is haunted; it's cursed the family are!" And I slip silently into the house and torment the hapless inhabitants a little more.

I could have killed them all, but I let them stay and survive. Why?

If I were of a more violent disposition, I would have ousted the usurpers long ago. I prefer to play a long and subtle game. How much more sense it makes to let them stay, to enjoy the slow burn of revenge over a century or three.

I tolerate them for the pure pleasure of haunting them.

"Just a sip, just a drop of your lifeblood," I whisper to Elizabeth in the darkness. "It must be freely given. Without it, I'll fade from Earth and be dragged into hell." In the euphoric convulsions of our love-making I draw on her neck as she groans with delight and pain. I resist the urge to take too much; she's too delightful to me, alive. And so she thinks she's saving a poor damned soul from the abyss!

For a while, anyway. By the time she realises the falsehood, she no longer cares.

It helps that I have this supernatural glow of beauty – the honey in the trap – that her new husband lacks. And she has the darkness in her soul that welcomes me, loving the danger and deception of it, loving the sheer sin.

I was right about the husband. He's some remote cousin of hers and his name is George. He's an older man, experienced in the ways of the world to the point of debauchery. He's handsome enough in his way; tall and strong, with a ruggedly arrogant face, thick brown hair, an overpowering sense of arrogant masculine entitlement. (Probably I would have been just like him, had my human life progressed as planned). George has made a fortune from trade in Dublin. He's been everywhere and done everything, and yet he expects as his due a shimmering, untouched maiden on his wedding night! To me, he seems coarse and charmless. There can be no love in this match. Society has shackled her to him, but her hidden self writhes and lashes against it like a serpent.

Elizabeth acts well the part of his new bride. How innocently she glides from church to bridal chamber, trembling and virginal, God-fearing and full of nervous anticipation. How flawlessly she feigns pain and inexperience! Attentive to detail, she even covertly pricks her finger on a pin to fake a few drops of virgin blood (ah, her sweet blood) on the sheets. Drunk on wine, blind in his triumphal lust, the husband suspects nothing.

As he takes her, grunting and oblivious, she looks at me over his shoulder. Her lips part and her eyes shine as she smiles at me, her secret lover in the shadows.

Every girl should have one.

I am standing once again in the courtyard, which still seems to echo with the screams of Mary and her pallid weed of a lover as I tear them apart, feasting on their blood, ripping the still-moving foetus from her womb to suck the tender fluids from it as if from an unborn lamb...

I write about all this as if I still cared, but in truth, I don't. When the unholy trinity of vampires came to feed on my blood and grief in the rain – golden Simon, dark Rasmila and pale Fyodor, as white as ectoplasm – I entered a clearer state of consciousness in which human pain no longer tore me. Since I was determined to burn down Blackwater Hall at the time, you could say that they saved the house, my three demon-angels. Should I thank them?

Whenever Elizabeth and George are absent, I walk through the salons as if I own the place. It has an eerie grandeur. There are high ceilings with elaborate plaster decoration, impressive fireplaces surmounted by coats of arms, rows of long windows hung with gorgeous curtains. Exotic rugs sprawl on polished floorboards. Along the walls are the antlered heads of stags, staring out with black marble eyes. And countless dark portraits of ancestors, fixing their painted gazes on mine.

Double doors lead from one great room to the next; here a drawing room that is insistently golden; wallpaper, frames, curtains, the scrolled woodwork of chairs, all gold. There are chairs lush with needlepoint roses, tapestry stools and fire-screens. Too many ornaments; clocks, statuettes, vases, elephants carved of onyx and jade. More paintings, huge mirrors rimmed with gilt.

None of this stuff is mine. Only the shell matters.

These great rooms – which feel so alien to me, even though I commissioned them – fill me with delicious, creeping awe. This place has the feel of a theatre, each room a lavish set waiting endlessly for the actors to arrive. The house creaks. Speaks. Upstairs there are nurseries and playrooms where expensive toys have been played with too little. Alas, the mortality rate of children has been tragically high over the decades – and not all my fault, far from it.

Feeding upon infants is a dull game, after all. True pleasure lies in toying with the adult inhabitants. I goad them, rather as a dog scratches at fleas, to remind them they should not be here.

Some regard the house as ugly. All things decay, of course. Each time I come I see further hints of weathering, paint peeling, rust-marks streaking the render. Perhaps Blackwater Hall is, as some claim, a brute of a place, as desolate as a prison fortress. Well, I don't ask anyone to admire it. It's the mirror of my soul. It is my soul.

In truth, I've no need to reclaim it, because it was never truly taken from me. It can't be taken; it's as if it exists partly in the Crystal Ring, an etheric house that transcends its earthly form. It transcends beauty itself.

If I speak of my house like a lover, it is because I regard it as a lover.

On the surface, Elizabeth is the good wife, attending church, managing her household, pretending to be thrilled when her husband brings her some trinket. She affects ignorance of his gambling, drinking and whoring when he's away in Dublin or in London. Like the dutiful wife she is, she turns a blind eye. But she has a secret.

Me.

Our limbs twine like snow in the moonlight, blood streaking darkly down her throat. Blood on snow. She knows by now that I'm no ghost, that my needs are nothing to do with saving my poor tormented soul – but she's beyond caring. We are both too addicted to this sensual game. When she feels faint, I hold her up and give her dark stout to drink, to strengthen the blood.

She knows that if we keep doing this, it will kill her, yet she cannot stop. Neither of us can. Urgently she welcomes me to her bed, whenever the husband is absent.

Then one night, panting in the aftermath of passion, she cries, "You must leave me alone, Sebastian." She pushes me away into the wreckage of bed sheets, her essence still sweet on my tongue. "I need to have children. Can you give me children?"

I laugh and reply, "I hardly think so. We both know that I can't."

Even in life, as I've mentioned, I failed to impregnate my wife. Whatever cold essence now spurts from my member, it is as clear as ice-water and as sterile as *poteen*. There is no life-force in it.

"Then you have to go, and leave me to my husband!"

So I do as she asks – out of curiosity, not compassion. I let her alone for a few years, and children she has. Three rosy daughters and two sons, who suck as greedily upon her breast as ever I have feasted on her neck. The beating urgency of life will always win out against the vampire.

Why did I indulge her? Well, I have patience. Of course the

temptation was there, to guzzle the life from those rosy children, from mother and father too, all in one debauched night – but I didn't. What am I, a fox in a flapping hen coop, to go on killing and killing until nothing moves anymore? No.

I was too soft on Elizabeth but, you see, if I'd destroyed her – and it would have been so easy, done in a moment – I'd have destroyed the very conditions that made my existence worthwhile. I was in love, a little. If not with her, then with the situation.

I still had to feed, of course, and so I went away for a while, a fair few years in fact, and found entertainment elsewhere. I might even have lost interest and never gone back at all – but by coincidence, nearly twenty years on, we meet at a ball in Dublin.

Elizabeth greets me with the same sly smile of recognition and, as I bow gallantly, we both know – the game is on again. She is tangibly older of course – flesh thickening, her stiff layers of corsetry and clothes giving her the grandeur of a duchess. Still a desirable woman, though. She still has the gleam in her violet eyes, once so innocent, now full of shrewdness; knowing and sultry. I still desire her – how not? Her flesh is as plump with blood as ever and the blood as sweet in its promise.

Later, at Blackwater Hall once more, we face each other in her bedchamber, but something is different. The first thing she says to me is, "Make me a vampire."

I only look at her. Somewhere deep inside me, dreary horror wells, a kind of tired revulsion.

"That's what I want," she insists. She clasps my arms, imploring me with luminous eyes. "Look at you, forever young and powerful, fearing nothing! I want that too!"

"Never." I tear myself from her. Surely my contempt must pierce her to the heart. "I couldn't do it, even if I wanted to. It's not a simple process. It takes three vampires to create a new one." And I explain a little about Rasmila, Fyodor and Simon.

"Then find two others to help you," she persists, addressing me as if I were some inept boot-boy.

"Don't you understand?" I say patiently. "The gathering of three means that the change can't happen by accident. It must be planned. Which means that it must be desirable."

"But it is. I desire it."

"Desirable to *them*. To me."

She looks at me as if I've lost my mind. The look makes me angry.

"Who do you think you are, Elizabeth?" I say with cold spite. "You were never anything to me but blood-filled flesh. What, you think you're worthy of immortality? No, you are not so special. You are no different from any other mortal. A lump of ageing flesh."

Strangely, she doesn't appear to react much. Her eyes narrow a little, but she keeps her burning, wounded anger contained inside her. She doesn't scream or beg. I'm too dismayed at her tiresome request to care about the feelings she is hiding.

Eventually she says, in a surprisingly cutting tone, "What you're telling me is that you, alone, lack the power to transform me. You can't do it without help. Poor Sebastian."

I should have killed her for that. Should have done so long before now. I hate it when I let them reach this stage.

I go away then, leaving her standing ghost-like in the centre of the large and shadowy bedroom that, so often, had witnessed our convulsions of ecstasy.

Unbelievable as it may seem, I almost entirely forget she ever made this request. It passes from my mind in the manner of a lover's tiff. Some months later I arrive at the house again, as jaunty as a young suitor who's gone off, got drunk, and returned later utterly oblivious to the fact that his lady friend has been seething with rage all this time.

I can't altogether have forgotten, though, because I feel wary. I don't approach her at once. Instead I haunt stairwells and alcoves for a time, watching the family from a distance. It amuses me to do this, but I'm sure Elizabeth knows I'm around. She's uneasy and over-sensitive, just as she used to be in the old days when I would look at the pale peach column of her neck with such delicious longing.

Actually, I have some vague intention of starting on one of the daughters now. Or maybe a son, for a change. Or all of them. They must be of an age to make it fun.

Alas, it seems I'm too late. Where did the time go? All but one of the offspring appear to have left – farmed out to schools or to relatives in order to become ladies and gentlemen, ready to marry money and enter society – they're out there in the world, but Elizabeth and her husband are still here. Their youngest is about eight, a plain bookish boy who doesn't interest me.

Still, I'm a patient man. I can wait for the son to grow up and come home with a trembling, fresh young wife, or even wait for grandchildren… After all, the house is mine. Generations will come and go but I will always be here, like a curse.

Only something is wrong.

I start to notice changes in Elizabeth. She's lost weight; she looks younger, more slender, her hair restored to its lustrous gold. She's languorous, pleased with herself – as she used to be in the early days with me. The changes aren't just in her, but in her husband George, too. It's as if his coarseness has been fine-polished away, and he no longer strides around like a drunken officer, slapping the furniture with a riding crop. Instead there's a thoughtful quality about him, a shine to his hair and a pale bloom to his skin.

Have I been blind? Isn't it strange, how we don't see what we don't *expect* to see? Some ghastly trick has been played upon me, here in my own house. Voices seem to be whispering and laughing at me from the corners of ceilings. Stags stare at me from black glass eyes. Something is pulling at me, an unseen current whirling me along, rendering me as wide-eyed and vulnerable as Elisabeth on that first night. As if in a trance, I walk into the drawing room and they are sitting in chairs on either side of the fireplace, George and Elizabeth, just as if they have been waiting for me to arrive. They sit perfectly composed, like brother and sister, hands lightly clasped in their laps. They are gazing at me with liquid eyes and their skin glows like candle-flames shining through the thinnest possible shell of wax.

"How did you do it?" My voice almost fails as I speak, emerging hoarse as an old man's.

"We met your angels," she answers simply. "Your three angels. They came back. I knew what they were and I persuaded them to transform us."

I should have remembered. The vampire's kiss, when it does not kill, brings madness. Not always in the form of wilting terror, but sometimes as a kind of megalomania.

"Why? They can't be persuaded. They take only those who are special, chosen. That is what they told me."

"And it's what they told us, too," she answers serenely. "You take yourself too seriously, Sebastian. Perhaps they changed us simply to annoy you."

"But him?" I point at the husband, who looks back at me. He sits motionless as only vampires can, fixing me with his all-knowing, pitiless gaze. "That – that coarse, arrogant, drink-raddled *merchant?*"

"Why would I want to be immortal, without my husband at my side?" she replies, genuinely surprised.

"You hate him, and all he represents!"

"No, I don't. It was your idea, that I hated him, that he maltreated me. Your perception, not reality. I love my husband. Have you no idea of the wonders I've shown him? We are one soul, George and I."

So, all the arts she learned from me, she has taught him in turn! And far from being suspicious at her knowledge, it turns out he was delighted with it, enthralled! Unbelievable.

And now they are holding hands, and he lifts hers to his mouth, pressing her knuckles to his lips. She laughs, showing the tips of her new fangs. "What, did you think you alone were the custodian of this delicious dark secret? Selfish Sebastian. You

171

wouldn't share, so we found another way, and now we don't need you anymore." And she laughs again. Laughs at me!

So this is what I did.

I went away and dressed myself up as a priest, and I arrived in the nearest village all dishevelled, with a crusading fire in my eye; a man of the cloth, on a mission from God. First I found the local priest and plied him with whisky as I span my story. Despite his unpromising appearance, he was soon full of holy ardour. He was a fiery fellow, eager to make his mark on the world, to impress his bishop and win the undying admiration of his congregation, or something on those lines. I wound him up and set him spinning.

He gathered the populace, and I spun my story; that Elizabeth and George were undead, that they'd sold their souls to the Devil in exchange for immortality, that I'd been hunting such creatures down across Europe, Britain and Ireland for years in order to bring them the mercy of death. Oh, a rare tale I wove.

I'd come to warn them, to help them purge the evil. Were they with me? Oh yes, by God, they were!

The priest fell in eagerly behind me like a captain behind a general. He took me for the scholar and holy man I purported to be and he wanted to play the hero, scrambling for his share of my glory. Turned out I'd walked into a community already possessed by rumour and fear. Elizabeth and George were young vampires, you see, not yet adept at hiding their tracks. There had been deaths, injuries that set a fair old fire of stories blazing. I'd walked in at the perfect time to become the saviour of the community.

All I had to do was to point and say, "They're the guilty ones," and the entire town became a mob, ablaze with righteous vengeance.

They will fight like tigers, I warned, so we'll go in a big band like an army. Some of us will probably die, but that's the risk we must take to be free of this curse.

They don't sleep in coffins, I told them, but they are more

dangerous by night and more apt to be off their guard during the day, from the necessity of pretending to be human. Don't bother with a stake to the heart, I said – that will only make them mad. No crosses, either; you'll only waste time while they laugh. Simply hack off their heads, I instructed. Hack the heads and the bodies into pieces, then throw the pieces onto a bonfire.

That should do the trick.

And so it happened that I led a vast, inflamed army to Blackwater Hall – priests and farmers, blacksmiths, washer-women and their big daughters, stomping along with rolled-up sleeves, everyone – and they took Elizabeth and her husband by surprise and overwhelmed them.

Too inexperienced to vanish into the shadows of the Crystal Ring, they fought for their lives with fangs and nails. They fought with all the desperation of mortals – and thus they fell, hacked to pieces.

The mob spared the little boy, who watched as his parents were cut down before his terrified eyes. Had he known what they'd become? How could he not? And yet, I still believe he didn't know. His parents had kept up a front of humanity for his sake, ensuring that he only saw what they wanted him to see.

I still wonder what nightmares haunted him down the rest of his years. At one time I would have been eager to know… would have sought him out wherever he was, and hidden in the shadows watching the liquid shine of his gaze questing for me in the darkness…

Strange, I never did. I lost my taste for it, somehow.

In the midst of this carnage, I slipped away.

A column of smoke rose behind me, turning the air bitterly fragrant like autumn – but it was a pyre that burned, not the house itself.

Their children survived. The older ones, I understand, never set foot in Blackwater Hall again. The youngest son, however – once he'd reached an age to make his own choice – lived there until his death; a bachelor. Quite eccentric, quite mad. He never

threw anything away, it seems. He filled the place with collections; with animals stuffed rigid under glass domes, with drawers full of fossils and coins, with butterflies pinned in glass cases and huge, ugly beetles impaled on cards. As if, by heaping talismans around himself, he built a great nest in which to hide from the darkness outside.

A grand job he did of tormenting himself; he didn't need any help from me at all.

Some years ago, he died and since then Blackwater Hall has lain empty, a shell loved by no one. And here it remains, falling into slow decline.

Sometimes I still come back.

I view the familiar sweeps of grass, magnificent lone trees, copses, the river gleaming like milk in the vaporous gloom. In the distance, the mountains are soaked in layers of folk-tale and myth, haunted forever by the black goddess Callee. And there it stands, Blackwater Hall; a great mansion, broodingly desolate. The walls are mottled and flaking, as if the place is shedding its skin with age. The windows, fogged like cataracts with dirt, stare indifferently at long-neglected gardens and stables.

I stand outside and gaze at it for hours, watching it decay by slow degrees. I'm filled with the sensation that it was not I who built the house after all, but some greater power acting through me. In darker moments I feel that I have simply been used in order to create a theatre for some great drama that has yet to unfold. In my mind the house is a sighing black tomb, and in place of antlered stags along the walls, there are horned demon heads.

Thus the house remains to this day – its walls grey with neglect, paint cracking, windows netted with cobwebs and dust. Somehow it withstands the vigorous, mindless invasion of life – the nesting of birds and bats, vegetation trying to drag it down with green tendrils. I wander the grand salons and bedrooms, corridors and attic nurseries, where rocking horses stand motionless under the soft, endless fall of dust. The edifice endures like an ancient castle fortress, tired yet impervious to time.

Was it I who sucked the life from this house? Will it ever be done with its revenge? I wanted the family gone and yet, without them, it is nothing. The house is dead yet here it stands, undead. Blackwater Hall draws me back, I swear, like a jealous lover. I know it is not done with me yet.

One day it may yet spring to life again. Some rich and enterprising young family might take on the Hall and restore it to glory, filling the rooms with fresh colours, with the chat and bustle of their lives, with scents of flowers and cooking; with the vigour of their own throbbing, blood-filled bodies. Children will run laughing and screaming along the endless corridors. Doll's house doors will be opened, gigantic child-faces staring in awe through the windows. Rocking horses will creak into life.

And on that day I will be here, waiting to claim my own.

Taken At His Word

Tanith Lee

1.

Olvero the Scholar left the Governor's court, intending to kill himself by drinking the poisonous ink from his ink-well. It was not long before sunrise. The sky was black as the intended ink, slit by one prescient, envenomed slash of red.

Consumed by self-pity Olvero leaned on a wall, and wept.

Yet, even while weeping, he heard the simultaneous nagging of that stern, pure, obdurate voice of his mind. Though he might have every justification for pitying himself, he must resist. Self-pity was useless. Just as suicide, in this instance, was despicable.

Others had a right to both self-pity and self-destruction, but Olvero (Olvero admonished himself) had not. He was young, strong, healthy, not ugly, and though his last cash had gone, still not entirely without potential funds. For could he not sell most of his possessions and so gain enough to support himself, at least another month? What, after all, did he need with the silver ring his adulterous mother had left him in place of herself? Or the little blue glass goblet he had rescued from a court official's banquet, where all else was being drunkenly smashed? Why too did Olvero need a quiet apartment with white walls and having a view of tall trees in which birds sang, at dawn and sunfall? Or, come to that, a supportive chair? A mattress? A roof? For God's sake, let him lose all and wander in rags and weather. See what gems he could write *then*, damn all his enemies to Hell.

Ah. The stern voice, as had been the weeping voice, was now subsumed in a raging one.

It was the City Governor's fault. *He* had deigned, after three months of the scholar's life spent in unaffordable bribes and waiting, to consider an epic drama the scholar had written. Tonight, however, the Governor had rejected the drama, having himself kept the scholar waiting thirteen months. This was done during a supper, to which the scholar had been summoned, and placed at a very low table. The rejection was staged just before the meat course when, having invited the scholar to stand up, the Governor and his courtiers regaled him with their censure and ridicule and – worse – 'disappointment' in the 'poorness' of his work.

"My last meal in a nest of ignorant vipers!" *Oh, God*, thought the scholar, wiping his eyes on his sleeve, *if I begin to write now as tritely as I speak – I deserve no better than a dose of poisoned ink.*

The birds were singing beautifully when he reached his room.

He stood by the window and stared at sun rising from river, turning the foliage of all the framing trees, and all the feathers of the flying birds, to gold, carmine and amber.

Then he poured himself a cup of chocolate. It was the very

178

last cup.

On the desk he spread his scorned epic, leafed through its pages, read here and there a line or two. His heart leapt. Though he would never claim perfection for any of his work, Olvero had known, since his eighteenth year, that what he did was of worth; was worthy too of notice. For it was not, really, *his*. That is, it was *given* him. It was a *gift* to him – or perhaps some *reward* he had earned by other work, in some other mystical and forgotten world inhabited before this one. Its glories came from *there*, that higher source, God, or gods, or angels – or even non-malignant demons possibly – which possessed him whenever he sat to the paper and dipped a quill into ink. Any flaws, of course, were due to his own misunderstanding – or mishearing – of the silent yet omniscient guidance which thereafter fired his brain and moved his hand.

He had been blessed. Olvero knew it. And yet if some vast power had chosen him as an imperfect yet acceptable conduit, the mortal power of men now spurned him. More, it seemed set to obliterate him.

At the thought, rage towered up again in Olvero, potent as lust. But he stamped upon the rage. He shut it in his heart, tightly bound it, locked on it the doors of his mind. For rage would interfere with the mediumistic process of his work. As indeed could great sorrow – the memory of his mother's departure, the later loss of a young woman he had deeply loved, who had fallen away from love of him . . . or extreme physical pain – as when he had been beaten by a gang of thieves for not having enough money to satisfy their rapacity. ..(also let it be said, for defending himself and breaking a pair of their noses).

Nevertheless, of these three distractions – rage, sorrow, pain – rage seemed the worst. It blocked and muddied the receptive channel. It must not break loose again. However many deserters, thieves, governors, *monsters* he was compelled to confront.

And so he sat down and closed the manuscript of his epic and drew towards him a piece of fresh paper – one of the hundred final sheets he had.

His urge was only to write a short piece, perhaps even a poem to praise the birds in the dawn. To bid them farewell, for the approaching day when he must leave his apartment.

But instead his mind slipped strangely askew. He thought first of a ghost story he had heard only yesterday, in the small tavern where sometimes he took a glass of wine. But the story was old now that he considered it. Then his mind – was it fumbling? After all still too dismayed to seek true dreams and images? – his mind slewed like a sailed craft to the wind. Olvero stared in vague surprise at an inner procession of odd, uncanny freaks. After the predatory ghost, a ghoul, said for years to prey on the burial ground of the city's cathedral. Next, an undine who lurked in a village well, drawing young men to their deaths. A murderous witch came after, with rats in her hair... a stone-inflicting gorgon whose own hair comprised snakes... a devil of the Eastern lands that danced in a sand storm, with ready teeth as pointed as awls.

Olvero stood up. He thrust away from the table.

To work with such nonsense was absurd.

He should sleep.

Yet even as he moved towards the mattress in the alcove, Olvero turned about again. He recrossed the room, leaned over the paper and, with the quill fresh dipped, wrote there very large and black, and with many curlicues of the sort he seldom if ever employed, one word. *Vampire*.

Stepping back once more, he regarded this effort.

He swore, both amused and disgusted. Best leave it all, go sleep, awake refreshed. Evidently, he could do nothing legitimate till then.

The Scholar Olvero sold his winter coat, (it was not yet autumn) a jacket reserved for grand occasions; (such as the Governor's disgraceful dinner); his boots, the blue goblet, one of the pillows from his mattress-bed... There were also things of lesser value. They all went. And with their unopulent returns, he kept himself in cheap lamp-oil, cheap ink, cheap food, dull husk-filled coffee and watered wine. His rent though seemed likely to plunge into arrears. Olvero borrowed from a usurer. (Leeches, all he dealt with, yet no worse than the Governor.)

During this while, a matter of eighteen days, Olvero found he could not write a single word.

Or, ultimately and bizarrely, that was all he *could* write.

Coming back to his desk on the very evening following his return from the Governmental palace, he had seated himself to construct the brief simple ode previously considered. Now to sunset birds, carolling a sinking disc.

The trees were falling into deep black, and stars scorching through them, when Olvero flung up from the table. He had written only gibberish, he believed. Masses of half-formed, unpunctuated sentences, verbs lacking nouns, and adjectives lacking meaning, and all of it with letters left out – things similar to *carlet* for scarlet, or *rung* for running, *ght* for night and *inggni* for singing.

Olvero thought he had gone mad, and became afraid. He set himself to write at least one word carefully, readably. And found he wrote again the word **Vampire**. Then he attempted the word *God* and instead wrote *Bark*. Next *Howl*.

After this he drank the last of his good wine, two cups. Then he wrote a prosaic list of things he must do – buying more cheap bread, stopping up a mouse-hole – and this all came out quite sensibly, spelled in the usual way and coherent.

But nothing else other than such lists *would* come. He could not even describe the darkness of the night, nor the narrow lighted windows across the street, nor a fisherman's fire on the river bank. This was like a horrible attack of lexicological hiccups or incurable stammering. Oh, he had known his ill-treatment by the Governor, (and by all those through the years who had belittled and tried to deny – or better, ruin – his gift) had harmed him. But surely not to such a pitch as to rob him of his true *life*, his ability to *work*.

In the end, drunk on the last of the strong wine, he sat and wrote over and over the one word he could now pen. *Vampire*. **Vampire**. **VAMPIRE**. And each time he ornamented it more and more. He draped it in coils and spirals, dots, slots, festoons of calligraphic decoration. Until, eventually, it seemed less a word than a briar-clump, or curving wall of thorns worthy of some fairy-tale imprisonment, that both shut in and shut out, threatening mutilation and death to any trying to get through it either way.

Next day then, and for seventeen days after, waking generally late, Olvero the Scholar wrote angrily across two, three, even four whole sheets of paper. He wrote over and over and only the ghastly and primitive word for a nightmare creature in which he, his enlightened self, did not believe. **Vampire**. **Vampire**. **VAMPIRE**. Vampire.

Then, not even pausing to sip water, he encumbered the word with swathes of inky ornament. He went out only reluctantly and after noon, in order to sell one or other more possession, or to visit the usurious establishment.

On the eighteenth day, Olvero did not leave his room.

He had nothing left to sell. Even his mother's ring was sold. Most of his paper was gone, too. Only one little stoop of ink remained.

Not even, now, enough to poison himself.

Perhaps, instead, he might eat the papers with their inky alphabetic briar forests of *vampire vampire vampire*.

The birds sang heartlessly at the dying sun.

Birds did not care for the sun's nightly death. Nor its morning birth-agonies. Nor would they care at all if Olvero, a mere human, could not sit and look at them, nor praise their voices. Another would do as well at the window. Or none at all.

By flickering, fading lamplight, **Vampire** wrote Olvero with enormous attention and in the last ink, across the height and width of a single sheet of paper.

Tomorrow he would wheedle another small loan, leaving his shoes as surety. He would then get drunk in the tavern on weak beer, next drowning himself in the river. Make the birds sing for that!

Vampire: deceiver, cheat, criminal, parasite, perpetrator of violence, adversary having implacable and undeserved powers, anti-god, un-thing, mindless drainer of blood and life...

Olvero dreamed he was still scribbling the word on and on. Yet there was a difference. Before, he had written *Vampire* first, then ensconced it in draperies of ink. Now in the dream, he *commenced* with a proliferation of inked coils and curls and curdles, and out of these gradually if remorselessly the letters of the word *Vampire* grew. Like a serpent it rose from two hundred score of looping, swirling talons.

The scholar opened his eyes. He was awake?

His room, in darkness after he had blown out the lamp, was now lit with a soft creamy radiance. Perhaps the moon had risen, and shone in at the window. No, it had not. The sky beyond the glass was black with latest night or most premature morning. The moon was dead. It would never shine again.

In here, however –

The pages covered with the word (*Vampire*) had somehow been dislodged and scattered in a loose heap on the floor. These were what gave off the glow, being now mostly pure white, unspoiled by marks. Instead the inked and thorn-like curlicues had also risen straight up, just as in the dream, right off the paper. In the white-lit air now the darkly molten spiky spiral hedges knotted and unreeled, embracing each other, *strangling* each other with wet-gleaming and spiny tentacles and feelers.

Olvero stared. He had become only eyes.

With those he watched what next emerged from the dance of the separated Word.

The shape was elongate and thin. Yet instantly solid, opaque and actual as marble and ebony. It also swayed and wriggled its long body, which while seeming legless as that of a huge worm, still displayed arms and hands, a neck, a face, a torrent of spooling hair, all of which wove and rippled in restless, ceaseless gesturings. The constant, almost tidal *flux* of it, having once formed, nevertheless retained a basic hardness and permanence. Nowhere was this more evident than in the awful *face*. It was a dead-white mask, equipped with all required features – but formed of a sort of – living? – alabaster. And where its eyes burned between the white lids they were only black – black as ink. And the lips were wet-black too, and between them showed a wet-ink-black mouth and an ink-black pointed tongue. And from the upper jaw extruded two extended canine teeth, the whitest things of all, and glittering.

Even as Olvero watched, this structure of animated writing folded suddenly as a closing fan. All motion stopped. Balanced on its black tail, the creature now represented utter stasis. Only the black tongue flicked once across the black lips, and the ink pools of the eyes were shut for a split second in a white-lidded blink.

Either it smiled at Olvero, or that was the thing's habitual expression in repose.

On the floor, the sheets of paper lay sodden and limp, not a single written mark on them. (Tomorrow the pages would have fallen to pieces. The ink-well – and the air – would be empty of darkness).

But now the creature hovered, elevated maybe an inch or so above the floor. It was quite impossible to tell if it had either or any gender. As for intelligence, it was not to be said. Yet intent it did seem to have. It smiled at Olvero, or *through* Olvero, a few more moments, during which the scholar, who had become only eyes, felt himself also adrift in the atmosphere of the room. Then the Vampire gathered itself together like a vast skein of black and snow-white wool. Mobile once more, it spun into itself, flattened, compressed, became like a twisted stalk of salty bitumen – and vanished.

At once all light was gone. All dark, too.

Olvero dropped away down miles of nothingness, and did not come back to himself again until light had refilled his window, and the rent-collecting landlord hammered on his door.

2.

There was plague in the city. Everyone spoke of it.

A man would, in the day, be healthy and about his business or pleasures as usual. Come next birdsong dawn, someone or other would find him – on the open street, tucked behind some wall of the tavern, in his own chamber, flung across floor or bed – a chalk-white corpse already stenchful and turning rotten, covered with peculiar lesions and wounds that were dryly black, since no blood remained in his body. Or *her* body; women were often victims too.

What kind of plague was it then? Most citizens knew the name for it but in the first days none would mention that name. Then they did, almost all of them. **Vampire**.

"Vampire," they said, whispered, muttered, shrieked, and hurried to the churches and cathedrals for blessed objects and holy water. None of these things did any good. It seemed the plague creature was not itself religious, had not the intellectual wit to reverence the might of God or gods – nor even demons – for counter-spells did no good either.

None had seen the **Vampire**. Or, only the dead had done so. (A wife, say, rousing from a sickening deathly sleep more like a trance, would wake beside her husband to find him a corpse. It would seem the night-fiend was selective, had *chosen* between them – while she had been spared any sight of it, or what it did).

It preyed everywhere, through all strata of society, from the lowest to the highest. Although... a certain partiality, aside even from its tendency to *choose*, might have been observed in its – what could one call it? – diet.

Fathers who bullied and whipped their sons, mothers who abandoned their sons while still children, girls who rejected their young suitors, tutors who scorned their pupils, thieves who beat those they robbed, officials who took bribes and patronizingly prevaricated... usurers, evicting landlords, tavern-keepers who refused an old customer a little beer gratis... Such were the feasts of the vampire. On these it supped, and left them whiter than their own bones, colder than winter, and riddled all over with black coils and curlicues of wounds, almost like a devilish scrivening.

3.

Veranilla the Courtesan went to the Governor 's palace, intending to provide him with sex, as their customary bargain was. It was late in the afternoon and the sky was rosy as a peach. Only the east showed a single hint of shadow.

Quite satisfied with her life, the courtesan felt neither unease nor resentment. She had been well-trained since her fourteenth year, and never used unkindly by her mother (also of the sorority) nor her early patrons. By the time she encountered any patrons of the rougher sort she was established, and able to make them rue the day they were born.

Having left her carriage, Veranilla entered the palace by a discreet way which led through charming gardens. In the vestibule she made her arrival known to a chamberlain, and was presently installed in a nice supper-room. Here she dined, as on her previous two visits, alone with the Governor.

She always found the Governor, the most powerful man in the city aside from the Bishop (whom she had also accommodated on several occasions), quite affable company. Descended from a mercantile family, the Governor was respectful of all the creative trades, including in his favour both artists and prostitutes. "But how I wish Heaven would spare me," he told her, as they reached the stage of sweets and fruit, "these bloody writers! Are they all quite mad? I don't refer to our popular playwrights, who so please the people – naturally not – nor those that work for the opera. But these others, the ones who wish only to entertain themselves with inept over-purpled gibberish, and may take seventeen stanzas of dross to reach some paltry climax – worthy only of putting on in a wine-shop latrine!"

The Governor did not once mention the plague. Let alone any plebeian chatter of a supernatural night-beast. The Governor, Veranilla suspected, did not even privately believe in the Supreme Being, but frequently alluded to the present age as an enlightened one. Men should, the Governor averred, have by now outgrown silly fancies.

That evening the sunset was prolonged and vivid and, just before the Governor went through into his bedroom, he and she paused to admire the crimsoning sky through a window of fine glass. Many small birds were flying over the garden trees, looking like swarms of bees against the red dusk, and Veranilla stayed to watch them, while the Governor stepped into the other room. Here he preferred to undress first and climb into the bed, sitting to observe as Veranilla took off her clothes. He left the door partly ajar, however, as normal. And so she heard at once when he let out a sudden wavering cry of what sounded like extreme terror.

Despite the relative reasonableness of her life so far, Veranilla had also been trained to be cautious.

She therefore turned from the window and walked softly in her satin shoes to the barely open door. Here she looked cautiously around its panelling and into the chamber beyond.

It too possessed long windows, and was filled by a deep wine-red brilliance. By this the young woman saw all, very clearly.

The Governor stood bolt upright by the bed, still in his shirt and breeches. He was transfixed. As well he might be. For there, in the middle of the floor, a million streaming jet-black rnuscular filaments circled and poured upward. They had come from nowhere, Veranilla surmised – for even as she stared, more and more of them evolved, apparently from nothing, to thicken and entwine the bristling mass already writhing on the tiles. It reminded her instantly of something: a sea-monster she had as a child once been shown, in a tank during carnival. Yet this apparition was the nastier, and much larger too. And all the while it swelled, rose upward, *grew*.

Veranilla did not scream. Nor did she remonstrate, not even calling out to the plainly panic-stricken Governor. *His* face was a study in insane horror. Hers in iron self-control.

All this time the fiery light, rather than dim, had intensified – as if the sun, just now down under the earth's edge, had exploded there like gunpowder.

Accordingly the Courtesan Veranilla was in no doubt when, from the tumult of thrashing thorny tentacles, a form began to consolidate itself. This form, not of a man, was of a creature. A creature like a black worm; with a black unspecified torso – less human than resembling the thorax of a giant insect. And from that came out the death-white arms and skinny hands and neck like a fungus stem and face like a mask, everything caught in a whirl of viper-like hairs, and other extended fringes, these all a liquid, poisonous black.

Just then the creature turned its head. Its flattish plate-like mask demonstrated a fixation with the casement. In this position also Veranilla was able to note the ink-pool of a single eye, the gleaming black lips and pointed tongue, the fangs. She was ready to hide herself more thoroughly should the obscene head turn further in her direction, but instead the creature's interest was, for that second, only in the window. Or rather, in the last flights of the birds beyond, as they went singing and settling to their roosts. She was to say later that she sensed a terrible hatred the creature had for these innocent birds. As if it resented their careless song and ability to fly. And Veranilla was glad that, being a monster of darkness, it might not manifest earlier in the day – and certainly not in the open sunset - to snatch any of them. Men though were to be snared both day and night.

At the hour, she nevertheless forgot about the birds, for next moment the *Vampire* (it was now to prove its title) sprang and dazzled through the air straight upon the Governor. Trapped in the thorns and tines, immediately borne to the ground beneath it, the Governor was able only to let out one deep, loud scream. Before the *Vampire* silenced him.

Veranilla had seen certain unpalatable events. But this surpassed them all.

At the theatrical maelstrom of ripped flesh and other bodily fragments, lit by sprays of scarlet that rivalled and then outshone the dying light, she did not look very long. In a minute, noiseless as a ghost herself, she fled through the outer room and into the corridor beyond.

As she had thought, the Governor's guards were seated some way off, playing cards. Any outcries they might have heard they would have put down to sensual transports, for the Governor had been inclined to voice his joys. No more, Veranilla believed. She knew but too well both guards must witness, as she had done, the awful scene in the bedroom. Or might she herself not be suspect? Might she still be, even should any think she had wrought the act through evil magic?

4.

The apartment where the scholar now lived lay two-thirds below the level of the street. Part of an old cellar, it had stayed cold, damp, fusty, dark, and redolent of wines long since drunk. A small hole provided a sort of window, but it was above Olvero's head. Along with admitting grudging daylight, the hole enabled rubbish sometimes to be kicked or pushed through into the cell, out of sheer malice.

In other areas of this establishment persons made raucous noise at all and any hour. That would have disturbed Olvero, had he had the inspiration to work. But he had none, let alone the means; paper, ink were gone. To get any money at all now he must carry out menial tasks, such as the porting of night-soil. He was unskilled in any craft save writing. He had in fact supposed at first he might be employed penning letters or other stuff for those unable to write at all. But obviously, as a general rule, those who could not write or read had acquaintances similarly unequipped. The one oaf who hired Olevro, to construct a note to a creditor, refused to pay until said creditor ceased his harrying. Worse, when the creditor read the note and continued merciless, the oaf returned and attacked Olvero. (Curiously, the oaf was discovered dead of the blood-draining plague only a night or so after.)

The scholar anyway had lost not only the knack for writing, but for living. He sat in his cellar-cell most of the time brooding on his ill-fortune. From the beginning, he had put down his sight of a **Vampire** rising from its written name as a dream or hallucination, brought on by anger and despair. That the paper had been made soggy and broken up in shreds the scholar attributed to some spillage, or to rain or dew somehow seeping through the unopened window of his former room.

The scholar did not believe in vampires.

Even when he heard the stories and affright from the lower city, the tally of 'vampiric' murders, Olvero dismissed them. He was a man of an Enlightened Era – if ironically too a genius persecuted by the lightless ignorance of fools. What could be more perfect in the cruel balance of existence?

He had been going on in this manner for a couple of months. A chill fall had meanwhile entered the city, hennaing the trees prior to shearing them, hanging early icicles from roofs, to provoke winter against the talented amateurism of autumn.

Olvero woke one morning with the foul taste of hunger in his mouth, and drank some stagnant water that did not relieve it.

When fists thundered on the door, he recalled the last landlord, who had demanded rent then slung him in the street. But the cell was in a ruin, it was free. The scholar thought those who knocked might, if left alone, depart.

But soon the door was broken down. Several of the Governor's soldiers came in.

"We have been searching for you," said one, with a grimace.

A wild hope gripped the scholar. He gaped at the men and half-remembered some tale he had heard a while before – when was that? – that the Governor had fallen sick. Could it be illness had slashed the veil from the Governor's eyes? The man now grasped that Olvero was a god-gifted writer, and so had sent to find and raise him from the mud to gold and glory?

Foolishly perhaps then, Olvero did not question the soldiers. Yet probably in any case it would not have mattered.

Olvero's dungeon cell was not so different from the cellar.

In fact it had certain superiorities. For example, the window could be looked through despite the bars. It afforded a glimpse of sky now and then blue. Nor was it accessible from the public road. Besides, food was provided and, if hardly tempting to a connoisseur, at least it was, fairly regularly, there. The water was no dirtier or more unhealthy than that available at the cellar.

Wretchedly Olvero told himself that, once freed (obviously, his imprisonment was an error), he would have much material to use in some future ode, epic or saga. Secretly he did not think he would ever be able to use it, however. His genius had died within him. Either that, or the gods had withdrawn their gift from him.

Eventually he was taken out and, to his dreary, added horror, chained. Up into an elegant cold room he was dragged. A great many officials and men of the Governor's court sat about, also priests in their own finery, each of whom glared at him with concentrated attention. The Governor himself was not present.

Olvero had no means of deducing that the Governor was dead – had been stone-dead indeed, from the first smiting of the **Vampire**. Few in the city had learned this. Only the Governor's immediate circle, his council, the Bishop, seven priests, three or four soldiers, and one woman knew. The murder was concealed, and the rumour of the Governor's sickness substituted, in order that the crime's perpetrator might not escape. Nevertheless, it took some while for any to find him. Since Olvero (for by then the perpetrator was known to be himself) had vanished from his accustomed lodging. The soldiers who next hunted for him, arrested and jailed him, had been given beforehand special safeguards from the Bishop. They had not known why. Nor luckily that, if put to the test, they would have been no use at all.

But Olvero the Scholar was not privy to any of this, either.

Now he stared about, blinking at the brightness of the room. And an official stood up and began to pronounce.

"Sirs, your Grace, my lord the Bishop, here then the felon is before us. In broad day, when alone we are secure from the vile beast he has conjured. Some thirty-seven significant persons of the city have by now perished through his midnight acts, and God knows how many of the lower orders, who inevitably have gone uncounted."

At this Olvero glanced around, wondering – *a felon?* – to whom they referred. Then it came to him that they meant none other than he. The scholar laughed bitterly, just as he had when the Governor had publically reviled him those months before.

"Hark," exclaimed the official, "he jeers at us, he is so certain of Satan's care of him. Come, let us get on. Bring in the woman Veranilla."

Then the doors were undone and the courtesan entered. Olvero gazed at her without much comprehension; though she was beautiful, she reminded him of no woman he had ever met.

Veranilla wore mourning, however, and seeing it Olvero came to realise quite abruptly that all save the priests did so. Therefore he was not very startled at the official's next words: "Now, Veranilla, inform us, if you will, of what occurred on the evening of the Governor's death."

The courtesan remained respectfully subdued, cool and self-possessed. As with much of what she did, she had rehearsed herself carefully in this monologue. She was blameless, and meant to be found so. Olvero, undeniably the culprit, must suffer solo for his disgusting deeds.

After a moment she spoke.

She explained that she had been visiting the Governor on an occasion of business, for he had graciously consented to offer her advice about a mercantile venture. (This, it went without saying, was a politeness, for only a mere handful were not aware of the true nature of their transaction. There would be other little politenesses and euphemisms in her account. Some to uphold decorum. Others, more personal to herself, were employed to make sure that she appeared quite beyond reproach.)

Veranilla told them how the Governor had gone into an adjoining room to fetch a book he wished to refer to. Presently she heard an awful cry. Rushing to the door she saw the *Vampire* already evolved from nothing – for there was no way in at all, the outer door and all the windows shut. More, it had already felled the Governor, slain him, and was busy ripping him wide open with its long white nails and teeth, and lashes of its black, whip-like tentacles of hair. Even the inky pointed tongue,

Veranilla vowed (with the most sensitive yet couth shudder), sliced the flesh like a knife. Blood flew everywhere. They might have seen it – most of those present had – sprayed about the walls of the bedroom, as if the ghastly crimson sunset had permanently stained them. The *Vampire* by then guzzled amid the carnage on the Governor's wounds. Powerless to help the poor dead gentleman, yet herself unnoted by the creature, Veranilla had run to fetch the guard. Thereafter the three of them witnessed the final horror.

The courtesan was at pains to stress that the *Vampire* had also the skill of beglamouring bystanders with a sort of deathly trance. It was because of that no other survivor had ever seen the beast, so she believed, even when it supped on their closest companion or spouse in the very same chamber, or even the same bed. But as things had this time happened, the *Vampire* had itself not at first seen Veranilla. (This aspect of her account was demonstrably true). Now though, she added, when she and the brave guardsmen reached the doorway, the creature, even while engaged in its grisly feast, did detect them and cast on them an immobilising spell. Only the absorption of the monster in its supper presumably prevented it from rendering them fully unconscious. Therefore they had seen, but been forced to stand like statues, unable to move hand or limb. (In actuality, this was another of Veranilla's little lies. The guards, on viewing the Vampire had certainly become frozen – with utter terror. But she had no intention of telling the officials of the court such a thing. She had even convinced the guards themselves that they had all the while been straining to leap to the Governor's aid, and only ill-magic had held them back. It had never been her task to make enemies among those who might be useful).

In the end, Veranilla continued, total night consumed the world. And at last the *Vampire* rose from its victim. A curious glow played about it, revealing how the creature seemed to unwind from itself, like a knot of serpentine vines untwisting from a stock. These fell away into the dark, sizzled out, and all illumination ceased. The fiend had vanished into thin air. Only then were any of the three able to move once more.

At once lights were kindled. And so they beheld the dreadful remains of the Governor, and saw, each one of them, what no other ever had: the freshness of the marks and wounds, and through that freshness, what they portended. For in every other previous case the drained bodies had dried and sunk upon themselves before they were discovered, thus distorting what was, in the first one or two hours, entirely visible. An alarm was next raised. Certain others were brought in haste into the room, among them even his Grace the Bishop himself.

Vampires – such did not exist. All these people had lost their minds. Olvero gazed superciliously upon them. And they, in turn, glared venomously at *him*.

"You are a male witch," announced the official. "You will not even merit cleansing torture, nor the offer that you recant, and beg God's forgiveness. For you, Olvero, such amenities are valueless. Your own creature, the Vampire, has itself betrayed you to the gallows."

Olvero finally felt a wave of fear.

He rose from it gasping, as a man briefly might when drowning in an icy river.

"Betrayed me – what lunacy is this? Such a demon does not exist. So how – *betray?*"

The official composed himself to granite. He replied in a voice of steel.

"The marks upon the body of our lord, the Governor, were closely examined. Drawings even were made of them by two of the leading artists of the city. Other bodies then, previously killed by your conjuration, were exhumed and studied, and the type of their wounds, decipherable in the light of this *later* evidence, displayed infallibly that *you* were the sole instigator. The monster is *your* creation – *yours* the will behind the wicked butchery – *yours* the despicable sorcery. You are damned. God will have *no* pity on your soul. Our work is only to expunge you, for your creature too will perish with you. That has been made plain by its own method."

Olvero blinked. He felt greatly tired, and the chains weighed him to the earth, or to Hell perhaps. He knew at last he was guilty, yes, he must know it. Why else had his genius abandoned him?

Humbly; or simply brokenly, he asked, "Still I fail to grasp – what *method*? *What* was the *type* of the wounds? How – did they reveal my – guilt?"

"Their pattern."

"I fail still—"

"He has gone mad," said the official. "The weight of his own infamy already destroys him. Show him one of the drawings," he added to a clerk. "Be aware, Olvero, each corpse we have found is signed the same."

In this way, just before they took him from the room, and so that very afternoon to his execution, Olvero saw drawn in ink on artist's paper a sketch of the body of the slaughtered Governor. The corpse seemed covered in black curlicues and chirographic decorations – and these were the slashes, punctures, slicing, bites and tears the **Vampire** had performed. While entangled in their centre – with slight effort Olvero came to perceive three words, which were also made of wounds, and also ornamentally defined. They were black as blackness, and might be discerned by any seeing, literate eye. ***Olvero the Scholar***, they read.

Time passes. Some one hundred and forty years after, various manuscripts of Olvero's were accidentally located. They caused a sensation and shot to fame. To this day several of his plays are still performed, if necessary in translation, in many of the great theatres of the world. His poetry is included in erudite volumes, and quoted by modern writers of acknowledged talent; even taught in universities. Certain sources claim his two unfinished novels have had nearly as many reprintings as the most popular of the wonderful works of Defoe.

As to the stories that surround Olvero's defamation and death, they are ascribed to superstition and moronic inanity. The slow will always try to pull down the faster runner. In this instance, seemingly, they succeeded.

> *And the Word was made flesh*
> Gospel of John, Ch.1, V. 14.

Coldrush

Kari Sperring

The tigermoth limped in from the Deep Dark, his body crumpled and curled, his wings thinned out to filigree with privation, his limbs almost too weak to grasp the edges of the docking leaves. Under his thorax, the remains of his habitat hung, sides buckled and warped, straps cracking. The call scent that rose from him was sickness and decay: the patterns and bands that should have further identified him were long lost to Dark Dust. The scavengers of Vine Authority SanWanWuShi circled him slowly, antennae sharp with nerves, none of them more willing that the others to be the first to come closer and brave whatever fate it was that haunted him. From the safe shelter of the heart leaves, the docking authorities and vine masters watched and waited. Long and long since any moth had returned so battered and abused. Longer still since any moth had returned from that quadrant, from the depths of the Dark.

SanWanWuShi grew almost on the borders of Vine Space, as far out as it was routinely considered safe to sail and then further. Its etiolated leaves sheltered the moths of prospectors and dreamers, youngest children and exiles, bankrupts and once-criminals. Its personnel were drawn from the ranks of the crazed and the failed and the loathed. From its heartwood, travellers might view the fragile spires of Vine End, the pallor of thin-aether leaves and the blank vastness of the Deep Dark, where the vine-lines thinned to leafless thread and only emptiness remained. It was said that most of those who travelled out to view such things were already mad, and that of the handful of thrill-seekers who had retained their sanity thus far, more than half came back to Vine Space with their minds cracked beyond repair.

The tigermoth had flown out into that void and somehow returned. That he had any mind left was unlikely – no sane creature would have made that attempt in the first place. As for his colleague and pilot... In the Vine Station heartwood, bets were placed that he had none at all, or that he had somehow contrived to kill the pilot before setting out on that last flight. None of the scavengers wanted to be the first to find out the truth. The moth was dying, but he was not yet dead and his mandibles were still strong. The scavengers hung back together, touching limbs and wings for comfort, humming their low songs of worry and concern. At the very edge of their circle the Youngest clung. She was yet only two-thirds grown, her carapace still marked with the bands of youth. She hung under the shadow of the nearest leaf, voice almost silent, hoping and hoping to go unremarked. The antennae of the youngest were always the most sensitive, yet at the same time their lack of experience made them of the least value. If the elders recalled her, if she sang too loudly or moved too suddenly, she would be the one sent first to probe the mysteries of the dying tigermoth. In her leaf shelter, she rubbed her rear limbs on her abdomen for reassurance and struggled to keep her fear from her scent. Here in leafshadow, where the aether was dense, emotions were too readily smelled and acted on. Fear perturbed, disturbed, was always swiftly punished with duty. And the nearest duty, now, was one she did not want at all. Better to be ignored, forgotten. Better to let the tigermoth die and fall apart before he was approached. Better to be safe, better to be slow and careful... *Better*, hummed the Youngest, soft under the words of her elders, *safer, better.*

Action, demanded the Vine Authorities, protected and impatient in their heartwood. *Investigate threat. Clear it. End disruptions.* The pack of scavengers shifted and the Youngest, intent on her song, lost her grip on the leaf and tumbled out into the space before the pack.

Six sixes of facetted eyes turned towards her. The Youngest curled herself small, aping childhood. The scavengers considered her for slow moments, then as one began to hum: *Go. Investigate. Report.* She dared not hesitate so close to the mandibles of her elders. Head tucked down, she flew obediently to the side of the great dying moth. His wings threw their shadows over her, his decayed musk choked her spiracles. She hovered, not wanting to come too close to the habitat, and behind her the elders hummed a threat. The Youngest set her front claws to the hatch and wrenched at it with all her strength. It gave way easily, gone to rust and bone and dropped away into the darkness around the station. Trembling, the Youngest crept into the sour space beyond and picked her way through the frost-scarred fragments of equipment. Here, an electric vein hung lose and flaccid; there, the skeleton of an aether-sensor gaped at the room. There was nothing left of value, unless some pampered collector sought possession of old dust. At the very rear of the habitat, bound to the ceiling by moth silk, hung the remnants of the pilot. The Youngest extended a foot, sniffing delicately through the air holes on its tip. Age and dirt and dying. She inched closer and, in its yellowed cocoon, the knot of bones twitched.

The Youngest leapt backwards, sending shards of consoles skittering. The cocoon twitched again, and then a long thin head broke through its end. The Youngest froze. Cracked white eyes peered at her; the stump of an antenna leaned towards her. She shuddered, felt her wings begin to hum her alarm.

Wait. The vibration was almost too slight to hear. Inside the cocoon, the pilot's wings struggled, setting its sides heaving. Its voice was a thin rattle, a ghost, a shred. *Hear*, it said, pale and low. *Listen.* Against all instinct, the Youngest crept closer. *Starflower*, whispered the pilot. *Moth knows. Bones know.* Another twitch in the cocoon, and a broken limb poked out. *Eyes know. Eat...eat eyes.*

The Youngest gave off a blast of terror, wings chattering and banging, scent peaking. The distant hum of her fellow scavengers grew sharper. The pilot struggled again in its cocoon, once, twice, three times. The cocoon bucked, rippled and tore: the pilot dropped to the smooth floor in a flurry of tatters. A lump of something dropped from between its middle legs, bounced, spattered flecks and specks of brilliance all around. The Youngest cried out as fragments struck her carapace and clung. Petals dropped around her, raw pieces of an unborn star. *Starflower*, whispered the dying pilot once more. *Bones know. Moth knows. Eat. Eat.*

The rumour flew out from SanWanWuShi on hasty moth wings, fluttered into ports and nodes, heartwoods and root-masses, spread its way through all the twists and bindings of Vine Space. A new flower, somewhere out there in the Deep Dark. A starflower, mother of light, birther of stars, a new centre from which a network of vine lines might grow. Prospectors and dreamers came from all directions, converged on SanWanWuShi with light moths and dark, great moths and small, in bands and clans and colonies, each of them hungering to claim the new flower and its promises. The Authorities could not contain them. SanWanWuShi's leaves drooped under their weight; its heartwood groaned and shivered. Almost before each new expedition sent forth into the Dark, another had come to take up its place. The port scavengers were amongst the very first to leave, each clutching a piece of the pilot's chitin tight against their own. The Youngest watched them go, one by one, on the moths they had stolen or begged. No one would sponsor her to fly with them, she was too young, too small, and her carapace was scarred with the marks of the star petals. She worked the leaves as before, finding and collecting debris before it damaged the vines and she watched the prospectors. Some used SanWanWuShi as a base, making careful reconnaissance flights into the Deep Dark and returning to log and collate their information. Some simply launched themselves out into the depths. But as the leaves grew and the hours passed, not one of them returned with the location of the new flower. At first, the hopeful crowded round the old moth as he hung in the leaf-shadow, studying the scars on his body, the holes in his wings, as if those might be read like a map. The old moth endured them, giving nothing away. In the down watches, the Youngest also crept to his side, to groom his flanks and weave patches for his wings. The moth gave nothing away, told them of nothing save his fatigue and age. The prospectors chattered their disdain and gave up on him. At last only the Youngest troubled with him, bringing titbits of simple foods, keeping the water vents filled. And under her carapace, her secret burned.

Eat. She had had scant seconds, once the petals dropped, before her elders rushed into the habitat to seize what they could. The pilot's body had been cut apart in instants, the fragments of flower gathered and hoarded. But under the plates of the Youngest's thorax a shard of eye was secreted. In her few private moments, she had darted forward and grabbed it as the pilot had demanded. The shard scratched her, irritated her, dragged at the movements of her front limbs and prevented her scales from lying as they should. She hunched herself about it, playing on her youth and expected timidity. And day on day she nursed and petted and watched over the old tigermoth. His smell of decay hung about her, and the denizens of the vine station avoided her. She did not care. Under her outer skin, the eye whispered to her of riches, of life, of success. *Starflower. Eat.*

Time passed and no flower was found though many prospectors were lost and many more wasted all their resources. But though they failed, replacements continued to arrive. And at last, many vine crowns of time after the old moth had limped into SanWanWuShi, he spoke to the Youngest as she curled up to stroke his wings. *Time*, he said, and his voice was soft as new leaves, *eat, mount, fly*. The Youngest was no longer afraid. With her front limbs, she tugged the eye fragment from under her scales and swallowed it. For a long moment nothing happened. Then, from within, heat began to grow. The Youngest reared up, batting her wings, convulsing as that glow began to spread. *Now,* shouted her scent, her sound, out across the station. *Come, follow, now.* Over her carapace, the petal scars lit up, cold and strong. She clung to the old moth, struggled her way into the remains of the habitat and the glow spun out over that also.

The tigermoth spread his great wings, taking up the call. *Come. Follow. Now.* Everywhere in SanWanWuShi activities stopped. The prospectors dropped their maps and their sap-bowls, their meals and their dances, and rushed to their moths. The authorities sat in their node, ignoring alarms and requests, staring out into the leaves. The tigermoth lifted off from his dock and set out towards the Deep Dark with long, slow wing beats. One by one, the prospectors followed in his wake, out into the cold where the aether grew thin and weak. On and on they flew, a great flotilla, drawn by the calling of that glow. The Youngest lay on the floor of the habitat, feeling herself burn, vibrating under the rush of wings. Somewhere out there, far ahead, something called back to her, called to the glow within and around her, lifted the moth, carried him outwards and onwards. The moth carried her up beyond the topmost frail tendril of the last vine, out to where the nearest stars were no more than specks of remembered light. The glow did not diminish; the old moth did not tire. Behind them, the prospectors struggled after, moth wings growing thin, limbs and carapaces flaking away in the cold. From time to time, debris tumbled past, perhaps shed from the convoy, perhaps wreckage left by earlier, lost explorers. The Youngest neither knew nor cared. That was not her job any more. She had no job, save to follow that deep sonorous call.

It thundered, whispered, rattled, sang. She rocked with the call, lulled and bound by the beats of the great moth's wings. Inside, she was heat and fire. Her whole body blazed, although she could not see that. Her eyes stared into the Deep Dark and, at last, found an answering glow. *There. Starflower.* Her cry echoed out through her train of followers, on and on, back and back, *Starflower. New starflower.* Now, the whole fleet could hear the call, the clear voice of new light, new growth. Their wings beat faster and the flower came into view.

There it hung before them, sole fruit of an ancient, blackened vine. Where that came from not one of them knew: the stem stretched back into the depths, thin and taut and leafless. But the flower... It hovered on the cusp of blooming, calyx lips parted to show a hint of petals. The great moth flew onwards, straight for the heart of the flower and the flotilla followed. From the Youngest came one last great burst of heat. The petals unfurled, vast and soft and darker than the deep itself.

The centre rippled, shimmered with a light that was not light. *New star*, cried the fleet, *new vine, new node.* Yet under their voices there was alarm. Surely no star before this one had ever awoken so dark, so chill? At the last moment before reaching the star's centre, the tigermoth veered aside, up, out, over the edge of the petals. The Youngest rolled, cried out as the edges of the habitat cut into her. The star shuddered again and began to breathe.

To inhale. The first breath took the vanguard of the fleet, still tracking the tigermoth. The star widened, inhaled again, swallowed down a second tranche of the pack. In tens and hundreds, it drew them in, drew out their energies into itself and grew, vast and dark and hungry.

In her broken habitat, the Youngest rejoiced and shook and shivered until the black corona reached out to suck her and the ancient moth also into its depths.

Lord of the Lyceum

Donna Scott

The vein in his temple throbbed; he focused his mind to push the pain down and away. No time, No time. Tonight was opening night: he couldn't claim a minute of the day for himself.

Bram gathered up the prompts in his arms, curved his little fingers round the arched handles of two flower baskets and, with no space for the third, clamped the handle between his teeth and pushed through the office door. A runner coming the other way flattened himself against the corridor wall to let him pass. Of course, Bram was a big man; not fat, but these backstage corridors were not built for a lady and her skirts, never mind the likes of this burly scrub-bearded man. Wonderful design, he thought: the spout of the kettle.

He poured into the green room and carefully set down the baskets on the one chair he could see that was not piled with clutter.

"My, you look like a setter; a red setter. Should be an Irish one, but there you go." Henry Irving was seated at a table, getting ready to sign a fresh pile of cabinet cards. Irving held the pen as though it were made of lead and seemed to be contemplating the black ink pool on the nib, watching it drip onto the blotter with fascination, shoulders rounded.

On the cabinet cards, Irving's pose was like a matador, hands on hips, head back and proud, but there was still no way of 'Kodaking' all that he could be on stage. There was no other actor in London, no, *in the nation* who could hold a candle to Irving's power, and yet he could pass through the streets of London like a shadow, if he so wished. A wonderful friend to have... of sorts.

"Oh Henry, you know they'll be queuing back a mile tonight." Papers fell from his hand, and Bram groaned as he saw them slip out of order.

Irving sighed. "It's perfectly fine. I have all the time in the world for this, whereas you... no one can ever be as busy as you, Bram. It's not humanly possible."

Bram took the implied instruction, quickly grabbed up the papers and busied himself out of the way. Yes, he had a lot to do. His main concern was front of house, but sometimes it was a case of 'all hands on deck', and tonight the house had more need for that than ever. One of the lights had broken; he would have to go back shortly and check that it had been fixed, make sure that he knew whatever the stage-manager knew for reporting back to Irving: had the shadows been painted on that last piece of scenery? If not, little Edy could do that; make sure the head carpenter was happy that all the ropes had been *made sure*, make sure everyone had their prompts, make sure the cast were all in house, make sure front of house had the right guest names... and Henry had arranged a post-performance gathering in the Beefsteak Room for a toast. Had the champagne arrived? Oh pray Irving would not pretend to forget his lines tonight, for Bram could say nothing, *nothing*.

Backstage was noisy with hammering, actors and actresses shouting lines to each other over the clamour, taking advantage of Irving's absence to cram the words in. Most people still had to act after all; only Irving could *be*.

The air was thick with sweat, hair oil and talcum, hemp-rope, paint and sawdust: the musk of the theatre. Ellen was at the back of the space thumbing through a copy of *Punch*. Bram muttered, "Excuse me," and made his way over to her. She began laughing.

"Not your usual reading matter, Nell?"

"Oh Bram, no. I do not read it. Only the cartoons."

She pointed at the page and showed him John Tenniel's latest illustration: A woman lay prone on the ground while a hideous bat-winged creature loomed over her: a creature with a hard stare… and a bushy beard. Beneath, the caption: *The Irish Vampire*.

"Oh," said Bram, for want of anything else.

"Isn't it just *ridiculous?*" laughed Ellen. "That woman on the ground is so obviously *me*, but I'm not sure what is meant by that monster. It might have Henry's eyes, I suppose, but that beard is *yours* if anyone's. Yet why would they be drawing *you?*"

"Well they haven't, have they? It is mere politics, and that macabre humour that is so popular these days… You know, Nell, you're not *always* the subject of *Punch's* cartoons—"

"No, but I'm often the object. Is Henry coming?"

"He'll be a while. Are you all set?"

"All I need is Henry."

"Good, good. Well, I am about if you should need me."

Bram walked off towards the stairwell that led to the dressing rooms, casting a glance back at Ellen. Her eyes looked wide today: perhaps it was a little of Margaret in her, to look so worried at a silly cartoon. Irving had wanted *Faust* and would have none but Ellen play the sweet, innocent Margaret; no girl could wear those chains so well when Irving played the devil.

The noise, the heat; Bram suddenly craved the outside air. He shoved his way past some young stagehands, through the corridors, breathing with effort as his palms slid on the frame of the stage door.

Outside, the light was sharp. Bram steadied himself and looked around. The back of the Lyceum theatre was deserted, the street noise muffled and distant, as though he were hearing things from inside a bell jar. He took out a handkerchief and wiped the sweat from his brow. Another world entirely existed here at the back of the theatre: sloped walls and stairwells crossed at odd angles; all was closed-in with dark brickwork, windows small and blank as sightless eyes. Later, this area would doubtless be thronged with ardent admirers of Irving's fearful Mephistopheles, and love-struck boyish men bearing bouquets for Miss Terry, but when there were no people around, what a little cauldron the space became, what a mousetrap!

A slight breeze cooled Bram's face momentarily and he heard a fluttering at his feet. Looking down, he could see it was a photograph: one of Ellen Terry's cabinet cards for the new production. In the photograph, her eyes were full of terror, her arms swaddled in the sleeves of her white robe as though she were an inmate of Bedlam, clasped hands shackled together, the chain swathed across her body. Bram picked the card up and tutted, hoping it had been left there for some accidental reason rather than because someone in the company was helping themselves to stock. Ellen's admirers had Bram's sympathy, but the accounts were down to him; a mere ha'penny-worth or not, he'd rather deal with a thief than one who wasted money through carelessness. He stuffed the card in his pocket and went back indoors.

By six o'clock the audience – and many who hoped to be among them – were queuing halfway down the Strand. Prior to the performance, the queues at the pisser were almost as long as everyone had suddenly realised at the last minute just how full their bladders were, and just how full the house was going to be. Bram had scarce enough time to attend to his own needs, being required both front and back of house. He had the final checks for the Beefsteak Room to attend to; another night of display for Irving's Artists' Benevolence Fund, the charity for "Decayed and Distressed Actors" as Irving had first called it, before Bram and others had persuaded him to change the title (though not before he had sent out numerous letters to important potential benefactors with the charity's name mentioned as such, much to Bram's chagrin).

Soon though, the house lights were down, and the spot was lit on the stage for Ellen. Bram watched from the wings. She was a virgin girl once more, smiling into the lights as a daydreamer smiles in the sunshine, all her sweetness conjured and focused, braiding the ends of her hair just as Goethe had described. Bram's nails dug into his palms. He could scarce breathe for watching her. This, *this*, was as powerful as her Ophelia had been. Excited, he tried glancing around to see who was in the audience: was Dodgson in? A fair review would be marvellous!

"Bram."

Irving had merely whispered, but Bram near forgot where he was and almost exclaimed... if Irving had spoken at all: the creature that stood there, pale-faced, formidable, would surely need no human words. It *was* Irving, of course: Bram had been present in the dress rehearsals, had seen Irving take this shape many a time. Bram nodded an acknowledgment and stepped back into the shadows, out of the devil's way.

When Irving stepped onto the stage, the air changed; the audience could sense some powerful magic at work, the gathering of thunderclouds. The lightning came when Faust tried to defy Mephistopheles, who cried out, "*I am a spirit!*" Irving looked to grow to a gigantic height – to hover over the ground instead of walking on it – marvellous what could be done with some discreetly-placed ropes. Bram, still watching from the wings, shivered; he grinned, thinking of the company's success, Irving's triumph. Then something strange occurred: Bram thought for an instant that he had seen his reflection in the opposite wing, as if there were a mirror there; the semblance of a man which, as Bram stared, resolved itself into shadows, into nothing. How odd, he thought, but then he realised he did perhaps feel a little tired and weak – and hungry.

The lights fell, then came up for the curtain call. The audience were in loud voice, near bellowing when Ellen and Irving took their bows. The stage was littered with loose flowers. Many bouquets would be presented backstage; those who wished for a personal word from their favourite actor and actress would need to run from the theatre to be able to get near the backstage door for the merest hope of gaining access. On opening night, they stood no chance! Conway, who had played Faust with considerably less skill than the part required, if Bram was honest, obliged the crowd with dutiful bows before leaving the stage to its true stars. The master and his stage wife had no need to act their triumph. Bram clapped them as they quit the stage and approached him in the wings.

"Bravo! Bravo!"

"Indeed, Bram," said Irving. "We shall have something to celebrate this evening, shall we not?"

"Of course. The diners are gathering as we speak." He beamed at Irving and Ellen. Her smile in return bore the semblance of Margaret's: girlish, pleasing. Bram frowned lightly. "And you, Ellen, you have plans?"

"Yes, with my children." She made a dismissive gesture. "Then I have letters to write. I want to get memories of tonight down while they're *fresh*."

"Good, good, well have a pleasant evening, Ellen" said Irving. "Bram, I will join you shortly in the Beefsteak Room. If you could tend to our guests?"

"Of course. Good night, Ellen."

"Good night."

Such soirées of Irving's were revivals of the old 'Sublime Society of Beef-Steaks' that used to meet in the room to eat beef and drink port – at least it seemed that way when the fellows met. Nellie Melba, Sarah Bernhardt and all the celebrated women of the day had been invited at one time or another for a little supper and reading in that room with Irving and his stage wife, but Irving had stipulated that this night was one just for the boys.

Bram had duly removed Whistler's paintings from the wall so that the artist wouldn't prattle about himself all night, and ordered in extra port.

The guest list for the Beefsteak Room read like a *Who's Who* of the art world: besides Whistler, there was John Singer Sargent, his pupil Walter Sickert, not to mention a significant connoisseur, young Eddy, who accompanied Sickert this evening, a rakish-looking chap with sly eyes and a soft mouth; pleasant enough considering he was a prince, Bram supposed. He was not entirely sure if etiquette required him to shake hands with Eddy on this occasion as he did with the others, it being a rather informal gathering, but Eddy saved him his doubts by extending his hand. Bram took it, trying not to grip too firmly. The party milled around the table, wineglasses in hand as they waited for Irving to make his grand entrance, which he could do, not because he was Master Mason, but because he was Mephistopheles and tonight was his night.

Irving flung open the door and strode into the velvet-red room, cape swirling, and made his way to the ornate President's Chair. A cheer went up from the assembled guests and Whistler began a chorus of 'For he's a Jolly Good Fellow' which seemed slightly incongruous given Irving's still-devilish appearance, though it did charm a smile from beneath his greasepaint sneer.

The wine was in full flow; the supper was brought in on a silver salver and placed before Irving to be served to the guests. In keeping with custom it was roast beef, served rare. Irving sliced into the deep pink flesh and forked slivers onto plates, near salivating as the juices oozed out: "A trifle underdone perhaps, but all the better for it."

"I'll say," said Eddy.

"A wonderful production tonight, Henry," said Whistler.

"Quite," Sickert added. "Your Mephistopheles was excellent, terrifying. Though I fear my heart now belongs to Miss Terry's Margaret."

"Your heart, Walter?" Eddy speared his beef with a fork.

"You told me quite plainly it was some other organ that the sight of Miss Terry had possessed."

Bram twisted the napkin in his lap. Sickert's response was a nervous laugh: "I'm sure I said nothing so blunt, Eddy."

"Yes you did. It was during that scene where Margaret takes her clothes off. It seems Miss Terry quite forgets there's an audience there and almost goes too far." His eyes widened. "It was wonderful. The front few rows looked quite mesmerised!"

Bram glanced over at Irving, trying to read his expression, but it was all shadow and greasepaint. Irving merely watched, swirling the liquid around in his wine glass without touching it to his lips even once. He would say nothing, then. It was up to Bram to intervene. "I am sure Miss Terry would be most displeased to hear that her *acting* had caused any distress to those of a genteel disposition in our audience—"

"Well, *I* was far from distressed, my good fellow."

"That is understood, but what I meant to say is that Miss Terry has worked tirelessly to raise the appreciation of actresses within *polite* society—"

"I dare say she has." Eddy took a swig from his glass. "I am full of admiration. I gather her Ophelia is a wonder to behold. Such sensuality! Such madness! Tell me, wasn't Miss Terry once also 'found drowned'?"

Bram scowled. "You saw her on stage tonight. She is quite alive."

"Indeed. Though I recall a story in *The Times* not so long back. A body had been pulled from the Thames that was thought to be hers. Of course, that was back when it was fashionable for whores to wash up in the river with their heads *still on*. Not like these days, eh, Walter?" he laughed. "I gather Miss Terry's own mother identified the corpse? Hadn't seen her for a while, thought she might end up in the drink... some shame that she'd run away from?"

Bram felt a knot in his stomach. Even Sickert looked to shift in his seat. "No shame of hers, Your Highness." Bram struggled to keep the disdain from his voice. "Miss Terry has a talent that convention should never have tried to subdue. Acting should be considered an art, no less a vocation, a higher calling, not a last refuge for the fallen woman. We are all here as its devotees – its abbots and abbesses. We are all about pretence, and yet, we hide nothing. I often wonder, Your Highness, if some people outside our profession can make the same claim?"

"Well," Eddy said and laughed, "they say honesty is the province of thieves and whores, so I would hesitate to make further comment." Before Bram could object, Eddy had raised his glass. Staring Bram hard in the eye, he proposed a toast to the Actors' Benevolent Fund before making a very generous pledge. All raised their glasses, though Bram's toast was somewhat muted.

Bram swallowed any retort down with the wine, then excused himself from the room for a few moments.

On coming back to the room, Sickert was waiting for him in front of the door. "Might I have a word?"

"Of course."

"I would just like to let you know, away from our esteemed friend there, that I hold in my heart only the utmost admiration for Miss Terry. I am afraid though that our friend has known a few *actresses* and thinks he knows them all."

"I see."

"Watching Miss Terry perform this evening, I was truly bewitched... her vulnerability..." Sickert swallowed. "Mr. Stoker, I must ask... I should be utterly delighted if you could arrange a private audience for me with Miss Terry." His face reddened. "She is, I'm aware, the muse for many an artist... but I am beginning to make quite a name for myself now..."

"You wish her to sit for you?"

"No, I should like to speak with her, that is all."

"Oh. Well, I cannot make any promise. As you can see, we have just embarked on a major production that will, I'm sure, pack the house out for months to come. There are always many people waiting to speak to Miss Terry after a performance, and she is bound to be very popular after *Faust*. I will do my best though."

"Thank you." Sickert hesitated for a moment before holding out his hand. There was no option but to take it.

The following morning, Bram had arranged to meet Irving and Ellen at breakfast in the green room. A lad was sent to fetch the newspapers, which he took an age to return with; meantime, the tea cooled in the pot and the kippers congealed on their plates.

Eventually, they heard the lad's boots as he approached the green room door. Bram snatched it open and grabbed the bundle from the open-mouthed boy. He threw the newspapers on a table and began riffling through them. Irving observed, lolling in a chair, while Ellen paced up and down, hands clasped under her chin.

"Have you found any yet, Bram?"

"No, Henry… wait, yes, here's one. What?"

"What is it?" cried Ellen. "What have they said?"

"*The Times* calls it 'clap-trap'. Clap-trap!"

"Stuff and nonsense," Ellen said, taking the paper from Bram's hands. "Ah, I see. They sent one of their idiots to write the review."

"Who is still full of praise for you, Ellen."

"Still an imbecile. Clap-trap indeed! I certainly don't think the rest of the audience thought that. They bellowed and cheered and stomped their feet – I thought my heart would burst!" She sighed.

"We'll be lucky to sell a single ticket tonight, then," said Irving.

"Oh Henry, don't be so dour," said Ellen, fetching her hat and pin from its box on the chair. "Only one course of action to take in such an instance as this."

"And that is…?"

"Henry, dear, don't be silly. I'm going shopping."

New gloves, Ellen had decided: the next best thing to new skin. Perhaps she would choose some more stationery; cream or blue, whichever looked the best. The air was paper-dry, gentle sunlight making everything seem green, fresh. A good day for walking around London, banishing critics from the brain. Oh Henry would be fine; he'd think of a cruel joke to play on some stagehand and displace the embarrassment. It was all very tiresome, really.

The centre of London was almost as busy as Christmas-time; a good excuse to head near the more select shopping areas and avoid the denser crowds. She strolled along Bond Street, paused a while outside an elegant window where jewelled cases were displayed on black velvet. Her eyes were reflected back to her as opals. She looked at herself, the wisps of copper-gold hair escaping from under her hat, her undone collar, which she fastened again and straightened. There was a man standing behind her, quite still while people moved around him. She turned and looked at him. He was just watching her, not smiling, not waving. Did she know him? Ellen couldn't be sure. The man then looked away. Perhaps he had not been staring after all. Ellen quickly looked down until he had moved off, strolling very slowly down the route she has just travelled.

Ellen continued walking in the direction of a shop that she knew sold the most exquisite gloves. No need to pause at the window; they would know exactly the sort of thing she wanted. She stepped inside the doorway and was greeted by the shop girls. Glancing out of the bow window, she could see the man standing on the opposite pavement. Surely he wasn't waiting for her to come out?

"Madam?" said one shop girl. Ellen smiled at her then turned back to the window. The man had gone.

At the Lyceum, Bram was taking the accounts down to Irving when he felt a breeze on his face. The papers in his hand fluttered. Had someone left a window open? He followed the source of the breeze; it led to the backstage door which was wide open. Bram tutted and was about to close it when he noticed something wedged between the inner and outer frame: another cabinet card. He pulled it out, cursing, then cursed again as he turned it over. It was another card of Ellen as Margaret, only this time the surface had been smeared with red and black paint, still slightly tacky to the touch. Worse still, the face had been scratched out using something akin to a blade or needle. Had any attempt been made at concealing this, Bram would have supposed it a curse, from a jealous actress perhaps, but like this? He looked out behind the Lyceum. The card may have been left like that hours before; the place was deserted now.

Ellen must never know.

The reviews had not deterred the eager theatregoers attending the Lyceum that night; if anything the numbers had increased. They spilled like blood through the Doric columns, their chatter sounding like the buzz of flies through the heavy curtains. Bram had been pacing around, checking the back door every few minutes, looking out for someone, anyone who shouldn't be at the back of house. Ellen had spent most of the time in her dressing room, but he saw her emerge every now and then, her gaze darting up and down the corridors.

She caught Bram watching her and smiled. "I am feeling all cooped up in here," she said.

"Soon you'll be on stage and free, little bird." Bram replied. He laughed as Ellen rolled her eyes at him and shut the door. It was good to know she was there, safe.

That night, Ellen's performance was crystalline, as though her gift were a diamond in her bosom, radiating through her and out to the world. As she trembled before Mephistopheles, Bram felt a delicious anxiety: his friend Irving was truly terrifying. Perhaps he was taking his poor reviews out on Ellen; the way he towered over her was unearthly. Once again, he felt privileged to be… what? Not exactly one of them. *Needed* by them, that was it.

Applause, applause! Then once more Bram was swept aside by the performers rushing past him to take their places on the stage. Blinking under the gaslight, the audience began to move from their seats, most slowly, but some racing along the rows to be able to make the backstage. Behind him, the stagehands were already at the rear doors, escorting a protesting man holding a bouquet back to the door. He felt a chill plunge within. He strode briskly to the doors. "Who is here? Who have you let through?"

"Mr. Stoker, sir," the elder lad began, "the only civilians back here are the guests of Mr. Irving. They have been taken through to the Beefsteak Room."

"The Beefsteak Room? The Beefsteak Room, lad? We had no supper guests planned for this evening!"

The lad gulped. "Mr. Irving said it was all right, sir. We left some ruby port in there for 'em."

Bram exhaled, rubbed the lad's arm. "No matter, Ben. Not your fault, I should have been told, is all."

He moved as quickly as his frame would allow to the Beefsteak Room and rapped on the door. There was no answer. He pushed open the door and could see the bottle of port on the table and two glasses, untouched.

Perhaps whoever it was had gone to the green room. He rushed back down the stairs and along the corridor until he reached it. The room was full of actors in full costume, chattering and knocking back wine. Irving was at the back in his favoured chair, re-reading the newspapers.

"Henry, Henry!" Bram pushed through the throng until he reached his boss. "Did you tell young Ben that you had guests, and to put some port out for them in the Beefsteak Room?"

Irving's greasepaint frown deepened. "No, Bram, I did not. Why? Has the lad been plundering my booze?"

"Hasn't touched a drop." Bram ran his fingers through his beard. "Have you seen Ellen?"

"I believe she is in her dressing room."

"Then I shall head that way. I will join you later, Henry."

Bram began pushing back through the room, feeling Irving's scowl on his back.

The corridors leading to the dressing rooms were empty; the distorted sound of carousing and banter carrying down from the green room. Bram reached Ellen's door. No sound came from within the room, but then Bram could mostly hear his own breathing, his heartbeat. He rapped on the door. There was no answer. He rapped again, before trying the handle. The door was not locked and swung open. There was an ambience to the room like powder settling, as though there had been a presence within just a fraction of a second before. Ellen's bustle dress lay on a peacock chair, draped as though she were sitting in it. Of Ellen though, there was no sign.

"Mr. Stoker?"

Bram turned round to see Sickert. In his hand he gripped a single rose, so deep a red it was near black.

"Sickert."

"It was perhaps audacious of me, but I thought I might call on Miss Terry whilst I was in the vicinity to offer my congratulations on another wonderful performance this evening."

"Audacious, sir?" Bram closed the door behind him. "This is a lady's dressing room."

"Indeed, indeed." Sickert lowered his eyes. "Though might I wait for her here?"

Bram flung up his hands. "Be dashed, fellow, no! Who was it that permitted you access to this area? And without an escort!"

Sickert's mouth moved as a goldfish's. "I-I-I came here by myself! I am *quite* familiar with the underbelly of the Lyceum. I painted enough scenery for you when I was younger. I am Lyceum through and through and know that guests are often permitted to meet the actors in their dressing rooms."

Bram tugged at his beard. What to do with the man...? "Might

I suggest we retire to the green room with the others, maybe have a slug of brandy? Miss Terry may have returned there."

Sickert's shoulders dropped.

Ellen was not in the green room, and neither now was Irving. They paused by the door as Bram stared into the crowded room, scratching his beard.

"Mr. Stoker, sir," Sickert began, "I imagine Miss Terry and Mr. Irving may have designed to dine in town this evening and have already stepped out. You have been burdened with my company for long enough now... I should really leave you be. I can find my own way out."

"Hold a moment, Sickert. This place is like a labyrinth. It is possible we have passed by them both and not noticed." Sickert was looking at him with an intensity he couldn't quite fathom. Bram narrowed his eyes. "I think we should keep looking, we're bound to bump into them sooner or later. Follow me."

The route took them back by the corridor that led to the backstage entrance. Ben was standing guard behind the closed door; the murmur of admirers from outside had begun to soften as the waiting crowd realised the Lyceum was admitting no admirers that evening and so had strarted to leave. The adolescent was nervous; Bram could tell from the dampness of the hair on the nape of his neck, and, as he turned, the bulge of his eyes. Bram and Sickert walked past, turned the corner and went along the corridor that led to the Beefsteak Room.

The President's Chair being a throne of sorts, Eddy had taken it and was leaning across the table, his wan face lit orange by candle flame; he had lit the candles himself, and was now pouring port from the decanter into the two glasses that had been left on the table. He proffered a glass: "Miss Terry."

"Your Highness." Ellen took the glass and set it down again.

"Miss Terry, it is a great honour to be in the company of England's finest actress."

"Mmm," Ellen touched the glass to her lips. "You have seen our play?"

"My dear, you are as talented as you are beautiful. You play to perfection."

He smiled for a little too long. Ellen sighed and cast down her eyes: "Your Highness, you flatter me, but I am afraid I have known too much sadness of late to be affected... death of love, and death... my art is all I have."

"Miss Terry. Ellen." He grasped her hand and she started, almost spilling her still-full glass. "I do not need to see you perform to know your art." He pulled her hand, quite sharply.

"Your Highness—"

"I am sorry, Miss Terry. Sometimes I do not know the extent of my own strength. I merely wish to... may I?" He took her hand and kissed it. Ellen remained steady, her smile tight. The prince gazed at her. "Miss Terry, the girl in you shines within the woman; that is how you can play Margaret with such intensity and conviction. If I could, I would immortalise you, so that the Lyceum would never lose you."

"I doubt it ever shall, Your Highness."

"So long as you remain in Irving's favour... yes? But what happens when he cannot have his Ophelia from you, his Juliet, his Margaret? When you have grey hair will those parts be yours?"

"I can play Lady Macbeth just as well."

The prince laughed. Then his fingernails were biting into her wrist. Ellen could not scream from the shock of this; she was pulled up onto her feet, the breath knocked out of her. The red room swirled in her vision, and she could feel the front of her robe soaked by warm, wet liquid, a ruby-coloured stain spreading over her breast, the glass singing through the air, drops flying, before crashing to the floor, before Ellen took one breath.

"Remember this, Ellen. You came to me because I willed it, because you willed it. You needn't be in Irving's power when a prince calls. You come to me."

Ellen saw his red tongue, his white teeth as he pulled her towards him. She thought of her children, Edy and Craig, somewhere in the Lyceum, wished she had hurried to be with them after the show. But she had not. She closed her eyes, but then, like a burning heat inside her, she felt her courage rise, and with a banshee cry used her strength to push the prince away. He was strong, but not so strong that she could not unsteady him, though he held tight to her wrist. He staggered back, pulling her with him, knocking into a painting.

For a moment, there was a pause and Ellen caught her breath. At any second, he could let go, apologise, begin to weep, but that moment passed and she watched in horror as his look grew thunderous. Shaking almost as much as she, he held Ellen's hand up to his face.

"You will bear my mark!"

With that he bit her. She felt his teeth pierce and crush her wrist. As she screamed, he sucked, hyperventilating, his pink-stained saliva stringing onto the carpet below. Ellen could feel the bruise coming; the pain growing dull instead of sharp – almost becoming bearable. Then, bizarrely, the prince released her wrist only to bite the end of her ring finger. Ellen cried out anew. She thought he would near bite off her fingertip. She tried to pull away again, but the more she did so, the more he gripped.

Ellen could scarce see through the pain, the tears in her eyes, though she knew that someone else was now in the room with them.

"Let her go!" Bram shouted, striding across the room to where the prince held Ellen, before Sickert ran in front of him.

"Stop! He is the son of the Prince of Wales! You cannot harm him!"

"Sickert, you idiot. I'm twice the size of both of you. Now get out of my way."

Sickert ducked, but not before Eddy had dropped Ellen and sped from the room. Bram hesitated for a moment, seeing Ellen bloodied and dishevelled.

"I'm fine Bram," she said. "Now go!"

Bram puffed like a steam engine, running down the corridors after the prince's shadow, but the prince was sprightlier and had soon made it to the backstage door.

"Hold, Ben!" Bram called out. "Don't open the door!" But Ben only hastened to let the prince through. Perhaps he had misheard?

Only two youngish men were still hanging around the door, and the prince shot through with such ferocity that they scampered from the locale with cries of "Spring-Heeled Jack!" not seeing the prince crash into a low wall and tumble down a stairwell.

Bram was silhouetted in the doorway. "Come out, Eddy. Show yourself!"

Wheezing, the prince emerged. "I'll wager I can still outrun you, Mr. Stoker." He spat a bloodied lump of spittle to the ground. "But there is no need for any of that. We are Brothers. Is that not so?"

Bram squeezed and unsqueezed his fists, cursed under his breath.

"You seem to be under some misapprehension." Bram and Eddy both turned to see the fearsome Mephistopheles, cape floating behind, eyes glowering. He seemed to grow taller as he spoke his next words: "You are enticed by the ritual and secrecy, yet think less of our moral code, our obligations. What is more, you seem to think the Lyceum is set up like some gentlemen's club, for those that do not wish to relinquish their hedonism. What you seem to forget..." and here he appeared to levitate, to almost float towards the prince, who stood round-eyed, round-mouthed. "What you seem to forget... the founding principle of our meetings here... and that principle is *meat!*"

With that Irving flew at the prince, who tried to run, but found all routes blocked by Bram and Irving. Finally Irving caught the prince, then, grasping his lapels, pulled the man's face close to his own. "Prince Albert Victor. Eddy. There are some things we shall never share, but there is one thing that we always shall and that is our vow to keep silent." Irving then ripped away the prince's shirt front. With a long fingernail, he made two swift cutting motions along his collarbone and neck. "Remember, Your Highness, to remain discreet. And stay away from my theatre! This is my domain!"

Irving released the prince, who with trembling hands drew his bloodied shirt back across his throat and refastened the pearl buttons as best he could.

"You are a fool, Irving. You will *die* in the theatre. It will use up all you have and you will grow old and weak and just *die*. Whereas I – I—"

"Whereas you will degenerate until you become a creature so loathsome and inhuman, none shall ever recognise you as a prince." He sneered. "I serve the Great Architect now."

With that, the devil-that-once-was turned on his heel and walked back to the Lyceum to where his faithful assistant and stage wife were waiting for him. As he reached the doorway, Sickert ran out from behind Bram, and so did young Ben (it was he who had told Ellen that the prince was waiting for her in the Beefsteak Room). The acolytes helped the crumpled prince to his feet and then assisted him towards the street where a cab could be found.

Epilogue:

Ellen's injury was so painful that she spent the rest of rehearsals wearing a sling, telling everyone she was suffering a whitlow. Her very next role was to be... Lady Macbeth.

Walter Sickert became a famous painter and remained friends with Eddy, 'introducing' him to some of his models... and doubtless you have already heard the tales of the troubles that *those* encounters led to.

Irving's *Faust* ran for twelve seasons, selling out every night. It was Irving himself who brought the production to an abrupt halt in the summer of 1888 out of consideration for heightened sensitivities in the wake of a series of grisly murders that had occurred in Whitechapel.

And Bram Stoker of course wrote *Dracula* – read it again and you will see that both Ellen Terry and Henry Irving are very heavily featured in it!

Fool's Gold

Sam Stone

The blood was what first alerted me to the problem. It just *smelt* wrong. So I dipped my finger in the congealing pool and lifted some to my lips. It tasted like milk with all the cream and goodness sucked out. Something was missing. At that point I wasn't sure what.

I'd been experimenting with blood for years. It was, after all, crucial to my survival. I'd realised that there were several types of blood, and each had a unique flavour. My favourite, and most rare, was later called Rhesus negative. This had a citric bite to it that appealed more to my once human taste than the sweeter 'O' positive – the common variety. Of course, when I was starving I didn't really care. But once I found Rhesus, it became a luxury I occasionally indulged in.

The dead girl's blood, though, lacked nutrition. All the integrity had been removed. I was hungry, but I knew after one taste that this thin, watery substance would never sustain me.

"Mmmm. Interesting," I murmured.

I heard a Peeler's whistle in the distance. Someone had raised the alarm. The girl must have died screaming. Not surprising really since her guts had been ripped out. It was obvious that the throat wound was there to shut her up; I'd have done the same.

I blended into the cold, damp fog and slipped into the shadows hanging around the nearest house as two Bobbies rounded the corner. For a moment their appearance was supernatural. The denseness of the air clung to the uniforms until one of them almost skidded in the rapidly spreading spillage and they came to a halt before the body. I shrunk back deeper into the mist; it wouldn't be good for them to find something like me at the scene.

They stared at the body for a long moment, as though paralysed, and then one of them turned his head and abruptly vomited on the ground. The other took off his tall hat and rubbed his forehead while wrinkling his nose in disgust at the odour his colleague had created.

"Jeee-zuss, Hobbs," he said. "That's a sorry mess if ever I saw one."

Hobbs dry heaved, his hands on his thighs.

"Pull yourself together."

The Peeler who'd spoken placed his hat back on his head and pulled out his pocket watch. He tutted, then began tapping his foot impatiently until his weak-stomached partner pulled himself upright, his trembling hand outstretched to the wall as he steadied himself.

"I'm alright," Hobbs murmured. "Just took me by surprise is all…"

"Well you better get over here and help me, 'cos I'm not examining her alone," the other replied.

Shaking, Hobbs wiped his mouth with the back of his hand.

"Yes, Bennett. I'm going to help… like I said, just shock is all."

Bennett waited impatiently as Hobbs fiddled with his tie, tugged his black jacket down and brushed invisible marks from his uniform while trying to compose himself. He'd already lost face with his senior colleague; he didn't want to lose anymore.

"So, what d'you think?" asked Hobbs.

Bennett crouched down; the air billowed around him as he

unwittingly mimicked my gesture by touching a chubby finger to the blood. "Still warm. He's nearby I reckon. Bet the murdering bastard is watching us even now."

Hobbs grew pale. Self-consciously I looked around. I hadn't even thought of that and I wondered now if the killer had seen me kneel down and taste his victim's blood. Careless.

"Same bloke?" Hobbs asked stepping forward with renewed curiosity, all sign of his earlier revulsion dissipated. A sickening gleam came into his eyes as he began to survey the crime scene.

"I think so," said Bennett, his mouth set into a thin line of distaste as he studied the woman's wounds.

"D'you think the papers will print our names?"

Bennett turned his head and glared at Hobbs for a moment. Hobbs didn't notice as he moved closer to the body.

Her throat was severed by two deep cuts, as though the first strike had failed to silence her. Her blood had dripped down her low-cut dress and over her bosom. It drew a line down to her abdomen where a long, uneven wound ripped through the faded and soiled dress, leaving a gaping, bloody hole. I'd noticed that some of her organs had been removed. The left kidney and a large part of her uterus were missing. The killer must have taken them for some perverse reason of his own.

"This don't look the same as the other one we found," Hobbs sulked. "I think it's a different killer."

"No," Bennett answered. "Look. The knife wounds on the neck... Bet he was disturbed on the other one, that's why he done this one."

Bennett turned the woman's head. The left side of her face was slashed. The knife had cut so deeply that part of her skull was visible. A clump of hair and flesh was sliced away right down to her eyebrow, where her eye stareed sightlessly from its socket.

"Fuck!" Bennett gasped, pulling back his hand in disgust.

Hobbs looked on dumbly as Bennett began to blow his whistle. In response, several running feet could be heard from all sides of Whitechapel and soon more Peelers poured into Mitre

Square.

I pulled a hood over my blonde curls and slipped away into the fog as the police surrounded the dead girl. No one noticed me, and if they had all they would have seen was a petite woman in a black cloak – nothing like the killer they were focussed on finding. But then appearances could be deceptive.

"Extra! Extra! Read all about it! 'Double event' as two more killed in Whitechapel."

I paid the newsboy and tucked the paper under my arm before crossing the busy street to a small park where I sat on my favourite bench. The fog from the previous night had lifted and the late September sun was shining weakly. I placed the paper across my knees and looked around. The park was quiet. It was as though the locals were afraid to be out alone, even in broad daylight. London was in a state of panic.

I shook the paper, straightening out the wrinkles with a small, gloved hand. 'Jack' had struck again. This time they were calling it 'The Double Event'. There had been two deaths that night. Elizabeth Stride, found in Dutfield's Yard, and apparently the woman I'd found in Mitre Square had been called Catherine Eddowes.

Jack claims two more in a double event. Four women dead so far...

The newspaper referred to them as women of 'questionable virtue' as though the common terms of 'whore' or the more formal name of 'prostitute' was too offensive for their readers. I looked back at the street again where the newsboy was rapidly selling his stack to passers-by. Humans loved the macabre. This was the most exciting news they'd had in a long time and the virtuous had no need to fear. They could hide at night, peeping through their shuttered windows while the destitute, like Annie Chapman, Jack's second victim, became nothing more than a ghoulish fascination. Perhaps tour guides would soon be touting for the 'Walk of Fear' to new world visitors and ghoulish locals.

Through the ages, serial killers had never been my concern, but one that could change the composition of blood, that was something else entirely. And so I had returned to the scene, shortly after the police took away Catherine Eddowes' body, and scraped up some of the dried blood that stained the pavement.

Back in my lab I'd mixed the blood with water to create a soft paste and smeared it roughly on a slide. Under the keen lens of the microscope, the blood had revealed some interesting facts. It was decomposing faster than usual because, as I'd expected, the composite had changed. The red blood cells were severely depleted. This was the most severe case of hypochromic anaemia I'd ever seen. One of the main minerals that helped the red blood cells reproduce, iron, was completely absent from Eddowes' blood. This accounted for the thin, tasteless, watery remains. If Eddowes' injuries hadn't killed her then the iron deficiency would have.

"Miss Collins."

I looked up from the paper and found my lawyer approaching across the park.

"Good morning, Mr Perry," I answered smiling.

"Good Lord, you aren't reading that gruesome stuff, are you?"

"One has to keep abreast of the times. Besides, it is important to be reminded that the streets of London are no fit place for a woman at night," I continued, giving him the 'expected' answer.

"What a sensible young woman you are, Miss Collins. Really one would believe at times that you held the wisdom of years in your youthful person."

I smiled politely at his patronising tone.

"Of course, I know your father was a doctor of some note, and I understand he did some pioneering research. I suppose that explains your interest in such things."

"Indeed, Mr Perry. Blood has long interested me," I remarked with a slight smile as I stood, leaving the newspaper on the bench.

"May I escort you home?" Perry said, offering his arm.

I glanced down at the paper, which was still open on the story. *Inspector Frederick Abberline said, 'We have many leads and several suspects that are helping us with our enquiries …'*

Interesting. Now I knew Freddie was involved I just *had* to shadow the police investigation. It would assuage my curiosity if nothing else and I'll confess to feeling a little nervous knowing there was a monster in town that was capable of contaminating my food source.

"Miss Collins?"

I looked back at Perry and found him scrutinising me carefully. Obediently I slipped my hand into the crook of his elbow. We walked slowly away from the park.

"Mr Perry, have you any news on the offer I made to purchase the house in Covent Garden?" I asked, quickly changing the subject.

"Why yes. That is precisely why I was so pleased to see you."

"I don't understand why this is of interest to you," Frederick Abberline said.

He was sitting behind his desk trying hard to look professional, but I noticed the slight tremble of his tightly clasped hands as he placed them before him on the desk. Oh yes, Freddie would tell me everything I needed to know. I smiled.

"Freddie, you know I've always been curious about your work. Do you really have suspects?"

"Miss Collins… Lucy. I can't discuss police matters with you. That would be highly inappropriate."

Frederick kept his face serious; it was part of his appeal. When he was angry with me he always took on the austere countenance of a bank manager and he had good cause to be annoyed. I hadn't been near him for months.

"Freddie…" I moved closer, touched his arm.

"Oh my God, Lucy," he cried as his composure broke.

His hands reached for me as he tried to rise from his chair to take me in his arms.

I stayed him with one hand on his shoulder, pressing him firmly back into his seat.

"No."

"When? When will you take from me again?" he begged.

I'd fed from Freddie several times over the years. We'd met on the streets before his promotion to Inspector. He'd mistaken me for one of the local whores until I bit him and drew his sweet nectar into my mouth for the first time. Frederick was the walking blood bank of my favourite brand. My luxury. My Rhesus donor. Though I'd made the mistake of revisiting him too often and now he was somewhat addicted to my bite; he craved it and unlike my other donors, he always remembered it.

"Soon, Freddie. But you know it can't be too often," I soothed.

"Tonight, please…"

I looked into his eyes knowing if I wanted to I could take every little bit of information about the case directly from his mind. But that wouldn't be much fun and I was starving; I hadn't eaten in days.

"All right. You help me and I will help you."

He pulled me to him and I let him kiss me. I didn't remind him about Emma, his wife. That would have been too cruel, even for me.

I walked the streets of Whitechapel every night for more than a month but all remained quiet. It seemed that Jack's frantic killings had ceased and it wasn't long before the whores of the city fell into a false sense of security once more. Even so, many had ceased doing trade out in the open. As I searched the city, I rarely saw the frantic rutting in the back alleys and corners of quiet streets anymore. The girls were taking clients back to their tiny hovels now. The occasional drunk and the Bobby on the beat were the only midnight occupants of the mausoleum streets.

"What are you doing out on your own, Miss?"

The Peeler was standing under a gaslight watching me quietly. He looked jaded. He was holding a small lump of rock, which he turned over and over in his fingers in a subconscious gesture to allay his boredom. The light hit the rock as it moved; it had the shine of precious metal.

"Nice respectable lady like you shouldn't be out here with that monster on the loose," he continued.

"I'm not afraid of monsters," I answered quietly.

"'Ere. Where you from? That's a nice little accent you got there. French are you?"

"Italian." I smiled walking towards him. I was suddenly very hungry.

"Long ways from home then?"

"Yes."

He continued to play with the rock as I approached him. I reached out and held his hand briefly, taking the stone from his compliant fingers. His mouth opened and froze in an 'O' shape as he met my gaze. I knew the gaslight would make the green in my eyes seem like cool fire.

"What is this?" I asked, opening my hand to gaze down at the rock breaking his paralysis.

"Fool's gold," he smiled. "There are bits of it scattered all over the city."

The rock gleamed. It was hard with shiny brass-yellow crystals peppering its surface. It looked and felt like a gold nugget.

"It's iron see," continued the Bobby. "Something happens to it to make it look like gold. Then a 'fool' might believe it's the real thing."

I knew what fool's gold was but I let him speak.

"… and you're no fool are you?" I flirted. "You say there have been many of these found around the city?"

"Yes. The Chief said it's because of the meteor shower we had a few months ago. D'you remember that, Miss?"

I nodded. I remembered the night well. It was in mid-May, I

was out hunting when the sky lit up and tiny balls of flame flew across London. I knew instantly that a small meteor had entered the Earth's atmosphere and was breaking up. It was quite a display, reminding me of the fireworks on Queen Victoria's coronation day.

"Reckon we are only just finding the remains of it now," the Peeler continued. "Keep this if you like."

I looked at the Bobby. He wasn't very old, maybe twenty-five. I sniffed the foggy, damp air around him. Despite the freezing, autumn weather, his body smelt warm in his big coat. I could feel the rush of blood in his veins as he noticed my scrutiny. I dropped the hood of my cloak back from my golden hair and felt the gaslight touch my scalp.

"You're a very pretty lady," he said quietly. "If you don't mind me saying."

"I find you very appealing too." I was famished and the pull of his blood made tiny hairs stand up on the back of my neck.

I stepped back out of the halo of the gaslight into the shadows as my teeth began to lengthen. The Bobby followed me meekly. I slipped the nugget of fool's gold into a pocket inside my cloak and took his hand. His body began to shudder as he felt the waves of blood lust trickle into his skin. I pulled him into a nearby alley and pressed him against the wall rubbing my body against him in a desperate gesture as I sniffed at his throat again. His blood smelt clean. One had to be so careful these days. His hands were inside my cloak and all over my body. I let him touch; it meant nothing to me as long as I fulfilled my needs. I felt his hand lifting my skirt and he spun us around so that I was now against the wall. With one hand, he reached down and unbuttoned himself, then yanked roughly at my undergarments until they fell around my ankles. He knelt then, helping me disentangle one leg from my pantaloons. He obviously used the whores on a regular basis and knew just what to do.

He lifted my legs, bracing me against the wall, and wrapped them around his waist, pushing inside me as hard and fast as he could. I let him rut for a moment, while I licked his throat. He shuddered at my touch. His sweat tasted of salt. I could feel the blood rushing beneath the skin, throbbing there. I listened to its call until I couldn't bear it any more. When I grew bored of having my back pounded into the hard wall, I sank my fangs deep into his straining neck. I sighed with pleasure. He went flaccid immediately and his member slipped uselessly free. He slumped against me. I was powerfully excited and I gripped my legs hard around him as I swallowed the blood I needed until I felt the strength leave his limbs. Then I put one leg down to steady us as he weakened. His eyes fluttered closed, and his mouth smiled in pleasure, as I gently licked at his throat. My saliva closed the puncture marks and stilled the flow of blood.

I propped him up against the wall and kneeled between his legs, buttoning him up before I left. He'd wake with a headache and the vague memory of having been with a whore in the alley – nothing more. There wouldn't be any marks by morning.

I pulled my cloak tight around me as I walked away and the fool's gold bounced against my leg. I took the rock from my pocket. Smelt it. Licked it. Iron: one of the flavours I liked most in blood, and, let's be honest, after three hundred years of living on it I am a bit of a connoisseur. I knew there had to be a link. Iron was missing from the victim's blood and fool's gold was being found around the city. But what did it mean?

I'd persuaded Freddie Abberline to let me see the body of the other victim, Elizabeth Stride. There had been a distinct lack of iron in her blood too, but not as much as Catherine Eddowes', which confirmed the police assumption that the killer had been disturbed while working on the first one. But I couldn't explain to Freddie what I knew, even though I wanted to help him solve the crime. The thing was, if this person – and I suspected it wasn't human at all – was able to drain one of the most important nutrients from blood, then its very existence was a threat to my future. I had every intention of finding this predator before the police did. There was only room for one monster in London and that was me.

"There was another one last night," Freddie said, as we lay naked in the large double bed of my suite at The Waldorf. "It was the worst I've yet seen."

"Mutilated?" I asked, licking his throat gently. The bite wounds in his neck healed and faded until two pale pink scars remained.

"Yes," Freddie sighed, as he snuggled deeper into my arms, "and... he'd slit her throat until he'd almost cut her head clean off."

"I see."

On the 9th November, 'Jack' had struck again. It was Saturday afternoon when I heard the news of Mary Jane Kelly's brutal murder at Miller's Court. Freddie told me how the girl's abdomen was emptied of most of her vital organs.

"The killer even took the heart this time," he continued.

"It seems more frantic, more desperate."

"Yes. That's what we think. I'm dreading the next one. But how much more can he possibly do to them?"

"It's interesting how you say 'he'," I murmured. "Couldn't the killer be of any gender?"

Freddie stared at me, horrified.

"No, I can't even bear to think that. To consider a man capable of such brutality is one thing. I couldn't even contemplate that kind of sickness in a female!"

If only Freddie knew. A monster can appear in any guise. I was a classic example. I supposed he thought my penchant for drinking blood was a sexual perversity but I hadn't always allowed my victims to live. Humans have such a selective grasp on reality.

That evening I went to Miller's Court and surveyed the crime scene. A policeman had been posted outside, presumably to keep the curious away, but I waited until he left his post for a hot toddy at the nearby tavern, and slipped in unseen.

The room was tiny. Mary Kelly had lived a solitary life in a single room with little more furniture than a bed, a small sideboard and a tiny table with one chair. Near the open fire was a small pot that she used to cook her meagre meals. Kelly had been all but destitute, like most women on the streets, but she at least had a dry place to sleep.

There was a strong odour in the room. Metallic. I touched the blood-soaked mattress of the bed. The blood was in the same condition as the other victims I'd seen, thin and depleted. I bent and sniffed the bed, detecting the iron deficiency; and then something glittering caught my eye. I turned to look at the fireplace. Among the ashes of the now dead fire, something gleamed. Walking to the fireplace, I looked down. *All that glitters is not gold* ...A large lump of fool's gold, oddly shaped like a human heart, blinked in the soot as light from the street filtered in through the slightly parted curtains on the window. I scooped it up and rubbed the ash away on the corner of my skirt. Black blood oozed over my fingers. I looked closely. So this was Mary Kelly's heart, oxidised and transformed, half iron, half human flesh. I dropped the mutated flesh back into the ashes and knelt to light the fire. I wanted to burn this monstrosity.

The fireplace was big and the chimney wide and sprawling. I heard the wind howling across the top and felt a breeze filter down into the room as I reached for the half-open box of matches on the hearth. I lit a taper and glanced up into the chimney but could only see as far as the first bend. It had been newly swept but a tiny glittering fragment could be seen perched on the corner. And then there was another gleam of light there.

I frowned. Something moved. I heard a shifting deep inside the chimney and a fine dusting of soot fell on my upturned face.

Then, golden eyes opened to stare down the chimney.

I fell back seconds before a knife-like iron claw swung at my face leaving a trail of rust particles in the air in its wake. The creature crawled down towards me, its imposing, impossibly stiff, wormlike body clattering down. Bits of iron pyrite broke off into the fireplace as it emerged with a mournful cry.

I backed away and in the shadow of the room I could barely make out the creature until the front part of its body reared up before me. The head almost touched the ceiling. The torso was a deformed mess. I could see human organs, partially absorbed, protruding from its body. A female uterus, the fallopian tubes ripped and jaggedly unattached were sprouting from the arm of the creature, and I realised that the monster had been incorporating the organs somehow. A claw swung again. I dived to the left, rolling across the room. The arm smashed into the wall, shattering the sharp blade at the end of the appendage. The monster roared in rage and pain. Howling, it rolled and thrashed on the floor, smashing the snake-like body into furniture. This made the being cry all the louder. I stepped back and crushed myself against the door narrowly avoiding the claw that reached for me. This time the arm thudded against the window, breaking a pane of glass while ripping the tattered curtains from the wall. Gaslight poured in through the exposed window with a rush of cold, foggy air. The being groaned and writhed as the damp air swirled into the room. Swivelling and writhing the creature tried to drag its damaged body back to the fireplace.

It all began to make sense. Fog *stung* the being's body like acid; corroding and rotting the metallic limbs even as I watched. Every particle of the iron-based composition was rusting away. The smog and damp of the London atmosphere was poison and, I speculated, this was just the final stages of a deterioration that had been occurring with frequent exposure: this explained the insatiable need to replenish iron and the fool's gold deposits scattered over the city. On instinct, I edged to the window, twisted the catch and threw the window as wide open as I could.

A gust of wind rushed into and through the room. The monster thrashed and doubled over. A damp miasma poured in, as though drawn to the creature like a magnet. The smog settled over the head and torso, eliciting a cry so sorrowful that my heart could not help but respond to the agonised sob. The creature tried to nurse broken and decaying limbs against a collapsing body. The fool's gold glint gradually dulled to brown rust as the metal oxidised. The pained cries ceased. Golden eyes glared in fury from a bulbous, deformed head as the carcass shrivelled; I sank to the floor below the window and watched.

An hour or more passed. No one came despite the commotion and I reasoned that they must have been too afraid, or that the lure of the tavern was too great on a cold night. The being had shrunk dramatically and now resembled a large, half-human foetus. The stolen human vital organs fell away as it rusted. I looked into a gaze that cried out to me. The monster wanted to live. In a flash of empathy I realised that this was nothing more than an alien child, probably stranded during the recent meteor shower.

Hunger and the will to survive drove even humans to animalistic instincts. I understood that more than most. The deaths of the women were borne of desperation. 'Jack the Ripper' was a starving baby, who only wanted to be fed the basic nutrients needed in order to endure.

The creature's eyes dimmed as its body oxidised. The damp, misty air from the chimney and window continued to blow around the body. The creature's chest cavity crumpled inwards, a burst of red dust puffing up into the atmosphere as the final breath huffed from the open torso. The being's slash-shaped maw gaped in a final silent cry and the fool's gold light went out finally from the pitiful gaze. With a shudder, the corpse disintegrated into a pile of red-brown rust.

I looked closely at the remains. A breeze picked up outside and a rush of air came down the chimney. Glancing back up the flue I could only surmise that the creature had sought heat and warmth where it could, even as the damp, London fog had slowly oxidized the alien flesh until it rotted away to nothing. The agony of the alien's death reverberated in my mind. A confusion of inarticulate screams left my body aching as I shook my head in a subconscious gesture. I wanted to wipe away all that I'd heard in those last few moments, but the memory stayed with me long into the night.

Opening the door I let in more of the London fog. On the floor the rust stirred and dispersed. Swirling like fallen leaves in the strong autumn breeze, the dust scattered, leaving no trace of the monster that had once been.

Leaving Kelly's house I headed into the fog. In the tavern I could see the bobby, who'd tired of guarding the crime scene, enjoying his drink in the company of several women of the night. 'Jack' was no more, and yet no one in this world but me would ever know who or what he had been.

I felt no remorse.

There really is room for only one monster in the city.

Wuthering Bites

Transcribed from the original manuscript
by Jon Courtenay Grimwood

Having moved to Thrushcross Grange in the Winter of 1801, I return from visiting my landlord, the only neighbour I shall be troubled with. In all England, I do not believe I could fix on a place so completely removed from society. A misanthropist's heaven: and Mr Heathcliff and I are a fine pair to divide the desolation between us; although I mean to have it to myself in time. He little imagines how I delight to behold his black scowl as he raises his lantern when I ride up. I know, what he does not, that I am not the first of my kind to use these roads.

"Mr Heathcliff?"

His expression says, 'Go to the Devil.' The gate he leans on moves not at all. I think this determines me to force an invitation. Here is a creature reserved as myself.

"Lockwood –" I state, before remembering my factor rented the grange from Mr Heathcliff entirely in his own name. Titles can be dispensed with. *Lockwood Ruthven* carries scandal already. There are only so many times I can be called *the dark lord* without starting to take it personally.

"My factor dealt for me."

He nods sourly.

When he sees my horse push at his gate, he puts out his hand to unchain the lock. "Enter then," he growls, little knowing he gives me run of his house, bleak as it is. "Joseph," he calls. "Take Mr. Lockwood's horse and bring some wine."

Joseph is old, very old. "Leave now," he whispers.

When I shake my head he shakes his own in peevish displeasure, while relieving me of my horse. Looking so sour I decide he must have trouble digesting his dinner.

Wuthering Heights this house is called. *Wuthering* being a provincial adjective, descriptive of tumult and storms. Pure, bracing ventilation they have up here at all times. The architect had sense to build the farm strong: the narrow windows are deep set in the walls, the corners defended with jutting stones. Wind-blasted trees lean towards the house on one side, and away on the other.

I doubt I've seen a residence this bleak since I took a crumbling villa on the shores of Lake Geneva once owned by a Calvinist lunatic, whose nephew was John Milton's lover. A fact you will find in neither the biographies of our greatest poet, nor guides to that strange city.

Before entering, I pause to admire a grotesque carving over the front door. Above which, among a wilderness of crumbling wolves and shameless little boys, I detect the date *1500*, and the name *Hareton Earnshaw*.

I would request a history from its surly owner; but Heathcliff's scowl demands my speedy entrance, or complete departure, and I have no desire to aggravate his impatience yet.

Above the chimney in the family room are sundry villainous old guns, and a couple of horse-pistols. The floor is of smooth, white flagstones; the chairs, high-backed and primitive, painted green. One or two heavy black ones lurk in the shade. Under the dresser reposes a huge, liver-hued hound, surrounded by squealing puppies. Other hounds haunt the room's recesses.

The room would be nothing extraordinary if belonging to a

homely, northern farmer, with a stubborn countenance, knee-breeches and gaiters. Such men sit in their armchairs, their mugs of ale frothing on round tables before them, everywhere in these hills. But Mr. Heathcliff is different. Dark-skinned, he dresses like a gentleman. That is, as much like a gentleman as many a squire. Slovenly perhaps, but not looking amiss in his negligence.

I take a seat, and fill an interval of silence by attempting to caress the hound, who has left her pups, and now sneaks wolfishly towards me, her lip curled up, and her yellowing teeth watering. My act provokes a long snarl.

"Let the bitch be," Heathcliff growls, baring his own teeth. "She will despise your kindness." He shrugs, carelessly. "She's always despised mine." Striding to a side door, he shouts, "Joseph!"

The old man yells from the depths of the cellar, but gives no sign of ascending; so his master goes down, leaving me with the bitch and a pair of grim sheep-dogs. Not anxious to be discovered I sit still. But, imagining she will scarce understand my insults, I curse her instead. My words being so irritating, she breaks into a fury and begins the change before my eyes. As she rise to her back legs, her muzzle shortens; I believe I grin at this monstrousness. Breasts grow, teats still hidden by wolfish hair, claws become twigged fingers. She turns to something near human on the cold stone in front of me.

"Know your place," I hiss.

She snarls and I fling her back, hastening to interpose a table between us. This arouses her pack: half-a-dozen four-footed fiends, of various sizes, issuing from hidden dens to the common centre. She alone changes; and parrying the bitch as effectually as I can with a poker, I am constrained to shout for assistance from her master in re-establishing peace. There are rules to be kept, even if Mr Heathcliff seems ignorant of them.

He and his man climb from the cellar with vexatious slowness. So slowly, the bitch begins changing back by the time I hear grumbling on the stairs. I don't think either moves one second faster than usual, though the room around me is an absolute tempest of worrying and yelping.

Happily, an inhabitant of the kitchen comes to my rescue. A lusty dame, with tucked-up gown, bare arms, and fire-flushed cheeks, rushes into the room flourishing a frying-pan: and uses it – and her tongue – to such purpose, the fury settles, and only she remains, heaving like a sea after a high wind.

"What the devil is the matter?" demands Mr Heathcliff on entering, eyeing us in a manner I can ill accept after this inhospitable shock.

"What indeed!" I mutter. "A herd of possessed swine could have had no worse spirits in them than that bitch of yours!"

"I said don't pet her," he remarks, putting wine before me, and restoring the displaced table. "She has her ways. Take a glass with me?"

"No, thank you."

"Not bitten, are you?"

"If I had been, I would have set my signet on the biter." At which, Heathcliff's countenance relaxes into a grin.

"Come," he says, "you're flurried. Here, take a little wine. Guests are so exceedingly rare in this house that I and my brood, I am willing to own, hardly know how to receive them. Your health, sir?"

I bow and return his pledge; beginning to perceive it would be foolish to sit sulking and wondering if he is simply ignorant of his hound's true shape. My kind and hers have long been at war. The reason is simple. We control our natures, they never can and resent us bitterly. She must be ancient though to live out her span in such changed state.

The next evening sets in grey, misty and cold. I have half a mind to spend it by my study fire, instead of wading across mud and blasted heath land to Wuthering Heights. However, on mounting the grange stairs with this lazy intention and stepping into my study, I see a servant-girl on her knees, surrounded by brushes and coal-scuttles, raising dust as she deals with heaps of cinders. Her shoulders are set low, her haunches raised high.

I could take her there, with or without her will.

The thought drives me out immediately; I take my hat, and, after a four-mile walk, under cloud-filled night, arrive at Heathcliff's garden-gate just in time to escape the first feathery flakes of a snow-shower.

On that bleak hill-top the earth is black frost, and the wind would make an ordinary man shiver through every limb. Being unable to remove the chain, I jump over, and, running up a path bordered by straggling gooseberry-bushes, knock for admittance, until my knuckles tingle and the bitch inside howls.

The door is locked.

Cursing the howling bitch, and deciding her species deserves perpetual isolation for its churlish inhospitality, I grasp the latch and shake it vehemently. Vinegar-faced Joseph juts his head from a round window in the barn.

"What are ye for?" he shouts. "The Master's down in the fold. Go round by the end of the lane if ye want to spake to him."

"Is nobody inside?"

"There's no one but t'missis. She'll not open even if you make that din all night."

"Can't you tell her who I am?"

"Not me! I'll have no hand in it," he yells, vanishing.

I seize the latch to essay another trial, when a broad-shouldered young man without coat and shouldering a pitchfork appears behind me. He growls I'm to follow him, and, after marching through a wash-house and pigeon-cot, brings me to the huge room I was in yesterday. It glows in the light of an immense fire, compounded of coal, peat, and wood. And near the table, laid for a plentiful evening meal, I'm pleased to see the 'missis,' mentioned earlier.

She is barely more than a child. Fair ringlets fall over bare shoulders. Her neck is long and – I confess, at this point I have to look away.

"Madam."

I bow and wait, thinking she will bid me sit. She stares instead, leaning back in her chair, and remains motionless and mute.

"Rough weather!" I remark. "I'm afraid, Mrs Heathcliff, the door must bear the consequence of your servants' slow attendance: they had hard work hearing me."

She never opens her mouth. I stare, she stares also: at any rate, she keeps her eyes on me in a cool, regardless manner, exceedingly embarrassing and disagreeable.

"Sit down," says the young man, gruffly. "He'll be in soon."

I obey; and call the bitch, who deigns at this second interview to move the extreme tip of her tail, in token of owning my acquaintance.

"Do you intend parting with her brood, madam?"

"They are not mine," she replies, her tone colder than Heathcliff himself could have managed. "You should not have come," she adds, rising and reaching from the chimney-piece for the painted canisters.

Her position before was sheltered from the light.

Now, I have a clear view of her whole figure and countenance. She is slender, and, as said, scarcely past girlhood: an admirable shape, and the most exquisite face that I have had the pleasure of beholding. Small features, very fair; flaxen ringlets, or rather golden, framing that enticing neck.

Her eyes, were they agreeable in expression, would be irresistible: fortunately for my susceptible heart, the only sentiment they show hovers between scorn and a bitter desperation, unnatural in one so young. The canisters are out of her reach, so I move to aid her and she turns on me, as a miser might turn if one attempted to assist him in counting his gold.

"I don't need your help," she snaps. "I can manage for myself."

"I beg your pardon!" I reply.

"Were you asked to tea?" she demands, tying an apron over her neat black frock, and standing with a spoonful of the leaf

248

poised over the pot.

"I shall be glad to have a cup."

"Were you asked?" she repeats.

"No," I say, half smiling. "You are the proper person to ask me."

She flings the tea back, spoon and all, and resumes her chair in a sulk; her flat forehead corrugated, and her red under-lip pushed out, like a child's about to cry; salt water wells in those beautiful blue eyes and is blinked furiously away.

Meanwhile, the young oaf has slung on a decidedly shabby upper garment and stands before the blaze, looking from the corner of his eyes, for all the world as if there is some mortal feud unavenged between us.

I begin to doubt he is a servant, though his dress and speech are crude, entirely devoid of the breeding observable in Mr and Mrs Heathcliff; his thick brown curls are rough and uncultivated, his whiskers encroach bearishly on his cheeks, and his hands are calloused like those of a labourer. But his bearing is free, almost haughty, and he shows none of a domestic's assiduity in attending the lady of the house.

Whatever the answer, he cannot think to challenge me. Glancing towards the bitch, unseen by the scowling sulking child in the chair, I catch the young man's eye.

"Your mother?"

His fists tighten, then slacken as he forces himself to relax, the monumental effort of will flooding his face with a sanguinary hue. In the absence of clear proof of his status, I decide to abstain from noticing him altogether. And, five minutes afterwards, the entrance of Heathcliff relieves me, in some measure, from the oaf's crude company.

"You see, Sir, I am come!" I exclaim, adding, "I fear I shall be weather-bound this half hour, if you can afford me shelter during that space."

"Half an hour?" he says, shaking white flakes from his coat. "I wonder you should select a snowstorm in which to wander. Do you understand the risk of being lost in the marshes? People familiar with these moors miss their road on such nights. There is no chance of a change at present."

"Perhaps I can get a guide among your lads, and he might stay at the Grange till morning. Could you spare me one?"

"No, I could not."

"Oh, indeed! Well, then, I must trust to my own sagacity."

"Umph!"

Ignoring our exchange, the oaf shifts his ferocious gaze from me to the young lady. "Are you going to make tea?"

"Is *he* to have any?" she asks, appealing to Heathcliff.

"Yes, damn it," the man hisses, words so savage that I start. The tone in which the words are said reveals a very bad nature. I no longer feel inclined to trust this man, if I ever did. When the preparations are finished, he says:

"Now, Sir, bring forward your chair."

We all, including the oaf, draw round the table. A grim silence prevailing while we drink our tea. Since I have caused the cloud, I feel it my duty to dispel it. They cannot, every day, sit so grim and taciturn; and it is impossible, however vile-tempered they might be, that the universal scowl they wear is their everyday countenance.

"It is strange," I say lightly. "How custom fixes taste. Many cannot imagine the existence of happiness in a life of such complete exile from the world as you spend, Mr Heathcliff. Yet, I'll venture, that, surrounded by your family, and with your amiable lady as the presiding genius over your home…"

"My amiable lady!" he interrupts, with an almost diabolical sneer on his face. "Where is she? This amiable lady?"

"Mrs Heathcliff, your wife." I say innocently.

"Well, yes. You suggest her spirit has taken its post of ministering angel, and guards the fortunes of Wuthering Heights, even when her body is gone?" The bitterness in his voice would have soured milk.

Finding myself in an obvious blunder, I nod placatingly. There is, my nod says, too great a disparity between the parties to make it likely they are man and wife. One is about forty: a period of mental vigour at which men seldom cherish the delusion of being married for love. The other not seventeen.

A new understanding shows in my countenance.

The oaf at my elbow, who is drinking tea from a saucer and eating his bread with unwashed hands, must be her husband. Heathcliff junior, of course. Here, my expression suggests, is the consequence of being buried alive. She has thrown herself away from sheer ignorance that better exists.

The last reflection may seem conceited to them. It is not. My neighbour at the table borders on the repulsive. I know, through experience, my kind are tolerably attractive. To a young girl like this, sometimes oppressively so.

"My daughter-in-law," says Heathcliff. As he speaks he shoots a vicious scowl in her direction. A look of pure hatred, unless he has a most perverse set of facial muscles that will not, like those of other humans, interpret the language of his soul.

"Ahh," I remark lightly, turning to the oaf. "So *you* are her favoured possessor?" At which he grows crimson and clenches his fists, with every appearance of an impending assault; but he disappoints me, smothering his fury in a brutal curse. Obviously, I appear not to notice…

"Again," observes my host; "unhappy conjecture, Sir. Neither of us have the privilege of owning your good fairy. Her mate is dead. I said she was my daughter-in-law: therefore, she must have married my son."

"And this young man is——?"

"Not mine, assuredly." Heathcliff smiles, as if it is rather too bold a jest to attribute the paternity of that oaf to him.

"My name is Hareton Earnshaw," the oaf growls. "I counsel you respect it!"

"I've shown no disrespect," is my reply, smiling at the solemnity with which he announces this. And then I remember why it sounds familiar. It is the name carved over the front door, above the date 1500.

Three centuries ago.

A descendant or the original? If the latter, how old does that make his dam? That liver-hued bitch watching me sharp-eyed from her retreat beneath the huge dresser; she fixes her eye on me longer than I care to return her stare, for fear one of us will reveal ourselves. I begin to feel out of place in this circle. The dismal atmosphere overcomes, and more than neutralises, the glowing physical comforts round me; and I resolve to be cautious about venturing under these rafters a third time.

The business of eating concluded, and no one uttering a word of sociable conversation, I approach a window to examine the weather. A sorrowful sight I see: sky and hills mingled in one bitter whirl of wind and suffocating snow. The night holds no fear for such as me; but that snow, and the fury of the wind, it could trap me out there until daybreak.

"I will need that guide," I can't help exclaiming. "The roads are buried already; and, if they were bare, I could scarcely see beyond my face."

"Hareton, drive those sheep into the barn. They'll be covered if left in the fold all night: and put a plank before them," Heathcliff orders.

"And me?" I ask, with rising irritation.

There is no reply to my question; and on looking round, I see why. Only Joseph bringing in a pail of slops for the dogs, and Mrs Heathcliff knelt by the fire, amusing herself burning long matches, which fell from the over-mantle when she restored the tea-canister to its place, now remain.

Joseph, having deposited his pail, takes a critical look at us, and in cracked tones grates, "I wonder ye can be so idle. Bud ye's nowt, and it's no use talking. You'll never mend yer ill ways, but go right to hell, like yer mother afore ye!"

For a moment I imagine this piece of rural rudeness addressed to me; and step towards him with an intention of hurling him outdoors. Mrs Heathcliff, however, halts me with her answer.

"Aren't you afraid of being carried away, whenever you mention the devil? Refrain from provoking me, or I'll ask him your abduction as a special favour!"

The ancient gapes at her.

"Stop! Look here, Joseph," she continues, taking a book from a shelf; "I'll show you how far I've progressed in the Black Arts. The red cow didn't die by chance; and your rheumatism is getting worse, isn't it?"

"Oh, wicked!" gasps the elder. "May the Lord deliver us from evil!"

"Be off, or I'll hurt you seriously! I'll model you, him and that oaf in wax and clay! The first who passes the limits I fix shall… I'll not say what now. But, you'll see! Go, I'm looking at you!"

The little witch puts a mock malignity into her beautiful eyes, and Joseph, trembling with sincere horror, hurries out, praying as he goes.

"Mrs Heathcliff," I say smiling. "Pray, point me out some landmark by which I may know my way home."

"Take the road you used," she answers, sitting in a chair, with a candle, and the long book open before her. "Brief advice, but as sound as any."

"And if you hear of me tragically dead in a bog or a ditch full of snow, your conscience won't whisper it is partly your fault?"

Neither will happen, of course, but her manner intrigues me, and her character is, to me, as opaque as her blue eyes are clear.

"How my fault?"

"Would it not be, at least partly?"

She shrugs. "I cannot escort you, even if I would. They won't let me beyond the garden wall. He fears what is out there."

"I would not ask you to go," I say, stepping closer. "I simply need you to tell me my way. Or else tell Mr Heathcliff to give me a guide."

"Who? There is himself, Earnshaw, the cook, Joseph and I. Which would you have?"

"No boys at the farm?"

"Those are all of us."

"Then, it follows I am compelled to stay."

"That you may settle with him. I have nothing to do with the matter."

"I hope this is a lesson to you to make no more rash journeys on these hills," comes Heathcliff's stern voice from the door. "As to staying here, I don't keep rooms for visitors: you must share a bed with Hareton or Joseph, if you stay."

"I can sleep on a chair in this room."

"No! A stranger is a stranger, be he rich or poor. It will not suit us to give anyone the range of this place."

With this insult my patience appears to end. Uttering an expression of disgust, I push past him to the yard, running into Earnshaw in my haste. It snows so hard I could not see the means of exit; and, as I peer round, I hear another example of their behaviour behind me. At first the oaf Earnshaw appears on my side.

"I'll go with him as far as the park."

"You'll go with him to hell!" exclaims his master, or whatever relation Heathcliff bears. "Who will look after my horses, eh?"

"His life," Mrs Heathcliff says, "is of more consequence than one evening's neglect of your nags. Besides, one of you must see him gone."

"Not at your command!" Earnshaw retorts.

"If he dies his ghost will haunt you; and I hope Mr Heathcliff never gets another tenant till the Grange is a ruin," she answers, sharply.

Joseph sits within earshot of all this, milking cows by the light of a lantern, which I seize unceremoniously, and, calling out that I will send it back on the morrow, head for the nearest postern.

"He's stealing t' lamp!" shouts the ancient.

On this cry, a reeking-breathed monster flies at my throat, bearing me down, and extinguishing the light; while a mingled guffaw from Earnshaw puts the copestone on my rage. Fortunately, the bitch is now more bent on stretching her paws, and yawning widely, and flourishing her tail, than fighting me.

The vehemence of my anger brings on a nose bleed, and Heathcliff laughs, until I stand, the stoniness of my gaze abruptly halting his laughter. The bitch goes back on her hind legs, aware my charity is gone.

I don't know what would conclude this scene, if not for Zillah, the stout housewife and cook; who issues forth to inquire into the nature of the uproar. She thinks they are laying violent hands on me; and, not daring to attack her master, turns her vocal artillery against the oaf.

"Well, Mr Earnshaw," she cries, "I wonder what next. Are we going to murder folk on our very door-stones? Come in, Sir, and I'll cure that. There now, hold ye still."

With these words she pours a pint of icy water onto my face, and pulls me into the kitchen. Mr. Heathcliff follows, his merriment long expired and replaced by his habitual moroseness.

\While leading the way upstairs, Zilliah recommends I hide the candle, and not make a noise; for her master has odd notions about the room she will put me in, and never lets anybody sleep there. I ask the reason. She does not know; she has only been there a year, and there are so many queer goings on she cannot afford to be curious.

"Can I get you anything else?" she asks.

I shake my head but she waits in the doorway, then steps into the small room and shuts the door behind her, carefully. She is in her late twenties; unmarried or more likely widowed in the war against Bonaparte. She has the thickness at her waist of a woman who has carried to term at least one child; and the ripe breasts of a woman who has fed that child also.

"Come here," I say.

She approaches without hesitation. Stopping, to stand in silence when she reaches me, although she quivers as I raise my hand to her neck and count the feathered pulse beneath my fingers. It is a night of temptations, but I have travelled too far and too fiercely to choose an easy road now. She shivers and quivers and gasps under my touch. Then steps back, eyes wide and countenance suddenly afraid. But her bosom still rises and falls, and a sheen of fresh dew dots her forehead and upper lip. She drops me a curtsy as she leaves. The first I have seen in my time here.

The whole furniture consists of a chair, a clothes-press, and a large oak case, with squares cut near the top resembling coach windows. Approaching this structure, I look inside and find an old-fashioned bed, designed to obviate the necessity for every member of the family to have a room to himself. In fact, the oak case forms a little closet, and the ledge of a window, which it encloses, serves as a table. I slide back the panels, get in with my light and pull the panels together, feeling secure against Heathcliff's distrust, the liver-hued bitch's knowledge of my true nature, and everyone else in that place.

The window ledge, where I place my candle, has mildewed books in one corner, and lettering scratched into it. This writing, however, is nothing but a name repeated endlessly, in childish and less childish writing. Catherine Earnshaw, varied to Catherine Heathcliff, and finally Catherine Linton.

I have found, I suspect, what I came to find; or at least, proof that it is here to find at all. In vapid listlessness I lean my head against the window and continue spelling over the Catherines, till my thoughts wander to older days; but they're not wandering five minutes when a flicker of white letters start from the dark. The air swarming with *Catherines* and, rousing myself to dispel them, I discover my candle against an antique book, stinking the place with roasted calf-skin.

Its fly-leaf bears the inscription, 'Catherine Earnshaw, her book,' and a date some quarter century back. I shut it, and take up another and another. Her library is select, and its state of dilapidation proves it well used; though not altogether for legitimate purposes: scarcely one chapter has escaped, and scrawls cover every morsel of blank the printer left. Some are detached sentences; others take the form of a regular diary, scrawled in an unformed, childish hand.

An awful Sunday, commences a paragraph. *'I wish my father alive again. My brother Hindley is a detestable substitute. His conduct to Heathcliff is atrocious. He and I are going to rebel, we took our first step this evening.*

All day has been rain; we could not go to church, so Joseph must needs get up a congregation in the garret; while Hindley and his wife bask downstairs before a fire. The service lasts three hours; and yet my brother has the face to exclaim, when he sees us descending, "What, done already?" On Sunday evenings we were once permitted to play, if we did not make much noise; now a mere titter is sufficient to send us into corners.

"You forget you have a master here," says the tyrant. "I'll demolish the first who puts me out of temper! I insist on perfect sobriety and silence.

I take my dingy volume by the spine, and hurl it into the dog-kennel, vowing I hate a good book. Heathcliff kicks his to the same place.

Then there is a hubbub!

"Maister Hindley!" shouts our chaplain. "Miss Cathy's riven the back off 'The Helmet o' Salvation,' and' Heathcliff's put his foot into 'The Broad Way to Destruction!'"

Hurrying from his warm hearth, Hindley seizes one of us by the collar, and the other by the arm, and hurls us both outside; where, Joseph swears, "Old Nick will fetch us as sure as we are living." And, so comforted, we each seek shelter to await his arrival. Taking this book, and a pot of ink from a shelf, I push the house-door ajar to give me light, and I spend my time writing these twenty minutes; if the surly old man comes, he may believe his prophecy verified — we cannot be damper, or colder, in the rain than we are here.'

I suppose Catherine fulfilled her project, for her next sentence takes up another subject: she waxes lachrymose.

How little did I dream Hindley would ever make me cry so! My head aches, till I cannot keep it on the pillow; and still I can't give over. Poor Heathcliff! Hindley calls him a vagabond, and won't let him sit with us, nor eat with us anymore. He says we may not play together, and threatens to turn him out of the house if I break these orders. Hindley blames our father (how dare he?) for treating Heathcliff too liberally; and swears he will reduce him to his right place—

Alas, for the effects of bad blood and bad temper! What else could it be that makes me pass such a restless night? I don't remember another that I can compare with it since I changed to whom I am now.

My heightened senses give me every creak and sound in that desolate place. Heathcliff's dark muttering, his daughter-in-law's tearful prayers to a deity she outwardly mocks, the noise of the oaf opening wine in the kitchen after everyone is supposed to be in bed. Old Jacob, hypocrite that his kind is, being turned back from the cook's bedroom door.

I hear distinctly the gusty wind beyond the windows, and even the driving of the snow; I hear, also, a fir bough at my little leaded window, endlessly repeating its teasing sound. It annoys me so much I resolve to silence it; and rising, endeavour to unhasp the window catch. The hook is soldered to the staple: a circumstance observed by me earlier, but forgotten.

Noise is pain to me. My ruined villas and desolate castles and lonely country houses like Thrushcross Grange are chosen as readily for their silence as their isolation and lack of troubling neighbours. Knocking my knuckles through a single leaded diamond of glass, I stretch an arm to seize the importunate branch. Instead of which, my fingers close on the fingers of a little, ice-cold hand.

She has come to me.

I did not even have to call! I start to draw in my arm, but the hand cling tight, and a most melancholy voice sobs, "They won't invite me in!"

"Tell me your name," I say, struggling to disengage myself.

"Catherine Linton," she replies, shiveringly. "I'm come home. I'd lost my way in the darkness!" As she speaks, I discern, obscurely, a girl's face through the window. She is the reflection of the girl by the fire, although her hair is dark not fair, and her sorrow more obvious.

"Invite me in."

Necessity makes me cruel; and, finding myself unable to shake her off, I grind her wrist onto broken glass, and drag it so until her flesh rips and bone becomes visible.

"Please," she begs.

Her tenacious grip on the memories of life, her hatred and my wrist is impressive in one so freshly changed. "Let go if you want me to let you in!" She does, and I withdraw my hand instead. "I am the wrong one," I tell her. "Not if you beg for twenty years will I let you in."

"It is twenty years. That's how long I've been a waif!"

"Still no," I tell her.

Her howl rips though the room, banshee-like and bitter, so obviously from beyond the grave that it brings the odour of corpses; and the wax of my candle seems to glow for a few moments with the yellowing sheen of old bones.

Hasty footsteps approach my chamber door, and somebody pushes it open, with a vigorous hand, and light glimmers through the panels of my closet. I sit, waiting, while the intruder hesitates and mutters to himself. At last, he says, in a half-whisper, plainly not expecting an answer.

"Is anyone here?"

I shall not soon forget the effect opening the panel has.

Standing in the doorway, in his long shirt, with a candle dripping wax on his fingers, Heathcliff looks as white as the wall. The first creak of the panel startles him so badly, the candle leaps from his grasp some feet, and his agitation is so extreme, he can hardly pick it up.

"It is only your guest," I say, sparing him the humiliation of exposing his cowardice further. "I'm sorry to disturb you."

"Disturb me?"

I nod amiably, my face now visible in the candlelight.

"God damn you, Mr Lockwood! I wish you were—" Setting his candle on a chair, because he finds it impossible to hold steady, he demands, "Who showed you up to this room? I've a mind to turn them out this instant."

"Zillah," I reply, reclaiming my garments. "I suppose she wanted proof this place is haunted. Well, it is. Swarming with ghosts and goblins! I will go now. I feel my time to leave is come."

"What can you mean?" Heathcliff growls. "Finish out the night, damn you, since you are here; but, for God's sake don't repeat that scream: nothing can excuse it, unless you are having your throat cut!"

"My throat is safe," I tell him. "Yours, less so. If that little fiend ever gets in here she will bleed you dry." I wait for him to demand to which little fiend I refer; but his countenance looks whiter than before, and his hands tremble.

I have shaken every bone in his body, reanimated the corpse of every bitter memory he tries to keep dead and safely buried. He hates the young woman downstairs, who hates him. The oaf resents him. The liver-hued bitch simply bides her time. The only person he has loved he hates too bitterly to invite in. I would tell him that I understand his troubles far more acutely than he can realise; but no man wants to compare his misery with another.

So I simply add more miseries to those he has.

"She told me she'd been walking the night these twenty years!"

Scarcely were these words uttered than Heathcliff falls back into the shelter of the bed, finally sitting down by the window, almost concealed behind the panels. I guess, by his irregular and intercepted breathing, that he struggles with an excess of violent emotions.

Not wishing to show that I hear the conflict, I dress rather noisily, look at my watch, and comment pointlessly on the length of the night: "Not three o'clock yet! I could have sworn it was six. Time stagnates here; we must surely have retired to rest at eight!"

"Retire at nine, rise at four," he mutters, suppressing a groan; and, as I fancy, by the motion of his shadow, dashing a tear from his eyes. "Mr Lockwood," he says, "you may take my room.

You'll only be in the way, coming down so early; and your outcry has sent sleep to the devil for me."

"For me, too," I reply smiling. "I'll walk the yard briefly, and then I'll be off; and you need not dread a repetition of my intrusion. I'm now quite cured of seeking pleasure in your society."

"Delightful," mutters Heathcliff. "Take the candle, and go where you please. Keep out of the yard, though, the dogs are unchained."

I obey, so far as to quit the chamber; then stand still and witness a piece of desperation on the part of my wretched landlord. Wrenching at the lattice, he bursts the window's weld, as he pulled at it, in an uncontrollable passion of tears.

"I was wrong," he says. "To keep you out. Please, come in... Cathy, do come. Oh, do. Once more. My heart's darling. Hear me!"

The spectre shows a spectre's ordinary caprice, and gives no sign of hearing; but I know she does, and I begin to make my way downstairs; ready to return to the Grange before daybreak. Cathy will come, and Heathcliff will go with her – that is the way this works – because that is the way this always works and has done since the changes began. The liver-hued bitch will get used to me, die or leave. The choice will be hers at first, and mine at last. I open the yard door, unconcerned by the thought of the dogs, who will be wise to avoid me this time. And the snow and the wind whirl welcomely through the opening, reaching me, and blowing out my light.

The Abomination
of Beauty

Ian Whates

Samsa came awake. For him this was no gradual thing, no gentle drift through levels of increasing consciousness, but instead an instant transition from dreamless sleep to full-blown alertness. He rose and moved to the mouth of the cave. The sun had already taken its leave, bowing down beneath the horizon and vacating the sky in favour of its colder, paler sister; a lingering nimbus around distant peaks the only testament to its passage. Even as he watched, that final defiant glow faded to leave night's dominion unchallenged.

He strode forward into the open, pausing to savour the air – heavy with potent scents and flavours. For brief seconds he stood there, a tall pale Adonis with hair as black as a raven's wing and a body that challenged perfection barring one ancient scar. Then he raised his head and keened: a high, piercing call that rose and swelled over the peaks, giving greeting to the sun-sister, the three-quarter moon that bathed the world in silver light. Other voices joined his to produce a haunting, ululating song that would have sounded both beautiful and chilling to the human ear; an eerie parody of dawn's joyous chorus. As the voices fell and their song died away, Samsa spread his wings: glorious and dark, feathers as black as his hair. Fully extended, he surrendered to the pull of wind and night and flung himself at the sky, where he rose to join those of his brethren already aloft. They soared and circled, revelling in the rebirth of darkness whilst waiting for late-comers to join them. Once all were gathered the whole band turned as one and headed east, following Samsa and leaving behind the mountains and the caves that had sheltered them through the long daylight hours.

It was time to feed.

Sara was elated. She danced around her room; quietly, since her parents were asleep. At least her father was – the tide of rumbling snores that ebbed and flowed through the whole house assured her of that much. How anybody could sleep in the same room as that noise was beyond her, but she supposed her mother benefited from a great deal of practice. Perhaps her own concern about disturbing them was unnecessary, but experience had taught her not to take such things for granted.

Sara should have been asleep herself at this late hour but she was too excited. Nathan and Daniel had fought each other today… over *her*. She was fifteen and it would soon be time to wed. Everyone seemed so certain she was destined to walk down the aisle with Daniel. The new house was almost complete and before summer ended it would be time… their time.

Yet Sara had always been a wilful child and, although the prospect of wedding Daniel was pleasant enough, Nathan with his dark and brooding ways had intrigued her increasingly of late. She'd been trying to catch his eye for weeks and in the last couple of days knew the satisfaction of success. If the flirting had been fun, the fight that ensued once Daniel caught them was even more so. She watched, feeling more alive than ever before –

knowing she was the cause and excited by this physical manifestation of the fact that the two best-looking boys in the village both wanted *her*. And why should they not? False modesty had never been one of Sara's failings. Even at fifteen she was aware of her own beauty and conscious of the effect this had on many of the village's men, even the married ones.

Perhaps, she dared to think – there in the privacy of her room and her own thoughts – she might yet have both Daniel *and* Nathan. Could she not marry one and still welcome the other as a lover? Oh, she would marry Daniel and, of course, her husband would have to be the first, while knowing on their wedding night that he *was* her first, but afterwards…

Such musings were scandalous, but were all the more thrilling for being so.

Instinctively aware of a sudden presence behind her, she stopped dancing and spun around… to find herself facing a god; a figure seemingly escaped from one of her own pubescent and unfocussed erotic fantasies. The breath caught in her throat as she drank him in. Tall and muscular, with night-black hair and eyes that spoke of dark secrets and even darker desires. Here was a *man*, beside whom Nathan and Daniel were no more than boys, instantly forgotten.

Suddenly, without her being conscious of his moving, he was before her, a hand caressing her cheek. She raised her lips to meet his kiss, tasting cool night and intoxicating sweetness. When the kiss ended, her gown lay on the floor though she had not been conscious of disrobing.

He trailed a finger gently down her nakedness. As it casually caressed a breast she shivered, an electric thrill tingling down her spine. The bed pressed against the back of her legs and without hesitation she eased herself down upon it. He lay with her and she was aware of a ferocious need within him that mirrored her own. *He* would be her first, not some fumbling village lad. Dimly, a primordial corner of her hinterbrain recognised that he would also be her last and quailed, but that tiny spark of self-preservation was drowned beneath the torrent of desire.

He kissed her cheek, moving down to nuzzle her neck, shifting his position on top of her. She tilted her chin back, thrilled at the touch of his lips and exposing her throat, at the same time parting her legs to welcome him there as well.

No gentleness as he entered her; instead it was a single powerful thrust that ruptured her maidenhood at the exact same instant as his teeth bit into her neck. She convulsed at the shock of twinned pain that seemed to pierce her very being. The small spark of warning roared into full panic but too little and far, far too late. For a brief second it blazed, urging her body to react, to take flight... to make some response. As rapidly as it had ignited, her will broke entirely and all defiance drained away. Sara could do nothing but lie there, legs and arms clasping her doom to her, holding her death in place.

Awareness narrowed down to just two sensations: the red hot agony/ecstasy of his rhythmic penetration and the numb coldness of life flowing away. Then even that faded to nothing.

The girl had been young and fresh and beautiful – deserving of a virtuoso performance, and Samsa had timed things to perfection. As the first of his dead seed exploded into her loins, so she breathed her last and the final drop of her life's blood trickled onto his lapping tongue.

He rose, renewed. The girl's sweet blood had strengthened him but he was not yet sated. The previous night's journey had been long and hard with little chance to feed. His body now craved more.

Then he heard the snoring.

Swiftly and soundlessly he left the girl's room and entered the next. A cramped space almost filled by a bed which contained two occupants, presumably the girl's parents. Both had slept soundly through their daughter's deflowering and death, unaware.

The man's snoring was a minor irritation that would have to stop. Samsa leaned forward and nipped the man's neck, tasting blood. It was the lightest of bites, the gentlest of touches that fell a long way short of being fatal yet still had its effect. The snoring ceased as the man came awake but was unable to move. The careful bite had paralysed, leaving only his eyes free. The wife slept on, oblivious.

Samsa paused to look at the woman, seeing in her a distant echo of the daughter's beauty, yet even relaxed in sleep the face showed signs of hardship, tell-tale lines of premature aging. Clearly hers had not been the easiest of lives. Nor would it have a chance to improve.

She slept on her side, back turned to the man who shared her bed. Samsa knelt to blow on her face. She awoke, her eyes staring directly into his own. He smiled, and so did she. Samsa stood, drew off the bedclothes and cast them to the floor. Then he gently turned her onto her back before ripping the coarse nightgown from her body and throwing it after the sheets. She had eyes only for him, taking no notice of the husband who lay motionless beside her. He kissed her, sampling her breath in advance of the act that would stop it forever. Then he treated her as he had her daughter.

As he lay on top of her she reached out with all four limbs, drawing him into her. With practiced ease he matched the lapping of blood to the rhythm of his pelvis. He wanted to slow down, to prolong the process for the husband's sake, but she was that much older than the girl, her life-force that much weaker. Pride would not permit him to mistime, so he savoured her blood and judged how quickly the spark of life faded, matching the rhythm of his thrusts accordingly. As ever, he managed to coincide his climax with the exact instant of her passing.

He stood up, fully sated, a little light-headed. The woman's blood had been thinner and less vigorous than the girl's but enjoyable nonetheless. A glance at the husband showed the man to have moisture running down his cheeks. Interesting: evidently the paralysis did not reach as far as the tear-ducts. He'd never noticed that before.

Not for one instant did Samsa consider killing the man. Quite apart from the fact that he was full it would be so much sweeter to let the husband live, carrying with him the images of the wife's passing, never able to escape the knowledge of how she had welcomed her killer as a lover even unto death.

Come morning the paralysis would lift, banished by the first rays of the cursed sun. The man would think that he had experienced the depths of despair, that nothing could be worse. That belief would last only until he found the remains of Samsa's hors-d'oeuvres, the drained and withered husk that had once been his daughter. Then he would discover just how deeply despair could reach.

Samsa left the small home fully sated, rising into the air on languid wings to circle above the rooftops and wait for his brethren to join him. They did so gradually, as if reluctant to leave the feast, drifting up in ones and twos until the sky was dark with wings. Then they departed – well ahead of the sun – flapping lazily toward the mountains and their sheltering caves, leaving behind them a village that would waken to a day of dark despair.

Come dawn the village seemed deceptively peaceful, the prevailing silence broken only by muffled sounds of a child crying somewhere. A single dog trotted down the deserted street, seemingly lost, as if looking for somebody... anybody.

It was well past sunrise before the first person dared to peek out from their door. Slowly the survivors emerged. The grief-stricken, the terrified, the disbelieving and the traumatised; they gravitated towards the church without any spoken consensus to do so. The Priest was among the living, having slept through the night whilst his flock were slaughtered around him. In the absence of any other authority, he started to organise this fractured community. He walked among them, talking to each person in turn, comforting and soothing, taking to one side those who seemed most able to function. He led them in prayer, then in song, attempting to raise first their voices and then their spirits.

The most capable-seeming he sent to scour the village, calling on every house in hope of finding others who might have survived but not yet emerged, perhaps too shocked to do so alone.

One such pair found Ned Baker, on his knees and crying, while cradling what looked to be the shrivelled body of an old woman. This proved to be Sara, Ned's daughter, who only yesterday had been the prettiest girl in the valley.

They burned the bodies. In part because of the fear that the dead might rise again once the sun set – they'd heard rumours. In fact this particular concern was groundless. It took a deft touch to effect such conversion. The tiniest drop of blood and life force had to remain, so that the victim would forever hover in a state of limbo, precariously balanced between life and death. Samsa and his people had been far too hungry to consider such niceties or to play such games.

There was also a more practical reason for cremation. The dead outnumbered the living. In a single night some two-thirds of the village had perished. Those that remained were in no fit state to dig graves or shift so much earth.

Instead they built an enormous pyre, using every scrap of wood to be found: the logs stockpiled against winter, pickets, poles and planks from fences and dilapidated old sheds, even chairs and pieces of furniture from homes that would no longer need them.

The sun had passed its zenith and begun the steady slide back towards the horizon before they were done. After sombre prayer the fire was set, while the Priest tried to raise a hymn amongst the tears and the anguish.

Through all of this Ned Baker said nothing, did nothing, made no response to anybody.

That night the remaining people gathered together in the church, sitting or lying on the pews, in hastily slung hammocks, on pallets or simply on the floor. Their number seemed pitifully few. The pyre still blazed at the edge of the village, bathing the church in its eerie, shifting glow. The Priest gave a sermon, but doubted its effectiveness. Torches were lit and maintained, since none welcomed the prospect of darkness. Exhausted by their terror and the day's labour most slept, despite vowing loudly that they would not. All there listened, all strained to catch the first sounds that might herald the vampires' return.

Yet the night passed undisturbed, the bloodsuckers having evidently turned their attention elsewhere. In the morning the villagers began the process of packing. There was no question of staying here. None believed that one night's reprieve meant they were by any measure safe. It was only a question of time before the vampires came again and only a fool would gamble on how much time. Carts and horses were laden with only those things deemed essential. They began soon after dawn and were soon finished, every horse and ox that the village could muster pressed into service as either mount or dray animal. They left as early as possible, hurrying the ditherers. No one wished to still be on the road when night fell.

So it was that a community died and its survivors fled, leaving both their dead and their past behind them, but not their fears; nor their memories.

Ned Baker would likely have remained behind were it not for the Priest. Ned had still not spoken since his ordeal, had still not responded to anything. Nobody knew exactly what had befallen him, but all agreed it must have been especially dreadful. Ned had always been a strong man, yet now he seemed as weak and pliant as a babe – not even eating without being prompted. "It's as if his soul has fled the real world and hidden," one former neighbour observed.

The Priest had taken a special interest in Ned, who seemed the most damaged of all his remaining parishioners and who had no surviving family to care for him.

When the Priest led him to the wagon, Ned made no objection and docilely went where instructed. Throughout the journey he sat listless, gazing at the world with an unchanging, vacant expression.

The small rag-tag caravan headed east, away from the mountains and towards Lylesford, the nearest sizeable town. Semi-fortified, Lylesford straddled a deep river and was the major local centre for trade. The town boasted a large population and a garrison of resident soldiers, so offered a measure of security that the villagers were desperate for. The journey would take two days but along the way were a number of hamlets at which the refugees hoped to find shelter whilst giving warning. It was a trip none of them would ever forget. Even in daylight they found themselves constantly glancing over their shoulders or watching the skies. It would be a long while before any of them truly felt safe again.

If asked about church or religion, a typical resident of Lylesford would most likely mention one name: Father Andrew Galleon.

For his part, Father Galleon knew himself to be nobody special and was puzzled that anyone should think otherwise. He did his best to be pious, dedicated and chaste – all things his vocation dictated – and for the most part believed that he succeeded, but at the same time knew that he was only human and no more perfect than the next man. True, he hated to see others suffer, either through injustice, misfortune or malicious intent, and it was also true that he sought to help those less fortunate than himself, both within his church and beyond. But what of that? God had blessed him with a compassionate nature. Any good deed he might effect was therefore due to God's grace, not his own. He was merely the vessel through which the Lord chose to act. So how did that make him special?

He supposed it was the exorcism that cemented his reputation. After that he was celebrated throughout Lylesford; a ridiculous state of affairs. While still a novice Galleon had recognised that demons were the most immediate enemies of the Church, so it seemed only natural to study them. This grew into a hobby and he became something of an expert, collecting an impressive library over the years and, indeed, publishing the occasional well-received paper on the subject himself. So when he was called upon to minister to an ailing parishioner he had little trouble in identifying the condition as demonic possession. Of course, he had no first-hand knowledge of such matters, but there were many accounts of similar events to call upon. He also found in his collection procedural instructions from several renowned exorcists. It was his library that saved the man and drove out the demon, not himself. Again, he was merely the vessel through which the appropriate knowledge had been channelled.

For some reason no one else seemed to see it that way, which was most perplexing.

Father Galleon was used to finding people in his church at all hours. He believed God's house to be an open one and never turned the needy away. Afterwards, he could not have said what drew his attention to the stranger, except that something about the man's demeanour called out to him. Perhaps it was the eyes, which seemed focused on some distant inner place, or perhaps it was just the way the man sat, but something told Father Galleon that here was a soul in torment, a man in desperate need.

Galleon approached him and waited for acknowledgement. When none came he sat down. Still there was no response. The stranger's clothes were grimy and looked to have been worn for several days, yet the man was clearly no vagrant. This reinforced the Priest's impression that he was from out of town, newly arrived in Lylesford, the dirt being a by-product of the journey. After watching in silence for several seconds and considering his options, the elderly Priest reached out to place a comforting hand on the man's shoulder. The words he had eventually decided upon were left unsaid, for as his hand alighted the other looked round, and for the first time in days Ned Baker focused on something outside of his own head.

When he spoke, his voice was dry and cracked through disuse, his words little more than a whisper. "Help me Father, for I have been touched by the Devil!"

Then he began to cry, for with the opening of his eyes and his mind he had also relaxed the iron grip that will-power had held on his heart. Father Galleon took him to the vestry, which offered the most immediate opportunity for privacy, and listened to Ned's tale. It was a story that shook him to the core.

How Ned had ended up at Galleon's church none could say, least of all Ned himself, who had only the dimmest recollection of anything following the night of his family's murder. It later transpired that upon the refugees' arrival at Lylesford Ned had simply wandered off, presumably while the village priest was distracted with other concerns. He reached the church in advance of gossip over the vampire attack which even then was spreading in waves across the town. Father Galleon never questioned the mechanism of his appearance. To him the whole incident had 'divine intervention' written all over it.

Ned told of his experience in detached, impersonal tones, as if relating events that had happened to someone else. Galleon listened with as little intervention as possible, only able to guess at the torture such a retelling must cause, but aware also that this was the foundation of healing. Only once did he interrupt. An apparently trivial matter amongst such horror, mentioned only in passing, yet he found himself quizzing Ned about it even whilst apologising for doing so. "You say there was a scar?"

"Yes on his..." He struggled for composure. "...on his arse. Least it looked like a scar... or a brand. You know, like a sheep or horse might carry."

A brand mark; why did that sound familiar? "I know this is hard, Ned, but I really think it might be important; are you certain this mark was regular, like a brand, rather than an irregular scar?"

"Well..." Ned paused, trying to reach past the pain and remember. "The sun," he said at last. "It looked like the sun."

Galleon fumbled in his robes for the pad and crayon that he habitually carried and proceeded to sketch a crude circle which he showed to Ned. "Like this?"

"No. More pointed, like a star."

Galleon took back the pad, thought for a second and then sketched in a crown of rays, completely surrounding the circle. Again he showed it to Ned.

"Yes, that's more like it... sort of." He closed his eyes and shuddered. "Do you really think this will help?"

Galleon sighed. "I don't know Ned, I really don't know."

He felt certain that he'd once read of such a branding but for the life of him could not think where or in what context.

Long after Ned had fallen into exhausted sleep Galleon sat up, poring through the contents of his library. Not for one moment did he consider Ned's arrival on his doorstep to be a coincidence, nor was he one to duck responsibility. Whatever God's plan, clearly he had a part.

Deep into the hours of morning Father Galleon finally gave in to his body's tiredness, accepting the need for sleep and abandoning his books. He had read much and learned a great deal without discovering what was needed. As he lay down to snatch a few precious hours rest his mind still churned. Never in his long life had he felt so driven, both by the horror of Ned Baker's ordeal and by the desperate certainty that time was running out.

Ned Baker and his fellow villagers proved to be only the first to seek the sanctuary of Lylesford. The day following their arrival others started to appear. They came in ones and twos, in families and in larger groups. Most had fled their homes simply as a precaution, having heard of the vampires and their atrocities and deciding to seek the perceived safety of the town; but towards late afternoon a second band of survivors arrived. Another village had been attacked, its populace slaughtered.

The authorities marshalled their resources as best they could, hastily detailing the militia to organise accommodation and provisions for the growing influx of refugees and seeking help on other measures from the only proven exorcist in town: the renowned Father Galleon.

Galleon did what he could, offering advice on the various

defences said to discourage vampires and imploring all who would listen to take every precaution possible, all the while begrudging time spent away from his books and chafing to return to them. He felt guilty about such an uncharitable attitude but, as the hours continued to slip past, grew increasingly certainty that his research was vital. By the day's end the pressure had built to become a near-physical weight bearing down upon his chest, restricting his breath. Finally he was able to cut his civic duties short and rush back to the library. Only when sat in the familiar chair with books all around him was he able to relax and breathe more easily. Certain that this urgency had once more been the guiding hand of God, he threw himself into the research with renewed vigour. Yet still the answer eluded him.

Inspiration only struck the next day, arriving in a most unlooked for manner. He caught himself humming the tune to a favourite hymn, his attention snagged by a single word of the lyric: *angels*.

Galleon stopped humming, stopped walking, and stood in stunned realisation. All his fruitless research had centred on the myths and conflicting theories about demons and vampirism. It had never occurred to him to look at angels. Yet something about angels and a brand mark struck a chord. He dashed to the library, took down a further selection of books and once more became immersed in the written knowledge and wisdom of lives past.

Hours later he paused; lunch had gone unnoticed, as had a long-scheduled meeting with a young couple about to be wed. Yet by the time he lifted his attention from the books a picture had begun to emerge; one that filled him with both horror and hope.

As Galleon's awareness returned to the external world, having been totally enmeshed in the fascination of research and the quickening thrill of revelation, he found a special courier waiting for him. The dispatch he was handed bore a seal that required instant attention; its contents brought a bitter smile.

William of Thissoury was en-route to Lylesford, bringing with him his lauded Church Knights.

Galleon had no great love of Thissoury or his order. Though unquestionably devout and far from stupid, the man's thinking was rigid and blinkered, his manner arrogant. Thissoury was a fanatic and Galleon had always considered fanaticism a dangerous trait, whatever its creed. As for his order, their posturing and self-importance irked him beyond measure. They styled themselves 'The Soldiers of Christ' and 'The Church Militant'. Galleon had always been taught that it was the duty of every Christian to actively save souls, welcoming them into the church and opening the way to the Kingdom of Heaven. *That* was The Church Militant – a title that every Christian and particularly every clergyman should claim with pride; yet Thissoury and his knights had usurped it for their own. Galleon found their presumption galling and unpalatable.

However, he was not blind to the timing of the courier's arrival, coinciding so exactly with the breakthrough in his research: clear indication of a plan in action. He might not like Thissoury, but since when had God's will required his approval?

Ned Baker was still staying with him, having no relatives in Lylesford and nowhere else to go. True to his name and profession, Ned had conjured up some wonderful loaves, and the fragrance of their baking lingered in the kitchen. Galleon made some tea, cut a generous slice of strong crumbling cheese from the larder and helped himself to a ham-fisted chunk of the fresh bread. He loaded these onto a precariously balanced tray and carried them back to the library. Again working long into the night, he reread and checked all that had been done before, ranging further afield in search of corroboration. All that he found served to strengthen his conviction that this was the right track.

Exhaustion eventually drove him to bed, where he fell into a deep sleep, untroubled by any dreams that consciousness could retrieve.

Garlic and crosses. This house was warded, if poorly. Samsa reached up, snatched a pungent bulb and crushed it in one hand. These things meant nothing to him but they would to his brethren, the lesser ones, who might well baulk at even such crude defences.

The night had not gone well. In search of prey they had ranged far and wide across a land suddenly bereft of vulnerable people. Word of their presence had clearly spread. Darkness was already well-advanced with few of the flock fed before he caught scent of this distant concentration of blood.

At first the town seemed open, inviting; a harvest ready for the reaping. The place had once been protected by walls but had long since outgrown them, dwellings bursting out to spread across the land. Not that walls meant anything to beings who could fly. Perhaps to signal his contempt for such measures, Samsa led the way over the wall and toward the houses within. A single sentry paced the top of the irrelevant defence. Samsa gestured and one of the brethren dropped down. He glanced back to see a slender figure crowned by a mane of white-gold hair draw the unresisting soldier into her embrace before the view was hidden by his descent into the inner town; into narrow streets that were dark, silent and ripe with the stench of humanity and effluent. Around him the brethren alighted, to be confronted by doors that were barred and buildings that were warded against them.

This was a defiance not to be tolerated.

There were two ways to challenge his sort: power and faith. He sensed no local emanation of the former, which left faith. A church: this town was large enough to boast more than one and it was in such buildings that faith was most likely to be found. He sprang into the air, calling as he rose. Half a dozen dark shapes answered his summons and followed. Almost at once he spotted a building larger than those around it, with a cross mounted prominently, brazenly, above its door.

Faith was a defence against him, but to be a perfect defence that faith had to be pure, which it rarely was. The church itself – a place of worship, a concentration of belief and prayer – was repugnant and difficult to approach; the house beside it less so.

He led them inside, black shadows emboldened by his presence, wisps of smoke that slipped silently past ineffective wards.

The Priest was a small and bloated man; short in stature, short of breath and short of faith, which he gave lip-service to when appropriate. His congregation believed him to be pious and holy. After all, did he not take in waifs and strays, providing home and shelter to young lads who would otherwise live on the streets and doubtless turn to crime? The Priest accepted these high opinions humbly, whilst at night satisfying his lusts and warming his bed with whichever of the young boys took his fancy. All of this Samsa saw.

The man's faith was thus a fragile thing, hollow and flawed, providing no protection against Samsa and his kind. They found him asleep, arm cradled around a lad of no more than eight or nine, the stink of freshly spilled semen heavy in the air. They flowed into the room, surrounded the bed and as one moved forward to feed. There was no sexual act this time, just the simple taking of blood: a flock of vultures feasting on helpless carrion. With such a group it was over in seconds.

They found the rest of the boys asleep in a back room, huddled together on pallets on the floor. Samsa stood to one side, allowing his brethren to enter.

Samsa had no great love of fire, which reminded him too much of the cursed sun, but nor did he have cause to fear it. Drawing embers that still smouldered from the living room hearth and dashing them against the base of the wooden church walls proved to be a simple matter. There they would doubtless have cooled and achieved little, had he not unfurled his mighty wings and fanned the coals with eldritch winds until they glowed red hot and the church walls started to smoulder. In a matter of seconds the flames leapt forth, spreading upward and outward with unnatural haste.

The building burned nicely: one less place for people to worship the hateful God of Betrayal.

There was movement, as some of the townsfolk came forth to see what was happening. Excellent! Not all the brethren would go hungry tonight.

Father Galleon awoke the next morning to find a populace traumatised by what had befallen them. Many people chose to leave, fleeing by both river and road. He couldn't blame them but had no thought of doing likewise. Having accepted responsibility for the spiritual welfare of the people of Lylesford, he would not desert them now when guidance and support were most needed.

Besides, flight was not the answer. The abomination had to be stopped.

From what he could make of the garbled reports, two members of the militia, two priests, nearly a dozen orphan boys and a similar number of ordinary citizens had lost their lives. Whilst even one loss to such creatures was one too many, it seemed to Galleon that in truth the town had escaped lightly.

Churches appeared to have been particularly targeted. Two had been burned down, their priests and households slaughtered. His own had been passed by, despite its being the largest in Lylesford. Clearly he had been spared by God's grace but he was not about to take such blessings for granted. Just because he had survived one night did not guarantee his safety the next. That realisation bought home a harsh fact; his personal welfare was far from a priority in the present circumstances. As yet he had imparted his suspicions and theories to no one and were he to die that knowledge would die with him. So it was that he sat down and began to write a letter.

He wrote carefully but swiftly, in flowing hand. First he described Ned's experience, then his own subsequent discoveries and the conclusions he had reached. The irony that this letter was for William of Thissoury did not escape him. He was pinning his hopes on a martial order he had vehemently opposed all his clerical life. Now it seemed that they were part of God's plan after all. His faith should have been stronger.

When the letter was finished and sealed he went in search of Ned, his nose guiding the way. Ned was baking again and the heartening aroma of fresh bread wafted throughout the house. In truth they already had more than enough for their own needs thanks to Ned's efforts, but Galleon was not about to stop him. He instinctively realised that baking was something the man needed to do, both as a form of therapy and as his way of making some repayment for whatever help Galleon had provided.

They chatted about bread making, pointedly avoiding all mention of the night's events, though both must have been aware of them. Galleon made some tea whilst Ned wiped the work surfaces clean of surplus flour, then they adjourned to the Priest's study.

"I need your help, Ned."

"My help? Of course, Father… but how can the likes of me possibly help *you*?"

Galleon smiled. "By delivering a letter for me, a very important letter. Have you ever ridden a horse, Ned?"

"Well… yes." It was a grudging admission and the Priest could almost hear the unspoken caveat *but not well or often*. No matter.

"I have a horse, one of my few vanities." A passion he had been unable to indulge much of late. "He's strong and fast, easy to ride. I need you to ride as hard as you can for West Morton. If you leave immediately you should reach it by nightfall. There you must seek out a man named William of Thissoury and deliver the letter. He should be easy enough to spot; he generally is. Thissoury is a man of God and a warrior – on his way here to rid us of the vampires. It's vital he learns what I've discovered." Galleon pulled a ring from his finger, one that Thissoury would know, and handed it across. "This plus the letter's seal should gain you an audience." Then, on impulse, he began to tell Ned what the letter contained, detailing all that he had learned and all that he suspected.

Samsa chose Lilith for the task. He couldn't recall her mortal name, nor indeed whether he had ever known it. Lilith was a whim of his own, the name given to her at the time of taking; since she was the first mortal he brought across to the state of Vampyra. It seemed appropriate.

Lilith possessed extraordinary beauty. In life she had inspired artists to paint her, minstrels to compose sonnets and married men to forget their vows. She had even been the cause of a minor but extremely bloody war. Since crossing over, her natural allure had been enhanced beyond measure.

The Priest was preparing for bed when they entered. He looked up, saw her, and stopped. Samsa stood back, knowing the man would see nothing beyond Lilith: a vision of woman personified.

Samsa, who came into the world with wings fully formed, snow-white and mighty, could never shed them; they were part of him, not to be denied. Lilith and the rest of his flock were different. Born human, their night-dark wings were of his making, bestowed upon them in mockery of his former brethren.

The wings had now disappeared. In their place she wore a long, dark cloak, clasped at the throat. With a shrug the cloak fell away, slithering down her body, clinging to every curve in sensuous caress. She stepped forward, young, pale and magnificent, raven hair flowing free. Lilith smiled. The Priest gawped.

He was strong in faith, this man; but faith was not enough.

Samsa was familiar with faith, knew it with an intimacy that no human could ever imagine. Against the likes of Samsa, faith alone could never be enough.

To his credit the man tried to resist, his face reddening with the effort of struggle, of trying to move against the combined will of Samsa and the very first of his flock, who both expressly commanded him not to. The effort was impressive, but futile.

Samsa watched as the priest's body twitched in resistance. From somewhere, the man found enough strength to see beyond the seductress and lock eyes with him, spitting out a name. It emerged as a strangled hiss but was still intelligible.

"Samael…"

The vampire froze. That was a name he had not heard in a long time, a name he believed lost and forgotten. It was as well that they had acted quickly, dealing with this priest before he had opportunity to cause any serious trouble. He locked eyes with the old man, finding there something other than he expected. Was it triumph? If so, it was misplaced.

Samsa turned away as Lilith came forward, to shred the Priest's cassock and lay him gently, almost tenderly on the bed, her mouth already clamped to his throat whilst her bare limbs encircled his body. Perhaps due to the Priest's inexperience, the sexual act did not last long. Even though in thrall the man's body shook and bucked as he shot his seed, which was doomed to perish the instant it entered her. The life-force took a little longer to draw forth and Samsa watched dispassionately as Lilith continued to feed. He found the whole process strangely unsatisfying and knew himself to be troubled, more unsettled by the Priest's unearthing of that name than he cared to admit.

Part of him wished to join Lilith, to take more personal vengeance on this man who had dared to defy him. Almost he wanted to have her roll over, so that the Priest was on top, buttocks exposed, allowing him to bugger the man at the same time as sharing the wretch's blood and life. But his preference had never truly run to men. It was women he lusted for, women's blood he craved, women who demanded his greatest wrath. After all, it was the lust for mortal Woman and her charms that had brought about his downfall those long ages past. Because of Woman he had been cast down, because of Woman he had been humiliated and branded. So Woman it was that he preferred to defile.

Samsa turned and departed before the Priest was fully drained, leaving Lilith to complete her feeding.

They did not return to the mountains that night, Samsa and

his flock, the distance too great. Instead they found shelter in the deserted houses cellars and barns of abandoned villages, many of which now littered the countryside. They had no fear of discovery. Local people had either been bled or fled.

On the whole, this night had gone better than the last; even though for the first time since they crossed the mountains one of the brethren had fallen. Somehow all the small defences and charms that the town employed had conspired to kill one of his children.

For that, Lylesford would pay.

They tore in with a vengeance. The outer skirts of the town had been abandoned, its inhabitants retreating behind the imagined security of the old defensive walls. Torches sputtered and soldiers waited atop those walls, far more than on previous nights. A few puny arrows arced towards them as they swept by. Samsa paused, signalling for some of the brethren to deal with this irritation. His own attention was focused elsewhere.

Ahead, almost in the centre of the town, there roared a fire; a beacon drawing him in. A challenge.

Samsa sensed that this night would be different. Like some cornered beast the town had decided to turn and fight. How delightful. Of course, in such a fight there could be but one winner.

Arrows continued to rise from darkened windows. None came close to him and he paid no heed to what occurred behind. A very special arrow would be needed to harm the brethren.

As he came closer to the town square he realised the beacon fire burned in the shape of a cross, and before it stood a figure silhouetted against the flames. Having outstripped his flock, Samsa alighted a score or so paces from his foe – a knight in full armour, crimson cross upon his chest. The man stood casually, hands meeting on the pommel of a great sword, the tip of which rested on the ground.

He knew this sort at once: Church Knight.

Even as Samsa landed the man barked a word of command. The vampire felt a great surge of power all around. Of course it was a trap; he had surmised that much but hadn't anticipated anything quite so sophisticated, or so dangerous.

Behind him Lilith and another of the brethren slammed against an unseen barrier, wings beating impotently, halted in mid-flight. He had entered a very carefully laid snare – a prepared area around which spells had been cast and guardian wards primed but not activated. The knight had evidently shouted the trigger-word needed to trip the shields.

Two more knights stepped from behind the fire, one to either side. They carried bows. The first took careful aim and let fly a fraction ahead of the other. As the arrow sped Samsa felt its passage, sensed its efficacy; dipped in silver, tempered in holy water, and blessed by a high servant of the treacherous God. Unhindered by the wards, the dart struck Lilith squarely in the chest. Here it achieved what no ordinary missile could ever have done, releasing the tiny spark of life that had been trapped within the vampire for centuries, suspended like an insect in amber. In an instant the spark was extinguished. Samsa screamed a pointless 'No' as Lilith withered and crumbled away before his eyes. The arrow clattered to the ground amidst a cloud of dust, to be followed seconds later by another as a second of his children perished.

Samsa turned to the knights in his rage… and paused. He would not have hesitated to take on a single knight, but here stood three of them, armed with weapons capable of harming even him, and still others were now moving out from behind the fire. The knight he had first seen, who appeared to be the leader, then spoke, his voice rich and resonant. "Samael of the Fallen, be aware that you are known. Prefect of the Grigori, teacher of the sun's secrets; Samsaveel, Shamsiel…"

That was enough for Samsa. There had always been power in a name and this knight seemed to know his, perhaps all of them. But how?

The old Priest; somehow he must have sent word. Truly afraid for the first time since the Fall, Samsa took to the wing and fled.

The shields wouldn't stop him for long. He had once been among the powers called upon to set such wards – how could they hope to resist him? Even as he landed at the base of the shield he was reaching out with his mind, divining its structure. Then, suddenly, a new force intervened, blinding his perception. Startled, disorientated, hemmed in by unfamiliar energies and barely able to move, he cast about for an explanation. He found it on the ground: a pentagram. He had landed inside a pentagram. A trap within a trap. Yet how had they known where to place it, which direction he would flee in when this had been no conscious choice but a random selection?

The knight with the sword stood before him and gave answer, as if reading his very thoughts. "We are all creatures of instinct, of habit; even you. As Samael you were Warden of the East. Since crossing the mountains you have moved inexorably in a single direction: east. When driven to mindless flight you instinctively chose to flee... east." He indicated the pentagram. "Thank you."

The knight grinned; a smile that lacked all hint of humour. "Had you not done so, we would still have had our arrows and our swords."

The knight stepped back. Others moved around the outskirts of the pentagram now, sprinkling water and intoning prayers. He stood helpless.

Only once before had Samsa felt so impotent, but *that* had been before God, whereas these were merely men.

As the night wore on the certainty of his fate grew all the more stark. He was to be left to the mercies of the cursed sun, ever his bane. He tested his bonds with both mind and body, flinging himself with all his strength one minute, then reaching out to fathom the nature of the holding spells the next, but it was as if his thoughts slid across a polished surface while his body was rebuffed by unyielding iron. From time to time one of the brethren would attempt to break through and aid him. An arrow would fly and he would have to watch another of his children die.

As morning approached, such attempts ceased; the survivors undoubtedly seeking somewhere dark to wait out the day. There would certainly be survivors, but without his guidance they would not stay as a group but splinter, becoming individual skulkers of shadows, forever fearing discovery and inevitable death. Hunters become the hunted.

Someone watched him; a man who was evidently not one of the knights. He looked vaguely familiar but did not merit recollection. Samsa turned his attention to the ever-lightening horizon.

Ned Baker might have lacked formal education but he was not wanting for intelligence. He'd never learned to read beyond his own name, but then he never found need to. Perhaps in compensation for this, he had developed an excellent memory. On seeing again the creature that had defiled and murdered his family, those images cried out to be relived. They were resisted. Instead, he concentrated his mind on that final meeting with Father Galleon, when the Father had revealed to him the nature of abomination.

"It *is* mentioned in the Bible, though only briefly," Galleon had explained. "Other texts cover the subject in greater detail and more again mention the event or refer to associated incidents and legends. Long ago, the Lord God sent down two hundred of his heavenly host; two hundred blessed angels to walk among men and to watch. But these Watchers fell into temptation. Against the Lord's decree they took for themselves mortal women as wives and fathered children – a bastard race history records as the Nephilim. One can well imagine that these angels would have been viewed in awe by human kind, looked up to as gods. Maybe they were flattered by this; because the Watchers, or Grigori, then compounded their sins by teaching our ancestors all manner of forbidden knowledge: sorcery, weapons, warfare… things mankind was not yet ready to learn.

"When the Lord learned of these transgressions his wrath was terrible, his punishment severe. He caused the hybrid Nephilim to be slain and had the Grigori themselves flung into Tartarus: a dank, dark Hell-pit surrounded by night and said to be one of the oldest parts of all creation.

"This much we know from a single record whose origins are reputedly entwined with those of the Holy Bible itself. Other texts flesh out the story, telling of associated events and rumoured occurrences. Some even suggest that not all the Grigori were secured in Tartarus, that one or more escaped. One such source states that those senior amongst the renegades – Shemyaza and his prefects – were singled out for specific punishments appropriate to their sins. For example, it is said of Shamsiel, who taught men the signs of the sun, that to him the sun became anathema, that from then on its rays would pain him unto death. Further, it is recorded that the sun's sign was burned into his flank as visible symbol of his disgrace; a mark that will never fade."

Apparently Shamsiel was also known by other names – which Ned failed to keep track of – though whether some or all of these were linguistic corruptions of the one root name or represented different aspects of the same heavenly entity was unclear. Such considerations were very much incidental to Ned, who was still trying to come to terms with the idea that the monster which had tortured him so, which was responsible for raping and butchering those he loved, had once been an angel; holiest of all creatures. An abomination if ever there were one.

It was a clear morning. The cross of fire had burned away long ago. As the air brightened an increasing number of knights appeared, returning from their positions throughout the town, where they had fought and killed the dark host. All now gathered to see the great vampire's passing. Ned promised himself that he would watch until the end, until the cleansing sun wiped this creature from the face of the Earth forever.

At that instant the first rays peeked over the horizon. As they struck the creature he began to smoulder, to burn; and he began to scream.

Revenge proved a hollow trophy, tasting far less sweet than Ned had expected. It did nothing to bring back those he'd lost. What was left to him? His wife and daughter were gone and now even the short-lived quest for vengeance was coming to an end. What was there left in the world for Ned Baker?

Samsa, haunter of men's nightmares, formerly the seraphim Samael, who had once been a guardian power of the east and as Shamsiel had been the Watcher who taught the signs of the sun to men, screamed anew as his nemesis rose further and the fire burned deeper.

Cast out of heaven, he had spurned hell's invitation, refusing to bow down before Satan – after all, what was Satan but a fallen angel like himself? Instead he had found his own way here on Earth, determined to establish his own dominion. Yet it seemed he was to be denied this realm too. What future was there for a being who could claim no place in Heaven, Hell or Earth?

That question formed his final thought. All that followed was the inevitable answer.

Nothing.

Vanities

Gail Z. Martin

I was dead when I first saw Antwerp.

The year was 1565. I had only been dead for about one hundred years.

"Isn't it beautiful?" Alard was my travelling companion, and the vampire who made me. It was night time, and we came up to the deck of the ship to see the city as we came into port.

"I didn't realize the city was quite so…big." Alard had been telling me about the city for years. But even so, the sight would have taken my breath away, if I still had breath to take. Ships filled the port. Buildings towered over the shoreline, and the lights of the torches and candles glittered in the River Scheldt. Above it all were the spires of the Cathedral of our Lady, not yet one hundred years old, one of the newest of Antwerp's wonders. Behind the cathedral, brooding and old, hunkered the fortified castle of Het Steen, still watching over the city and the river from the empty, darkened eye sockets of its deep-set windows.

"Big and full of diamonds," Alard said with a grin that showed his elongated eye teeth plainly.

Before Alard turned me, I had been a petty thief in Bruges. A very good thief, meaning, I was good at what I did, although my marks might not have thought me a good person. I ate regularly, had a warm place to live, and eluded the Watch, which is to say, I was at the top of my game. Until I died.

I'd got myself into the home of a well-heeled nobleman, and managed to work all twenty of the mechanical locks on his infernal strongbox. That was my specialty, lockboxes. I had the touch for the gears and an ear for the way they fit together. The job had been worth the risk. The box was full of gold and jewels. I'd even thought that I might quit thieving and open a respectable pub if the take was large enough. Oh, I had plenty of dreams, until things went sour.

That night, I was spotted by the Watch when I was almost over the wall. I might have outrun them, except that I landed badly when I jumped from the top of the wall and turned my ankle. I ran blindly, and took shelter in an abandoned warehouse. Alard found me before the guards did. I knew what the Watch would do if they caught me. First, they'd cut off my hands for thieving, and then my head.

I can still remember what Alard said to me. *Do you want to be the best thief in the world?* Since the choice was between truly dead and dead with benefits, I took him up on his offer

And now, here we were sailing into Antwerp for the biggest theft of our, um, lives. For the first time in a long while I missed the way my heart used to beat faster before a job, the way my breath came short and quick, and the feel of a light sheen of sweat on my brow. But now I was stronger, faster and immortal, and I could levitate, a little. I still thought I'd made a good trade.

"Sorren, are you listening to me at all?" There was exasperation in Alard's voice, but beneath it, joviality. On the whole, he was a very good-natured dead man, not at all the way I'd pictured a vampire back when I thought such things were only in children's tales.

"When was the last time you were in Antwerp?" I hurried to bring my focus back to our conversation.

Alard thought for a moment. "I was here quite a bit during the textile 'wars.' And before that, I made most of my fortune in the silver exchange with the Spaniards. But the first time I saw Antwerp, none of this was here." He swept his arm to encompass the waterfront crowded full of buildings and wharves. "The Het Steen was newly built, and I always thought it glowered over the river." I could guess where his thoughts went after that. He'd been the youngest son of a noble family, thrown into the Het Steen's prison as security for his father's debts. There he had languished, until a visitor came one evening and offered him a different sort of freedom. By my reckoning, that made Alard over three hundred years old. But to everyone else, with his blond hair, crisp blue eyes and slightly crooked nose in an otherwise perfect face, he looked like the young aristocrat he had once been, just over the cusp of thirty and certainly in his prime.

I wasn't convinced that, despite the care Alard devoted to teaching me to choose a wardrobe befitting my new station in life, I'd ever look the part of a noble with as much grace as he did. I'd been in my late twenties when he'd turned me. My hair was a dark, unremarkable blond and I was wiry and thin-built. Great for slipping through windows, but not so good for impressing women with my physique. Alard told me once that I had good enough looks to not stand out, and not quite perfect enough looks to be remembered. I wasn't sure whether or not that was a compliment, but being easily forgettable is good for a thief. In fact, the only feature anyone had ever really remarked on was my eyes. They're blue-gray, and my mother said they were the colour of the sea when a storm's coming. I worried, a bit, that being dead might change them. It didn't.

"We've got a busy schedule ahead," Alard said, with a note of resignation as if he realized I'd been woolgathering again. "Let's get below and take our bags. We'll wait until the rest of the passengers are off the ship. The less notice we attract, the better."

We'd taken a night passage ship for obvious reasons. There were few other passengers, and the inside cabins were ridiculously cheap. The ship had seen better days, and its captain was happy for the coin. Even so, I had the feeling that Alard knew the man.

Alard knew everyone. Now, with a big job in front of us, that could be both a blessing and a curse.

Alard left me with the bags. "I thought we were supposed to be two gentlemen on holiday," I grumbled. I wasn't surprised to find Alard's bag was heavier than mine.

"Who told you that?" Alard's tone was flat, but a smile quirked around the corners of his mouth.

"Forget it." While I would have found the bags heavy as a mortal, their weight wasn't what bothered me. They were bulky and awkward, and I wasn't happy being the valet.

"Two gentlemen might be remembered. As a collector of fine art and artefacts, I might even be remembered. No one will take a second look at my valet."

"Thanks a lot."

I followed Alard through the winding, cobblestone streets, taking every opportunity to twist my neck to see the buildings around me. I hadn't existed for enough centuries to become jaded yet, and part of me hoped I never would. Even Alard, as old as he was, still managed to have a spark of curiosity about him. He'd told me once that the vampires who survived the changing times were the ones who never stopped being curious. Then he told me that by that measure, I'd outlive them all. I'm still not sure whether that was meant to be a good thing or not. I took it as a plus. So far, being dead (perhaps 'undead' was a better word) had been good to me.

Alard stopped in front of a small shop several streets behind the waterfront. A sign said "Vanities," and, from the window I could see that it was one of the antiques and curio shops that Alard favoured.

"In here. Be quick about it." Alard motioned for me to maneuver our bags through the narrow door. The shop looked closed. I was about to protest that breaking into a shop might attract the attention we were trying to escape, when a lamp flared behind us, its glow shaded to avoid making it too easy for passers-by to see.

"Alard. Come in."

I put the bags where Alard bid and followed as Alard and our host continued, more than began, a lively conversation. Two things stood out to me: they were obviously old friends, and our host was clearly mortal.

"Drink this." Alard must have known that after the voyage my hunger might endanger our host. I usually had good control, but it wasn't wise to be in close quarters with such fresh, delicious blood when I hadn't eaten. He handed me a goblet of blood, goat blood by the smell, and although while not my favourite, I was hungry enough not to quibble.

"I thought you might be hungry, so there's a flagon for each of you." For the first time, I got a good look at our host. He was an older man, perhaps in his late sixties. Spry but beginning to show his age. He had a bald head with wisps of white hair that refused to lie flat. He squinted like a scholar, and he wore a jacket that looked worn at the elbows. "I'm Carel. Welcome to Antwerp. You must be Sorren."

Carel motioned for us both to take a seat. We were in a fairly large sitting room. Everywhere I looked there were manuscripts: old, leather-bound illuminated manuscripts, and such a multitude of trifles and treasures that I hardly knew where to look first. The books alone would have been worth a small fortune. Alard had been expanding my thiefly education to recognize value that the commoner might overlook.

"What do you see, Sorren?" Alard downplayed my guesses that he could, as my maker, at least partly read my thoughts. But there were too damn many coincidences for me to doubt. I'd learned to keep my mouth shut when I was mortal. Now, I'd learned to keep unflattering comments in the back of my head, where they hadn't quite taken form as words. I was grumbling a bit to myself like that now, and if Alard read it, he didn't respond.

"I see pottery, probably Greek, definitely ancient. The gold jewellery on the desk: Egyptian. I'd have to be up close to know the dynasty. The brooches on the shelf are ancient Celtic. Nice

work, too. From the number of manuscripts, I'd guess someone ransacked a monastery. The inlaid box is a miracle, but I've no idea where it comes from."

"India," Carel replied offhandedly. "Not surprised you couldn't place that."

"You're a collector?"

Carel gave a smile that didn't quite reach his eyes. "Of sorts. It was dark in the shop when you came in, and we hurried you through, so you probably didn't get much of a look around. I deal in treasures and antiquities, most legal; some not so much."

"You're our fence."

Carel chuckled. "Really, Alard. You can take the thief out of the alley, but have you taken the alley out of the thief? I prefer 'merchant,' thank you."

Before we could quibble more over wording, the door opened. Alard moved before the handle turned, and I was just a blink behind him. Without a word, we'd both flattened ourselves against the ceiling. Mortals rarely look up when they're indoors.

"You're at the shop late, aren't you?" A young man walked into the room, and from his manner and the resemblance, I knew he had to be Carel's son. To my surprise, he glanced upwards. "Hello, Alard. You need to change your hiding place."

Alard grinned and drifted down to the floor. I followed him. "No one but you ever looks up in here, Dietger."

I took another look at Dietger. He was about my age, or at least the age I appeared. He had light brown hair, and his eyes were a cold blue, like mine. His jacket was newer and less worn than his father's, and I noticed that someone had replaced its buttons with old Roman coins. A chain with an amulet hung around his neck. When he shifted his stance, it disappeared into his shirt, but I'd seen enough to know that it was Etruscan, and magic.

"I guess father didn't tell you that I think he ought to cut down on the side deals," Dietger said, directing his comments to Alard. "He's getting too old for this kind of thing. It's dangerous."

Alard chuckled. "From my perspective, he's still a young pup."

Dietger rolled his eyes. "Easy for you to say. But it's too dangerous. You and…" He looked at me and realized we hadn't been introduced.

"Sorren," I supplied.

"…Sorren can get yourselves out of a jam if a deal goes bad. You're not what you appear to be. But father doesn't have your defences. I thought we'd covered this last time you came."

"We did."

"But you're back."

Alard shrugged. "It was too good of an opportunity to miss."

"I don't want to know."

"We're going after the Black Dragon." Carel spoke. Alard raised an eyebrow. I probably looked surprised. No one had told me anything except that the job would be big, dangerous, and worth it. Dietger's eyes widened.

"No. Tell me you're not."

"It's the best chance we've had in a century," Alard said, and his voice had gone serious. He wasn't trying to use his vampire powers to sway Dietger's mind, so I figured he actually liked the young man. He was trying to persuade him. Obviously, we were going to do this the hard way.

"Seventy men have died trying to destroy the Black Dragon," Dietger said. His tone had grown resolute. "I don't want father to be the seventy-first."

"Who said we were going to destroy him? The Black Dragon can't be destroyed. He can be bound. He can be weakened. His alliances with mortals can be subverted." Alard clucked his tongue. "My dear boy, I haven't survived all these centuries picking fights I can't win."

"It only takes one." Dietger was going to be stubborn.

"This might be a good time to tell the thief what he's stealing." Everyone had forgotten about me, but I knew that when it really came down to the wire, I'd be the one doing the real work.

"Now's as good a time as any." Alard withdrew a folded piece of parchment from his vest pocket and laid it out carefully on the cluttered desk. Carel and I clustered around it. Dietger gave a sigh and joined us after a moment. I took a good look at the drawing. It was of a necklace with a pendant made from what appeared to be a cluster of small gemstones set in an unusual pattern. Rather garish, but no one asked my opinion.

"That's the Verheen Brooch," Carel said in a low voice. "No one's seen it in over a hundred years. I thought it was lost."

"Not lost. Purposely hidden. We made a deal with the Verhoeveren family to be the guardians of the brooch once Edmund finally tracked the thing down the last time it got away." I heard a note of anger creeping into Alard's voice that made me look up. "The fools were supposed to keep it inside the magical wards and out of sight."

"What happened?" Carel asked. He looked worried, too. Even Dietger appeared concerned. I was obviously the only one who hadn't been in on the story.

"Their dim-witted granddaughter, Anique, found it after her parents died in that carriage accident a few months ago. I'd brokered the arrangement myself with the grandfather, and come back for good measure when he died to make my point to his eldest son. They understood how dangerous the brooch was. Obviously," Alard said, disdain clear in his voice, "the girl's parents never took her into their confidence. So we've got a debutante planning to wear the Verheen Brooch out in public at Lady Evelien's ball."

"The only thing more dangerous than wearing that... thing... is trying to sell it. Are you trying to get us all killed?" Dietger was angry now. I could smell his anger. Underneath it lay fear.

"I'm not going to sell the brooch," Carel replied calmly. "Alard and I are just going to make sure it gets into the hands of a responsible guardian."

"If the brooch is so dangerous, why not just destroy it?" As soon as I'd spoken, I felt like I must have sprouted a second head. Everyone stared at me. It was my turn to feel righteously annoyed. "How come the mortals here know all about this, and I don't – even though I'm the one stealing it? You said this was a 'big' job. You didn't tell me there was a dragon involved."

Carel sighed and exchanged glances with Alard. "Perhaps we should all sit down. This could take a while. I'll fetch more tea and blood."

"I'll get those, father." Dietger looked happy to leave the room. I suspected he would have been even happier if Alard and I had been the ones leaving.

"The Black Dragon isn't a dragon," Alard said. "He's a very old spirit, one that finds a new body to possess every lifetime or so. I don't think he ever was completely human. Someone imprisoned him long ago in the New World, but the damned Spaniards set him free in their quest for gold and silver, and brought him over with their loot. That idiot, Pizarro, never even wondered why the people he conquered had so many relics hidden and locked away. All he saw was treasure. Never occurred to him that it could be anything else."

"What was it, if not treasure?" Mention gold, and my fingertips get itchy. I can't help that. Thieving is in my blood.

"Oh, some of the pieces were decoys. But several of those beautiful breastplates and necklaces of gold, silver and gemstones were magical. They were objects of power, and strong magic users had charged them with spells to keep what was bound beneath those towers bound forever."

"And it's taken us several lifetimes to find those pieces again and get them back into the hands of people trained to use them as intended," Carel said tartly as Dietger returned with the drinks, and a hunk of bread and cheese with ale for himself.

"So this Verheen Brooch is an object of power?" I sipped the blood. That kept me from watching the pulse beat in Dietger's neck.

"And if the granddaughter is wearing it, that means the brooch has been taken out of the vault where it was sealing in something

that really shouldn't get out," Carel finished.

"Antwerp is built on a very old, very large, mound of earth. There are stories from the city's beginning about strange creatures exacting a terrible price for crossing the river," Dietger said, and I guessed he'd been an unwilling pupil of his father's. "Legend says that the city was made possible when a hero battled a giant and cut off his hand. Hundreds of years ago, those dark creatures were imprisoned in the mound beneath the city, and in the deepest caves. Objects of power guard the entrances to that prison. In this case, the home of our debutante lies directly over one of the main shafts into the caves where the spirits are imprisoned. That's why we felt the need to ward it with the brooch. Now that the warding is compromised…" Alard let his voice drift.

"The Black Dragon may be able to escape." It was Dietger who spoke.

"Who, exactly, did the imprisoning? Who's the "we" you mention?" I didn't like what I was hearing, and I liked less that Alard had obviously had just this kind of thing in mind when he turned me.

"'We' are a loose alliance of vampires, shifters, magic users and mortals who would prefer to keep the dark things buried," Alard replied. "A similar coalition imprisoned the Black Dragon and spirits like him. This sort of thing has been going on since long before I was turned. I'm one of the elders now, and, unfortunately, these kind of responsibilities fall to me."

"What happens if they get out, these spirits?"

Alard's eyes grew dark. "Imagine beings whose hunger for blood is never sated. Things that are unwilling to slake their thirst from goats and deer. The Black Dragon and his kin feed off blood, but they also feed from life itself. They can drain a man's life without opening a vein. Can you picture what that would be like, loosed across the kingdoms? Even the Black Death would pale in comparison to the horror."

"So my job is to steal the brooch – and then what?"

Alard turned away. I had a bad feeling that this job even made him nervous. "We steal the brooch. Carel helps us get it into the hands of a trusted guardian. The Black Dragon stays buried."

"But what about the passages under the granddaughter's house? Won't they be unguarded?"

"It seems that Anique wants to travel. She'll be leaving Antwerp for Paris right after the ball, and isn't expected home for more than a year. If she finds a nice young man, perhaps never."

"And while she's gone, someone puts the brooch back, but in a secret hiding place?"

"Exactly."

Two nights later, Alard was dressed for a reception at the Verhoeveren house. Anique's home. Even I was impressed. He wore a black doublet with slashed sleeves that showed glimpses of his red silk shirt. A wide, stiff ruff around his neck and cuffs seemed to decrease the contrast between Alard's pale skin and the stark black velvet of his coat. Alard was trim enough to look good in the heavy hose tights, and soft leather boots came up above his knees. I knew that, under his ruff, Alard wore several charms and amulets against dark magic. A short cape set off the outfit nicely.

"You expect to hide in that?" I was put out more over my outfit than his. I was in solid, form-fitting black from head to toe, the epitome of a well-dressed valet. A waist-length jacket covered a black shirt with full sleeves. The jacket held thieves' tools and the spelled dagger Alard insisted on giving me. I had a variety of lock picks and other items of dubious legality hidden about my person, though since I'd become a vampire I'd relied more on enhanced hearing, sight and touch than on gadgets.

"I expect to hide in plain sight." Alard picked at the stiff fabric at his ruffs and jerked his head to move his chin out of range of the abrasive ruff. "I'm the guest of one of Carel's friends, a professor at the university. That will get me invited over the threshold and once I'm inside, I can invite you."

"Does your patron know you're dead?"

Alard smiled. I looked again, and saw that there was a tinge of pink in his cheeks and lips, and that his hands had lost their pallor. "You've fed. On whom?" Again, I was jealous. I got goat blood. Alard had dined on a human. Nothing but human blood works as well to warm us and revive our colour. Alard was no more pale than a scholar who spent his days indoors.

"The wharves have more than their share of cutpurses and murderers. Let's say that my dining companion won't be missed by anyone except the Watch."

"I used to be one of those cutpurses," I muttered.

"You didn't make a habit of slittng your mark's throat for the sheer joy of watching them bleed."

I couldn't argue with that. I'd found my thrill in liberating heavily guarded objects. Hurting people had never been something I'd enjoyed, and I'd managed to do most of my thieving without causing physical harm to anyone.

"You have the knife?" Something in Alard's voice was tighter than usual. This was the third time he'd asked me. Maybe he really was nervous.

"I have it, although why is beyond me. I've never stabbed anything except a side of beef."

"You've got the knife for the same reason I had Carel give you the amulets. The charms should get you past the wardings on the vault. The knife is just in case anything's got loose."

"Got loose? Now wait a second!" Alard had begun to walk away from me. I started to follow, and came to an abrupt halt. "Hold on. If I need charms to get into the vault because it's protected, how did Anique get the brooch in the first place?"

"Because her charm is in her blood." Alard turned to look at me. "The Verhoeveren family has a long history of magic. In generations past, they also chose one of their most talented sons to take the Dark Gift. That certainly didn't hurt the family fortunes." He grimaced. "Unfortunately, the recent generations have moved away from those practices. And magic, as well as common sense, certainly seem to have skipped the granddaughter."

Alard hailed a rented carriage several streets over from Vanities, not wanting anything to tie us to Carel's shop should we be noticed. For the same reason, we had agreed to travel separately. Alard got the fine carriage. I was on foot, sticking to the back alleys where I could use my supernatural speed without attracting the attention of anyone except the gutter drunks and the doorway strumpets.

The Verhoeveren home was as impressive as I'd expected. A grand home rising four floors high, the house was a step-gabled masterpiece of Gothic style. The home stood shoulder to shoulder against other homes, each equally luxurious. Tonight, the house glittered with candles and lanterns. I watched from a safe distance, hidden in the shadows, as Alard met his new friend and they went in together, already busily talking. If all went well, Alard would have a wonderful evening chatting about art and antiquities with a professor while I did all the heavy lifting.

In the old days, when I was still alive, I would have taken a couple of deep breaths to get myself in the mood to work. Now, I made do with rubbing my hands together. Oh, I could make myself breathe if I really wanted to, make my chest rise and fall the same way I'd raise and lower my left foot, but the breathing would stop if I stopped thinking about it, and since I didn't need the air, the process felt strange. I rubbed my hands together and found that even dead, my nerves could still feel jangled.

In the dark, I slipped easily around to the back. The servants' door was ajar. I approached carefully, and heard Alard whisper, "Come in." There it was, my invitation across the threshold. I was in.

Alard was gone by the time I opened the door. In the distance, I could hear the clatter of pots and dishes. I might be dead, but I was newly crossed enough that the smell of food woke a hunger in me for more than blood. I'd learned the hard way not to give in to that hunger. My body no longer tolerated anything but blood, and so what else I ate had to come back out the way it went in. Once was enough. But the memory of how food tastes still haunted me. That was one of only two things I missed about being mortal. Getting drunk was the other one.

I had work to do. I slipped past the kitchen and down the back stairs. I thought I'd moved silently before I'd been turned. Now, I moved like a ghost. I didn't have the same skill Alard had at clouding mortal minds so that they didn't see me, but I hardly ever had the need. Not being seen was my one of my specialties.

The wooden stairs creaked for the servants who passed me in the shadows without noticing. I moved on silently, levitating just a bit with each step to avoid putting stress on the old wooden stair treads. Carel had got his hands on the original plans to the house. I didn't ask how. Alard knew where the modifications had been made for the vault. I'd memorized the plans, and now I moved through the darkened cellar as surely as if I'd lived there all my life.

A servant laden with wine bottles came down the corridor singing to himself. I stepped into the shadows and disappeared. A few more steps and I was in front of a door. When I'd been mortal, I'd relied on my gut feeling as much as any lock picking equipment. Now, my gut told me that the door led to somewhere I didn't want to go. Alard had said that my intuition was a type of magic, a form of second sight. I wasn't sure I believed that, but my second sight sure didn't want to see what was behind that door.

I set my jaw and stepped up to the door. While I wasn't certain about intuition being magic, I didn't doubt that what I was about to do qualified. I'd learned quite young that with enough concentration I could work a lock just by touching the wood. Gradually, I got good enough to work locks through metal, even thick iron. It was almost as if my fingers could "see" right through the door and turn the tumblers.

Right off, I knew this door would be a challenge. Alard had warned me it had layers of locks. I closed my eyes, trusting in my vampire hearing to alert me before any passer-by came close enough to see me. I needed my eyes closed to work the locks. I made myself relax, and pressed my fingers to the first lock. Alard told me that the locks began simple and became increasingly complex – and dangerous. The first challenge was a padlock, intricately forged to look like the head of a dragon in black iron. Subtle. I had a master key infused with a bit of magic that could sense the shape of the mechanism inside and adapt. The key had been expensive to make, pricy enough to keep such a useful tool out of the hands of the average thief. Alard had given me the master key as a present on the first anniversary of my turning.

The key hesitated in the lock for a moment, and then turned smoothly. I reclaimed the key and left the lock hanging. I'd need to be able to put everything back as I found it, or Anique would suspect. Next came a door secured with an elaborately knotted rope. I knew before I touched it that the deceptively silken cord was infused with magic. I withdrew one of the amulets from beneath my tunic and held it up. The cord glowed a faint blue, and then went dark, and the tingle that warned of magic vanished in my mind. I was good at knots, and without its magical enhancement, the cord gave way to me within a minute.

The next door had a lock like a chest lid, with a complicated series of bolts and gears. The gears turned when I "felt" the lock, moving my fingers to align the bolts and pins. The bolts slid back, and I smiled.

In the distance, I could hear the sounds of the party. My goal was to be through the locks and gone with the brooch before the guests moved on to their third course. The final door had a set of pin tumblers. Again, I'd use my ear and my fingers to feel my way into the vault. I touched the lock, and frowned. The first attempt to turn the lock felt wrong. At the same time, one of the charms around my neck had grown suddenly warm, then hot. Irritated, I pulled the thing out from beneath my shirt, and it glowed. I was about to stash it beneath my jacket when I glanced at the lock in the amulet's glow. The sequence of figures on the lock that I saw

in the light of the amulet was completely different from the way the sequence appeared without the talisman. Just to make sure, I shielded the amulet's light, and looked again. It hadn't been a trick of my eyes. Leaving the amulet out, I worked in its dim glow. The lock turned smoothly for me now, and I had the satisfaction of feeling the tumblers drop into place.

Lock by lock, I made my way into the vault. Alard had warned me that the last trap was on the floor. Unless Verhoeveren blood flowed in my veins to counter the charm, I'd need to cross a span too wide for a man to jump without touching down on the floor between here and there. The tiles, Alard warned, were actually carefully balanced, and they would set off a series of alarm bells if disturbed. Difficult to impossible for a mortal, but not for a vampire. I couldn't fly properly yet, not like Alard and the old ones could, but I could float. Floating was all I needed.

I made a small sound of triumph as the last door opened. Inside lay the spelled chest that held the Verheen Brooch. Alard had assured me that the words he made me memorize would open the chest, although they sounded like nonsense to me. He'd drilled me on how to pronounce them correctly, until I heard them in my sleep.

"Nonnes javar viciat, alrum valonas fideras."

I could hear the magical locks working, hear the bolts sliding and the gears turning, hear the pins falling into place. It was a joyous sound. I rubbed my hands together in anticipation, and floated over to claim my prize.

The chest was empty.

Empty! If I'd had a heartbeat, it would have been racing. All this work, all this time, and no brooch. Alard hadn't said anything about it being charmed, or invisible. I felt around the velvet-lined bottom of the chest. Nothing. I tapped at the bottom of the chest, inside and out, listening for a false bottom. I examined the sides of the chest for hidden openings. I even searched the inside of the chest lid, and sized up the chest to see if the dimensions inside compared to the outside suggested a secret compartment

I'd missed. I came up empty, as empty as the chest. Panicked, I looked around the vault. It was empty, too, except for the chest.

Think. Where would the brooch be if not in the vault? And then it hit me. The answer would have been obvious, if Alard and I hadn't been men. It would have been doubly obvious if we'd been thinking of the brooch as a piece of jewellery instead of a priceless magical object.

The granddaughter thinks it's just a nice, shiny necklace. Valuable, but no more so than the other sparklies she's got. It's in her goddamn room, probably lying right out on her dressing table. Damn, damn, damn.

Angry and resigned, I worked my way back out of the vault. I'd just wasted precious time, and used up some of my luck. It was a rule I'd thieved by all my life, and breaking it had got me dead. Only pull one job in a house at a time. Get in, get the goods and get out. Sure, there could be silver in the dining room, diamonds in the lady's jewellery case and gold coins in the master's desk, but roaming from room to room looking for treasure increased the odds of getting caught. Greed catches more thieves than the Watch. I'd forgotten that just one time, and I died because of it. Now, I was going to have to break that rule again. And whilst I was already dead, Alard had impressed upon me that getting caught would create problems that made death look simple. I didn't want to find out.

Someone was coming. I got the last lock latched and plastered myself against the ceiling just in time. It was a barrel vaulted chamber, and the bricks were uncomfortable at my back, but I stayed hidden until the servants passed. The one saving grace in having to look for the brooch in Anique's room was that she was likely to be down among the guests tonight. Alard thought she was saving the brooch to make a big splash at Lady Evelien's ball tomorrow. Now that I thought about it, a silly young woman would want to keep a treasure like the brooch handy where she could try it on with her dress and admire herself in the mirror. Did the brooch's magic speak to her blood? Could she feel the power of the brooch, or was it just a pretty, shiny, dead thing?

Working my way up the stairs to the living quarters was harder than slipping into the basement. As I moved through the house, I caught a glimpse of the party. Banks of candles and huge candelabra laden with dozens of candles lit the room, which was walled with mirrors.

I found the back stairs, the servants' passageway, and I grabbed a tea tray from near the kitchen to carry, hoping no one looked closely at my face. I got up the stairs without a challenge, and set the tray aside. As a vampire, I could usually sense where mortals were. I could hear their heartbeats, smell their blood. As I listened to my senses, I did not feel any mortals nearby. I'd got lucky.

I slipped down the hallway, trying the doorknobs. None of the rooms looked as if they belonged to a spoiled young rich girl. I came to the last door, and turned the knob. The room was decorated with delicately-sized, feminine furnishings, and swathed in luxurious fabrics and sumptuous pillows. Mirrors reflected candlelight, making the whole room glitter. The tables and chests were littered with extravagant trinkets of silver and crystal, playthings that cost more than a workingman might make in years. A dressing table sat against the wall with a large mirror and a pink velvet-cushioned chair. The top was cluttered with exquisite bottles of perfume, silver-handled combs and a variety of cosmetics.

A small chest, covered with ornate inlay, sat amid the clutter. It was a lady's jewellery chest, and I went straight to it, digging carefully through the strands of pearls, gemstones and diamonds. In the old days, I'd have just grabbed the chest and run. Alard had taught me patience. But despite my thorough search, the Verheen Brooch was not in the box.

"Looking for this?"

I spun around. A blonde young woman stood just inside the doorway. She was dressed for a dinner party, her long hair braided up. She was dressed in a black gown, as was the fashion, but the jewels in her earrings and bracelets dispelled any thought that somber colours meant simplicity. Pinned to her gown, just above the swell of her breasts lay the prize, the Verheen Brooch.

I should have heard her approach. I *would* have heard her approach, if she'd been mortal.

"What are you?" My heightened senses were practically screaming an alarm. The body was young, but around it, inside it, enveloping it was an ancient evil.

"I'm just a silly, spoiled rich girl with a fondness for pretty things." The voice was mocking, but the eyes were dead serious. No, the eyes were just dead. Whatever was looking out through them had never been a silly, spoiled girl.

"You don't know what you've got."

Her laugh chilled me. Hard to scare a dead man, but she managed. "Oh, yes. I know." Her fingers fondled the brooch like it was a lover. "I've got something that will make everyone take me very seriously."

They say that the devil whispers in everyone's ear the thing he or she wants most. For some it's money, for others, social status, power, beauty. She was born with all those things, and Alard told me she was already courted by the most desirable men in the city.

"You thought I was nothing but a stupid girl."

She was right. Alard and I made the same mistake everyone else made. But the Black Dragon didn't. And he'd whispered the one prize she couldn't buy when he'd seduced her. Not just power. Respect.

"What did it offer you?" I asked. I kept my eyes on hers. What looked out at me through her eyes wasn't human, and it certainly wasn't a vapid socialite. What glinted in those blue eyes was cold, calculating, and ancient.

She laughed, and I shuddered. Something in that sound felt as if her long nails had raked down my spine. "My father thought I was too stupid for him to trust me with the family secret. He forgot that Verhoeveren blood doesn't play favourites. I've heard the voices since I was just a little girl. Everyone else ordered me about or spoke to me like a child. Not the voices. They saw my

true potential."

Your true potential to be a pawn, I thought, but didn't say. I didn't know how much of Anique was still inside, and how much was the Black Dragon. "When did you take the brooch out of the vault?"

"Just before my dear, dear parents had their tragic accident."

Alard and Carel had been expecting the girl to be an innocent. The Black Dragon had recognized her as an ally, willing to do anything to get what she craved most.

"What did he promise you?"

Anique smiled. Although she was a beautiful girl, her smile bared her teeth in a way that said she shared a hunger for blood. "He promised me that I'd be free from an arranged marriage. Free from my father. Free from the lawyers that tried to steal my money after father died. I want what would have been mine if I'd been a son instead of a daughter."

"All it needed was your blood."

Her face twitched a little when I said that. I wondered if the Black Dragon was whispering to her while she spoke to me.

"The brooch didn't lock him inside the vault, you know," she said smugly. "The brooch *is* the vault. They bound his spirit inside the brooch to contain it, just like father's stupid rules tried to keep me locked in a box. But together, we got out of the box."

"Now what?" I wanted to keep her talking while I thought of something brilliant. I was a thief, not a fighter. I'd made my way robbing empty homes where I never had to encounter the prize's owner. I hadn't counted on having to do more than grab the necklace and run.

"Now you die, permanently."

Anique moved with the speed of a vampire. She came at me and, as I threw myself out of the way, it was almost as if there were two images, not just one, when I looked at her. I saw Anique, beautiful, greedy and deadly, coming at me with her teeth bared and her hands raised like claws. But the image was blurred, as if a painter had tried to paint a second portrait over the top of an existing one. In that blurred image I saw a black shadow with real claws and real fangs, and I didn't want to find out whose jaws I'd feel if they clamped down on me.

Something else stirred in the room, and before I'd truly had time to process what I'd seen, Alard had tackled Anique from behind. He'd come in prepared to fight, and I was certain that the telepathy he'd always refused to confirm played a big part in his perfect timing.

Anique gave a shriek, but the band downstairs had begun to play a loud tune, covering the noise. The black shadow seemed to fill her, leeching the colour out of her skin until she was a dull grey, the colour of a corpse. Filled with the Black Dragon's power, she tore free from Alard's grip, something a mortal could never do. Alard stumbled backwards, and Anique came at me again, matching my speed and reflexes in a game of cat and mouse.

I'll hold her. Use your dagger. It was Alard's voice sounding clear in my mind. I guess he'd decided to stop pretending. Alard told me that the dagger was spelled. That had made me feel pretty good, until I got a look at the Black Dragon. Now, it seemed like a puny weapon against a monster.

Too late for second thoughts. Alard was already launching himself at Anique, and I was moving too, trying to get a clear strike at her heart. Taking a vampire's heart destroyed the vampire. I was going to have to hope that putting a knife through Anique's heart would at least slow down the Black Dragon long enough for me to get my hands on that damn brooch.

Alard grabbed Anique from behind, locking his arms around her waist in a grip that should have crushed a mortal woman. I threw myself towards her, expecting Anique to struggle, or to buck and kick. Instead, the darkness around her shape grew more solid, and she arched, reaching back with both hands to grasp Alard's head.

My knife plunged into her chest, and for good measure, my fangs sank into the artery that pulsed at the base of that beautiful

white neck. Suddenly, I was covered by a fountain of blood. Warm blood, spurting from the gaping wound in Anique's chest and the bright red liquid that filled my mouth from her throat. And cold blood, dark blood. Anique's arms came back down holding their prize. In her hands, she held Alard's head, torn from his body with the Black Dragon's inhuman strength. The whole house seemed to shake as if the earth suddenly moved beneath it, and from the lower levels of the house, I heard the revellers scream.

Anique crumpled and I stumbled backwards. Alard's voice was suddenly silent, and I knew then that I'd accepted his presence as a constant background hum in all the years since I'd been turned without thinking about it. Now that it was gone, I reeled, as if blinded. Anique had killed my maker, my source. I'd taken her heart with my knife, but she'd wounded me far worse. The middle of a battle is the wrong time to learn how to deal with the death of your maker. I fell to my knees as Anique's body dropped to the ground, my dagger still sticking out of her blood soaked bodice.

Then I realized that the shadow was shifting. A dark mist coalesced above Anique's body. The Black Dragon was taking its true shape, and in that dark mist I saw every nightmare I'd ever dreamed.

The shape grew taller and darker, a giant that stretched to the ceiling. Its arms were too long for its body, and the hands ended with talons. Faceless, eyeless, it still found me. I had to get that brooch. The Black Dragon swung clawed hands at me, but I dodged, barely. I felt hot slashes open down my back. It dived at me, and again I scrambled out of the way as long teeth snapped just a breath away from my leg.

I threw myself at Anique, trying not to see Alard's headless corpse behind her. She was still breathing, which meant my knife had missed its mark, or whatever spell it held didn't work as Alard had planned. I wrapped my fingers around that damned brooch and pulled, but the clasp held.

The dark mist swirled back around me, and as I watched in horror, it streamed back into Anique's body, entering through her eyes, her nose, her mouth, her ears. I jerked my spelled blade out of Anique's chest and stumbled backwards. Anique's body began to tremble, as if the power that filled her was too much for her dying form to handle. But the Black Dragon brought Anique to her knees, and then to her feet. The disdainful sneer that twisted her finely drawn lips was all Anique, regardless of the power that animated her.

Anique came at me again, even as I heard something in the hallway. The distraction slowed me down just enough for Anique to nearly close the distance. A loud blast came from the doorway, sending flame and smoke into the room. Anique's head exploded in a shower of blood and gore and I dove aside as a musket ball tore through bone and flesh, taking off her head the way she had torn Alard's from his body.

As she fell, I grabbed for the brooch. The edge of the brooch tore a gash in my palm from the strength I used to jerk it clear. The brooch was slick with blood: Anique's, Alard's and my own.

Dietger stood in the doorway with a matchlock.

Everything happened at once. The black shadow shed Anique's dead body and came after me. And in that instant, I had a plan. I held up the brooch.

"Come and get it."

The Black Dragon streaked toward me and stopped, and I began to laugh, a high-pitched sound born more of nerves and fear than my normal chuckle.

"You can't touch me." I had Verhoeveren blood in my veins. Anique's blood, which I'd drunk from the punctures in her neck. Verhoeveren blood not only ran in my veins, but now, it covered my clothes in bloody gobbets, and it ran down my arm where I held the brooch that was sticky with her blood.

I held the brooch in my left hand. In my right was the spelled dagger. Now, I knew why Alard had insisted that I bring it.

It wasn't meant for Anique.

Antwerp has its own way of dealing with monsters.

Brandishing the Verheen Brooch like a weapon, I charged at the Black Dragon. With a war cry, I brought down the spelled dagger not in its chest, but across its right arm at the wrist. The dagger cut through the cold, dark mist and met resistance, but I brought all my vampire strength to bear, knowing that my existence, and Dietger's, depended on it.

An inhuman wail tore from the Black Dragon. I had no free hand to clap to my ears, and the sound seemed to tear at every fibre in my body. Dietger fell to his knees, dropping the gun and covering his ears in pain. I was shaking all over, but I forced myself to move forward, still brandishing the brooch.

"Verhoeveren blood runs in my veins. You must obey the blood. Return to the brooch."

This time, when the Black Dragon came at me, I thought I was ready. Some say that the dead don't feel fear. They're wrong. Terror filled me as that black mist swirled towards me, no longer bothering to take a shape. The air around me became freezing cold, and I braced myself with all my immortal strength to hold up the brooch as the mist entered it, and the dome of the brooch began to glow. In a moment, it was over, but I stood, trembling, unable to speak.

Only then did I realize that smoke was seeping into the room from the hallway behind Dietger.

Dietger seemed to come back to himself. He grabbed up his gun and gave a pained glance to where Alard's body had collapsed into dust. "Great job with the brooch, but I'm afraid there's no way out. The house is on fire."

"How's that?" I heard him, but I wasn't processing the information. I still felt as if I were making my way through molasses; everything seemed to take enormous effort.

"Something rocked the house while I was on the way up here. Damn near knocked me down the steps. It must have knocked over the candles."

All those candles, and the tinderbox of fine, billowing skirts and kindling-dry wigs. The smoke was thicker now.

I looked to Dietger. Either we took our only chance, or we burned with the brooch. "On my count, we run for the windows."

"We're four stories in the air."

"Trust me."

Dietger gave me a look that told me clearly that self-preservation had more to do with it than any kind of trust, but on my count, we ran for the window and burst through the glass. The brooch was clasped tightly in my left hand. I flung out my right arm, letting the dagger fall, and caught Dietger around the waist as we fell.

"You can fly?"

"No."

We plummeted. Beneath us, I could see flames shooting from the lower windows of the once-grand home, and chaos in the street. No one looked up to see us fall. Mortals never look up. They didn't see us until we were almost on them, and they scrambled out of the way, expecting us to hit the ground in a spatter of blood. To Dietger's credit, he did not scream, but I could hear him reciting a prayer. I didn't pray. Instead, I focused all my will on what I could do.

I couldn't fly, but I could float.

We fell like a cast stone. Then, when we were only about the length of a man's arm above the unyielding pavement, we slowed with a jerk that must have sent Dietger's heart into his throat. We hovered for a moment, and then touched down gently. But before the crowd around us could react, I ran, carrying Dietger with me, still clutching the brooch. To the mortals in the street, we must have disappeared in a blur. I hoped that they would take it as a trick of the smoke, but I had more important things to worry about.

Dietger whispered directions, taking me through the winding streets. We made enough switchbacks and turns to deter even the more dogged pursuer. I came to a stop in front of Vanities, and

put him down.

Dietger looked pale as one of the undead. He swallowed, and straightened his waistcoat. The door to the shop opened, although the front of the shop was dark.

"Come in. Hurry."

We didn't need light. Dietger and Carel knew the shop's crowded layout by heart. I could see in the dark. We followed Carel to the same parlour where he had greeted Alard and me just a night before. Only then did I feel the magnitude of my loss.

Alard was gone.

I collapsed into the chair where Alard had sat and put my head in my hands. The Dark Gift denied me the release of tears, but my whole body shook with grief. More than grief. Alard had brought me across. For the first hundred years of my undead existence, it had been his power that sustained me. I was only just at the threshold when fledglings could leave their maker and survive. Now that the battle with the Black Dragon was over, I felt Alard's destruction in every sinew of my body. For the first time since my turning, I felt like a dead thing.

I can give you what you crave.

For a moment, I didn't know where the voice was coming from. And then, I knew. It was the Verheen Brooch. I had jammed it into my vest pocket during the escape. Now, it called to the same Verhoeveren blood that had enabled me to imprison it, and I understood why Anique's family had kept this thing locked away, buried beneath stone and iron.

I can make you rich. Powerful. Respected.

With a cry, I tore the damned brooch from my pocket and hurled it across the room.

Dietger and Carel looked up from where they were huddled in conversation, respecting my need to grieve. I saw that Carel had tears running down his cheeks. He, too, mourned my maker, his friend.

"It speaks to him," Carel said to Dietger, with a nod toward where I'd thrown the brooch.

Dietger went to retrieve the brooch, and held it warily, dangling it from the chain Anique had used to hang it around her neck. "Alard was right. Once he had Verhoeveren blood in his veins, the Black Dragon had to obey."

A bitter smile touched the edges of Carel's mouth. "Fortunately, that will pass."

I nodded. It took about twelve hours for a feeding to spend itself. I would not carry Verhoeveren blood in me forever, and when it passed, the Verheen Brooch would be a dead thing to me.

Carel brought me a goblet of blood and pressed it into my hand. "Eat. You've been through a lot." The thick strip of linen wrapped around his arm told me whose blood it was. I looked at him, questioning.

"Alard and I were friends for a long time," Carel said quietly. "Over the years, I gained immunity to his powers, and he used his Gift to extend my life. Many a time, I gave him human blood when nothing else would suffice. This is one of those times when naught but human blood will sustain you. Drink."

The blood cleared my head and steadied me. Only then did Carel's words sink in. I turned to him. "Alard extended your life?"

Carel nodded, and I could see the answer to my next question in his face. Just since our first meeting, it looked as if he had aged decades. His eyes were sunken, and his skin had grown paper-thin. "There's not much time left," he said. He looked from me to Dietger, and motioned for Dietger to join us. Dietger knelt next to his father, watching with a mixture of horror and grief as the man aged in front of our eyes.

"Swear to me, both of you, that you will carry on the work."

"What work?" I looked from Carel to Dietger.

"The Alliance Alard and I created has kept the Black Dragon and things like it from returning to the world. Dietger knows everything you need, even if he's never put the pieces together to realize it. What is bound must remain bound." Carel's voice had grown wavering, and he began to cough. "This store, Vanities, is much more than it appears. For decades, Alard and the Alliance brought me found objects, objects of power, and I moved them to places of safekeeping. Sometimes, other people brought me things they thought to be cursed or haunted, and I made them disappear."

Talking had become difficult, but determination flashed in his eyes. "You must take over for me," Carel said, reaching out a bony hand to clutch Dietger's arm. "You must take over the work."

Dietger bowed his head. I could see his struggle. He had only grudgingly acknowledged this part of his father's life, and now the full responsibility was about to fall on his shoulders. "I swear to."

Carel turned toward me. Cataracts now covered both of his eyes, but he stared at me as if he could still see. "Swear to me, Sorren. Swear that you'll take Alard's place. Swear it, and he won't have died in vain."

I didn't want to do this. Like Dietger, I wanted to be leagues away from this place. Then I thought of Alard, and how his dust by now was mingled with the ash of the Verhoeveren home. I swallowed hard. A million objections screamed in my mind, and they were my own objections, not the voice of the damned brooch. I didn't know how to reach the Alliance. I didn't know how to find the objects, or what to do with them. I didn't know anything, anything except that I owed a great debt to Alard, one I might spend my immortality repaying.

"I'll do it."

The light seemed to fade from Carel's eyes. "Good," he said in a raspy whisper. "Good." He began to sway, and Dietger reached out to grab his shoulders, but I knew that life left him before he slumped to the floor.

I looked at Dietger over his father's body. "Now what?"

Dietger took a deep breath to steady himself. I knew the grief he was feeling. Tonight, we had both lost our fathers. "Now, we bury our dead." He closed his eyes and seemed to give himself a shake to clear his head. When he looked at me, his blue eyes were clear, filled with the same determination I'd seen in Carel's eyes.

"Tomorrow, we carry on the work."

I thought about everything that had happened since my ship anchored in Antwerp. I'd crossed a vale as final as when Alard had brought me across, long ago. Then, my death gave me a new existence as an immortal. Now, Alard's death gave me a mission. I held out my hand to Dietger. A hand covered with soot and blood, which he shook.

When Alard turned me, I learned that death wasn't the end. Now, in the oath I'd given to Carel, I learned that my immortality could have purpose. I wasn't the same man who'd landed in Antwerp two days ago. "Let's see about burying your father," I said. "And then, I want rid of that damned brooch."